LOST IN THE DESERT

Tarzan stumbled and fell, and when he tried to rise he found that he could not; his strength was too far gone. With a final effort, he turned himself over on his back to see Ska the vulture wheeling above him.

"Is the end so near?" the ape-man wondered. Closing his eyes, he threw a forearm across them to protect them from Ska's sharp beak. It was restful lying there—and Tarzan was very tired.

Circling slowly, Ska dropped closer and closer to the dying man. Why did not Tarzan move? Had death claimed that mighty body?

Ska, filled with suspicion, circled warily. Twice he almost alighted upon the great, naked breast, only to wheel suddenly away. But the third time his talons touched the brown skin of his intended victim . . .

Edgar Rice Burroughs
TARZAN NOVELS

COMPLETE AND UNABRIDGED!

TARZAN
THE UNTAMED

Edgar Rice Burroughs

BALLANTINE BOOKS • NEW YORK

ISBN 0-345-27697-3

This edition published by arrangement with
Edgar Rice Burroughs, Inc.

Manufactured in the United States of America

First U.S. Printing: July 1963
Seventh U.S. Printing: February 1978

First Canadian Printing: December 1963
Second Canadian Printing: February 1973

Cover art by Boris Vallejo

CONTENTS

1

Murder and Pillage

HAUPTMANN FRITZ SCHNEIDER trudged wearily through the somber aisles of the dark forest. Sweat rolled down his bullet head and stood upon his heavy jowls and bull neck. His lieutenant marched beside him while Underlieutenant von Goss brought up the rear, following with a handful of askaris the tired and all but exhausted porters whom the black soldiers, following the example of their white officer, encouraged with the sharp points of bayonets and the metal-shod butts of rifles.

There were no porters within reach of Hauptmann Schneider so he vented his Prussian spleen upon the askaris nearest at hand, yet with greater circumspection since these men bore loaded rifles—and the three white men were alone with them in the heart of Africa.

Ahead of the hauptmann marched half his company, behind him the other half—thus were the dangers of the savage jungle minimized for the German captain. At the forefront of the column staggered two naked savages fastened to each other by a neck chain. These were the native guides impressed into the service of Kultur and upon their poor, bruised bodies Kultur's brand was revealed in divers cruel wounds and bruises.

Thus even in darkest Africa was the light of German civilization commencing to reflect itself upon the undeserving natives just as at the same period, the fall of 1914, it was shedding its glorious effulgence upon benighted Belgium.

It is true that the guides had led the party astray; but this is the way of most African guides. Nor did it matter that ignorance rather than evil intent had been the cause of their failure. It was enough for Hauptmann Fritz Schneider to know that he was lost in the African wilderness and that he had at hand human beings less powerful than he who could be made to suffer by torture. That he did not kill them outright was partially due to a faint hope that they might eventually prove the means of extricating him from his difficulties and partially that so long as they lived they might still be made to suffer.

The poor creatures, hoping that chance might lead them at last upon the right trail, insisted that they knew the way and so led on through a dismal forest along a winding game trail trodden deep by the feet of countless generations of the savage denizens of the jungle.

Here Tantor, the elephant, took his long way from dust wallow to water. Here Buto, the rhinoceros, blundered blindly in his solitary majesty, while by night the great cats paced silently upon their padded feet beneath the dense canopy of overreaching trees toward the broad plain beyond, where they found their best hunting.

It was at the edge of this plain which came suddenly and unexpectedly before the eyes of the guides that their sad hearts beat with renewed hope. Here the hauptmann drew a deep sigh of relief, for after days of hopeless wandering through almost impenetrable jungle the broad vista of waving grasses dotted here and there with open parklike woods and in the far distance the winding line of green shrubbery that denoted a river appeared to the European a veritable heaven.

The Hun smiled in his relief, passed a cheery word with his lieutenant, and then scanned the broad plain with his field glasses. Back and forth they swept across the rolling land until at last they came to rest upon a point near the center of the landscape and close to the green-fringed contours of the river.

"We are in luck," said Schneider to his companions. "Do you see it?"

The lieutenant, who was also gazing through his own glasses, finally brought them to rest upon the same spot that had held the attention of his superior.

"Yes," he said, "an English farm. It must be Greystoke's, for there is none other in this part of British East Africa. God is with us, Herr Captain."

"We have come upon the English schweinhund long before he can have learned that his country is at war with ours," replied Schneider. "Let him be the first to feel the iron hand of Germany."

"Let us hope that he is at home," said the lieutenant, "that we may take him with us when we report to Kraut at Nairobi. It will go well indeed with Herr Hauptmann Fritz Schneider if he brings in the famous Tarzan of the Apes as a prisoner of war."

Schneider smiled and puffed out his chest. "You are right, my friend," he said, "it will go well with both of us; but I shall have to travel far to catch General Kraut before he reaches Mombasa. These English pigs with their contemptible army will make good time to the Indian Ocean."

It was in a better frame of mind that the small force set out across the open country toward the trim and well-kept farm buildings of John Clayton, Lord Greystoke; but disappointment was to be their lot since neither Tarzan of the Apes nor his son was at home.

Lady Jane, ignorant of the fact that a state of war existed between Great Britain and Germany, welcomed the officers most hospitably and gave orders through her trusted Waziri to prepare a feast for the black soldiers of the enemy.

Far to the east, Tarzan of the Apes was traveling rapidly from Nairobi toward the farm. At Nairobi he had received news of the World War that had already started, and, anticipating an immediate invasion of British East Africa by the Germans, was hurrying homeward to fetch his wife to a place of greater security. With him were a score of his ebon warriors, but far too slow for the ape-man was the progress of these trained and hardened woodsmen.

When necessity demanded, Tarzan of the Apes sloughed the thin veneer of his civilization and with it the hampering apparel that was its badge. In a moment the polished English gentleman reverted to the naked ape man.

His mate was in danger. For the time, that single thought dominated. He did not think of her as Lady Jane Greystoke, but rather as the she he had won by the might of his steel thews, and that he must hold and protect by virtue of the same offensive armament.

It was no member of the House of Lords who swung swiftly and grimly through the tangled forest or trod with untiring muscles the wide stretches of open plain—it was a great he ape filled with a single purpose that excluded all thoughts of fatigue or danger.

Little Manu, the monkey, scolding and chattering in the upper terraces of the forest, saw him pass. Long had it been since he had thus beheld the great Tarmangani naked and alone hurtling through the jungle. Bearded and gray was Manu, the monkey, and to his dim old eyes came the fire of recollection of those days when Tarzan of the Apes had ruled supreme, Lord of the Jungle, over all the myriad life that trod the matted vegetation between the boles of the great trees, or flew or swung or climbed in the leafy fastness upward to the very apex of the loftiest terraces.

And Numa, the lion, lying up for the day close beside last night's successful kill, blinked his yellow-green eyes and twitched his tawny tail as he caught the scent spoor of his ancient enemy.

Nor was Tarzan senseless to the presence of Numa or Manu or any of the many jungle beasts he passed in his rapid flight towards the west. No particle had his shallow probing of English society dulled his marvelous sense faculties. His nose had picked out the presence of Numa, the lion, even before the majestic king of beasts was aware of his passing.

He had heard noisy little Manu, and even the soft rustling of the parting shrubbery where Sheeta passed before either of these alert animals sensed his presence.

But however keen the senses of the ape-man, however swift his progress through the wild country of his adoption, however mighty the muscles that bore him, he was still mortal. Time and space placed their inexorable limits upon him; nor was there another who realized this truth more keenly than Tarzan. He chafed and fretted that he could not travel with the swiftness of thought and that the long tedious miles stretching far ahead of him must require hours and hours of tireless effort upon his part before he would swing at last from the final bough of the fringing forest into the open plain and in sight of his goal.

Days it took, even though he lay up at night for but a few hours and left to chance the finding of meat directly on his trail. If Wappi, the antelope, or Horta, the boar, chanced in his way when he was hungry, he ate, pausing but long enough to make the kill and cut himself a steak.

Then at last the long journey drew to its close and he was passing through the last stretch of heavy forest that bounded his estate upon the east, and then this was traversed and he stood upon the plain's edge looking out across his broad lands towards his home.

At the first glance his eyes narrowed and his muscles tensed. Even at that distance he could see that something was amiss. A thin spiral of smoke arose at the right of the bungalow where the barns had stood, but there were no barns there now, and from the bungalow chimney from which smoke should have arisen, there arose nothing.

Once again Tarzan of the Apes was speeding onward, this time even more swiftly than before, for he was goaded now by a nameless fear, more product of intuition than of reason. Even as the beasts, Tarzan of the Apes seemed to possess a sixth sense. Long before he reached the bungalow, he had almost pictured the scene that finally broke upon his view.

Silent and deserted was the vine-covered cottage. Smoldering embers marked the site of his great barns. Gone were the thatched huts of his sturdy retainers, empty the fields, the pastures, and corrals. Here and there vultures rose and circled above the carcasses of men and beasts.

It was with a feeling as nearly akin to terror as he ever had experienced that the ape-man finally forced himself to enter his home. The first sight that met his eyes set the red haze of hate and bloodlust across his vision, for there, crucified against the wall of the living-room, was Wasimbu, giant son of the faithful Muviro and for over a year the personal body-guard of Lady Jane.

The overturned and shattered furniture of the room, the brown pools of dried blood upon the floor, and prints of bloody hands on walls and woodwork evidenced something of the frightfulness of the battle that had been waged within the narrow confines of the apartment. Across the baby grand piano lay the corpse of another black warrior, while before the door of Lady Jane's boudoir were the dead bodies of three more of the faithful Greystoke servants.

The door of this room was closed. With drooping shoulders and dull eyes Tarzan stood gazing dumbly at the insensate panel which hid from him what horrid secret he dared not even guess.

Slowly, with leaden feet, he moved toward the door. Gropingly his hand reached for the knob. Thus he stood for another long minute, and then with a sudden gesture he straightened his giant frame, threw back his mighty shoulders and, with fearless head held high, swung back the door and stepped across the threshhold into the room which held for him the dearest memories and associations of his life. No change of expression crossed his grim and stern-set features as he strode across the room and stood beside the little couch and the inanimate form which lay face downward upon it; the still, silent thing that had pulsed with life and youth and love.

No tear dimmed the eye of the ape-man; but the God who made him alone could know the thoughts that passed through that still half-savage brain. For a long time he stood there just looking down upon the dead body, charred beyond recognition, and then he stooped and lifted it in his arms. As he turned the body over and saw how horribly death had been meted he plumbed, in that instant, the uttermost depths of grief and horror and hatred.

Nor did he require the evidence of the broken German rifle in the outer room, or the torn and blood-stained service cap upon the floor, to tell him who had been the perpetrators of this horrid and useless crime.

For a moment he had hoped against hope that the blackened corpse was not that of his mate, but when his eyes discovered and recognized the rings upon her fingers the last faint ray of hope forsook him.

In silence, in love, and in reverence he buried, in the little rose garden that had been Jane Clayton's pride and love, the poor, charred form and beside it the great black warriors who had given their lives so futilely in their mistress' protection.

At one side of the house Tarzan found other newly made graves and in these he sought final evidence of the identity of the real perpetrators of the atrocities that had been committed there in his absence.

Here he disinterred the bodies of a dozen German askaris and found upon their uniforms the insignia of the company and regiment to which they had belonged. This was enough for the ape-man. White officers had commanded these men, nor would it be a difficult task to discover who they were.

Returning to the rose garden, he stood among the Hun-trampled blooms and bushes above the grave of his dead— with bowed head he stood there in a last mute farewell. As the sun sank slowly behind the towering forests of the west, he turned slowly away upon the still-distinct trail of Hauptmann Fritz Schneider and his blood-stained company.

His was the suffering of the dumb brute—mute; but though voiceless no less poignant. At first his vast sorrow numbed his other faculties of thought—his brain was overwhelmed by the calamity to such an extent that it reacted to but a single objective suggestion: She is dead! She is dead! She is dead! Again and again this phrase beat monotonously upon his brain —a dull, throbbing pain, yet mechanically his feet followed the trail of her slayer while, subconsciously, his every sense was upon the alert for the ever-present perils of the jungle.

Gradually the labor of his great grief brought forth another emotion so real, so tangible, that it seemed a companion walking at his side. It was Hate—and it brought to him a measure of solace and of comfort, for it was a sublime hate that ennobled him as it has ennobled countless thousands since— hatred for Germany and Germans. It centered about the slayer of his mate, of course; but it included everything German, animate or inanimate. As the thought took firm hold upon him he paused and raising his face to Goro, the moon, cursed with upraised hand the authors of the hideous crime that had been perpetrated in that once peaceful bungalow behind him; and he cursed their progenitors, their progeny, and all their kind the while he took silent oath to war upon them relentlessly until death overtook him.

There followed almost immediately a feeling of content, for, where before his future at best seemed but a void, now it was filled with possibilities the contemplation of which brought him, if not happiness, at least a surcease of absolute grief, for before him lay a great work that would occupy his time.

Stripped not only of all the outward symbols of civilization, Tarzan had also reverted morally and mentally to the status of the savage beast he had been reared. Never had his civilization been more than a veneer put on for the sake of her he loved because he thought it made her happier to see him thus. In reality he had always held the outward evidences of so-called culture in deep contempt. Civilization meant to Tarzan of the Apes a curtailment of freedom in all its aspects—freedom of action, freedom of thought, freedom of love, freedom of hate. Clothes he abhorred—uncomfortable, hideous, confining things that reminded him somehow of bonds securing him to the life he had seen the poor creatures of London and Paris living. Clothes were the emblems of that hypocrisy for which civilization stood—a pretense that the wearers were ashamed of what the clothes covered, of the human form made in the semblance of God. Tarzan knew how silly and pathetic the lower orders of animals appeared in the clothing of civilization, for he had seen several poor creatures thus appareled in various traveling shows in Europe, and he knew, too, how silly and pathetic man appears in them since the only men he had seen in the first twenty years of his life had been, like himself, naked savages. The ape-man had a keen admiration for a well-muscled, well-proportioned body, whether lion, or antelope, or man, and it had ever been beyond him to understand how clothes could be considered more beautiful than a clear, firm, healthy skin, or coat and trousers more graceful than the gentle curves of rounded muscles playing beneath a flexible hide.

In civilization Tarzan had found greed and selfishness and cruelty far beyond that which he had known in his familiar, savage jungle, and though civilization had given him his mate and several friends whom he loved and admired, he never had come to accept it as you and I who have known little or nothing else; so it was with a sense of relief that he now definitely abandoned it and all that it stood for, and went forth into the jungle once again stripped to his loin cloth and weapons.

The hunting knife of his father hung at his left hip, his bow and his quiver of arrows were slung across his shoulders, while around his chest over one shoulder and beneath the opposite arm was coiled the long grass rope without which Tarzan would have felt quite as naked as would you should you be suddenly thrust upon a busy highway clad only in a union suit. A heavy war spear which he sometimes carried in

one hand and again slung by a thong about his neck so that
it hung down his back completed his armament and his
apparel. The diamond-studded locket with the pictures of
his mother and father that he had worn always until he had
given it as a token of his highest devotion to Jane Clayton
before their marriage was missing. She always had worn it
since; but it had not been upon her body when he found her
slain in her boudoir, so that now his quest for vengeance included also a quest for the stolen trinket.

Toward midnight Tarzan commenced to feel the physical
strain of his long hours of travel and to realize that even
muscles such as his had their limitations. His pursuit of the
murderers had not been characterized by excessive speed; but
rather more in keeping with his mental attitude, which was
marked by a dogged determination to require from the Germans more than an eye for an eye and more than a tooth for
a tooth, the element of time entering but slightly into his
calculations.

Inwardly as well as outwardly Tarzan had reverted to beast
and in the lives of beasts, time, as a measurable aspect of
duration, has no meaning. The beast is actively interested
only in *now*, and as it is always *now* and always shall be, there
is an eternity of time for the accomplishment of objects. The
ape-man, naturally, had a slightly more comprehensive realization of the limitations of time; but, like the beasts, he moved
with majestic deliberation when no emergency prompted him
to swift action.

Having dedicated his life to vengeance, vengeance became
his natural state and, therefore, no emergency, so he took his
time in pursuit. That he had not rested earlier was due to
the fact that he had felt no fatigue, his mind being occupied
by thoughts of sorrow and revenge; but now he realized that
he was tired, and so he sought a jungle giant that had harbored
him upon more than a single other jungle night.

Dark clouds moving swiftly across the heavens now and
again eclipsed the bright face of Goro, the moon, and fore-
warned the ape-man of impending storm. In the depth of
the jungle the cloud shadows produced a thick blackness that
might almost be felt—a blackness that to you and me might
have proven terrifying with its accompaniment of rustling
leaves and cracking twigs, and its even more suggestive intervals of utter silence in which the crudest of imaginations
might have conjured crouching beasts of prey tensed for the
fatal charge; but through it Tarzan passed unconcerned, yet
always alert. Now he swung lightly to the lower terraces
of the overarching trees when some subtle sense warned him
that Numa lay upon a kill directly in his path, or again he

sprang lightly to one side as Buto, the rhinoceros, lumbered toward him along the narrow, deep-worn trail, for the ape-man, ready to fight upon necessity's slightest pretext, avoided unnecessary quarrels.

When he swung himself at last into the tree he sought, the moon was obscured by a heavy cloud, and the tree tops were waving wildly in a steadily increasing wind whose soughing drowned the lesser noises of the jungle. Upward went Tarzan toward a sturdy crotch across which he long since had laid and secured a little platform of branches. It was very dark now, darker even than it had been before, for almost the entire sky was overcast by thick, black clouds.

Presently the man-beast paused, his sensitive nostrils dilating as he sniffed the air about him. Then, with the swiftness and agility of a cat, he leaped far outward upon a swaying branch, sprang upward through the darkness, caught another, swung himself upon it and then to one still higher. What could have so suddenly transformed his matter-of-fact ascent of the giant bole to the swift and wary action of his detour among the branches? You or I could have seen nothing—not even the little platform that an instant before had been just above him and which now was immediately below—but as he swung above it we should have heard an ominous growl; and then as the moon was momentarily uncovered, we should have seen both the platform, dimly, and a dark mass that lay stretched upon it—a dark mass that presently, as our eyes became accustomed to the lesser darkness, would take the form of Sheeta, the panther.

In answer to the cat's growl, a low and equally ferocious growl rumbled upward from the ape-man's deep chest—a growl of warning that told the panther he was trespassing upon the other's lair; but Sheeta was in no mood to be dispossessed. With upturned, snarling face he glared at the brown-skinned Tarmangani above him. Very slowly the ape-man moved inward along the branch until he was directly above the panther. In the man's hand was the hunting knife of his long-dead father—the weapon that had first given him his real ascendency over the beasts of the jungle; but he hoped not to be forced to use it, knowing as he did that more jungle battles were settled by hideous growling than by actual combat, the law of bluff holding quite as good in the jungle as elsewhere—only in matters of love and food did the great beasts ordinarily close with fangs and talons.

Tarzan braced himself against the bole of the tree and leaned closer toward Sheeta.

"Stealer of balus!" he cried. The panther rose to a sitting position, his bared fangs but a few feet from the ape-man's taunting face. Tarzan growled hideously and struck at the cat's face with his knife. "I am Tarzan of the Apes," he roared. "This is Tarzan's lair. Go, or I will kill you." Though he spoke in the language of the great apes of the jungle, it is doubtful that Sheeta understood the words, though he knew well enough that the hairless ape wished to frighten him from his well-chosen station past which edible creatures might be expected to wander sometime during the watches of the night.

Like lightning the cat reared and struck a vicious blow at his tormentor with great, bared talons that might well have torn away the ape-man's face had the blow landed; but it did not land—Tarzan was even quicker than Sheeta. As the panther came to all fours again upon the little platform, Tarzan unslung his heavy spear and prodded at the snarling face, and as Sheeta warded off the blows, the two continued their horrid duet of blood-curdling roars and growls.

Goaded to frenzy the cat presently determined to come up after this disturber of his peace; but when he essayed to leap to the branch that held Tarzan he found the sharp spear point always in his face, and each time as he dropped back he was prodded viciously in some tender part; but at length, rage having conquered his better judgment, he leaped up the rough bole to the very branch upon which Tarzan stood. Now the two faced each other upon even footing and Sheeta saw a quick revenge and a supper all in one. The hairless ape-thing with the tiny fangs and the puny talons would be helpless before him.

The heavy limb bent beneath the weight of the two beasts as Sheeta crept cautiously out upon it and Tarzan backed slowly away, growling. The wind had risen to the proportions of a gale so that even the greatest giants of the forest swayed, groaning, to its force and the branch upon which the two faced each other rose and fell like the deck of a storm-tossed ship. Goro was now entirely obscured, but vivid flashes of lightning lit up the jungle at brief intervals, revealing the grim tableau of primitive passion upon the swaying limb.

Tarzan backed away, drawing Sheeta farther from the stem of the tree and out upon the tapering branch, where his footing became ever more precarious. The cat, infuriated by the pain of spear wounds, was overstepping the bounds of caution. Already he had reached a point where he could do little more than maintain a secure footing, and it was this moment that Tarzan chose to charge. With a roar that mingled with the booming thunder from above he leaped toward the panther, who could only claw futilely with one huge paw while he clung to the branch with the other; but the ape-man did not come within that parabola of destruction. Instead he leaped

above menacing claws and snapping fangs, turning in mid-air
and alighting upon Sheeta's back, and at the instant of impact
his knife struck deep into the tawny side. Then Sheeta, impelled by pain and hate and rage and the first law of Nature,
went mad. Screaming and clawing he attempted to turn
upon the ape-thing clinging to his back. For an instant he
toppled upon the now wildly gyrating limb, clutched frantically to save himself, and then plunged downward into the
darkness with Tarzan still clinging to him. Crashing through
splintering branches the two fell. Not for an instant did the
ape-man consider relinquishing his death-hold upon his adversary. He had entered the lists in mortal combat and true
to the primitive instincts of the wild—the unwritten law of
the jungle—one or both must die before the battle ended.

Sheeta, catlike, alighted upon four out-sprawled feet, the
weight of the ape-man crushing him to earth, the long knife
again imbedded in his side. Once the panther struggled to
rise; but only to sink to earth again. Tarzan felt the giant
muscles relax beneath him. Sheeta was dead. Rising, the
ape-man placed a foot upon the body of his vanquished foe,
raised his face toward the thundering heavens, and as the
lightning flashed and the torrential rain broke upon him,
screamed forth the wild victory cry of the bull ape.

Having accomplished his aim and driven the enemy from
his lair, Tarzan gathered an armful of large fronds and
climbed to his dripping couch. Laying a few of the fronds
upon the poles he lay down and covered himself against the
rain with the others, and despite the wailing of the wind and
the crashing of the thunder, immediately fell asleep.

2

The Lion's Cave

THE rain lasted for twenty-four hours and much of the time
it fell in torrents so that when it ceased, the trail he had
been following was entirely obliterated. Cold and uncomfortable—it was a savage Tarzan who threaded the mazes of
the soggy jungle. Manu, the monkey, shivering and chattering in the dank trees, scolded and fled at his approach. Even
the panthers and the lions let the growling Tarmangani pass
unmolested.

When the sun shone again upon the second day and a wide,
open plain let the full heat of Kudu flood the chilled, brown
body, Tarzan's spirits rose; but it was still a sullen, surly brute
that moved steadily onward into the south where he hoped
again to pick up the trail of the Germans. He was now in
German East Africa and it was his intention to skirt the mountains west of Kilimanjaro, whose rugged peaks he was quite
willing to give a wide berth, and then swing eastward along
the south side of the range to the railway that led to Tanga,
for his experience among men suggested that it was toward
this railroad that German troops would be likely to converge.

Two days later, from the southern slopes of Kilimanjaro, he
heard the boom of cannon far away to the east. The afternoon had been dull and cloudy and now as he was passing
through a narrow gorge a few great drops of rain began to
splatter upon his naked shoulders. Tarzan shook his head
and growled his disapproval; then he cast his eyes about for
shelter, for he had had quite enough of the cold and drenching.
He wanted to hasten on in the direction of the booming noise,
for he knew that there would be Germans fighting against the
English. For an instant his bosom swelled with pride at the
thought that he was English and then he shook his head
again viciously. "No!" he muttered, "Tarzan of the Apes is
not English, for the English are men and Tarzan is Tarmangani;" but he could not hide even from his sorrow or from his
sullen hatred of mankind in general that his heart warmed

18

at the thought it was Englishmen who fought the Germans. His regret was that the English were human and not *great white apes* as he again considered himself.

"Tomorrow," he thought, "I will travel that way and find the Germans," and then he set himself to the immediate task of discovering some shelter from the storm. Presently he espied the low and narrow entrance to what appeared to be a cave at the base of the cliffs which formed the northern side of the gorge. With drawn knife he approached the spot warily, for he knew that if it were a cave it was doubtless the lair of some other beast. Before the entrance lay many large fragments of rock of different sizes, similar to others scattered along the entire base of the cliff, and it was in Tarzan's mind that if he found the cave unoccupied he would barricade the door and insure himself a quiet and peaceful night's repose within the sheltered interior. Let the storm rage without— Tarzan would remain within until it ceased, comfortable and dry. A tiny rivulet of cold water trickled outward from the opening.

Close to the cave Tarzan kneeled and sniffed the ground. A low growl escaped him and his upper lip curved to expose his fighting fangs. "Numa!" he muttered; but he did not stop. Numa might not be at home—he would investigate. The entrance was so low that the ape-man was compelled to drop to all fours before he could poke his head within the aperture; but first he looked, listened, and sniffed in each direction at his rear—he would not be taken by surprise from that quarter.

His first glance within the cave revealed a narrow tunnel with daylight at its farther end. The interior of the tunnel was not so dark but that the ape-man could readily see that it was untenanted at present. Advancing cautiously he crawled toward the opposite end imbued with a full realization of what it would mean if Numa should suddenly enter the tunnel in front of him; but Numa did not appear and the ape-man emerged at length into the open and stood erect, finding himself in a rocky cleft whose precipitous walls rose almost sheer on every hand, the tunnel from the gorge passing through the cliff and forming a passageway from the outer world into a large pocket or gulch entirely inclosed by steep walls of rock. Except for the small passageway from the gorge, there was no other entrance to the gulch which was some hundred feet in length and about fifty in width and appeared to have been worn from the rocky cliff by the falling of water during long ages. A tiny stream from Kilimanjaro's eternal snow cap still trickled over the edge of the rocky wall at the upper end of the gulch, forming a little pool at the

bottom of the cliff from which a small rivulet wound downward to the tunnel through which it passed to the gorge
beyond. A single great tree flourished near the center of the
gulch, while tufts of wiry grass were scattered here and there
among the rocks of the gravelly floor.

The bones of many large animals lay about and among them
were several human skulls. Tarzan raised his eyebrows. "A
man-eater," he murmured, "and from appearances he has held
sway here for a long time. Tonight Tarzan will take the lair
of the man-eater and Numa may roar and grumble upon the
outside."

The ape-man had advanced well into the gulch as he in-
vestigated his surroundings and now as he stood near the
tree, satisfied that the tunnel would prove a dry and quiet
retreat for the night, he turned to retrace his way to the outer
end of the entrance that he might block it with bowlders
against Numa's return; but even with the thought there came
something to his sensitive ears that froze him into statuesque
immobility with eyes glued upon the tunnel's mouth. A
moment later the head of a huge lion framed in a great black
mane appeared in the opening. The yellow-green eyes glared,
round and unblinking, straight at the trespassing Tarmangani,
a low growl rumbled from the deep chest, and lips curled
back to expose the mighty fangs.

"Brother of Dango!" shouted Tarzan, angered that Numa's
return should have been so timed as to frustrate his plans for
a comfortable night's repose. "I am Tarzan of the Apes, Lord
of the Jungle. Tonight I lair here—go!"

But Numa did not go. Instead he rumbled forth a menacing roar and took a few steps in Tarzan's direction. The ape-
man picked up a rock and hurled it at the snarling face. One
can never be sure of a lion. This one might turn tail and run
at the first intimation of attack—Tarzan had bluffed many in
his time—but not now. The missile struck Numa full upon
the snout—a tender part of a cat's anatomy—and instead of
causing him to flee it transformed him into an infuriated
engine of wrath and destruction.

Up went his tail, stiff and erect, and with a series of frightful roars he bore down upon the Tarmangani at the speed of
an express train. Not an instant too soon did Tarzan reach
the tree and swing himself into its branches and there he
squatted, hurling insults at the king of beasts while Numa
paced a circle beneath him, growling and roaring in rage.

It was raining now in earnest adding to the ape-man's dis-
comfort and disappointment. He was very angry; but as only
direct necessity had ever led him to close in mortal combat
with a lion, knowing as he did that he had only luck and

agility to pit against the frightful odds of muscle, weight, fangs, and talons, he did not now even consider descending and engaging in so unequal and useless a duel for the mere reward of a little added creature comfort. And so he sat perched in the tree while the rain fell steadily and the lion padded round and round beneath, casting a baleful eye upward after every few steps.

Tarzan scanned the precipitous walls for an avenue of escape. They would have baffled an ordinary man; but the ape-man, accustomed to climbing, saw several places where he might gain a foothold, precarious possibly; but enough to give him reasonable assurance of escape if Numa would but betake himself to the far end of the gulch for a moment. Numa, however, notwithstanding the rain, gave no evidence of quitting his post so that at last Tarzan really began to consider seriously if it might not be as well to take the chance of a battle with him rather than remain longer cold and wet and humiliated in the tree.

But even as he turned the matter over in his mind Numa turned suddenly and walked majestically toward the tunnel without even a backward glance. The instant that he disappeared, Tarzan dropped lightly to the ground upon the far side of the tree and was away at top speed for the cliff. The lion had no sooner entered the tunnel than he backed immediately out again and, pivoting like a flash, was off across the gulch in full charge after the flying ape-man; but Tarzan's lead was too great—if he could find finger or foothold upon the sheer wall he would be safe; but should he slip from the wet rocks his doom was already sealed as he would fall directly into Numa's clutches where even the Great Tarmangani would be helpless.

With the agility of a cat Tarzan ran up the cliff for thirty feet before he paused, and there finding a secure foothold, he stopped and looked down upon Numa who was leaping upward in a wild and futile attempt to scale the rocky wall to his prey. Fifteen or twenty feet from the ground the lion would scramble only to fall backward again defeated. Tarzan eyed him for a moment and then commenced a slow and cautious ascent toward the summit. Several times he had difficulty in finding holds but at last he drew himself over the edge, rose, picked up a bit of loose rock, hurled it at Numa and strode away.

Finding an easy descent to the gorge, he was about to pursue his journey in the direction of the still-booming guns when a sudden thought caused him to halt and a half-smile to play about his lips. Turning, he trotted quickly back to the outer opening of Numa's tunnel. Close beside it he listened for a moment and then rapidly began to gather large rocks and pile them within the entrance. He had almost closed the aperture when the lion appeared upon the inside—a very ferocious and angry lion that pawed and clawed at the rocks and uttered mighty roars that caused the earth to tremble; but roars did not frighten Tarzan of the Apes. At Kala's shaggy breast he had closed his infant eyes in sleep upon countless nights in years gone by to the savage chorus of similar roars. Scarcely a day or night of his jungle life—and practically all his life had been spent in the jungle—had he not heard the roaring of hungry lions, or angry lions, or love-sick lions. Such sounds affected Tarzan as the tooting of an automobile horn may affect you—if you are in front of the automobile it warns you out of the way, if you are not in front of it you scarcely notice it. Figuratively Tarzan was not in front of the automobile—Numa could not reach him and Tarzan knew it, so he continued deliberately to choke the entrance until there was no possibility of Numa's getting out again. When he was quite through he made a grimace at the hidden lion beyond the barrier and resumed his way toward the east. "A man-eater who will eat no more men," he soliloquized.

That night Tarzan lay up under an overhanging shelf of rock. The next morning he resumed his journey, stopping only long enough to make a kill and satisfy his hunger. The other beasts of the wild eat and lie up; but Tarzan never let his belly interfere with his plans. In this lay one of the greatest differences between the ape-man and his fellows of the jungles and forests. The firing ahead rose and fell during the day. He had noticed that it was highest at dawn and immediately after dusk and that during the night it almost ceased. In the middle of the afternoon of the second day he came upon troops moving up toward the front. They appeared to be raiding parties, for they drove goats and cows along with them and there were native porters laden with grain and other foodstuffs. He saw that these natives were all secured by neck chains and he also saw that the troops were composed of native soldiers in German uniforms. The officers were white men. No one saw Tarzan, yet he was here and there about and among them for two hours. He inspected the insignia upon their uniforms and saw that they were not the same as that which he had taken from one of the dead soldiers at the bungalow and then he passed on ahead of them, unseen in the dense bush. He had come upon Germans and had not killed them; but it was because the killing of Germans at large was not yet the prime motive of his existence —now it was to discover the individual who slew his mate.

After he had accounted for him he would take up the little matter of slaying *all* Germans who crossed his path, and he meant that many should cross it, for he would hunt them precisely as professional hunters hunt the man-eaters.

As he neared the front lines the troops became more numerous. There were motor trucks and ox teams and all the impedimenta of a small army and always there were wounded men walking or being carried toward the rear. He had crossed the railroad some distance back and judged that the wounded were being taken to it for transportation to a base hospital and possibly as far away as Tanga on the coast.

It was dusk when he reached a large camp hidden in the foothills of the Pare Mountains. As he was approaching from the rear he found it but lightly guarded and what sentinels there were, were not upon the alert, and so it was an easy thing for him to enter after darkness had fallen and prowl about listening at the backs of tents, searching for some clew to the slayer of his mate.

As he paused at the side of a tent before which sat a number of native soldiers he caught a few words spoken in native dialect that riveted his attention instantly: "The Waziri fought like devils; but we are greater fighters and we killed them all. When we were through the captain came and killed the woman. He stayed outside and yelled in a very loud voice until all the men were killed. Underlieutenant von Goss is braver—he came in and stood beside the door shouting at us, also in a very loud voice, and bade us nail one of the Waziri who was wounded to the wall, and then he laughed loudly because the man suffered. We all laughed. It was very funny."

Like a beast of prey, grim and terrible, Tarzan crouched in the shadows beside the tent. What thoughts passed through that savage mind? Who may say? No outward sign of passion was revealed by the expression of the handsome face; the cold, gray eyes denoted only intense watchfulness. Presently the soldier Tarzan had heard first rose and with a parting word turned away. He passed within ten feet of the ape-man and continued on toward the rear of the camp. Tarzan followed and in the shadows of a clump of bushes overtook his quarry. There was no sound as the man beast sprang upon the back of his prey and bore it to the ground for steel fingers closed simultaneously upon the soldier's throat, effectually stifling any outcry. By the neck Tarzan dragged his victim well into the concealment of the bushes.

"Make no sound," he cautioned in the man's own tribal dialect as he released his hold upon the other's throat.

The fellow gasped for breath, rolling frightened eyes upward to see what manner of creature it might be in whose power he was. In the darkness he saw only a naked brown body bending above him; but he still remembered the terrific strength of the mighty muscles that had closed upon his wind and dragged him into the bushes as though he had been but a little child. If any thought of resistance had crossed his mind he must have discarded it at once, as he made no move to escape.

"What is the name of the officer who killed the woman at the bungalow where you fought with the Waziri?" asked Tarzan.

"Hauptmann Schneider," replied the black when he could again command his voice.

"Where is he?" demanded the ape-man.

"He is here. It may be that he is at headquarters. Many of the officers go there in the evening to receive orders."

"Lead me there," commanded Tarzan, "and if I am discovered I will kill you immediately. Get up!"

The black rose and led the way by a roundabout route back through the camp. Several times they were forced to hide while soldiers passed; but at last they reached a great pile of baled hay from about the corner of which the black pointed out a two-story building in the distance.

"Headquarters," he said. "You can go no farther unseen. There are many soldiers about."

Tarzan realized that he could not proceed farther in company with the black. He turned and looked at the fellow for a moment as though pondering what disposition to make of him.

"You helped to crucify Wasimbu, the Waziri," he accused in a low yet none the less terrible tone.

The black trembled, his knees giving beneath him. "He ordered us to do it," he plead.

"Who ordered it done?" demanded Tarzan.

"Underlieutenant von Goss," replied the soldier. "He, too, is here."

"I shall find him," returned Tarzan, grimly. "You helped to crucify Wasimbu, the Waziri, and, while he suffered, you laughed."

The fellow reeled. It was as though in the accusation he read also his death sentence. With no other word Tarzan seized the man again by the neck. As before there was no outcry. The giant muscles tensed. The arms swung quickly upward and with them the body of the black soldier who had helped to crucify Wasimbu, the Waziri, described a circle in the air—once, twice, three times, and then it was

flung aside and the ape-man turned in the direction of General
Kraut's headquarters.

A single sentinel in the rear of the building barred the way.
Tarzan crawled, belly to the ground, toward him, taking advantage of cover as only the jungle-bred beast of prey can
do. When the sentinel's eyes were toward him, Tarzan hugged
the ground, motionless as stone; when they were turned away,
he moved swiftly forward. Presently he was within charging
distance. He waited until the man had turned his back once
more and then he rose and sped noiselessly down upon him.
Again there was no sound as he carried the dead body with
him toward the building.

The lower floor was lighted, the upper dark. Through the
windows Tarzan saw a large front room and a smaller room
in rear of it. In the former were many officers. Some moved
about talking to one another, others sat at field tables writing.
The windows were open and Tarzan could hear much of the
conversation; but nothing that interested him. It was mostly
about the German successes in Africa and conjectures as to
when the German army in Europe would reach Paris. Some
said the Kaiser was doubtlessly already there, and there was a
great deal of damning Belgium.

In the smaller back room a large, red-faced man sat behind a table. Some other officers were also sitting a little in
rear of him, while two stood at attention before the general,
who was questioning them. As he talked, the general toyed
with an oil lamp that stood upon the table before him. Presently there came a knock upon the door and an aide entered
the room. He saluted and reported: "Fräulein Kircher has
arrived, sir."

"Bid her enter," commanded the general, and then nodded
to the two officers before him in sign of dismissal.

The Fräulein, entering, passed them at the door. The
officers in the little room rose and saluted, the Fräulein
acknowledging the courtesy with a bow and a slight smile.
She was a very pretty girl. Even the rough, soiled riding habit
and the caked dust upon her face could not conceal the fact,
and she was young. She could not have been over nineteen.

She advanced to the table behind which the general stood
and, taking a folded paper from an inside pocket of her coat,
handed it to him.

"Be seated, Fräulein," he said, and another officer brought
her a chair. No one spoke while the general read the contents of the paper.

Tarzan appraised the various people in the room. He
wondered if one might not be Hauptmann Schneider, for two
of them were captains. The girl he judged to be of the intel-

ligence department—a spy. Her beauty held no appeal for
him—without a glimmer of compunction he could have wrung
that fair, young neck. She was German and that was enough;
but he had other and more important work before him. He
wanted Hauptmann Schneider.

Finally the general looked up from the paper.

"Good," he said to the girl, and then to one of his aides,
"Send for Major Schneider."

Major Schneider! Tarzan felt the short hairs at the back
of his neck rise. Already they had promoted the beast who
had murdered his mate—doubtless they had promoted him
for that very crime.

The aide left the room and the others fell into a general
conversation from which it became apparent to Tarzan that
the German East African forces greatly outnumbered the
British and that the latter were suffering heavily. The ape-
man stood so concealed in a clump of bushes that he could
watch the interior of the room without being seen from within,
while he was at the same time hidden from the view of anyone who might chance to pass along the post of the sentinel
he had slain. Momentarily he was expecting a patrol or a
relief to appear and discover that the sentinel was missing,
when he knew an immediate and thorough search would be
made.

Impatiently he awaited the coming of the man he sought
and at last he was rewarded by the reappearance of the aide
who had been dispatched to fetch him accompanied by an
officer of medium size with fierce, upstanding mustaches. The
newcomer strode to the table, halted and saluted, reporting.
The general acknowledged the salute and turned toward the
girl.

"Fräulein Kircher," he said, "allow me to present Major
Schneider—"

Tarzan waited to hear no more. Placing a palm upon the
sill of the window he vaulted into the room into the midst of
an astounded company of the Kaiser's officers. With a stride
he was at the table and with a sweep of his hand sent the
lamp crashing into the fat belly of the general who, in his
mad effort to escape cremation, fell over backward, chair and
all, upon the floor. Two of the aides sprang for the ape-man
who picked up the first and flung him in the face of the other.
The girl had leaped from her chair and stood flattened against
the wall. The other officers were calling aloud for the guard
and for help. Tarzan's purpose centered upon but a single
individual and him he never lost sight of. Freed from attack
for an instant he seized Major Schneider, threw him over his
shoulder and was out of the window so quickly that the

astonished assemblage could scarce realize what had occurred.

A single glance showed him that the sentinel's post was still vacant and a moment later he and his burden were in the shadows of the hay dump. Major Schneider had made no outcry for the very excellent reason that his wind was shut off. Now Tarzan released his grasp enough to permit the man to breathe.

"If you make a sound you will be choked again," he said.

Cautiously and after infinite patience Tarzan passed the final outpost. Forcing his captive to walk before him he pushed on toward the west until, late into the night, he recrossed the railway where he felt reasonably safe from discovery. The German had cursed and grumbled and threatened and asked questions; but his only reply was another prod from Tarzan's sharp war spear. The ape-man herded him along as he would have driven a hog with the difference that he would have had more respect and therefore more consideration for a hog.

Until now Tarzan had given little thought to the details of revenge. Now he pondered what form the punishment should take. Of only one thing was he certain—it must end in death. Like all brave men and courageous beasts Tarzan had little natural inclination to torture—none, in fact; but this case was unique in his experience. An inherent sense of justice called for an eye for an eye and his recent oath demanded even more. Yes, the creature must suffer even as he had caused Jane Clayton to suffer. Tarzan could not hope to make the man suffer as he had suffered, since physical pain may never approach the exquisiteness of mental torture.

All through the long night the ape-man goaded on the exhausted and now terrified Hun. The awful silence of his captor wrought upon the German's nerves. If he would only speak! Again and again Schneider tried to force or coax a word from him; but always the result was the same—continued silence and a vicious and painful prod from the spear point. Schneider was bleeding and sore. He was so exhausted that he staggered at every step, and often he fell only to be prodded to his feet again by that terrifying and remorseless spear.

It was not until morning that Tarzan reached a decision and it came to him then like an inspiration from above. A slow smile touched his lips and he immediately sought a place to lie up and rest—he wished his prisoner to be fit now for what lay in store for him. Ahead was a stream which Tarzan had crossed the day before. He knew the ford for a drinking place and a likely spot to make an easy kill. Cautioning the German to utter silence with a gesture the two approached the stream quietly. Down the game trail Tarzan

saw some deer about to leave the water. He shoved Schneider
into the brush at one side and, squatting next him, waited.
The German watched the silent giant with puzzled, frightened
eyes. In the new dawn he, for the first time, was able to obtain a good look at his captor, and, if he had been puzzled
and frightened before, those sensations were nothing to what
he experienced now.

Who and what could this almost naked, white savage be?
He had heard him speak but once—when he had cautioned
him to silence—and then in excellent German and the well-
modulated tones of culture. He watched him now as the
fascinated toad watches the snake that is about to devour it.
He saw the graceful limbs and symmetrical body motionless
as a marble statue as the creature crouched in the concealment of the leafy foliage. Not a muscle, not a nerve moved.
He saw the deer coming slowly along the trail, down wind
and unsuspecting. He saw a buck pass—an old buck—and
then a young and plump one came opposite the giant in ambush, and Schneider's eyes went wide and a scream of terror
almost broke from his lips as he saw the agile beast at his side
spring straight for the throat of the young buck and heard
from those human lips the hunting roar of a wild beast. Down
went the buck and Tarzan and his captive had meat. The
ape-man ate his raw, but he permitted the German to build
a fire and cook his portion.

The two lay up until late in the afternoon and then took up
the journey once again—a journey that was so frightful to
Schneider because of his ignorance of its destination that he at
times groveled at Tarzan's feet begging for an explanation
and for mercy; but on and on in silence the ape-man went,
prodding the failing Hun whenever the latter faltered.

It was noon of the third day before they reached their
destination. After a steep climb and a short walk they halted
at the edge of a precipitous cliff and Schneider looked down
into a narrow gulch where a single tree grew beside a tiny
rivulet and sparse grass broke from a rock-strewn soil. Tarzan
motioned him over the edge; but the German drew back in
terror. The Ape-man seized him and pushed him roughly
toward the brink. "Descend," he said. It was the second
time he had spoken in three days and perhaps his very silence,
ominous in itself, had done more to arouse terror in the breast
of the Boche than even the spear point, ever ready as it always was.

Schneider looked fearfully over the edge; but was about
to essay the attempt when Tarzan halted him. "I am Lord
Greystoke," he said. "It was my wife you murdered in the

Waziri country. You will understand now why I came for you. Descend."

The German fell upon his knees. "I did not murder your wife," he cried. "Have mercy! I did not murder your wife. I do not know anything about—"

"Descend!" snapped Tarzan, raising the point of his spear. He knew that the man lied and was not surprised that he did. A man who would murder for no cause would lie for less. Schneider still hesitated and pled. The ape-man jabbed him with the spear and Schneider slid fearfully over the top and began the perilous descent. Tarzan accompanied and assisted him over the worst places until at last they were within a few feet of the bottom.

"Be quiet now," cautioned the ape-man. He pointed at the entrance to what appeared to be a cave at the far end of the gulch. "There is a hungry lion in there. If you can reach that tree before he discovers you, you will have several days longer in which to enjoy life and then—when you are too weak to cling longer to the branches of the tree Numa, the man-eater, will feed again for the last time." He pushed Schneider from his foothold to the ground below. "Now run," he said.

The German trembling in terror started for the tree. He had almost reached it when a horrid roar broke from the mouth of the cave and almost simultaneously a gaunt, hunger-mad lion leaped into the daylight of the gulch. Schneider had but a few yards to cover; but the lion flew over the ground to circumvent him while Tarzan watched the race with a slight smile upon his lips.

Schneider won by a slender margin, and as Tarzan scaled the cliff to the summit, he heard behind him mingled with the roaring of the baffled cat, the gibbering of a human voice that was at the same time more bestial than the beast's.

Upon the brink of the cliff the ape-man turned and looked back into the gulch. High in the tree the German clung frantically to a branch across which his body lay. Beneath him was Numa—waiting.

The ape-man raised his face to Kudu, the sun, and from his mighty chest rose the savage victory cry of the bull ape.

3

In the German Lines

TARZAN was not yet fully revenged. There were many millions of Germans yet alive—enough to keep Tarzan pleasantly occupied the balance of his life, and yet not enough, should he kill them all, to recompense him for the great loss he had suffered—nor could the death of all those million Germans bring back his loved one.

While in the German camp in the Pare Mountains, which lie just east of the boundary line between German and British East Africa, Tarzan had overheard enough to suggest that the British were getting the worst of the fighting in Africa. At first he had given the matter but little thought, since, after the death of his wife, the one strong tie that had held him to civilization, he had renounced all mankind, considering himself no longer man, but ape.

After accounting for Schneider as satisfactorily as lay within his power he circled Kilimanjaro and hunted in the foothills to the north of that mightiest of mountains as he had discovered that in the neighborhood of the armies there was no hunting at all. Some pleasure he derived through conjuring mental pictures from time to time of the German he had left in the branches of the lone tree at the bottom of the high-walled gulch in which was penned the starving lion. He could imagine the man's mental anguish as he became weakened from hunger and maddened by thirst, knowing that sooner or later he must slip exhausted to the ground where waited the gaunt man-eater. Tarzan wondered if Schneider would have the courage to descend to the little rivulet for water should Numa leave the gulch and enter the cave, and then he pictured the mad race for the tree again when the lion charged out to seize his prey as he was certain to do, since the clumsy German could not descend to the rivulet without making at least some slight noise that would attract Numa's attention.

But even this pleasure palled, and more and more the ape-man found himself thinking of the English soldiers fighting against heavy odds and especially of the fact that it was Germans who were beating them. The thought made him lower his head and growl and it worried him not a little—a bit, perhaps, because he was finding it difficult to forget that he was an Englishman when he wanted only to be an ape. And at last the time came when he could not longer endure the thought of Germans killing Englishmen while he hunted in safety a bare march away.

His decision made, he set out in the direction of the German camp, no well-defined plan formulated; but with the general idea that once near the field of operations he might find an opportunity to harass the German command as he so well knew how to do. His way took him along the gorge close to the gulch in which he had left Schneider, and, yielding to a natural curiosity, he scaled the cliffs and made his way to the edge of the gulch. The tree was empty, nor was there sign of Numa, the lion. Picking up a rock he hurled it into the gulch, where it rolled to the very entrance to the cave. Instantly the lion appeared in the aperture; but such a different-looking lion from the great sleek brute that Tarzan had trapped there two weeks before. Now he was gaunt and emaciated, and when he walked he staggered.

"Where is the German?" shouted Tarzan. "Was he good eating, or only a bag of bones when he slipped and fell from the tree?"

Numa growled. "You look hungry, Numa," continued the ape-man. "You must have been very hungry to eat all the grass from your lair and even the bark from the tree as far up as you can reach. Would you like another German?" and smiling he turned away.

A few minutes later he came suddenly upon Bara, the deer, asleep beneath a tree, and as Tarzan was hungry he made a quick kill, and squatting beside his prey proceeded to eat his fill. As he was gnawing the last morsel from a bone his quick ears caught the padding of stealthy feet behind him, and turning he confronted Dango, the hyena, sneaking upon him. With a growl the ape-man picked up a fallen branch and hurled it at the skulking brute. "Go away, eater of carrion!" he cried; but Dango was hungry and being large and powerful he only snarled and circled slowly about as though watching for an opportunity to charge. Tarzan of the Apes knew Dango even better than Dango knew himself. He knew that the brute, made savage by hunger, was mustering its courage for an attack, that it was probably accustomed to man and therefore more or less fearless of him and so he unslung his heavy spear and laid it ready at his side while he continued his meal, all the time keeping a watchful eye upon the hyena.

He felt no fear, for long familiarity with the dangers of his wild world had so accustomed him to them that he took whatever came as a part of each day's existence as you accept the homely though no less real dangers of the farm, the range, or the crowded metropolis. Being jungle bred he was ready to protect his kill from all comers within ordinary limitations of caution. Under favorable conditions Tarzan would face even Numa himself and, if forced to seek safety by flight, he could do so without any feeling of shame. There was no braver creature roamed those savage wilds and at the same time there was none more wise—the two factors that had permitted him to survive.

Dango might have charged sooner but for the savage growls of the ape-man—growls which, coming from human lips, raised a question and a fear in the hyena's heart. He had attacked women and children in the native fields and he had frightened their men about their fires at night; but he never had seen a man-thing who made this sound that reminded him more of Numa angry than of a man afraid.

When Tarzan had completed his repast he was about to rise and hurl a clean-picked bone at the beast before he went his way, leaving the remains of his kill to Dango; but a sudden thought stayed him and instead he picked up the carcass of the deer, threw it over his shoulder, and set off in the direction of the gulch. For a few yards Dango followed, growling, and then realizing that he was being robbed of even a taste of the luscious flesh he cast discretion to the winds and charged. Instantly, as though Nature had given him eyes in the back of his head, Tarzan sensed the impending danger and, dropping Bara to the ground, turned with raised spear. Far back went the brown, right hand and then forward, lightning-like, backed by the power of giant muscles and the weight of his brawn and bone. The spear, released at the right instant, drove straight for Dango, caught him in the neck where it joined the shoulders and passed through the body.

When he had withdrawn the shaft from the hyena Tarzan shouldered both carcasses and continued on toward the gulch. Below lay Numa beneath the shade of the lone tree and at the ape-man's call he staggered slowly to his feet, yet weak as he was, he still growled savagely, even essaying a roar at the sight of his enemy. Tarzan let the two bodies slide over the rim of the cliff. "Eat, Numa!" he cried. "It may be that I shall need you again." He saw the lion, quickened to new life at the sight of food, spring upon the body of the deer and then he left him rending and tearing the flesh as he bolted great pieces into his empty maw.

The following day Tarzan came within sight of the German lines. From a wooded spur of the hills he looked down upon the enemy's left flank and beyond to the British lines. His position gave him a bird's-eye view of the field of battle, and his keen eyesight picked out many details that would not have been apparent to a man whose every sense was not trained to the highest point of perfection as were the ape-man's. He noted machine-gun emplacements cunningly hidden from the view of the British and listening posts placed well out in No Man's Land.

As his interested gaze moved hither and thither from one point of interest to another he heard from a point upon the hillside below him, above the roar of cannon and the crack of rifle fire, a single rifle spit. Immediately his attention was centered upon the spot where he knew a sniper must be hid. Patiently he awaited the next shot that would tell him more surely the exact location of the rifleman, and when it came he moved down the steep hillside with the stealth and quietness of a panther. Apparently he took no cognizance of where he stepped, yet never a loose stone was disturbed nor a twig broken—it was as though his feet saw.

Presently, as he passed through a clump of bushes, he came to the edge of a low cliff and saw upon a ledge some fifteen feet below him a German soldier prone behind an embankment of loose rock and leafy boughs that hid him from the view of the British lines. The man must have been an excellent shot, for he was well back of the German lines, firing over the heads of his fellows. His high-powered rifle was equipped with telescope sights and he also carried binoculars which he was in the act of using as Tarzan discovered him, either to note the effect of his last shot or to discover a new target. Tarzan let his eye move quickly toward that part of the British line the German seemed to be scanning, his keen sight revealing many excellent targets for a rifle placed so high above the trenches.

The Hun, evidently satisfied with his observations, laid aside his binoculars and again took up his rifle, placed its butt in the hollow of his shoulder and took careful aim. At the same instant a brown body sprang outward from the cliff above him. There was no sound and it is doubtful that the German ever knew what manner of creature it was that alighted heavily upon his back, for at the instant of impact the sinewy fingers of the ape-man circled the hairy throat of the Boche. There was a moment of futile struggling followed by the sudden realization of dissolution—the sniper was dead.

Lying behind the rampart of rocks and boughs, Tarzan looked down upon the scene below. Near at hand were the trenches of the Germans. He could see officers and men moving about in them and almost in front of him a well-hidden machine gun was traversing No Man's Land in an oblique direction, striking the British at such an angle as to make it difficult for them to locate it.

Tarzan watched, toying idly with the rifle of the dead German. Presently he fell to examining the mechanism of the piece. He glanced again toward the German trenches and changed the adjustment of the sights, then he placed the rifle to his shoulder and took aim. Tarzan was an excellent shot. With his civilized friends he had hunted big game with the weapons of civilization and though he never had killed except for food or in self-defense he had amused himself firing at inanimate targets thrown into the air and had perfected himself in the use of firearms without realizing that he had done so. Now indeed would he hunt big game. A slow smile touched his lips as his finger closed gradually upon the trigger. The rifle spoke and a German machine gunner collapsed behind his weapon. In three minutes Tarzan picked off the crew of that gun. Then he spotted a German officer emerging from a dugout and the three men in the bay with him. Tarzan was careful to leave no one in the immediate vicinity to question how Germans could be shot in German trenches when they were entirely concealed from enemy view.

Again adjusting his sights he took a long-range shot at a distant machine-gun crew to his right. With calm deliberation he wiped them out to a man. Two guns were silenced. He saw men running through the trenches and he picked off several of them. By this time the Germans were aware that something was amiss—that an uncanny sniper had discovered a point of vantage from which this sector of the trenches was plainly visible to him. At first they sought to discover his location in No Man's Land; but when an officer looking over the parapet through a periscope was struck full in the back of the head with a rifle bullet which passed through his skull and fell to the bottom of the trench they realized that it was beyond the parados rather than the parapet that they should search.

One of the soldiers picked up the bullet that had killed his officer, and then it was that real excitement prevailed in that particular bay, for the bullet was obviously of German make. Hugging the parados, messengers carried the word in both directions and presently periscopes were leveled above the parados and keen eyes were searching out the traitor. It did not take them long to locate the position of the hidden sniper and then Tarzan saw a machine gun being trained upon him. Before it had gotten into action its crew lay dead about it; but there were other men to take their places, reluctantly perhaps; but driven on by their officers they were forced to it and at the same time two other machine guns were swung around toward the ape-man and put into operation.

Realizing that the game was about up Tarzan with a farewell shot laid aside the rifle and melted into the hills behind him. For many minutes he could hear the sputter of machine-gun fire concentrated upon the spot he had just quit and smiled as he contemplated the waste of German ammunition.

"They have paid heavily for Wasimbu, the Waziri, whom they crucified, and for his slain fellows," he mused; "but for Jane they can never pay—no, not if I killed them all."

After dark that night he circled the flanks of both armies and passed through the British out-guards and into the British lines. No man saw him come. No man knew that he was there.

Headquarters of the Second Rhodesians occupied a sheltered position far enough back of the lines to be comparatively safe from enemy observation. Even lights were permitted, and Colonel Capell sat before a field table, on which was spread a military map, talking with several of his officers. A large tree spread above them, a lantern sputtered dimly upon the table, while a small fire burned upon the ground close at hand. The enemy had no planes and no other observers could have seen the lights from the German lines.

The officers were discussing the advantage in numbers possessed by the enemy and the inability of the British to more than hold their present position. They could not advance. Already they had sustained severe losses in every attack and had always been driven back by overwhelming numbers. There were hidden machine guns, too, that bothered the colonel considerably. It was evidenced by the fact that he often reverted to them during the conversation.

"Something silenced them for a while this afternoon," said one of the younger officers. "I was observing at the time and I couldn't make out what the fuss was about; but they seemed to be having a devil of a time in a section of trench on their left. At one time I could have sworn they were attacked in the rear—I reported it to you at the time, sir, you'll recall—for the blighters were pepperin' away at the side of that bluff behind them. I could see the dirt fly. I don't know what it could have been."

There was a slight rustling among the branches of the tree above them and simultaneously a lithe, brown body dropped in their midst. Hands moved quickly to the butts of pistols; but otherwise there was no movement among the officers. First they looked wonderingly at the almost naked white man standing there with the firelight playing upon rounded muscles,

took in the primitive attire and the equally primitive armament and then all eyes turned toward the colonel.

"Who the devil are you, sir?" snapped that officer.

"Tarzan of the Apes," replied the newcomer.

"Oh, Greystoke!" cried a major, and stepped forward with
outstretched hand.

"Preswick," acknowledged Tarzan as he took the proffered
hand.

"I didn't recognize you at first," apologized the major. "The
last time I saw you you were in London in evening dress.
Quite a difference—'pon my word, man, you'll have to admit
it."

Tarzan smiled and turned toward the colonel. "I overheard
your conversation," he said. "I have just come from behind
the German lines. Possibly I can help you."

The colonel looked questioningly toward Major Preswick
who quickly rose to the occasion and presented the ape-man
to his commanding officer and fellows. Briefly Tarzan told
them what it was that brought him out alone in pursuit of the
Germans.

"And now you have come to join us?" asked the colonel.

Tarzan shook his head. "Not regularly," he replied. "I
must fight in my own way; but I can help you. Whenever I
wish I can enter the German lines."

Capell smiled and shook his head. "It's not so easy as you
think," he said; "I've lost two good officers in the last week
trying it—and they were experienced men; none better in the
Intelligence Department."

"Is it more difficult than entering the British lines?" asked
Tarzan.

The colonel was about to reply when a new thought appeared to occur to him and he looked quizzically at the ape-
man. "Who brought you here?" he asked. "Who passed you
through our out-guards?"

"I have just come through the German lines and yours and
passed through your camp," he replied. "Send word to as-
certain if anyone saw me."

"But who accompanied you?" insisted Capell.

"I came alone," replied Tarzan and then, drawing himself to
his full height, "You men of civilization, when you come into
the jungle, are as dead among the quick. Manu, the monkey,
is a sage by comparison. I marvel that you exist at all—only
your numbers, your weapons, and your power of reasoning
save you. Had I a few hundred great apes with your reasoning power I could drive the Germans into the ocean as quickly
as the remnant of them could reach the coast. Fortunate it is
for you that the dumb brutes cannot combine. Could they,

Africa would remain forever free of men. But come, can I help you? Would you like to know where several machine-gun emplacements are hidden?"

The colonel assured him that they would, and a moment later Tarzan had traced upon the map the location of three that had been bothering the English. "There is a weak spot here," he said, placing a finger upon the map. "It is held by blacks; but the machine guns out in front are manned by whites. If—wait! I have a plan. You can fill that trench with your own men and enfilade the trenches to its right with their own machine guns."

Colonel Capell smiled and shook his head. "It sounds very easy," he said.

"It *is* easy—for me," replied the ape-man. "I can empty that section of trench without a shot. I was raised in the jungle—I know the jungle folk—the Gomangani as well as the others. Look for me again on the second night," and he turned to leave.

"Wait," said the colonel. "I will send an officer to pass you through the lines."

Tarzan smiled and moved away. As he was leaving the little group about headquarters he passed a small figure wrapped in an officer's heavy overcoat. The collar was turned up and the visor of the military cap pulled well down over the eyes; but, as the ape-man passed, the light from the fire illuminated the features of the newcomer for an instant, revealing to Tarzan a vaguely familiar face. Some officer he had known in London, doubtless, he surmised, and went his way through the British camp and the British lines all unknown to the watchful sentinels of the out-guard.

Nearly all night he moved across Kilimanjaro's foothills, tracking by instinct an unknown way, for he guessed that what he sought would be found on some wooded slope higher up than he had come upon his other recent journeys in this, to him, little known country. Three hours before dawn his keen nostrils apprised him that somewhere in the vicinity he would find what he wanted, and so he climbed into a tall tree and settled himself for a few hours' sleep.

4

When the Lion Fed

K UDU, the sun, was well up in the heavens when Tarzan awoke. The ape-man stretched his giant limbs, ran his fingers through his thick hair, and swung lightly down to earth. Immediately he took up the trail he had come in search of, following it by scent down into a deep ravine. Cautiously he went now, for his nose told him that the quarry was close at hand, and presently from an overhanging bough he looked down upon Horta, the boar, and many of his kinsmen. Unslinging his bow and selecting an arrow, Tarzan fitted the shaft and, drawing it far back, took careful aim at the largest of the great pigs. In the ape-man's teeth were other arrows, and no sooner had the first one sped, than he had fitted and shot another bolt. Instantly the pigs were in turmoil, not knowing from whence the danger threatened. They stood stupidly at first and then commenced milling around until six of their number lay dead or dying about them; then with a chorus of grunts and squeals they started off at a wild run, disappearing quickly in the dense underbrush.

Tarzan then descended from the tree, dispatched those that were not already dead and proceeded to skin the carcasses. As he worked, rapidly and with great skill, he neither hummed nor whistled as does the average man of civilization. It was in numerous little ways such as these that he differed from other men, due, probably, to his early jungle training. The beasts of the jungle that he had been reared among were playful to maturity but seldom thereafter. His fellow-apes, especially the bulls, became fierce and surly as they grew older. Life was a serious matter during lean seasons—one had to fight to secure one's share of food then, and the habit once formed became lifelong. Hunting for food was the life labor of the jungle bred, and a life labor is a thing not to be approached with levity nor prosecuted lightly. So all work found Tarzan serious, though he still retained what the other beasts lost as they grew older—a sense of humor, which he gave play to when the mood suited him. It was a grim humor and sometimes ghastly; but it satisfied Tarzan.

Then, too, were one to sing and whistle while working on the ground, concentration would be impossible. Tarzan possessed the ability to concentrate each of his five senses upon its particular business. Now he worked at skinning the six pigs and his eyes and his fingers worked as though there was naught else in all the world than these six carcasses; but his ears and his nose were as busily engaged elsewhere—the former ranging the forest all about and the latter assaying each passing zephyr. It was his nose that first discovered the approach of Sabor, the lioness, when the wind shifted for a moment.

As clearly as though he had seen her with his eyes, Tarzan knew that the lioness had caught the scent of the freshly killed pigs and immediately had moved down wind in their direction. He knew from the strength of the scent spoor and the rate of the wind about how far away she was and that she was approaching from behind him. He was finishing the last pig and he did not hurry. The five pelts lay close at hand—he had been careful to keep them thus together and near him —an ample tree waved its low branches above him.

He did not even turn his head for he knew she was not yet in sight; but he bent his ears just a bit more sharply for the first sound of her nearer approach. When the final skin had been removed he rose. Now he heard Sabor in the bushes to his rear, but not yet too close. Leisurely he gathered up the six pelts and one of the carcasses, and as the lioness appeared between the boles of two trees he swung upward into the branches above him. Here he hung the hides over a limb, seated himself comfortably upon another with his back against the bole of the tree, cut a hind quarter from the carcass he had carried with him and proceeded to satisfy his hunger. Sabor slunk, growling, from the brush, cast a wary eye upward toward the ape-man and then fell upon the nearest carcass.

Tarzan looked down upon her and grinned, recalling an argument he had once had with a famous big-game hunter who had declared that the king of beasts ate only what he himself had killed. Tarzan knew better for he had seen Numa and Sabor stoop even to carrion.

Having filled his belly, the ape-man fell to work upon the hides—all large and strong. First he cut strips from them about half an inch wide. When he had sufficient number of these strips he sewed two of the hides together, afterwards piercing holes every three or four inches around the edges. Running another strip through these holes gave him a large bag with a drawstring. In similar fashion he produced four other like bags, but smaller, from the four remaining hides and had several strips left over.

All this done he threw a large, juicy fruit at Sabor, cached the remainder of the pig in a crotch of the tree and swung off toward the southwest through the middle terraces of the forest, carrying his five bags with him. Straight he went to the rim of the gulch where he had imprisoned Numa, the lion. Very stealthily he approached the edge and peered over. Numa was not in sight. Tarzan sniffed and listened. He could hear nothing, yet he knew that Numa must be within the cave. He hoped that he slept—much depended upon Numa not discovering him.

Cautiously he lowered himself over the edge of the cliff, and with utter noiselessness commenced the descent toward the bottom of the gulch. He stopped often and turned his keen eyes and ears in the direction of the cave's mouth at the far end of the gulch, some hundred feet away. As he neared the foot of the cliff his danger increased greatly. If he could reach the bottom and cover half the distance to the tree that stood in the center of the gulch he would feel comparatively safe for then, even if Numa appeared, he felt that he could beat him either to the cliff or to the tree, but to scale the first thirty feet of the cliff rapidly enough to elude the leaping beast would require a running start of at least twenty feet as there were no very good hand- or footholds close to the bottom —he had had to run up the first twenty feet like a squirrel running up a tree that other time he had beaten an infuriated Numa to it. He had no desire to attempt it again unless the conditions were equally favorable at least, for he had escaped Numa's raking talons by only a matter of inches on the former occasion.

At last he stood upon the floor of the gulch. Silent as a disembodied spirit he advanced toward the tree. He was half way there and no sign of Numa. He reached the scarred hole from which the famished lion had devoured the bark and even torn pieces of the wood itself and yet Numa had not appeared. As he drew himself up to the lower branches he commenced to wonder if Numa were in the cave after all. Could it be possible that he had forced the barrier of rocks with which Tarzan had plugged the other end of the passage where it opened into the outer world of freedom? Or was Numa dead? The ape-man doubted the verity of the latter suggestion as he had fed the lion the entire carcasses of a deer and a hyena only a few days since—he could not have starved in so short a time, while the little rivulet running across the gulch furnished him with water a-plenty.

Tarzan started to descend and investigate the cavern when

it occurred to him that it would save effort were he to lure
Numa out instead. Acting upon the thought he uttered a low
growl. Immediately he was rewarded by the sound of a movement within the cave and an instant later a wild-eyed, haggard
lion rushed forth ready to face the devil himself were he edible.
When Numa saw Tarzan, fat and sleek, perched in the tree
he became suddenly the embodiment of frightful rage. His
eyes and his nose told him that this was the creature respon-
sible for his predicament and also that this creature was good
to eat. Frantically the lion sought to scramble up the bole of
the tree. Twice he leaped high enough to catch the lowest
branches with his paws, but both times he fell backward to
the earth. Each time he became more furious. His growls
and roars were incessant and horrible and all the time Tarzan
sat grinning down upon him, taunting him in jungle billings-
gate for his inability to reach him and mentally exulting that
always Numa was wasting his already waning strength.

Finally the ape-man rose and unslung his rope. He arranged
the coils carefully in his left hand and the noose in his right,
and then he took a position with each foot on one of two
branches that lay in about the same horizontal plane and with
his back pressed firmly against the stem of the tree. There
he stood hurling insults at Numa until the beast was again
goaded into leaping upward at him, and as Numa rose the
noose dropped quickly over his head and about his neck. A
quick movement of Tarzan's rope hand tightened the coil and
when Numa slipped backward to the ground only his hind
feet touched, for the ape-man held him swinging by the neck.

Moving slowly outward upon the two branches Tarzan
swung Numa out so that he could not reach the bole of the
tree with his raking talons, then he made the rope fast after
drawing the lion clear of the ground, dropped his five pigskin
sacks to earth and leaped down himself. Numa was striking
frantically at the grass rope with his fore claws. At any moment he might sever it and Tarzan must, therefore, work
rapidly.

First he drew the larger bag over Numa's head and secured
it about his neck with the draw string, then he managed, after
considerable effort, during which he barely escaped being torn
to ribbons by the mighty talons, to hog-tie Numa—drawing
his four legs together and securing them in that position with
the strips trimmed from the pigskins.

By this time the lion's efforts had almost ceased—it was
evident that he was being rapidly strangled and as that did
not at all suit the purpose of the Tarmangani the later swung
again into the tree, unfastened the rope from above and
lowered the lion to the ground where he immediately fol-

lowed it and loosed the noose about Numa's neck. Then he drew his hunting knife and cut two round holes in the front of the head bag opposite the lion's eyes for the double purpose of permitting him to see and giving him sufficient air to breathe.

This done Tarzan busied himself fitting the other bags, one over each of Numa's formidably armed paws. Those on the hind feet he secured not only by tightening the draw strings but also rigged garters that fastened tightly around the legs above the hocks. He secured the front-feet bags in place similarly above the great knees. Now, indeed, was Numa, the lion, reduced to the harmlessness of Bara, the deer.

By now Numa was showing signs of returning life. He gasped for breath and struggled; but the strips of pigskin that held his four legs together were numerous and tough. Tarzan watched and was sure that they would hold, yet Numa is mightily muscled and there was the chance, always, that he might struggle free of his bonds after which all would depend upon the efficacy of Tarzan's bags and draw strings.

After Numa had again breathed normally and was able to roar out his protests and his rage, his struggles increased to Titanic proportions for a short time; but as a lion's powers of endurance are in no way proportionate to his size and strength he soon tired and lay quietly. Amid renewed growling and another futile attempt to free himself, Numa was finally forced to submit to the further indignity of having a rope secured about his neck; but this time it was no noose that might tighten and strangle him; but a bowline knot, which does not tighten or slip under strain.

The other end of the rope Tarzan fastened to the stem of the tree, then he quickly cut the bonds securing Numa's legs and leaped aside as the beast sprang to his feet. For a moment the lion stood with legs far outspread, then he raised first one paw and then another, shaking them energetically in an effort to dislodge the strange footgear that Tarzan had fastened upon them. Finally he began to paw at the bag upon his head. The ape-man, standing with ready spear, watched Numa's efforts intently. Would the bags hold? He sincerely hoped so. Or would all his labor prove fruitless?

As the clinging things upon his feet and face resisted his every effort to dislodge them, Numa became frantic. He rolled upon the ground, fighting, biting, scratching, and roaring; he leaped to his feet and sprang into the air; he charged Tarzan, only to be brought to a sudden stop as the rope securing him to the tree tautened. Then Tarzan stepped in and rapped him smartly on the head with the shaft of his spear. Numa reared upon his hind feet and struck at the ape-man and in return received a cuff on one ear that sent him reeling sideways. When he returned to the attack he was again sent sprawling. After the fourth effort it appeared to dawn upon the king of beasts that he had met his master, his head and tail dropped and when Tarzan advanced upon him he backed away, though still growling.

Leaving Numa tied to the tree Tarzan entered the tunnel and removed the barricade from the opposite end, after which he returned to the gulch and strode straight for the tree. Numa lay in his path and as Tarzan approached growled menacingly. The ape-man cuffed him aside and unfastened the rope from the tree. Then ensued a half-hour of stubbornly fought battle while Tarzan endeavored to drive Numa through the tunnel ahead of him and Numa persistently refused to be driven. At last, however, by dint of the unrestricted use of his spear point, the ape-man succeeded in forcing the lion to move ahead of him and eventually guided him into the passageway. Once inside, the problem became simpler since Tarzan followed closely in the rear with his sharp spear point, an unremitting incentive to forward movement on the part of the lion. If Numa hesitated he was prodded. If he backed up the result was extremely painful and so, being a wise lion who was learning rapidly, he decided to keep on going and at the end of the tunnel, emerging into the outer world, he sensed freedom, raised his head and tail and started off at a run.

Tarzan, still on his hands and knees just inside the entrance, was taken unaware with the result that he was sprawled forward upon his face and dragged a hundred yards across the rocky ground before Numa was brought to a stand. It was a scratched and angry Tarzan who scrambled to his feet. At first he was tempted to chastise Numa; but, as the ape-man seldom permitted his temper to guide him in any direction not countenanced by reason, he quickly abandoned the idea.

Having taught Numa the rudiments of being driven, he now urged him forward and there commenced as strange a journey as the unrecorded history of the jungle contains. The balance of that day was eventful both for Tarzan and for Numa. From open rebellion at first the lion passed through stages of stubborn resistance and grudging obedience to final surrender. He was a very tired, hungry, and thirsty lion when night overtook them; but there was to be no food for him that day or the next—Tarzan did not dare risk removing the head bag, though he did cut another hole which permitted Numa to quench his thirst shortly after dark. Then he tied him to a tree, sought food for himself, and stretched out among the branches above his captive for a few hours' sleep.

Early the following morning they resumed their journey, winding over the low foothills south of Kilimanjaro, toward the east. The beasts of the jungle who saw them took one look and fled. The scent spoor of Numa, alone, might have been enough to have provoked flight in many of the lesser animals, but the sight of this strange apparition that smelled like a lion, but looked like nothing they ever had seen before, being led through the jungles by a giant Tarmangani was too much for even the more formidable denizens of the wild.

Sabor, the lioness, recognizing from a distance the scent of her lord and master intermingled with that of a Tarmangani and the hide of Horta, the boar, trotted through the aisles of the forest to investigate. Tarzan and Numa heard her coming, for she voiced a plaintive and questioning whine as the baffling mixture of odors aroused her curiosity and her fears, for lions, however terrible they may appear, are often timid animals and Sabor, being of the gentler sex, was, naturally, habitually inquisitive as well.

Tarzan unslung his spear for he knew that he might now easily have to fight to retain his prize. Numa halted and turned his outraged head in the direction of the coming she. He voiced a throaty growl that was almost a purr. Tarzan was upon the point of prodding him on again when Sabor broke into view, and behind her the ape-man saw that which gave him instant pause—four full-grown lions trailing the lioness.

To have goaded Numa then into active resistance might have brought the whole herd down upon him and so Tarzan waited to learn first what their attitude would be. He had no idea of relinquishing his lion without a battle; but knowing lions as he did, he knew that there was no assurance as to just what the newcomers would do.

The lioness was young and sleek, and the four males were in their prime—as handsome lions as he ever had seen. Three of the males were scantily maned but one, the foremost, carried a splendid, black mane that rippled in the breeze as he trotted majestically forward. The lioness halted a hundred feet from Tarzan, while the lions came on past her and stopped a few feet nearer. Their ears were upstanding and their eyes filled with curiosity. Tarzan could not even guess what they might do. The lion at his side faced them fully, standing silent now and watchful.

Suddenly the lioness gave vent to another little whine, at which Tarzan's lion voiced a terrific roar and leaped forward straight toward the beast of the black mane. The sight of this awesome creature with the strange face was too much for the lion toward which he leaped, dragging Tarzan after him, and with a growl the lion turned and fled, followed by his companions and the she.

Numa attempted to follow them; Tarzan held him in leash and when he turned upon him in rage, beat him unmercifully across the head with his spear. Shaking his head and growling, the lion at last moved off again in the direction they had been traveling; but it was an hour before he ceased to sulk. He was very hungry—half famished in fact—and consequently of an ugly temper, yet so thoroughly subdued by Tarzan's heroic methods of lion taming that he was presently pacing along at the ape-man's side like some huge St. Bernard.

It was dark when the two approached the British right, after a slight delay farther back because of a German patrol it had been necessary to elude. A short distance from the British line of out-guard sentinels Tarzan tied Numa to a tree and continued on alone. He evaded a sentinel, passed the out-guard and support, and by devious ways came again to Colonel Capell's headquarters, where he appeared before the officers gathered there as a disembodied spirit materializing out of thin air.

When they saw who it was that came thus unannounced they smiled and the colonel scratched his head in perplexity.

"Someone should be shot for this," he said. "I might just as well not establish an out-post if a man can filter through whenever he pleases."

Tarzan smiled. "Do not blame them," he said, "for I am not a man. I am Tarmangani. Any Mangani who wished to, could enter your camp almost at will; but if you have them for sentinels no one could enter without their knowledge."

"What are the Mangani?" asked the colonel. "Perhaps we might enlist a bunch of the beggars."

Tarzan shook his head. "They are the great apes," he explained; "my people; but you could not use them. They cannot concentrate long enough upon a single idea. If I told them of this they would be much interested for a short time— I might even hold the interest of a few long enough to get them here and explain their duties to them; but soon they would lose interest and when you needed them most they might be off in the forest searching for beetles instead of watching their posts. They have the minds of little children —that is why they remain what they are."

"You call them Mangani and yourself Tarmangani—what is the difference?" asked Major Preswick.

"*Tar* means white," replied Tarzan, "and *Mangani*, great ape. My name—the name they gave me in the tribe of Kerchak—means White-skin. When I was a little balu my skin,

I presume, looked very white indeed against the beautiful, black coat of Kala, my foster mother and so they called me Tarzan, the Tarmangani. They call you, too, Tarmangani," he concluded, smiling.

Capell smiled. "It is no reproach, Greystoke," he said; "and, by Jove, it would be a mark of distinction if a fellow could act the part. And now how about your plan? Do you still think you can empty the trench opposite our sector?"

"Is it still held by Gomangani?" asked Tarzan.

"What are Gomangani?" inquired the colonel. "It is still held by native troops, if that is what you mean."

"Yes," replied the ape-man, "the Gomangani are the great black apes—the Negroes."

"What do you intend doing and what do you want us to do?" asked Capell.

Tarzan approached the table and placed a finger on the map. "Here is a listening post," he said; "they have a machine gun in it. A tunnel connects it with this trench at this point." His finger moved from place to place on the map as he talked. "Give me a bomb and when you hear it burst in this listening post let your men start across No Man's Land slowly. Presently they will hear a commotion in the enemy trench; but they need not hurry, and, whatever they do, have them come quietly. You might also warn them that I may be in the trench and that I do not care to be shot or bayoneted."

"And that is all?" queried Capell, after directing an officer to give Tarzan a hand grenade; "you will empty the trench alone?"

"Not exactly alone," replied Tarzan with a grim smile; "but I shall empty it, and, by the way, your men may come in through the tunnel from the listening post if you prefer. In about half an hour, Colonel," and he turned and left them.

As he passed through the camp there flashed suddenly upon the screen of recollection, conjured there by some reminder of his previous visit to headquarters, doubtless, the image of the officer he had passed as he quit the colonel that other time and simultaneously recognition of the face that had been revealed by the light from the fire. He shook his head dubiously. No, it could not be and yet the features of the young officer were identical with those of Fräulein Kircher, the German spy he had seen at German headquarters the night he took Major Schneider from under the nose of the Hun general and his staff.

Beyond the last line of sentinels Tarzan moved quickly in the direction of Numa, the lion. The beast was lying down as Tarzan approached, but he rose as the ape-man reached his side. A low whine escaped his muzzled lips. Tarzan smiled for he recognized in the new note almost a supplication—it was more like the whine of a hungry dog begging for food than the voice of the proud king of beasts.

"Soon you will kill—and feed," he murmured in the vernacular of the great apes.

He unfastened the rope from about the tree and, with Numa close at his side, slunk into No Man's Land. There was little rifle fire and only an occasional shell vouched for the presence of artillery behind the opposing lines. As the shells from both sides were falling well back of the trenches, they constituted no menace to Tarzan; but the noise of them and that of the rifle fire had a marked effect upon Numa who crouched, trembling, close to the Tarmangani as though seeking protection.

Cautiously the two beasts moved forward toward the listening post of the Germans. In one hand Tarzan carried the bomb the English had given him, in the other was the coiled rope attached to the lion. At last Tarzan could see the position a few yards ahead. His keen eyes picked out the head and shoulders of the sentinel on watch. The ape-man grasped the bomb firmly in his right hand. He measured the distance with his eye and gathered his feet beneath him, then in a single motion he rose and threw the missile, immediately flattening himself prone upon the ground.

Five seconds later there was a terrific explosion in the center of the listening post. Numa gave a nervous start and attempted to break away; but Tarzan held him and, leaping to his feet, ran forward, dragging Numa after him. At the edge of the post he saw below him but slight evidence that the position had been occupied at all, for only a few shreds of torn flesh remained. About the only thing that had not been demolished was a machine gun which had been protected by sand bags.

There was not an instant to lose. Already a relief might be crawling through the communication tunnel, for it must have been evident to the sentinels in the Hun trenches that the listening post had been demolished. Numa hesitated to follow Tarzan into the excavation; but the ape-man, who was in no mood to temporize, jerked him roughly to the bottom. Before them lay the mouth of the tunnel that led back from No Man's Land to the German trenches. Tarzan pushed Numa forward until his head was almost in the aperture, then as though it were an afterthought, he turned quickly and, taking the machine gun from the parapet, placed it in the bottom of the hole close at hand, after which he turned again to Numa, and with his knife quickly cut the garters that held the bags

upon his front paws. Before the lion could know that a part
of his formidable armament was again released for action,
Tarzan had cut the rope from his neck and the head bag from
his face, and grabbing the lion from the rear had thrust him
partially into the mouth of the tunnel.

Then Numa balked, only to feel the sharp prick of Tarzan's
knife point in his hind quarters. Goading him on the ape-man
finally succeeded in getting the lion sufficiently far into the
tunnel so that there was no chance of his escaping other than
by going forward or deliberately backing into the sharp blade
at his rear. Then Tarzan cut the bags from the great hind
feet, placed his shoulder and his knife point against Numa's
seat, dug his toes into the loose earth that had been broken
up by the explosion of the bomb, and shoved.

Inch by inch at first Numa advanced. He was growling
now and presently he commenced to roar. Suddenly he
leaped forward and Tarzan knew that he had caught the
scent of meat ahead. Dragging the machine gun beside him
the ape-man followed quickly after the lion whose roars he
could plainly hear ahead mingled with the unmistakable
screams of frightened men. Once again a grim smile touched
the lips of this man-beast.

"They murdered my Waziri," he muttered; "they crucified
Wasimbu, son of Muviro."

When Tarzan reached the trench and emerged into it there
was no one in sight in that particular bay, nor in the next, nor
the next as he hurried forward in the direction of the German
center; but in the fourth bay he saw a dozen men jammed in
the angle of the traverse at the end while leaping upon them
and rending with talons and fangs was Numa, a terrific in-
carnation of ferocity and ravenous hunger.

Whatever held the men at last gave way as they fought
madly with one another in their efforts to escape this dread
creature that from their infancy had filled them with terror,
and again they were retreating. Some clambered over the
parados and some even over the parapet preferring the dangers of No Man's Land to this other soul-searing menace.

As the British advanced slowly toward the German trenches,
they first met terrified blacks who ran into their arms only
too willing to surrender. That pandemonium had broken
loose in the Hun trench was apparent to the Rhodesians not
only from the appearance of the deserters, but from the sounds
of screaming, cursing men which came clearly to their ears;
but there was one that baffled them for it resembled nothing
more closely than the infuriated growling of an angry lion.

And when at last they reached the trench, those farthest on

the left of the advancing Britishers heard a machine gun sputter suddenly before them and saw a huge lion leap over the German parados with the body of a screaming Hun soldier between his jaws and vanish into the shadows of the night, while squatting upon a traverse to their left was Tarzan of the Apes with a machine gun before him with which he was raking the length of the German trenches.

The foremost Rhodesians saw something else—they saw a huge German officer emerge from a dugout just in rear of the ape-man. They saw him snatch up a discarded rifle with bayonet fixed and creep upon the apparently unconscious Tarzan. They ran forward, shouting warnings; but above the pandemonium of the trenches and the machine gun their voices could not reach him. The German leaped upon the parapet behind him—the fat hands raised the rifle butt aloft for the cowardly downward thrust into the naked back and then, as moves Ara, the lightning, moved Tarzan of the Apes.

It was no man who leaped forward upon that Boche officer, striking aside the sharp bayonet as one might strike aside a straw in a baby's hand—it was a wild beast and the roar of a wild beast was upon those savage lips, for as that strange sense that Tarzan owned in common with the other jungle-bred creatures of his wild domain warned him of the presence behind him and he had whirled to meet the attack, his eyes had seen the corps and regimental insignia upon the other's blouse—it was the same as that worn by the murderers of his wife and his people, by the despoilers of his home and his happiness.

It was a wild beast whose teeth fastened upon the shoulder of the Hun—it was a wild beast whose talons sought that fat neck. And then the boys of the Second Rhodesian Regiment saw that which will live forever in their memories. They saw the giant ape-man pick the heavy German from the ground and shake him as a terrier might shake a rat—as Sabor, the lioness, sometimes shakes her prey. They saw the eyes of the Hun bulge in horror as he vainly struck with his futile hands against the massive chest and head of his assailant. They saw Tarzan suddenly spin the man about and placing a knee in the middle of his back and an arm about his neck bend his shoulders slowly backward. The German's knees gave and he sank upon them; but still that irresistible force bent him further and further. He screamed in agony for a moment—then something snapped and Tarzan cast him aside, a limp and lifeless thing.

The Rhodesians started forward, a cheer upon their lips—a cheer that never was uttered—a cheer that froze in their throats, for at that moment Tarzan placed a foot upon the carcass of his kill and, raising his face to the heavens, gave voice to the weird and terrifying victory cry of the bull ape.

Underlieutenant von Goss was dead.

Without a backward glance at the awe-struck soldiers Tarzan leaped the trench and was gone.

5

The Golden Locket

THE little British army in East Africa, after suffering severe reverses at the hands of a numerically much superior force, was at last coming into its own. The German offensive had been broken and the Huns were now slowly and doggedly retreating along the railway to Tanga. The break in the German lines had followed the clearing of a section of their left-flank trenches of native soldiers by Tarzan and Numa, the lion, upon that memorable night that the ape-man had loosed a famishing man-eater among the superstitious and terror-stricken blacks. The Second Rhodesian Regiment had immediately taken possession of the abandoned trench and from this position their flanking fire had raked contiguous sections of the German line, the diversion rendering possible a successful night attack on the part of the balance of the British forces.

Weeks had elapsed. The Germans were contesting stubbornly every mile of waterless, thorn-covered ground and clinging desperately to their positions along the railway. The officers of the Second Rhodesians had seen nothing more of Tarzan of the Apes since he had slain Underlieutenant von Goss and disappeared toward the very heart of the German position, and there were those among them who believed that he had been killed within the enemy lines.

"They may have killed him," assented Colonel Capell; "but I fancy they never captured the beggar alive."

Nor had they, nor killed him either. Tarzan had spent those intervening weeks pleasantly and profitably. He had amassed a considerable fund of knowledge concerning the disposition and strength of German troops, their methods of warfare, and the various ways in which a lone Tarmangani might annoy an army and lower its morale.

At present he was prompted by a specific desire. There was a certain German spy whom he wished to capture alive and take back to the British. When he had made his first visit

to German headquarters, he had seen a young woman deliver
a paper to the German general, and later he had seen that
same young woman within the British lines in the uniform of a
British officer. The conclusions were obvious—she was a spy.

And so Tarzan haunted German headquarters upon many
nights hoping to see her again or to pick up some clew as to
her whereabouts, and at the same time he utilized many an
artifice whereby he might bring terror to the hearts of the
Germans. That he was successful was often demonstrated by
the snatches of conversation he overheard as he prowled
through the German camps. One night as he lay concealed
in the bushes close beside a regimental headquarters he
listened to the conversation of several Boche officers. One of
the men reverted to the stories told by the native troops in
connection with their rout by a lion several weeks before and
the simultaneous appearance in their trenches of a naked,
white giant whom they were perfectly assured was some
demon of the jungle.

"The fellow must have been the same as he who leaped
into the general's headquarters and carried off Schneider,"
asserted one. "I wonder how he happened to single out the
poor major. They say the creature seemed interested in no
one but Schneider. He had von Kelter in his grasp, and he
might easily have taken the general himself; but he ignored
them all except Schneider. Him he pursued about the room,
seized and carried off into the night. Gott knows what his
fate was."

"Captain Fritz Schneider has some sort of theory," said
another. "He told me only a week or two ago that he thinks
he knows why his brother was taken—that it was a case of
mistaken identity. He was not so sure about it until von Goss
was killed, apparently by the same creature, the night the
lion entered the trenches. Von Goss was attached to Schneider's company. One of Schneider's men was found with his
neck wrung the same night that the major was carried off and
Schneider thinks that this devil is after him and his command
—that it came for him that night and got his brother by
mistake. He says Kraut told him that in presenting the major
to Fräulein Kircher the former's name was no sooner spoken
than this wild man leaped through the window and made for
him."

Suddenly the little group became rigid—listening. "What
was that?" snapped one, eyeing the bushes from which a
smothered snarl had issued as Tarzan of the Apes realized
that through his mistake the perpetrator of the horrid crime at
his bungalow still lived—that the murderer of his wife went
yet unpunished.

For a long minute the officers stood with tensed nerves, every eye rivetted upon the bushes from whence the ominous sound had issued. Each recalled recent mysterious disappearances from the heart of camps as well as from lonely out-guards. Each thought of the silent dead he had seen, slain almost within sight of their fellows by some unseen creature. They thought of the marks upon dead throats—made by talons or by giant fingers, they could not tell which—and those upon shoulders and jugulars where powerful teeth had fastened and they waited with drawn pistols.

Once the bushes moved almost imperceptibly and an instant later one of the officers, without warning, fired into them; but Tarzan of the Apes was not there. In the interval between the moving of the bushes and the firing of the shot he had melted into the night. Ten minutes later he was hovering on the outskirts of that part of camp where were bivouacked for the night the black soldiers of a native company commanded by one Hauptmann Fritz Schneider. The men were stretched upon the ground without tents; but there were tents pitched for the officers. Toward these Tarzan crept. It was slow and perilous work, as the Germans were now upon the alert for the uncanny foe that crept into their camps to take his toll by night, yet the ape-man passed their sentinels, eluded the vigilance of the interior guard, and crept at last to the rear of the officers' line.

Here he flattened himself against the ground close behind the nearest tent and listened. From within came the regular breathing of a sleeping man—one only. Tarzan was satisfied. With his knife he cut the tie strings of the rear flap and entered. He made no noise. The shadow of a falling leaf, floating gently to earth upon a still day, could have been no more soundless. He moved to the side of the sleeping man and bent low over him. He could not know, of course, whether it was Schneider or another, as he had never seen Schneider; but he meant to know and to know even more. Gently he shook the man by the shoulder. The fellow turned heavily and grunted in a thick guttural.

"Silence!" admonished the ape-man in a low whisper. "Silence—I kill."

The Hun opened his eyes. In the dim light he saw a giant figure bending over him. Now a mighty hand grasped his shoulder and another closed lightly about his throat.

"Make no outcry," commanded Tarzan; but answer in a whisper my questions. What is your name?"

"Luberg," replied the officer. He was trembling. The weird presence of this naked giant filled him with dread. He, too, recalled the men mysteriously murdered in the still watches of the night camps. "What do you want?"

"Where is Hauptmann Fritz Schneider?" asked Tarzan, "Which is his tent?"

"He is not here," replied Luberg. "He was sent to Wilhelmstal yesterday."

"I shall not kill you—now," said the ape-man. "First I shall go and learn if you have lied to me and if you have your death shall be the more terrible. Do you know how Major Schneider died?"

Luberg shook his head negatively.

"I do," continued Tarzan, "and it was not a nice way to die —even for an accursed German. Turn over with your face down and cover your eyes. Do not move or make any sound."

The man did as he was bid and the instant that his eyes were turned away, Tarzan slipped from the tent. An hour later he was outside the German camp and headed for the little hill town of Wilhelmstal, the summer seat of government of German East Africa.

Fräulein Bertha Kircher was lost. She was humiliated and angry—it was long before she would admit it, that she, who prided herself upon her woodcraft, was lost in this little patch of country between the Pangani and the Tanga railway. She knew that Wilhelmstal lay southeast of her about fifty miles; but, through a combination of untoward circumstances, she found herself unable to determine which was southeast.

In the first place she had set out from German headquarters on a well-marked road that was being traveled by troops and with every reason to believe that she would follow that road to Wilhelmstal. Later she had been warned from this road by word that a strong British patrol had come down the west bank of the Pangani, effected a crossing south of her, and was even then marching on the railway at Tonda.

After leaving the road she found herself in thick bush and as the sky was heavily overcast she presently had recourse to her compass and it was not until then that she discovered to her dismay that she did not have it with her. So sure was she of her woodcraft, however, that she continued on in the direction she thought west until she had covered sufficient distance to warrant her in feeling assured that, by now turning south, she could pass safely in rear of the British patrol.

Nor did she commence to feel any doubts until long after she had again turned toward the east well south, as she thought, of the patrol. It was late afternoon—she should long since have struck the road again south of Tonda; but she had found no road and now she began to feel real anxiety.

Her horse had traveled all day without food or water, night was approaching and with it a realization that she was hopelessly lost in a wild and trackless country notorious principally for its tsetse flies and savage beasts. It was maddening to know that she had absolutely no knowledge of the direction she was traveling—that she might be forging steadily further from the railway, deeper into the gloomy and forbidding country toward the Pangani; yet it was impossible to stop—she must go on.

Bertha Kircher was no coward, whatever else she may have been; but as night began to close down around her she could not shut out from her mind entirely contemplation of the terrors of the long hours ahead before the rising sun should dissipate the Stygian gloom—the horrid jungle night—that lures forth all the prowling, preying creatures of destruction.

She found, just before dark, an open meadow-like break in the almost interminable bush. There was a small clump of trees near the center and here she decided to camp. The grass was high and thick, affording feed for her horse and a bed for herself, and there was more than enough dead wood lying about the trees to furnish a good fire well through the night. Removing the saddle and bridle from her mount she placed them at the foot of a tree and then picketed the animal close by. Then she busied herself collecting firewood and by the time darkness had fallen she had a good fire and enough wood to last until morning.

From her saddlebags she took cold food and from her canteen a swallow of water. She could not afford more than a small swallow for she could not know how long a time it might be before she should find more. It filled her with sorrow that her poor horse must go waterless, for even German spies may have hearts and this one was very young and very feminine.

It was now dark. There was neither moon nor stars and the light from her fire only accentuated the blackness beyond. She could see the grass about her and the boles of the trees which stood out in brilliant relief against the solid background of impenetrable night, and beyond the firelight there was nothing.

The jungle seemed ominously quiet. Far away in the distance she heard faintly the boom of big guns; but she could not locate their direction. She strained her ears until her nerves were on the point of breaking; but she could not tell from whence the sound came. And it meant so much to her to know, for the battle lines were north of her and if she could but locate the direction of the firing she would know which way to go in the morning.

In the morning! Would she live to see another morning? She squared her shoulders and shook herself together. Such thoughts must be banished—they would never do. Bravely she hummed an air as she arranged her saddle near the fire and pulled a quantity of long grass to make a comfortable seat over which she spread her saddle blanket. Then she unstrapped a heavy, military coat from the cantle of her saddle and donned it, for the air was already chill.

Seating herself where she could lean against the saddle she prepared to maintain a sleepless vigil throughout the night. For an hour the silence was broken only by the distant booming of the guns and the low noises of the feeding horse and then, from possibly a mile away, came the rumbling thunder of a lion's roar. The girl started and laid her hand upon the rifle at her side. A little shudder ran through her slight frame and she could feel the goose flesh rise upon her body.

Again and again was the awful sound repeated and each time she was certain that it came nearer. She could locate the direction of this sound although she could not that of the guns, for the origin of the former was much closer. The lion was up wind and so could not have caught her scent as yet, though he might be approaching to investigate the light of the fire which could doubtless be seen for a considerable distance.

For another fear-filled hour the girl sat straining her eyes and ears out into the black void beyond her little island of light. During all that time the lion did not roar again; but there was constantly the sensation that it was creeping upon her. Again and again she would start and turn to peer into the blackness beyond the trees behind her as her overwrought nerves conjured the stealthy fall of padded feet. She held the rifle across her knees at the ready now and she was trembling from head to foot.

Suddenly her horse raised his head and snorted, and with a little cry of terror the girl sprang to her feet. The animal turned and trotted back toward her until the picket rope brought him to a stand, and then he wheeled about and with ears up-pricked gazed out into the night; but the girl could neither see nor hear aught.

Still another hour of terror passed during which the horse often raised his head to peer long and searchingly into the dark. The girl replenished the fire from time to time. She found herself becoming very sleepy. Her heavy lids persisted in drooping; but she dared not sleep. Fearful lest she might be overcome by the drowsiness that was stealing through her she rose and walked briskly to and fro, then she threw some more wood on the fire, walked over and stroked her horse's muzzle and returned to her seat.

Leaning against the saddle she tried to occupy her mind with plans for the morrow; but she must have dozed. With a start she awoke. It was broad daylight. The hideous night with its indescribable terrors was gone.

She could scarce believe the testimony of her senses. She had slept for hours, the fire was out and yet she and the horse were safe and alive, nor was there sign of savage beast about. And, best of all, the sun was shining, pointing the straight road to the east. Hastily she ate a few mouthfuls of her precious rations, which with a swallow of water constituted her breakfast. Then she saddled her horse and mounted. Already she felt that she was as good as safe in Wilhelmstal.

Possibly, however, she might have revised her conclusions could she have seen the two pairs of eyes watching her every move intently from different points in the bush.

Light-hearted and unsuspecting, the girl rode across the clearing toward the bush while directly before her two yellow-green eyes glared round and terrible, a tawny tail twitched nervously and great, padded paws gathered beneath a sleek barrel for a mighty spring. The horse was almost at the edge of the bush when Numa, the lion, launched himself through the air. He struck the animal's right shoulder at the instant that it reared, terrified, to wheel in flight. The force of the impact hurled the horse backward to the ground and so quickly that the girl had no opportunity to extricate herself; but fell to the earth with her mount, her left leg pinned beneath its body.

Horror-stricken, she saw the king of beasts open his mighty jaws and seize the screaming creature by the back of its neck. The great jaws closed, there was an instant's struggle as Numa shook his prey. She could hear the vertebrae crack as the mighty fangs crunched through them, and then the muscles of her faithful friend relaxed in death.

Numa crouched upon his kill. His terrifying eyes rivetted themselves upon the girl's face—she could feel his hot breath upon her cheek and the odor of the fetid vapor nauseated her. For what seemed an eternity to the girl the two lay staring at each other and then the lion uttered a menacing growl.

Never before had Bertha Kircher been so terrified—never before had she had such cause for terror. At her hip was a pistol—a formidable weapon with which to face a man; but a puny thing indeed with which to menace the great beast before her. She knew that at best it could but enrage him and yet she meant to sell her life dearly, for she felt that she must die. No human succor could have availed her even had it been there to offer itself. For a moment she tore her gaze from the hypnotic fascination of that awful face and breathed a last prayer to her God. She did not ask for aid, for she felt that she was beyond even divine succor—she only asked that the end might come quickly and with as little pain as possible.

No one can prophesy what a lion will do in any given emergency. This one glared and growled at the girl for a moment and then fell to feeding upon the dead horse. Fräulein Kircher wondered for an instant and then attempted to draw her leg cautiously from beneath the body of her mount; but she could not budge it. She increased the force of her efforts and Numa looked up from his feeding to growl again. The girl desisted. She hoped that he might satisfy his hunger and then depart to lie up; but she could not believe that he would leave her there alive. Doubtless he would drag the remains of his kill into the bush for hiding and, as there could be no doubt that he considered her part of his prey, he would certainly come back for her, or possibly drag her in first and kill her.

Again Numa fell to feeding. The girl's nerves were at the breaking point. She wondered that she had not fainted under the strain of terror and shock. She recalled that she often had wished she might see a lion, close to, make a kill and feed upon it. God! how realistically her wish had been granted.

Again she bethought herself of her pistol. As she had fallen, the holster had slipped around so that the weapon now lay beneath her. Very slowly she reached for it; but in so doing she was forced to raise her body from the ground. Instantly the lion was aroused. With the swiftness of a cat he reached across the carcass of the horse and placed a heavy, taloned paw upon her breast, crushing her back to earth, and all the time he growled and snarled horribly. His face was a picture of frightful rage incarnate. For a moment neither moved and then from behind her the girl heard a human voice uttering bestial sounds.

Numa suddenly looked up from the girl's face at the thing beyond her. His growls increased to roars as he drew back, ripping the front of the girl's waist almost from her body with his long talons, exposing her white bosom, which through some miracle of chance the great claws did not touch.

Tarzan of the Apes had witnessed the entire encounter from the moment that Numa had leaped upon his prey. For some time before, he had been watching the girl, and after the lion attacked her he had at first been minded to let Numa have his way with her. What was she but a hated German and a spy besides? He had seen her at General Kraut's headquarters

in conference with the German staff and again he had seen her
within the British lines masquerading as a British officer. It
was the latter thought that prompted him to interfere. Doubtless General Jan Smuts would be glad to meet and question
her. She might be forced to divulge information of value to
the British commander before Smuts had her shot.

Tarzan had recognized not only the girl, but the lion as well.
All lions may look alike to you and me; but not so to their
intimates of the jungle. Each has his individual characteristics
of face and form and gait as well defined as those that dif-
ferentiate members of the human family, and besides these
the creatures of the jungle have a still more positive test—
that of scent. Each of us, man or beast, has his own peculiar
odor, and it is mostly by this that the beasts of the jungle,
endowed with miraculous powers of scent, recognize individuals.

It is the final proof. You have seen it demonstrated a thousand times—a dog recognizes your voice and looks at you.
He knows your face and figure. Good, there can be no doubt
in his mind but that it is you; but is he satisfied? No, sir—he
must come up and smell of you. All his other senses may be
fallible, but not his sense of smell, and so he makes assurance
positive by the final test.

Tarzan recognized Numa as he whom he had muzzled with
the hide of Horta, the boar—as he whom he handled by a
rope for two days and finally loosed in a German front-line
trench, and he knew that Numa would recognize him—that
he would remember the sharp spear that had goaded him
into submission and obedience and Tarzan hoped that the
lesson he had learned still remained with the lion.

Now he came forward calling to Numa in the language of
the great apes—warning him away from the girl. It is open
to question that Numa, the lion, understood him; but he did
understand the menace of the heavy spear that the Tarmangani carried so ready in his brown, right hand, and so he drew
back, growling, trying to decide in his little brain whether
to charge or flee.

On came the ape-man with never a pause, straight for the
lion. "Go away, Numa," he cried, "or Tarzan will tie you up
again and lead you through the jungle without food. See
Arad, my spear! Do you recall how his point stuck into you
and how with his haft I beat you over the head? Go, Numa!
I am Tarzan of the Apes!"

Numa wrinkled the skin of his face into great folds, until
his eyes almost disappeared and he growled and roared and
snarled and growled again, and when the spear point came
at last quite close to him he struck at it viciously with his

armed paw; but he drew back. Tarzan stepped over the
dead horse and the girl lying behind him gazed in wide-eyed
astonishment at the handsome figure driving an angry lion
deliberately from its kill.

When Numa had retreated a few yards, the ape-man called
back to the girl in perfect German, "Are you badly hurt?"

"I think not," she replied; "but I cannot extricate my foot
from beneath my horse."

"Try again," commanded Tarzan. "I do not know how long
I can hold Numa thus."

The girl struggled frantically; but at last she sank back
upon an elbow.

"It is impossible," she called to him.

He backed slowly until he was again beside the horse, when
he reached down and grasped the cinch, which was still intact.
Then with one hand he raised the carcass from the ground.
The girl freed herself and rose to her feet.

"You can walk?" asked Tarzan.

"Yes," she said; "my leg is numb; but it does not seem to be
injured."

"Good," commented the ape-man. "Back slowly away behind me—make no sudden movements. I think he will not
charge."

With utmost deliberation the two backed toward the bush.
Numa stood for a moment, growling, then he followed them,
slowly. Tarzan wondered if he would come beyond his kill
or if he would stop there. If he followed them beyond, then
they could look for a charge, and if Numa charged it was
very likely that he would get one of them. When the lion
reached the carcass of the horse Tarzan stopped and so did
Numa, as Tarzan had thought that he would and the ape-man
waited to see what the lion would do next. He eyed them for
a moment, snarled angrily and then looked down at the tempting meat. Presently he crouched upon his kill and resumed
feeding.

The girl breathed a deep sigh of relief as she and the ape-
man resumed their slow retreat with only an occasional glance
from the lion, and when at last they reached the bush and had
turned and entered it, she felt a sudden giddiness overwhelm
her so that she staggered and would have fallen had Tarzan
not caught her. It was only a moment before she regained
control of herself.

"I could not help it," she said, in half apology. "I was so
close to death—such a horrible death—it unnerved me for an
instant; but I am all right now. How can I ever thank you?
It was so wonderful—you did not seem to fear the frightful
creature in the least; yet he was afraid of you. Who are you?"

"He knows me," replied Tarzan, grimly—"that is why he fears me."

He was standing facing the girl now and for the first time he had a chance to look at her squarely and closely. She was very beautiful—that was undeniable; but Tarzan realized her beauty only in a subconscious way. It was superficial—it did not color her soul which must be black as sin. She was German—a German spy. He hated her and desired only to compass her destruction; but he would choose the manner so that it would work most grievously against the enemy cause.

He saw her naked breasts where Numa had torn her clothing from her and dangling there against the soft, white flesh he saw that which brought a sudden scowl of surprise and anger to his face—the diamond-studded, golden locket of his youth —the love token that had been stolen from the breast of his mate by Schneider, the Hun. The girl saw the scowl but did not interpret it correctly. Tarzan grasped her roughly by the arm.

"Where did you get this?" he demanded, as he tore the bauble from her.

The girl drew herself to her full height. "Take your hand from me," she demanded, but the ape-man paid no attention to her words, only seizing her more forcibly.

"Answer me!" he snapped. "Where did you get this?"

"What is it to you?" she countered.

"It is mine," he replied. "Tell me who gave it to you or I will throw you back to Numa."

"You would do that?" she asked.

"Why not?" he queried. "You are a spy and spies must die if they are caught."

"You were going to kill me, then?"

"I was going to take you to headquarters. They would dispose of you there; but Numa can do it quite as effectively. Which do you prefer?"

"Hauptmann Fritz Schneider gave it to me," she said.

"Headquarters it will be then," said Tarzan. "Come!"

The girl moved at his side through the bush and all the time her mind worked quickly. They were moving east, which suited her, and as long as they continued to move east she was glad to have the protection of the great, white savage. She speculated much upon the fact that her pistol still swung at her hip. The man must be mad not to take it from her.

"What makes you think I am a spy?" she asked after a long silence.

"I saw you at German headquarters," he replied, "and then again inside the British lines."

She could not let him take her back to them. She must reach Wilhelmstal at once and she was determined to do so even if she must have recourse to her pistol. She cast a side glance at the tall figure. What a magnificent creature! But yet he was a brute who would kill her or have her killed if she did not slay him. And the locket! She must have that back —it must not fail to reach Wilhelmstal. Tarzan was now a foot or two ahead of her as the path was very narrow. Cautiously she drew her pistol. A single shot would suffice and he was so close that she could not miss. As she figured it all out her eyes rested on the brown skin with the graceful muscles rolling beneath it and the perfect limbs and head and the carriage that a proud king of old might have envied. A wave of revulsion for her contemplated act surged through her. No, she could not do it—yet, she must be free and she must regain possession of the locket. And then, almost blindly, she swung the weapon up and struck Tarzan heavily upon the back of the head with its butt. Like a felled ox he dropped in his tracks.

6

Vengeance and Mercy

I T WAS an hour later that Sheeta, the panther, hunting, chanced to glance upward into the blue sky where his attention was attracted by Ska, the vulture, circling slowly above the bush a mile away and downwind. For a long minute the yellow eyes stared intently at the gruesome bird. They saw Ska dive and rise again to continue his ominous circling and in these movements their woodcraft read that which, while obvious to Sheeta, would doubtless have meant nothing to you or me.

The hunting cat guessed that on the ground beneath Ska was some living thing of flesh—either a beast feeding upon its kill or a dying animal that Ska did not yet dare attack. In either event it might prove meat for Sheeta, and so the wary feline stalked by a circuitous route, upon soft, padded feet that gave forth no sound, until the circling *aasvogel* and his intended prey were upwind. Then, sniffing each vagrant zephyr, Sheeta, the panther, crept cautiously forward, nor had he advanced any considerable distance before his keen nostrils were rewarded with the scent of man—a Tarmangani.

Sheeta paused. He was not a hunter of men. He was young and in his prime; but always before he had avoided this hated presence. Of late he had become more accustomed to it with the passing of many soldiers through his ancient hunting ground, and as the soldiers had frightened away a great part of the game Sheeta had been wont to feed upon, the days had been lean, and Sheeta was hungry.

The circling Ska suggested that this Tarmangani might be helpless and upon the point of dying, else Ska would not have been interested in him, and so easy prey for Sheeta. With this thought in mind the cat resumed his stalking. Presently he pushed through the thick bush and his yellow-green eyes rested gloatingly upon the body of an almost naked Tarmangani lying face down in a narrow game trail.

Numa, sated, rose from the carcass of Bertha Kircher's horse and seized the partially devoured body by the neck and dragged it into the bush; then he started east toward the lair where he had left his mate. Being uncomfortably full he was inclined to be sleepy and far from belligerent. He moved slowly and majestically with no effort at silence or concealment. The king walked abroad, unafraid.

With an occasional regal glance to right or left he moved along a narrow game trail until at a turn he came to a sudden stop at what lay revealed before him—Sheeta, the panther, creeping stealthily upon the almost naked body of a Tarmangani lying face down in the deep dust of the pathway. Numa glared intently at the quiet body in the dust. Recognition came. It was *his* Tarmangani. A low growl of warning rumbled from his throat and Sheeta halted with one paw upon Tarzan's back and turned suddenly to eye the intruder.

What passed within those savage brains? Who may say? The panther seemed debating the wisdom of defending his find, for he growled horribly as though warning Numa away from the prey. And Numa? Was the idea of property rights dominating his thoughts? The Tarmangani was his, or he was the Tarmangani's. Had not the Great White Ape mastered and subdued him and, too, had he not fed him? Numa recalled the fear that he had felt of this man-thing and his cruel spear; but in savage brains fear is more likely to engender respect than hatred and so Numa found that he respected the creature who had subdued and mastered him. He saw Sheeta, upon whom he looked with contempt, daring to molest the master of the lion. Jealousy and greed alone might have been sufficient to prompt Numa to drive Sheeta away, even though the lion was not sufficiently hungry to devour the flesh that he thus wrested from the lesser cat; but then, too, there was in the little brain within the massive head a sense of loyalty, and perhaps this it was that sent Numa quickly forward, growling, toward the spitting Sheeta.

For a moment the latter stood his ground with arched back and snarling face, for all the world like a great, spotted tabby.

Numa had not felt like fighting; but the sight of Sheeta daring to dispute his rights kindled his ferocious brain to sudden fire. His rounded eyes glared with rage, his undulating tail snapped to stiff erectness as, with a frightful roar, he charged this presuming vassal.

It came so suddenly and from so short a distance that Sheeta had no chance to turn and flee the rush, and so he met it with raking talons and snapping jaws; but the odds were all against him. To the larger fangs and the more powerful jaws of his adversary were added huge talons and the preponderance of the lion's great weight. At the first clash Sheeta was crushed and, though he deliberately fell upon his back and drew up his powerful hind legs beneath Numa with the intention of disemboweling him, the lion forestalled him and at the same time closed his awful jaws upon Sheeta's throat.

It was soon over. Numa rose, shaking himself, and stood above the torn and mutilated body of his foe. His own sleek coat was cut and the red blood trickled down his flank; though it was but a minor injury, it angered him. He glared down at the dead panther and then, in a fit of rage, he seized and mauled the body only to drop it in a moment, lower his head, voice a single terrific roar, and turn toward the ape-man.

Approaching the still form he sniffed it over from head to foot. Then he placed a huge paw upon it and turned it over with its face up. Again he smelled about the body and at last with his rough tongue licked Tarzan's face. It was then that Tarzan opened his eyes.

Above him towered the huge lion, its hot breath upon his face, its rough tongue upon his cheek. The ape-man had often been close to death; but never before so close as this, he thought, for he was convinced that death was but a matter of seconds. His brain was still numb from the effects of the blow that had felled him, and so he did not, for a moment, recognize the lion that stood over him as the one he had so recently encountered.

Presently, however, recognition dawned upon him and with it a realization of the astounding fact that Numa did not seem bent on devouring him—at least not immediately. His position was a delicate one. The lion stood astraddle Tarzan with his front paws. The ape-man could not rise, therefore, without pushing the lion away and whether Numa would tolerate being pushed was an open question. Too, the beast might consider him already dead and any movement that indicated the contrary was true would, in all likelihood, arouse the killing instinct of the man-eater.

But Tarzan was tiring of the situation. He was in no mood to lie there forever, especially when he contemplated the fact that the girl spy who had tried to brain him was undoubtedly escaping as rapidly as possible.

Numa was looking right into his eyes now evidently aware that he was alive. Presently the lion cocked his head on one side and whined. Tarzan knew the note, and he knew that it spelled neither rage nor hunger, and then he risked all on a single throw, encouraged by that low whine.

"Move, Numa!" he commanded and placing a palm against the tawny shoulder he pushed the lion aside. Then he rose and with a hand on his hunting knife awaited that which might follow. It was then that his eyes fell for the first time on the torn body of Sheeta. He looked from the dead cat to the live one and saw the marks of conflict upon the latter, too, and in an instant realized something of what had happened—Numa had saved him from the panther!

It seemed incredible and yet the evidence pointed clearly to the fact. He turned toward the lion and without fear approached and examined his wounds which he found superficial, and as Tarzan knelt beside him Numa rubbed an itching ear against the naked, brown shoulder. Then the ape-man stroked the great head, picked up his spear, and looked about for the trail of the girl. This he soon found leading toward the east, and as he set out upon it something prompted him to feel for the locket he had hung about his neck. It was gone!

No trace of anger was apparent upon the ape-man's face unless it was a slight tightening of the jaws; but he put his hand ruefully to the back of his head where a bump marked the place where the girl had struck him and a moment later a half-smiled played across his lips. He could not help but admit that she had tricked him neatly, and that it must have taken nerve to do the thing she did and to set out armed only with a pistol through the trackless waste that lay between them and the railway and beyond into the hills where Wilhelmstal lies.

Tarzan admired courage. He was big enough to admit it and admire it even in a German spy, but he saw that in this case it only added to her resourcefulness and made her all the more dangerous and the necessity for putting her out of the way paramount. He hoped to overtake her before she reached Wilhelmstal and so he set out at the swinging trot that he could hold for hours at a stretch without apparent fatigue.

That the girl could hope to reach the town on foot in less than two days seemed improbable, for it was a good thirty miles and part of it hilly. Even as the thought crossed his mind he heard the whistle of a locomotive to the east and knew that the railway was in operation again after a shutdown of several days. If the train was going south the girl would signal it if she had reached the right of way. His keen ears caught the whining of brake shoes on wheels and a few minutes later the signal blast for brakes off. The train had stopped and started again and, as it gained headway and greater distance, Tarzan could tell from the direction of the sound that it was moving south.

The ape-man followed the trail to the railway where it ended abruptly on the west side of the track, showing that the girl had boarded the train, just as he thought. There was nothing now but to follow on to Wilhelmstal, where he hoped to find Captain Fritz Schneider, as well as the girl, and to recover his diamond-studded locket.

It was dark when Tarzan reached the little hill town of Wilhelmstal. He loitered on the outskirts, getting his bearings and trying to determine how an almost naked white man might explore the village without arousing suspicion. There were many soldiers about and the town was under guard, for he could see a lone sentinel walking his post scarce a hundred yards from him. To elude this one would not be difficult; but to enter the village and search it would be practically impossible, garbed, or ungarbed, as he was.

Creeping forward, taking advantage of every cover, lying flat and motionless when the sentry's face was toward him, the ape-man at last reached the sheltering shadows of an outhouse just inside the lines. From there he moved stealthily from building to building until at last he was discovered by a large dog in the rear of one of the bungalows. The brute came slowly toward him, growling. Tarzan stood motionless beside a tree. He could see a light in the bungalow and uniformed men moving about and he hoped that the dog would not bark. He did not; but he growled more savagely and, just at the moment that the rear door of the bungalow opened and a man stepped out, the animal charged.

He was a large dog, as large as Dango, the hyena, and he charged with all the vicious impetuosity of Numa, the lion. As he came Tarzan knelt and the dog shot through the air for his throat; but he was dealing with no man now and he found his quickness more than matched by the quickness of the Tarmangani. His teeth never reached the soft flesh—strong fingers, fingers of steel, seized his neck. He voiced a single startled yelp and clawed at the naked breast before him with his talons; but he was powerless. The mighty fingers closed upon his throat; the man rose, snapped the clawing body once, and cast it aside. At the same time a voice from the open bungalow door called: "Simba!"

There was no response. Repeating the call the man descended the steps and advanced toward the tree. In the light from the doorway Tarzan could see that he was a tall, broad-shouldered man in the uniform of a German officer. The ape-man withdrew into the shadow of the tree's stem. The man came closer, still calling the dog—he did not see the savage beast, crouching now in the shadow, awaiting him. When he had approached within ten feet of the Tarmangani, Tarzan leaped upon him—as Sabor springs to the kill, so sprang the ape-man. The momentum and weight of his body hurled the German to the ground, powerful fingers prevented an outcry and, though the officer struggled, he had no chance and a moment later lay dead beside the body of the dog.

As Tarzan stood for a moment looking down upon his kill and regretting that he could not risk voicing his beloved victory cry, the sight of the uniform suggested a means whereby he might pass to and fro through Wilhelmstal with the minimum chance of detection. Ten minutes later a tall, broad-shouldered officer stepped from the yard of the bungalow leaving behind him the corpses of a dog and a naked man.

He walked boldly along the little street and those who passed him could not guess that beneath Imperial Germany's uniform beat a savage heart that pulsed with implacable hatred for the Hun. Tarzan's first concern was to locate the hotel, for here he guessed he would find the girl, and where the girl was doubtless would be Hauptmann Fritz Schneider, who was either her confederate, her sweetheart, or both, and there, too, would be Tarzan's precious locket.

He found the hotel at last, a low, two-storied building with a veranda. There were lights on both floors and people, mostly officers, could be seen within. The ape-man considered entering and inquiring for those he sought; but his better judgment finally prompted him to reconnoiter first. Passing around the building he looked into all the lighted rooms on the first floor and, seeing neither of those for whom he had come, he swung lightly to the roof of the veranda and continued his investigations through windows of the second story.

At one corner of the hotel in a rear room the blinds were drawn; but he heard voices within and once he saw a figure silhouetted momentarily against the blind. It appeared to be the figure of a woman; but it was gone so quickly that he could not be sure. Tarzan crept close to the window and listened. Yes, there was a woman there and a man—he heard distinctly the tones of their voices although he could overhear no words, as they seemed to be whispering.

The adjoining room was dark. Tarzan tried the window and found it unlatched. All was quiet within. He raised the sash and listened again—still silence. Placing a leg over the sill he slipped within and hurriedly glanced about. The room was vacant. Crossing to the door he opened it and looked out into the hall. There was no one there, either, and he stepped out and approached the door of the adjoining room where the man and woman were.

Pressing close to the door he listened. Now he distinguished words, for the two had raised their voices as though in argument. The woman was speaking.

"I have brought the locket," she said, "as was agreed upon between you and General Kraut, as my identification. I carry no other credentials. This was to be enough. You have nothing to do but give me the papers and let me go."

The man replied in so low a tone that Tarzan could not catch the words and then the woman spoke again—a note of scorn and perhaps a little of fear in her voice.

"You would not dare, Hauptmann Schneider," she said, and then: "Do not touch me! Take your hands from me!"

It was then that Tarzan of the Apes opened the door and stepped into the room. What he saw was a huge, bull-necked German officer with one arm about the waist of Fräulein Bertha Kircher and a hand upon her forehead pushing her head back as he tried to kiss her on the mouth. The girl was struggling against the great brute; but her efforts were futile. Slowly the man's lips were coming closer to hers and slowly, step by step, she was being carried backward.

Schneider heard the noise of the opening and closing door behind him and turned. At sight of this strange officer he dropped the girl and straightened up.

"What is the meaning of this intrusion, Lieutenant?" he demanded, noting the other's epaulettes. "Leave the room at once."

Tarzan made no articulate reply; but the two there with him heard a low growl break from those firm lips—a growl that sent a shudder through the frame of the girl and brought a pallor to the red face of the Hun and his hand to his pistol; but even as he drew his weapon it was wrested from him and hurled through the blind and window to the yard beyond. Then Tarzan backed against the door and slowly removed the uniform coat.

"You are Hauptmann Schneider," he said to the German.

"What of it?" growled the latter.

"I am Tarzan of the Apes," replied the ape-man. "Now you know why I intrude."

The two before him saw that he was naked beneath the coat which he threw upon the floor and then he slipped quickly from the trousers and stood there clothed only in his loin cloth. The girl had recognized him by this time, too.

"Take your hand off that pistol," Tarzan admonished her. Her hand dropped at her side. "Now come here!"

She approached and Tarzan removed the weapon and hurled it after the other. At the mention of his name Tarzan had noted the sickly pallor that overspread the features of the Hun. At last he had found the right man. At last his mate would be partially avenged—never could she be entirely avenged. Life was too short and there were to many Germans.

"What do you want of me?" demanded Schneider.

"You are going to pay the price for the thing you did at the little bungalow in the Waziri country," replied the ape-man.

Schneider commenced to bluster and threaten. Tarzan turned the key in the lock of the door and hurled the former through the window after the pistols. Then he turned to the girl. "Keep out of the way," he said in a low voice. "Tarzan of the Apes is going to kill."

The Hun ceased blustering and began to plead. "I have a wife and children at home," he cried. "I have done nothing," I——"

"You are going to die as befits your kind," said Tarzan, "with blood on your hands and a lie on your lips." He started across the room toward the burly Hauptmann. Schneider was a large and powerful man—about the height of the ape-man but much heavier. He saw that neither threats nor pleas would avail him and so he prepared to fight as a cornered rat fights for its life with all the maniacal rage, cunning, and ferocity that the first law of nature imparts to many beasts.

Lowering his bull head he charged for the ape-man and in the center of the floor the two clinched. There they stood locked and swaying for a moment until Tarzan succeeded in forcing his antagonist backward over a table which crashed to the floor, splintered by the weight of the two heavy bodies.

The girl stood watching the battle with wide eyes. She saw the two men rolling hither and thither across the floor and she heard with horror the low growls that came from the lips of the naked giant. Schneider was trying to reach his foe's throat with his fingers while, horror of horrors, Bertha Kircher could see that the other was searching for the German's jugular with his teeth!

Schneider seemed to realize this too, for he redoubled his efforts to escape and finally succeeded in rolling over on top of the ape-man and breaking away. Leaping to his feet he ran for the window; but the ape-man was too quick for him and before he could leap through the sash a heavy hand fell upon his shoulder and he was jerked back and hurled across the room to the opposite wall. There Tarzan followed him, and once again they locked, dealing each other terrific blows, until Schneider in a piercing voice screamed, *"Kamerad! Kamerad!"*

Tarzan grasped the man by the throat and drew his hunting knife. Schneider's back was against the wall so that though his knees wobbled he was held erect by the ape-man. Tarzan brought the sharp point to the lower part of the German's abdomen.

"Thus you slew my mate," he hissed in a terrible voice. "Thus shall you die!"

The girl staggered forward. "Oh, God, no!" she cried. "Not that. You are too brave—you cannot be such a beast as that!"

Tarzan turned at her. "No," he said, "you are right, I cannot do it—I am no German," and he raised the point of his blade and sunk it deep into the putrid heart of Hauptmann Fritz Schneider, putting a bloody period to the Hun's last gasping cry: "I did not do it! She is not——"

Then Tarzan turned toward the girl and held out his hand. "Give me my locket," he said.

She pointed toward the dead officer. "He has it." Tarzan searched him and found the trinket. "Now you may give me the papers," he said to the girl, and without a word she handed him a folded document.

For a long time he stood looking at her before he spoke again.

"I came for you, too," he said. "It would be difficult to take you back from here and so I was going to kill you, as I have sworn to kill all your kind; but you were right when you said that I was not such a beast as that slayer of women. I could not slay him as he slew mine, nor can I slay you, who are a woman."

He crossed to the window, raised the sash and an instant later he had stepped out and disappeared into the night. And then Fräulein Bertha Kircher stepped quickly to the corpse upon the floor, slipped her hand inside the blouse and drew forth a little sheaf of papers which she tucked into her waist before she went to the window and called for help.

7

When Blood Told

TARZAN of the Apes was disgusted. He had had the German spy, Bertha Kircher, in his power and had left her unscathed. It is true that he had slain Hauptmann Fritz Schneider, that Underlieutenant von Goss had died at his hands, and that he had otherwise wreaked vengeance upon the men of the German company who had murdered, pillaged, and raped at Tarzan's bungalow in the Waziri country. There was still another officer to be accounted for; but him he could not find. It was Lieutenant Obergatz he still sought, though vainly, for at last he learned that the man had been sent upon some special mission, whether in Africa or back to Europe Tarzan's informant either did not know or would not divulge.

But the fact that he had permitted sentiment to stay his hand when he might so easily have put Bertha Kircher out of the way in the hotel at Wilhelmstal that night rankled in the ape-man's bosom. He was shamed by his weakness, and when he had handed the paper she had given him to the British chief of staff, even though the information it contained permitted the British to frustrate a German flank attack, he was still much dissatisfied with himself. And possibly the root of this dissatisfaction lay in the fact that he realized that were he again to have the same opportunity he would still find it as impossible to slay a woman as it had been in Wilhelmstal that night.

Tarzan blamed this weakness, as he considered it, upon his association with the effeminating influences of civilization, for in the bottom of his savage heart he held in contempt both civilization and its representatives—the men and women of the civilized countries of the world. Always was he comparing their weaknesses, their vices, their hypocrisies, and their little vanities with the open, primitive ways of his ferocious jungle mates, and all the while there battled in that same big heart with these forces another mighty force—Tarzan's love and loyalty for his friends of the civilized world.

The ape-man, reared as he had been by savage beasts amid savage beasts, was slow to make friends. Acquaintances he numbered by the hundreds; but of friends he had few. These few he would have died for as, doubtless, they would have died for him; but there were none of these fighting with the British forces in East Africa, and so, sickened and disgusted by the sight of man waging his cruel and inhuman warfare, Tarzan determined to heed the insistent call of the remote jungle of his youth, for the Germans were now on the run and the war in East Africa was so nearly over that he realized that his further services would be of negligible value.

Never regularly sworn into the service of the King, he was under no obligation to remain now that the moral obligation had been removed, and so it was that he disappeared from the British camp as mysteriously as he had appeared a few months before.

More than once had Tarzan reverted to the primitive only to return again to civilization through love for his mate; but now that she was gone he felt that this time he had definitely departed forever from the haunts of man, and that he should live and die a beast among beasts even as he had been from infancy to maturity.

Between him and destination lay a trackless wilderness of untouched primeval savagery where, doubtless in many spots, his would be the first human foot to touch the virgin turf. Nor did this prospect dismay the Tarmangani—rather was it an urge and an inducement, for rich in his veins flowed that noble strain of blood that has made most of the earth's surface habitable for man.

The question of food and water that would have risen paramount in the mind of an ordinary man contemplating such an excursion gave Tarzan little concern. The wilderness was his natural habitat and woodcraft as inherent to him as breathing. Like other jungle animals he could scent water from a great distance and, where you or I might die of thirst, the ape-man would unerringly select the exact spot at which to dig and find water.

For several days Tarzan traversed a country rich in game and watercourses. He moved slowly, hunting and fishing, or again fraternizing or quarreling with the other savage denizens of the jungle. Now it was little Manu, the monkey, who chattered and scolded at the mighty Tarmangani and in the next breath warned him that Histah, the snake, lay coiled in the long grass just ahead. Of Manu Tarzan inquired concerning the great apes—the Mangani—and was told that few inhabited this part of the jungle, and that even these were hunting farther to the north this season of the year.

"But there is Bolgani," said Manu. "Would you like to see Bolgani?"

Manu's tone was sneering, and Tarzan knew that it was because little Manu thought all creatures feared mighty Bolgani, the gorilla. Tarzan arched his great chest and struck it with a clinched fist. "I am Tarzan," he cried. "While Tarzan was yet a balu he slew a Bolgani. Tarzan seeks the Mangani, who are his brothers, but Bolgani he does not seek, so let Bolgani keep from the path of Tarzan."

Little Manu, the monkey, was much impressed, for the way of the jungle is to boast and to believe. It was then that he condescended to tell Tarzan more of the Mangani.

"They go there and there and there," he said, making a wide sweep with a brown hand first toward the north, then west, and then south again. "For there," and he pointed due west, "is much hunting; but between lies a great place where there is no food and no water, so they must go that way," and again he swung his hand through the half-circle that explained to Tarzan the great detour the apes made to come to their hunting ground to the west.

That was all right for the Mangani, who are lazy and do not care to move rapidly; but for Tarzan the straight road would be the best. He would cross the dry country and come to the good hunting in a third of the time that it would take to go far to the north and circle back again. And so it was that he continued on toward the west, and crossing a range of low mountains came in sight of a broad plateau, rock strewn and desolate. Far in the distance he saw another range of mountains beyond which he felt must lie the hunting ground of the Mangani. There he would join them and remain for a while before continuing on toward the coast and the little cabin that his father had built beside the land-locked harbor at the jungle's edge.

Tarzan was full of plans. He would rebuild and enlarge the cabin of his birth, constructing storage houses where he would make the apes lay away food when it was plenty against the times that were lean—a thing no ape ever had dreamed of doing. And the tribe would remain always in the locality and he would be king again as he had in the past. He would try to teach them some of the better things that he had learned from man, yet knowing the ape-mind as only Tarzan could, he feared that his labors would be for naught.

The ape-man found the country he was crossing rough in the extreme, the roughest he ever had encountered. The plateau was cut by frequent canyons the passage of which often entailed hours of wearing effort. The vegetation was sparse and of a faded brown color that lent to the whole landscape a most depressing aspect. Great rocks were strewn in every direction as far as the eye could see, lying partially

embedded in an impalpable dust that rose in clouds about him
at every step. The sun beat down mercilessly out of a cloud-
less sky.

For a day Tarzan toiled across this now hateful land and
at the going down of the sun the distant mountains to the west
seemed no nearer than at morn. Never a sign of living thing
had the ape-man seen, other than Ska, that bird of ill omen,
that had followed him tirelessly since he had entered this
parched waste.

No littlest beetle that he might eat had given evidence that
life of any sort existed here, and it was a hungry and thirsty
Tarzan who lay down to rest in the evening. He decided now
to push on during the cool of the night, for he realized that
even mighty Tarzan had his limitations and that where there
was no food one could not eat and where there was no water
the greatest woodcraft in the world could find none. It was a
totally new experience to Tarzan to find so barren and terrible
a country in his beloved Africa. Even the Sahara had its
oases; but this frightful world gave no indication of containing
a square foot of hospitable ground.

However, he had no misgivings but that he would fare forth
into the wonder country of which little Manu had told him,
though it was certain that he would do it with a dry skin and
an empty belly. And so he fought on until daylight, when he
again felt the need of rest. He was at the edge of another of
those terrible canyons, the eighth he had crossed, whose precipitous sides would have taxed to the uttermost the strength
of an untired man well fortified by food and water, and for the
first time, as he looked down into the abyss and then at the
opposite side that he must scale, misgivings began to assail
his mind.

He did not fear death—with the memory of his murdered
mate still fresh in his mind he almost courted it, yet strong
within him was that primal instinct of self-preservation—the
battling force of life that would keep him an active contender
against the Great Reaper until, fighting to the very last, he
should be overcome by a superior power.

A shadow swung slowly across the ground beside him, and
looking up, the ape-man saw Ska, the vulture, wheeling a wide
circle above him. The grim and persistent harbinger of evil
aroused the man to renewed determination. He arose and
approached the edge of the canyon, and then, wheeling, with
his face turned upward toward the circling bird of prey, he
bellowed forth the challenge of the bull ape.

"I am Tarzan," he shouted, "Lord of the Jungle. Tarzan of
the Apes is not for Ska, eater of carrion. Go back to the lair
of Dango and feed off the leavings of the hyenas, for Tarzan

will leave no bones for Ska to pick in this empty wilderness of death."

But before he reached the bottom of the canyon he again was forced to the realization that his great strength was waning, and when he dropped exhausted at the foot of the cliff and saw before him the opposite wall that must be scaled, he bared his fighting fangs and growled. For an hour he lay resting in the cool shade at the foot of the cliff. All about him reigned utter silence—the silence of the tomb. No fluttering birds, no humming insects, no scurrying reptiles relieved the deathlike stillness. This indeed was the valley of death. He felt the depressing influence of the horrible place setting down upon him; but he staggered to his feet, shaking himself like a great lion, for was he not still Tarzan, mighty Tarzan of the Apes? Yes, and Tarzan the mighty he would be until the last throb of that savage heart!

As he crossed the floor of the canyon he saw something lying close to the base of the side wall he was approaching—something that stood out in startling contrast to all the surroundings and yet seemed so much a part and parcel of the somber scene as to suggest an actor amid the settings of a well-appointed stage, and, as though to carry out the allegory, the pitiless rays of flaming Kudu topped the eastern cliff, picking out the thing lying at the foot of the western wall like a giant spotlight.

And as Tarzan came nearer he saw the bleached skull and bones of a human being about which were remnants of clothing and articles of equipment that, as he examined them, filled the ape-man with curiosity to such an extent that for a time he forgot his own predicament in contemplation of the remarkable story suggested by these mute evidences of a tragedy of a time long past.

The bones were in a fair state of preservation and indicated by their intactness that the flesh had probably been picked from them by vultures as none was broken; but the pieces of equipment bore out the suggestion of their great age. In this protected spot where there were no frosts and evidently but little rainfall, the bones might have lain for ages without disintegrating, for there were here no other forces to scatter or disturb them.

Near the skeleton lay a helmet of hammered brass and a corroded breastplate of steel while at one side was a long, straight sword in its scabbard and an ancient harquebus. The bones were those of a large man—a man of wondrous strength and vitality Tarzan knew he must have been to have penetrated thus far through the dangers of Africa with such a ponderous yet at the same time futile armament.

The ape-man felt a sense of deep admiration for this nameless adventurer of a bygone day. What a brute of a man he must have been and what a glorious tale of battle and kaleidoscopic vicissitudes of fortune must once have been locked within that whitened skull! Tarzan stooped to examine the shreds of clothing that still lay about the bones. Every particle of leather had disappeared, doubtless eaten by Ska. No boots remained, if the man had worn boots, but there were several buckles scattered about suggesting that a great part of his trappings had been of leather, while just beneath the bones of one hand lay a metal cylinder about eight inches long and two inches in diameter. As Tarzan picked it up he saw that it had been heavily lacquered and had withstood the slight ravages of time so well as to be in as perfect a state of perservation today as it had been when its owner dropped into his last, long sleep perhaps centuries ago.

As he examined it he discovered that one end was closed with a friction cover which a little twisting force soon loosened and removed, revealing within a roll of parchment which the ape-man removed and opened, disclosing a number of age-yellowed sheets closely written upon in a fine hand in a language which he guessed to be Spanish but which he could not decipher. Upon the last sheet was a roughly drawn map with numerous reference points marked upon it, all unintelligible to Tarzan, who, after a brief examination of the papers, returned them to their metal case, replaced the top and was about to toss the little cylinder to the ground beside the mute remains of its former possessor when some whim of curiosity unsatisfied prompted him to slip it into the quiver with his arrows, though as he did so it was with the grim thought that possibly centuries hence it might again come to the sight of man beside his own bleached bones.

And then, with a parting glance at the ancient skeleton, he turned to the task of ascending the western wall of the canyon. Slowly and with many rests he dragged his weakening body upwards. Again and again he slipped back from sheer exhaustion and would have fallen to the floor of the canyon but for merest chance. How long it took him to scale that frightful wall he could not have told, and when at last he dragged himself over the top it was to lie weak and gasping, too spent to rise or even to move a few inches farther from the perilous edge of the chasm.

At last he arose, very slowly and with evident effort gaining his knees first and then staggering to his feet, yet his indomitable will was evidenced by a sudden straightening of his shoulders and a determined shake of his head as he lurched forward on unsteady legs to take up his valiant fight for sur-

vival. Ahead he scanned the rough landscape for sign of another canyon which he knew would spell inevitable doom.
The western hills rose closer now though weirdly unreal as
they seemed to dance in the sunlight as though mocking him
with their nearness at the moment that exhaustion was about
to render them forever unattainable.

Beyond them he knew must be the fertile hunting grounds
of which Manu had told. Even if no canyon intervened, his
chances of surmounting even low hills seemed remote should
he have the fortune to reach their base; but with another
canyon hope was dead. Above them Ska still circled, and it
seemed to the ape-man that the ill-omened bird hovered ever
lower and lower as though reading in that failing gait the nearing of the end, and through cracked lips Tarzan growled out
his defiance.

Mile after mile Tarzan of the Apes put slowly behind him,
borne up by sheer force of will where a lesser man would have
lain down to die and rest forever tired muscles whose every
move was an agony of effort; but at last his progress became
practically mechanical—he staggered on with a dazed mind
that reacted numbly to a single urge—on, on, on! The hills
were now but a dim, ill-defined blur ahead. Sometimes he
forgot that they were hills, and again he wondered vaguely
why he must go on forever through all this torture endeavoring
to overtake them—the fleeing, elusive hills. Presently he
began to hate them and there formed within his half-delirious
brain the hallucination that the hills were German hills, that
they had slain someone dear to him, whom he could never
quite recall, and that he was pursuing to slay them.

This idea, growing, appeared to give him strength—a new
and revivifying purpose—so that for a time he no longer
staggered; but went forward steadily with head erect. Once
he stumbled and fell, and when he tried to rise he found that
he could not—that his strength was so far gone that he could
only crawl forward on his hands and knees for a few yards and
then sink down again to rest.

It was during one of these frequent periods of utter exhaustion that he heard the flap of dismal wings close above him.
With his remaining strength he turned himself over on his back
to see Ska wheel quickly upward. With the sight Tarzan's
mind cleared for a while.

"Is the end so near as that?" he thought. "Does Ska know
that I am so near gone that he dares come down and perch
upon my carcass?" And even then a grim smile touched those
swollen lips as into the savage mind came a sudden thought—
the cunning of the wild beast at bay. Closing his eyes he

threw a forearm across them to protect them from Ska's powerful beak and then he lay very still and waited.

It was restful lying there, for the sun was now obscured by clouds and Tarzan was very tired. He feared that he might sleep and something told him that if he did he would never awaken, and so he concentrated all his remaining powers upon the one thought of remaining awake. Not a muscle moved— to Ska, circling above, it became evident that the end had come—that at last he should be rewarded for his long vigil.

Circling slowly he dropped closer and closer to the dying man. Why did not Tarzan move? Had he indeed been overcome by the sleep of exhaustion, or was Ska right—had death at last claimed that mighty body? Was that great, savage heart stilled forever? It is unthinkable.

Ska, filled with suspicions, circled warily. Twice he almost alighted upon the great, naked breast only to wheel suddenly away; but the third time his talons touched the brown skin. It was as though the contact closed an electric circuit that instantaneously vitalized the quiet clod that had lain motionless so long. A brown hand swept downward from the brown forehead and before Ska could raise a wing in flight he was in the clutches of his intended victim.

Ska fought, but he was no match for even a dying Tarzan, and a moment later the ape-man's teeth closed upon the carrion-eater. The flesh was coarse and tough and gave off an unpleasant odor and a worse taste; but it was food and the blood was drink and Tarzan only an ape at heart and a dying ape into the bargain—dying of starvation and thirst.

Even mentally weakened as he was the ape-man was still master of his appetite and so he ate but sparingly, saving the rest, and then, feeling that he now could do so safely, he turned upon his side and slept.

Rain, beating heavily upon his body, awakened him and sitting up he cupped his hands and caught the precious drops which he transferred to his parched throat. Only a little he got at a time; but that was best. The few mouthfuls of Ska that he had eaten, together with the blood and rain water and the sleep had refreshed him greatly and put new strength into his tired muscles.

Now he could see the hills again and they were close and, though there was no sun, the world looked bright and cheerful, for Tarzan knew that he was saved. The bird that would have devoured him, and the providential rain, had saved him at the very moment that death seemed inevitable.

Again partaking of a few mouthfuls of the unsavory flesh of Ska, the vulture, the ape-man arose with something of his old force and set out with steady gait toward the hills of promise

rising alluringly ahead. Darkness fell before he reached them;
but he kept on until he felt the steeply rising ground that
proclaimed his arrival at the base of the hills proper, and then
he lay down and waited until morning should reveal the easiest
passage to the land beyond. The rain had ceased, but the sky
still was overcast so that even his keen eyes could not pene-
trate the darkness farther than a few feet. And there he slept,
after eating again of what remained of Ska, until the morning
sun awakened him with a new sense of strength and well-
being.

And so at last he came through the hills out of the valley of
death into a land of parklike beauty, rich in game. Below him
lay a deep valley through the center of which dense jungle
vegetation marked the course of a river beyond which a
primeval forest extended for miles to terminate at last at the
foot of lofty, snow-capped mountains. It was a land that
Tarzan never had looked upon before, nor was it likely that
the foot of another white man ever had touched it unless,
possibly, in some long-gone day the adventurer whose skeleton
he had found bleaching in the canyon had traversed it.

8

Tarzan and the Great Apes

THREE days the ape-man spent in resting and recuperating, eating fruits and nuts and the smaller animals that were most easily bagged, and upon the forth he set out to explore the valley and search for the great apes. Time was a negligible factor in the equation of life—it was all the same to Tarzan if he reached the west coast in a month or a year or three years. All time was his and all Africa. His was absolute freedom—the last tie that had bound him to civilization and custom had been severed. He was alone but he was not exactly lonely. The greater part of his life had been spent thus, and though there was no other of his kind, he was at all times surrounded by the jungle peoples for whom familiarity had bred no contempt within his breast. The least of them interested him, and, too, there were those with whom he always made friends easily, and there were his hereditary enemies whose presence gave a spice to life that might otherwise have become humdrum and monotonous.

And so it was that on the fourth day he set out to explore the valley and search for his fellow-apes. He had proceeded southward for a short distance when his nostrils were assailed by the scent of man, of Gomangani, the black man. There were many of them, and mixed with their scent was another—that of a she Tarmangani.

Swinging through the trees Tarzan approached the authors of these disturbing scents. He came warily from the flank, but paying no attention to the wind, for he knew that man with his dull senses could apprehend him only through his eyes or ears and then only when comparatively close. Had he been stalking Numa or Sheeta he would have circled about until his quarry was upwind from him, thus taking practically all the advantage up to the very moment that he came within sight or hearing; but in the stalking of the dull clod, man, he approached with almost contemptuous indifference, so that all the jungle about him knew that he was passing—all but the men he stalked.

From the dense foliage of a great tree he watched them pass—a disreputable mob of blacks, some garbed in the uniform of German East African native troops, others wearing a single garment of the same uniform, while many had reverted to the simple dress of their forbears—approximating nudity. There were many black women with them, laughing and talking as they kept pace with the men, all of whom were armed with German rifles and equipped with German belts and ammunition.

There were no white officers there, but it was none the less apparent to Tarzan that these men were from some German native command, and he guessed that they had slain their officers and taken to the jungle with their women, or had stolen some from native villages through which they must have passed. It was evident that they were putting as much ground between themselves and the coast as possible and doubtless were seeking some impenetrable fastness of the vast interior where they might inaugurate a reign of terror among the primitively armed inhabitants and by raiding, looting, and rape grow rich in goods and women at the expense of the district upon which they settled themselves.

Between two of the black women marched a slender white girl. She was hatless and with torn and disheveled clothing that had evidently once been a trim riding habit. Her coat was gone and her waist half torn from her body. Occasionally and without apparent provocation one or the other of the Negresses struck or pushed her roughly. Tarzan watched through half-closed eyes. His first impulse was to leap among them and bear the girl from their cruel clutches. He had recognized her immediately and it was because of this fact that he hesitated.

What was it to Tarzan of the Apes what fate befell this enemy spy? He had been unable to kill her himself because of an inherent weakness that would not permit him to lay hands upon a woman, all of which of course had no bearing upon what others might do to her. That her fate would now be infinitely more horrible than the quick and painless death that the ape-man would have meted to her only interested Tarzan to the extent that the more frightful the end of a German the more in keeping it would be with what they all deserved.

And so he let the blacks pass with Fräulein Bertha Kircher in their midst, or at least until the last straggling warrior suggested to his mind the pleasures of blackbaiting—an amusement and a sport in which he had grown ever more proficient since that long-gone day when Kulonga, the son of Mbonga, the chief, had cast his unfortunate spear at Kala, the ape-man's foster mother.

The last man, who must have stopped for some purpose, was fully a quarter of a mile in rear of the party. He was hurrying to catch up when Tarzan saw him, and as he passed beneath the tree in which the ape-man perched above the trail, a silent noose dropped deftly about his neck. The main body still was in plain sight, and as the frightened man voiced a piercing shriek of terror, they looked back to see his body rise as though by magic straight into the air and disappear amidst the leafy foliage above.

For a moment the blacks stood paralyzed by astonishment and fear; but presently the burly sergeant, Usanga, who led them, started back along the trail at a run, calling to the others to follow him. Loading their guns as they came the blacks ran to succor their fellow, and at Usanga's command they spread into a thin line that presently entirely surrounded the tree into which their comrade had vanished.

Usanga called but received no reply; then he advanced slowly with rifle at the ready, peering up into the tree. He could see no one—nothing. The circle closed in until fifty blacks were searching among the branches with their keen eyes. What had become of their fellow? They had seen him rise into the tree and since then many eyes had been fastened upon the spot, yet there was no sign of him. One, more venturesome than his fellows, volunteered to climb into the tree and investigate. He was gone but a minute or two and when he dropped to earth again he swore that there was no sign of a creature there.

Perplexed, and by this time a bit awed, the blacks drew slowly away from the spot and with many backward glances and less laughing continued upon their journey until, when about a mile beyond the spot at which their fellow had disappeared, those in the lead saw him peering from behind a tree at one side of the trail just in front of them. With shouts to their companions that he had been found they ran forwards; but those who were first to reach the tree stopped suddenly and shrank back, their eyes rolling fearfully first in one direction and then in another as though they expected some nameless horror to leap out upon them.

Nor was their terror without foundation. Impaled upon the end of a broken branch the head of their companion was propped behind the tree so that it appeared to be looking out at them from the opposite side of the bole.

It was then that many wished to turn back, arguing that they had offended some demon of the wood upon whose preserve they had trespassed; but Usanga refused to listen to them, assuring them that inevitable torture and death awaited them should they return and fall again into the hands of their cruel German masters. At last his reasoning prevailed to the end that a much-subdued and terrified band moved in a compact mass, like a drove of sheep, forward through the valley and there were no stragglers.

It is a happy characteristic of the Negro race, which they hold in common with little children, that their spirits seldom remain depressed for a considerable length of time after the immediate cause of depression is removed, and so it was that in half an hour Usanga's band was again beginning to take on to some extent its former appearance of carefree light-heartedness. Thus were the heavy clouds of fear slowly dissipating when a turn in the trail brought them suddenly upon the headless body of their erstwhile companion lying directly in their path, and they were again plunged into the depth of fear and gloomy forebodings.

So utterly inexplicable and uncanny had the entire occurrence been that there was not a one of them who could find a ray of comfort penetrating the dead blackness of its ominous portent. What had happened to one of their number each conceived as being a wholly possible fate for himself—in fact quite his probable fate. If such a thing could happen in broad daylight what frightful thing might not fall to their lot when night had enshrouded them in her mantle of darkness. They trembled in anticipation.

The white girl in their midst was no less mystified than they; but far less moved, since sudden death was the most merciful fate to which she might now look forward. So far she had been subjected to nothing worse than the petty cruelties of the women, while, on the other hand, it had alone been the presence of the women that had saved her from worse treatment at the hands of some of the men—notably the brutal, black sergeant, Usanga. His own woman was of the party—a veritable giantess, a virago of the first magnitude—and she was evidently the only thing in the world of which Usanga stood in awe. Even though she was particularly cruel to the young woman, the latter believed that she was her sole protection from the degraded black tyrant.

Late in the afternoon the band came upon a small palisaded village of thatched huts set in a clearing in the jungle close beside a placid river. At their approach the villagers came pouring out, and Usanga advanced with two of his warriors to palaver with the chief. The experiences of the day had so shaken the nerves of the black sergeant that he was ready to treat with these people rather than take their village by force of arms, as would ordinarily have been his preference; but now a vague conviction influenced him that there watched over this part of the jungle a powerful demon who wielded miraculous power for evil against those who offended him. First Usanga would learn how these villagers stood with this savage god and if they had his good will Usanga would be most careful to treat them with kindness and respect.

At the palaver it developed that the village chief had food, goats, and fowl which he would be glad to dispose of for a proper consideration; but as the consideration would have meant parting with precious rifles and ammunition, or the very clothing from their backs, Usanga began to see that after all it might be forced upon him to wage war to obtain food.

A happy solution was arrived at by a suggestion of one of his men—that the soldiers go forth the following day and hunt for the villagers, bringing them in so much fresh meat in return for their hospitality. This the chief agreed to, stipulating the kind and quantity of game to be paid in return for flour, goats, and fowl, and a certain number of huts that were to be turned over to the visitors. The details having been settled after an hour or more of that bickering argument of which the native African is so fond, the newcomers entered the village where they were assigned to huts.

Bertha Kircher found herself alone in a small hut to the palisade at the far end of the village street, and though she was neither bound nor guarded, she was assured by Usanga that she could not escape the village without running into almost certain death in the jungle, which the villagers assured them was infested by lions of great size and ferocity. "Be good to Usanga," he concluded, "and no harm will befall you. I will come again to see you after the others are asleep. Let us be friends."

As the brute left her the girl's frame was racked by a convulsive shudder as she sank to the floor of the hut and covered her face with her hands. She realized now why the women had not been left to guard her. It was the work of the cunning Usanga, but would not his woman suspect something of his intentions? She was no fool and, further, being imbued with insane jealousy she was ever looking for some overt act upon the part of her ebon lord. Bertha Kircher felt that only she might save her and that she would save her if word could be but gotten to her. But how?

Left alone and away from the eyes of her captors for the first time since the previous night, the girl immediately took advantage of the opportunity to assure herself that the papers she had taken from the body of Hauptmann Fritz Schneider were still safely sewn inside one of her undergarments.

Alas! Of what value could they now ever be to her beloved country? But habit and loyalty were so strong within her that she still clung to the determined hope of eventually delivering the little packet to her chief.

The natives seemed to have forgotten her existence—no one came near the hut, not even to bring her food. She could hear them at the other end of the village laughing and yelling and knew that they were celebrating with food and native beer—knowledge which only increased her apprehension. To be prisoner in a native village in the very heart of an unexplored region of Central Africa—the only white woman among a band of drunken Negroes! The very thought appalled her. Yet there was a slight promise in the fact that she had so far been unmolested—the promise that they might, indeed, have forgotten her and that soon they might become so hopelessly drunk as to be harmless.

Darkness had fallen and still no one came. The girl wondered if she dared venture forth in search of Naratu, Usanga's woman, for Usanga might not forget that he had promised to return. No one was near as she stepped out of the hut and made her way toward the part of the village where the revelers were making merry about a fire. As she approached she saw the villagers and their guests squatting in a large circle about the blaze before which a half-dozen naked warriors leaped and bent and stamped in some grotesque dance. Pots of food and gourds of drink were being passed about among the audience. Dirty hands were plunged into the food pots and the captured portions devoured so greedily that one might have thought the entire community had been upon the point of starvation. The gourds they held to their lips until the beer ran down their chins and the vessels were wrested from them by greedy neighbors. The drink had now begun to take noticeable effect upon most of them, with the result that they were beginning to give themselves up to utter and licentious abandon.

As the girl came nearer, keeping in the shadow of the huts, looking for Naratu she was suddenly discovered by one upon the edge of the crowd—a huge woman, who rose, shrieking, and came toward her. From her aspect the white girl thought that the woman meant literally to tear her to pieces. So utterly wanton and uncalled-for was the attack that it found the girl entirely unprepared, and what would have happened had not a warrior interferred may only be guessed. And then Usanga, noting the interruption, came lurching forward to question her.

"What do you want," he cried, "food and drink? Come with me!" and he threw an arm about her and dragged her toward the circle.

"No!" she cried, "I want Naratu. Where is Naratu?"

This seemed to sober the black for a moment as though he had temporarily forgotten his better half. He cast quick, fearful glances about, and then, evidently assured that Naratu had noticed nothing, he ordered the warrior who was still holding the infuriated black woman from the white girl to take the latter back to her hut and to remain there on guard over her.

First appropriating a gourd of beer for himself the warrior motioned the girl to precede him, and thus guarded she returned to her hut, the fellow squatting down just outside the doorway, where he confined his attentions for some time to the gourd.

Bertha Kircher sat down at the far side of the hut awaiting she knew not what impending fate. She could not sleep so filled was her mind with wild schemes of escape though each new one must always be discarded as impractical. Half an hour after the warrior had returned her to her prison he rose and entered the hut, where he tried to engage in conversation with her. Groping across the interior he leaned his short spear against the wall and sat down beside her, and as he talked he edged closer and closer until at last he could reach out and touch her. Shrinking, she drew away.

"Do not touch me!" she cried. "I will tell Usanga if you do not leave me alone, and you know what he will do to you."

The man only laughed drunkenly, and, reaching out his hand, grabbed her arm and dragged her toward him. She fought and cried aloud for Usanga and at the same instant the entrance to the hut was darkened by the form of a man.

"What is the matter?" shouted the newcomer in the deep tones that the girl recognized as belonging to the black sergeant. He had come, but would she be any better off? She knew that she would not unless she could play upon Usanga's fear of his woman.

When Usanga found what had happened he kicked the warrior out of the hut and bade him begone, and when the fellow had disappeared, muttering and grumbling, the sergeant approached the white girl. He was very drunk, so drunk that several times she succeeded in eluding him and twice she pushed him so violently away that he stumbled and fell.

Finally he became enraged and rushing upon her, seized her in his long, apelike arms. Striking at his face with clenched fists she tried to protect herself and drive him away. She threatened him with the wrath of Naratu, and at that he changed his tactics and began to plead, and as he argued with her, promising her safety and eventual freedom, the warrior he had kicked out of the hut made his staggering way to the hut occupied by Naratu.

Usanga, finding that pleas and promises were as unavailing as threats, at last lost both his patience and his head, seizing the girl roughly, and simultaneously there burst into the hut a raging demon of jealousy. Naratu had come. Kicking, scratching, striking, biting, she routed the terrified Usanga in short order, and so obsessed was she by her desire to inflict punishment upon her unfaithful lord and master that she quite forgot the object of his infatuation.

Bertha Kircher heard her screaming down the village street at Usanga's heels and trembled at the thought of what lay in store for her at the hands of these two, for she knew that to-morrow at the latest Naratu would take out upon her the full measure of her jealous hatred after she had spent her first wrath upon Usanga.

The two had departed but a few minutes when the warrior guard returned. He looked into the hut and then entered. "No one will stop me now, white woman," he growled as he stepped quickly across the hut toward her.

Tarzan of the Apes, feasting well upon a juicy haunch from Bara, the deer, was vaguely conscious of a troubled mind. He should have been at peace with himself and all the world, for was he not in his native element surrounded by game in plenty and rapidly filling his belly with the flesh he loved best? But Tarzan of the Apes was haunted by the picture of a slight, young girl being shoved and struck by brutal Negresses, and in imagination could see her now camped in this savage country a prisoner among degraded blacks.

Why was it so difficult to remember that she was only a hated German and a spy? Why would the fact that she was a woman and white always obtrude itself upon his consciousness? He hated her as he hated all her kind, and the fate that was sure to be hers was no more terrible than she in common with all her people deserved. The matter was settled and Tarzan composed himself to think of other things, yet the picture would not die—it rose in all its details and annoyed him. He began to wonder what they were doing to her and where they were taking her. He was very much ashamed of himself as he had been after the episode in Wilhelmstal when his weakness had permitted him to spare this spy's life. Was he to be thus weak again? No!

Night came and he settled himself in an ample tree to rest until morning; but sleep would not come. Instead came the vision of a white girl being beaten by black women, and again of the same girl at the mercy of the warriors somewhere in that dark and forbidding jungle.

With a growl of anger and self-contempt Tarzan arose, shook himself, and swung from his tree to that adjoining, and thus, through the lower terraces, he followed the trail that Usanga's party had taken earlier in the afternoon. He had little difficulty as the band had followed a well-beaten path and when toward midnight the stench of a native village assailed his delicate nostrils he guessed that his goal was near and that presently he should find her whom he sought.

Prowling stealthily as prowls Numa, the lion, stalking a wary prey, Tarzan moved noiselessly about the palisade, listening and sniffing. At the rear of the village he discovered a tree whose branches extended over the top of the palisade and a moment later he had dropped quietly into the village.

From hut to hut he went searching with keen ears and nostrils some confirming evidence of the presence of the girl, and at last, faint and almost obliterated by the odor of the Gomangani, he found it hanging like a delicate vapor about a small hut. The village was quiet now, for the last of the beer and the food had been disposed of and the blacks lay in their huts overcome by stupor, yet Tarzan made no noise that even a sober man keenly alert might have heard.

He passed around to the entrance of the hut and listened. From within came no sound, not even the low breathing of one awake; yet he was sure that the girl had been here and perhaps was even now, and so he entered, slipping in as silently as a disembodied spirit. For a moment he stood motionless just within the entranceway, listening. No, there was no one here, of that he was sure, but he would investigate. As his eyes became accustomed to the greater darkness within the hut an object began to take form that presently outlined itself in a human form supine upon the floor.

Tarzan stepped closer and leaned over to examine it—it was the dead body of a naked warrior from whose chest protruded a short spear. Then he searched carefully every square foot of the remaining floor space and at last returned to the body again where he stooped and smelled of the haft of the weapon that had slain the black. A slow smile touched his lips—that and a slight movement of his head betokened that he understood.

A rapid search of the balance of the village assured him that the girl had escaped and a feeling of relief came over him that no harm had befallen her. That her life was equally in jeopardy in the savage jungle to which she must have flown did not impress him as it would have you or me, since to

Tarzan the jungle was not a dangerous place—he considered one safer there than in Paris or London by night.

He had entered the trees again and was outside the palisade when there came faintly to his ears from far beyond the village an old, familiar sound. Balancing lightly upon a swaying branch he stood, a graceful statue of a forest god, listening intently. For a minute he stood thus and then there broke from his lips the long, weird cry of ape calling to ape and he was away through the jungle toward the sound of the booming drum of the anthropoids leaving behind him an awakened and terrified village of cringing blacks, who would forever after connect that eerie cry with the disappearance of their white prisoner and the death of their fellow-warrior.

Bertha Kircher, hurrying through the jungle along a well-beaten game trail, thought only of putting as much distance as possible between herself and the village before daylight could permit pursuit of her. Whither she was going she did not know, nor was it a matter of great moment since death must be her lot sooner or later.

Fortune favored her that night, for she passed unscathed through as savage and lion-ridden an area as there is in all Africa—a natural hunting ground which the white man has not yet discovered, where deer and antelope and zebra, giraffe and elephant, buffalo, rhinoceros, and the other herbivorous animals of central Africa abound unmolested by none but their natural enemies, the great cats which, lured here by easy prey and immunity from the rifles of big-game hunters, swarm the district.

She had fled for an hour or two, perhaps, when her attention was arrested by the sound of animals moving about, muttering and growling close ahead. Assured that she had covered a sufficient distance to insure her a good start in the morning before the blacks could take to her trail, and fearful of what the creatures might be, she climbed into a large tree with the intention of spending the balance of the night there.

She had no sooner reached a safe and comfortable branch when she discovered that the tree stood upon the edge of a small clearing that had been hidden from her by the heavy undergrowth upon the ground below, and simultaneously she discovered the identity of the beasts she had heard.

In the center of the clearing below her, clearly visible in the bright moonlight, she saw fully twenty huge, manlike apes —great, shaggy fellows who went upon their hind feet with only slight assistance from the knuckles of their hands. The moonlight glanced from their glossy coats, the numerous gray-tipped hairs imparting a sheen that made the hideous creatures almost magnificent in their appearance.

The girl had watched them but a minute or two when the little band was joined by others, coming singly and in groups until there were fully fifty of the great brutes gathered there in the moonlight. Among them were young apes and several little ones clinging tightly to their mothers' shaggy shoulders. Presently the group parted to form a circle about what appeared to be a small, flat-topped mound of-earth in the center of the clearing. Squatting close about this mound were three old females armed with short, heavy clubs with which they presently began to pound upon the flat top of the earth mound which gave forth a dull, booming sound, and almost immediately the other apes commenced to move about restlessly, weaving in and out aimlessly until they carried the impression of a moving mass of great, black maggots.

The beating of the drum was in a slow, ponderous cadence, at first without time but presently settling into a heavy rhythm to which the apes kept time with measured tread and swaying bodies. Slowly the mass separated into two rings, the outer of which was composed of shes and the very young, the inner of mature bulls. The former ceased to move and squatted upon their haunches, while the bulls now moved slowly about in a circle the center of which was the drum and all now in the same direction.

It was then that there came faintly to the ears of the girl from the direction of the village she had recently quitted a weird and high-pitched cry. The effect upon the apes was electrical—they stopped their movements and stood in attitudes of intent listening for a moment, and then one fellow, huger than his companions, raised his face to the heavens and in a voice that sent the cold shudders through the girl's slight frame answered the far-off cry.

Once again the beaters took up their drumming and the slow dance went on. There was a certain fascination in the savage ceremony that held the girl spellbound, and as there seemed little likelihood of her being discovered, she felt that she might as well remain the balance of the night in her tree and resume her flight by the comparatively greater safety of daylight.

Assuring herself that her packet of papers was safe she sought as comfortable a position as possible among the branches, and settled herself to watch the weird proceedings in the clearing below her.

A half-hour passed, during which the cadence of the drum increased gradually. Now the great bull that had replied to the distant call leaped from the inner circle to dance alone between the drummers and the other bulls. He leaped and crouched and leaped again, now growling and barking, again stopping to raise his hideous face to Goro, the moon, and, beating upon his shaggy breast, uttered a piercing scream—the challenge of the bull ape, had the girl but known it.

He stood thus in the full glare of the great moon, motionless after screaming forth his weird challenge, in the setting of the primeval jungle and the circling apes a picture of primitive savagery and power—a mightily muscled Hercules out of the dawn of life—when from close behind her the girl heard an answering scream, and an instant later saw an almost naked white man drop from a near-by tree into the clearing.

Instantly the apes became a roaring, snarling pack of angry beasts. Bertha Kircher held her breath. What maniac was this who dared approach these frightful creatures in their own haunts, alone against fifty? She saw the brown-skinned figure bathed in moonlight walk straight toward the snarling pack. She saw the symmetry and the beauty of that perfect body—its grace, its strength, its wondrous proportioning, and then she recognized him. It was the same creature whom she had seen carry Major Schneider from General Kraut's headquarters, the same who had rescued her from Numa, the lion; the same whom she had struck down with the butt of her pistol and escaped when he would have returned her to her enemies, the same who had slain Hauptmann Fritz Schneider and spared her life that night in Wilhelmstal.

Fear-filled and fascinated she watched him as he neared the apes. She heard sounds issue from his throat—sounds identical with those uttered by the apes—and though she could scarce believe the testimony of her own ears, she knew that this godlike creature was conversing with the brutes in their own tongue.

Tarzan halted just before he reached the shes of the outer circle. "I am Tarzan of the Apes!" he cried. "You do not know me because I am of another tribe; but Tarzan comes in peace or he comes to fight—which shall it be? Tarzan will talk with your king," and so saying he pushed straight forward through the shes and the young who now gave way before him, making a narrow lane through which he passed toward the inner circle.

Shes and balus growled and bristled as he passed closer, but none hindered him and thus he came to the inner circle of bulls. Here bared fangs menaced him and growling faces hideously contorted. "I am Tarzan," he repeated. "Tarzan comes to dance the Dum-Dum with his brothers. Where is your king?" Again he pressed forward and the girl in the tree clapped her palms to her cheeks as she watched, wide-eyed, this madman going to a frightful death. In another instant they would be upon him, rending and tearing until that perfect form had been ripped to shreds; but again the ring parted, and though the apes roared and menaced him they did not attack, and at last he stood in the inner circle close to the drum and faced the great king ape.

Again he spoke. "I am Tarzan of the Apes," he cried. "Tarzan comes to live with his brothers. He will come in peace and live in peace or he will kill; but he has come and he will stay. Which—shall Tarzan dance the Dum-Dum in peace with his brothers, or shall Tarzan kill first?"

"I am Go-lat, King of the Apes," screamed the great bull. "I kill! I kill! I kill!" and with a sullen roar he charged the Tarmangani.

The ape-man, as the girl watched him, seemed entirely unprepared for the charge and she looked to see him born down and slain at the first rush. The great bull was almost upon him with huge hands outstretched to seize him before Tarzan made a move; but when he did move his quickness would have put Ara, the lightning, to shame. As darts forward the head of Histah, the snake, so darted forward the left hand of the man-beast as he seized the left wrist of his antagonist. A quick turn and the bull's right arm was locked beneath the right arm of his foe in a jujutsu hold that Tarzan had learned among civilized men—a hold with which he might easily break the great bones, a hold that left the ape helpless.

"I am Tarzan of the Apes!" screamed the ape-man. "Shall Tarzan dance in peace or shall Tarzan kill?"

"I kill! I kill! I kill!" shrieked Go-lat.

With the quickness of a cat Tarzan swung the king ape over one hip and sent him sprawling to the ground. "I am Tarzan, King of all the Apes!" he shouted. "Shall it be peace?"

Go-lat, infuriated, leaped to his feet and charged again, shouting his war cry: "I kill! I kill! I kill!" and again Tarzan met him with a sudden hold that the stupid bull, being ignorant of, could not possibly avert—a hold and a throw that brought a scream of delight from the interested audience and suddenly filled the girl with doubts as to the man's madness —evidently he was quite safe among the apes, for she saw him swing Go-lat to his back and then catapult him over his shoulder. The king ape fell upon his head and lay very still.

"I am Tarzan of the Apes!" cried the ape-man. "I come to dance the Dum-Dum with my brothers," and he made a motion to the drummers, who immediately took up the cadence of the dance where they had dropped it to watch their king slay the foolish Tarmangani.

It was then that Go-lat raised his head and slowly crawled

to his feet. Tarzan approached him. "I am Tarzan of the Apes," he cried. "Shall Tarzan dance the Dum-Dum with his brothers now, or shall he kill first?"

Go-lat raised his bloodshot eyes to the face of the Tarmangani. "*Kagoda!*" he cried "Tarzan of the Apes will dance the Dum-Dum with his brothers and Go-lat will dance with him!"

And then the girl in the tree saw the savage man leaping, bending, and stamping with the savage apes in the ancient rite of the Dum-Dum. His roars and growls were more beastly than the beasts. His handsome face was distorted with savage ferocity. He beat upon his great breast and screamed forth his challenge as his smooth, brown hide brushed the shaggy coats of his fellows. It was weird; it was wonderful; and in its primitive savagery it was not without beauty—the strange scene she looked upon, such a scene as no other human being, probably, ever had witnessed—and yet, withal, it was horrible.

As she gazed, spell-bound, a stealthy movement in the tree behind her caused her to turn her head, and there, back of her, blazing in the reflected moonlight, shone two great, yellow-green eyes. Sheeta, the panther, had found her out.

The beast was so close that it might have reached out and touched her with a great, taloned paw. There was no time to think, no time to weigh chances or to choose alternatives. Terror-inspired impulse was her guide as, with a loud scream, she leaped from the tree into the clearing.

Instantly the apes, now maddened by the effects of the dancing and the moonlight, turned to note the cause of the interruption. They saw this she Tarmangani, helpless and alone and they started for her. Sheeta, the panther, knowing that not even Numa, the lion, unless maddened by starvation, dares meddle with the great apes at their Dum-Dum, had silently vanished into the night, seeking his supper elsewhere.

Tarzan, turning with the other apes toward the cause of the interruption, saw the girl, recognized her and also her peril. Here again might she die at the hands of others; but why consider it! He knew that he could not permit it, and though the acknowledgment shamed him, it had to be admitted.

The leading shes were almost upon the girl when Tarzan leaped among them, and with heavy blows scattered them to right and left; and then as the bulls came to share in the kill they thought this new ape-thing was about to make that he might steal all the flesh for himself, they found him facing them with an arm thrown about the creature as though to protect her.

"This is Tarzan's she," he said. "Do not harm her." It was

the only way he could make them understand that they must not slay her. He was glad that she could not interpret the words. It was humiliating enough to make such a statement to wild apes about this hated enemy.

So once again Tarzan of the Apes was forced to protect a Hun. Growling, he muttered to himself in extenuation:

"She is a woman and I am not a German, so it could not be otherwise!"

9

Dropped from the Sky

LIEUTENANT HAROLD PERCY SMITH-OLDWICK, Royal Air Service, was on reconnaissance. A report, or it would be better to say a rumor, had come to the British headquarters in German East Africa that the enemy had landed in force on the west coast and was marching across the dark continent to reinforce their colonial troops. In fact the new army was supposed to be no more than ten or twelve days' march to the west. Of course the thing was ridiculous—preposterous—but preposterous things often happen in war; and anyway no good general permits the least rumor of enemy activity to go uninvestigated.

Therefore Lieutenant Harold Percy Smith-Oldwick flew low toward the west, searching with keen eyes for signs of a Hun army. Vast forests unrolled beneath him in which a German army corps might have lain concealed, so dense was the overhanging foliage of the great trees. Mountain, meadowland, and desert passed in lovely panorama; but never a sight of man had the young lieutenant.

Always hoping that he might discover some sign of their passage—a discarded lorry, a broken limber, or an old camp site—he continued farther and farther into the west until well into the afternoon. Above a tree-dotted plain through the center of which flowed a winding river he determined to turn about and start for camp. It would take straight flying at top speed to cover the distance before dark; but as he had ample gasoline and a trustworthy machine there was no doubt in his mind but that he could accomplish his aim. It was then that his engine stalled.

He was too low to do anything but land, and that immediately, while he had the more open country accessible, for directly east of him was a vast forest into which a stalled engine could only have plunged him to certain injury and probable death; and so he came down in the meadowland

near the winding river and there started to tinker with his
motor.

As he worked he hummed a tune, some music-hall air that
had been popular in London the year before, so that one might
have thought him working in the security of an English flying
field surrounded by innumerable comrades rather than alone
in the heart of an unexplored African wilderness. It was
typical of the man that he should be wholly indifferent to his
surroundings, although his looks entirely belied any assump-
tion that he was of particularly heroic strain.

Lieutenant Harold Percy Smith-Oldwick was fair-haired,
blue-eyed, and slender, with a rosy, boyish face that might
have been molded more by an environment of luxury, indo-
lence, and ease than the more strenuous exigencies of life's
sterner requirements.

And not only was the young lieutenant outwardly careless
of the immediate future and of his surroundings, but actually
so. That the district might be infested by countless enemies
seemed not to have occurred to him in the remotest degree.
He bent assiduously to the work of correcting the adjustment
that had caused his motor to stall without so much as an upward glance at the surrounding country. The forest to the
east of him, and the more distant jungle that bordered the
winding river, might have harbored an army of bloodthirsty
savages, but neither could elicit even a passing show of interest on the part of Lieutenant Smith-Oldwick.

And even had he looked, it is doubtful if he would have
seen the score of figures crouching in the concealment of the
undergrowth at the forest's edge. There are those who are
reputed to be endowed with that which is sometimes, for want
of a better appellation, known as the sixth sense—a species of
intuition which apprises them of the presence of an unseen
danger. The concentrated gaze of a hidden observer provokes
a warning sensation of nervous unrest in such as these, but
though twenty pairs of savage eyes were gazing fixedly at
Lieutenant Harold Percy Smith-Oldwick, the fact aroused no
responsive sensation of impending danger in his placid breast.
He hummed peacefully and, his adjustment completed, tried
out his motor for a minute or two, then shut it off and descended to the ground with the intention of stretching his legs
and taking a smoke before continuing his return flight to
camp. Now for the first time he took note of his surroundings,
to be immediately impressed by both the wildness and the
beauty of the scene. In some respects the tree-dotted meadowland reminded him of a parklike English forest, and that
wild beasts and savage men could ever be a part of so quiet
a scene seemed the remotest of contingencies.

Some gorgeous blooms upon a flowering shrub at a little distance from his machine caught the attention of his aesthetic eye, and as he puffed upon his cigarette, he walked over to examine the flowers more closely. As he bent above them he was probably some hundred yards from his plane and it was at this instant that Numabo, chief of the Wamabo, chose to leap from his ambush and lead his warriors in a sudden rush upon the white man.

The young Englishman's first intimation of danger was a chorus of savage yells from the forest behind him. Turning, he saw a score of naked, black warriors advancing rapidly toward him. They moved in a compact mass and as they approached more closely their rate of speed noticeably diminished. Lieutenant Smith-Oldwick realized in a quick glance that the direction of their approach and their proximity had cut off all chances of retreating to his plane, and he also understood that their attitude was entirely warlike and menacing. He saw that they were armed with spears and with bows and arrows, and he felt quite confident that notwithstanding the fact that he was armed with a pistol they could overcome him with the first rush. What he did not know about their tactics was that at any show of resistance they would fall back, which is the nature of the native Negroes, but that after numerous advances and retreats, during which they would work themselves into a frenzy of rage by much shrieking, leaping, and dancing, they would eventually come to the point of a determined and final assault.

Numabo was in the forefront, a fact which taken in connection with his considerably greater size and more warlike appearance, indicated him as the natural target and it was at Numabo that the Englishman aimed his first shot. Unfortunately for him it missed its target, as the killing of the chief might have permanently dispersed the others. The bullet passed Numabo to lodge in the breast of a warrior behind him and as the fellow lunged forward with a scream the others turned and retreated, but to the lieutenant's chagrin they ran in the direction of the plane instead of back toward the forest so that he was still cut off from reaching his machine.

Presently they stopped and faced him again. They were talking loudly and gesticulating, and after a moment one of them leaped into the air, brandishing his spear and uttering savage war cries, which soon had their effect upon his fellows so that it was not long ere all of them were taking part in the wild show of savagery, which would bolster their waning courage and presently spur them on to another attack.

The second charge brought them closer to the Englishman, and though he dropped another with his pistol, it was not before two or three spears had been launched at him. He now had five shots remaining and there were still eighteen warriors to be accounted for, so that unless he could frighten them off, it was evident that his fate was sealed.

That they must pay the price of one life for every attempt to take his had its effect upon them and they were longer now in initiating a new rush and when they did so it was more skilfully ordered than those that had preceded it, for they scattered into three bands which, partially surrounding him, came simultaneously toward him from different directions, and though he emptied his pistol with good effect, they reached him at last. They seemed to know that his ammunition was exhausted, for they circled close about him now with the evident intention of taking him alive, since they might easily have riddled him with their sharp spears with perfect safety to themselves.

For two or three minutes they circled about him until, at a word from Numabo, they closed in simultaneously, and though the slender young lieutenant struck out to right and left, he was soon overwhelmed by superior numbers and beaten down by the hafts of spears in brawny hands.

He was all but unconscious when they finally dragged him to his feet, and after securing his hands behind his back, pushed him roughly along ahead of them toward the jungle.

As the guard prodded him along the narrow trail, Lieutenant Smith-Oldwick could not but wonder why they had wished to take him alive. He knew that he was too far inland for his uniform to have any significance to this native tribe to whom no inkling of the World War probably ever had come, and he could only assume that he had fallen into the hands of the warriors of some savage potentate upon whose royal caprice his fate would hinge.

They had marched for perhaps half an hour when the Englishman saw ahead of them, in a little clearing upon the bank of the river, the thatched roofs of native huts showing above a crude but strong palisade; and presently he was ushered into a village street where he was immediately surrounded by a throng of women and children and warriors. Here he was soon the center of an excited mob whose intent seemed to be to dispatch him as quickly as possible. The women were more venomous than the men, striking and scratching him whenever they could reach him, until at last Numabo, the chief, was obliged to interfere to save his prisoner for whatever purpose he was destined.

As the warriors pushed the crowd back, opening a space through which the white man was led toward a hut, Lieutenant Smith-Oldwick saw coming from the opposite end of the village a number of Negroes wearing odds and ends of German uniforms. He was not a little surprised at this, and his first thought was that he had at last come in contact with some portion of the army which was rumored to be crossing from the west coast and for signs of which he had been searching.

A rueful smile touched his lips as he contemplated the unhappy circumstances which surrounded the accession of this knowledge for though he was far from being without hope, he realized that only by the merest chance could he escape these people and regain his machine.

Among the partially uniformed blacks was a huge fellow in the tunic of a sergeant and as this man's eyes fell upon the British officer, a loud cry of exultation broke from his lips, and immediately his followers took up the cry and pressed forward to bait the prisoner.

"Where did you get the Englishman?" asked Usanga, the black sergeant, of the chief Numabo. "Are there many more with him?"

"He came down from the sky," replied the native chief "in a strange thing which flies like a bird and which frightened us very much at first; but we watched for a long time and saw that it did not seem to be alive, and when this white man left it we attacked him and though he killed some of my warriors, we took him, for we Wamabos are brave men and great warriors."

Usanga's eyes went wide. "He flew here through the sky?" he asked.

"Yes," said Numabo. "In a great thing which resembled a bird he flew down out of the sky. The thing is still there where it came down close to the four trees near the second bend in the river. We left it there because, not knowing what it was, we were afraid to touch it and it is still there if it has not flown away again."

"It cannot fly," said Usanga, "without this man in it. It is a terrible thing which filled the hearts of our soldiers with terror, for it flew over our camps at night and dropped bombs upon us. It is well that you captured this white man, Numabo, for with his great bird he would have flown over your village tonight and killed all your people. These Englishman are very wicked white men."

"He will fly no more," said Numabo. "It is not intended that a man should fly through the air; only wicked demons do such things as that and Numabo, the chief, will see that this white man does not do it again," and with the words he pushed the young officer roughly toward a hut in the center of the village, where he was left under guard of two stalwart warriors.

For an hour or more the prisoner was left to his own devices, which consisted in vain and unremitting attempts to loosen the strands which fettered his wrists, and then he was interrupted by the appearance of the black sergeant Usanga, who entered his hut and approached him.

"What are they going to do with me?" asked the Englishman. "My country is not at war with these people. You speak their language. Tell them that I am not an enemy, that my people are the friends of the black people and that they must let me go in peace."

Usanga laughed. "They do not know an Englishman from a German," he replied. "It is nothing to them what you are, except that you are a white man and an enemy."

"Then why did they take me alive?" asked the lieutenant.

"Come," said Usanga and he led the Englishman to the doorway of the hut. "Look," he said, and pointed a black forefinger toward the end of the village street where a wider space between the huts left a sort of plaza.

Here Lieutenant Harold Percy Smith-Oldwick saw a number of Negresses engaged in laying fagots around a stake and in preparing fires beneath a number of large cooking vessels. The sinister suggestion was only too obvious.

Usanga was eyeing the white man closely, but if he expected to be rewarded by any signs of fear, he was doomed to disappointment and the young lieutenant merely turned toward him with a shrug: "Really now, do you beggars intend eating me?"

"Not my people," replied Usanga. "We do not eat human flesh, but the Wamabos do. It is they who will eat you, but we will kill you for the feast, Englishman."

The Englishman remained standing in the doorway of the hut, an interested spectator of the preparations for the coming orgy that was so horribly to terminate his earthly existence. It can hardly be assumed that he felt no fear; yet, if he did, he hid it perfectly beneath an imperturbable mask of coolness. Even the brutal Usanga must have been impressed by the bravery of his victim since, though he had come to abuse and possibly to torture the helpless prisoner, he now did neither, contenting himself merely with berating whites as a race and Englishman especially, because of the terror the British aviators had caused Germany's native troops in East Africa.

"No more," he concluded, "will your great bird fly over our people dropping death among them from the skies—Usanga will see to that," and he walked abruptly away toward a group of his own fighting men who were congregated near the stake where they were laughing and joking with the women.

A few minutes later the Englishman saw them pass out of

the village gate, and once again his thoughts reverted to various futile plans for escape.

Several miles north of the village on a little rise of ground close to the river where the jungle, halting at the base of a knoll, had left a few acres of grassy land sparsely wooded, a man and a girl were busily engaged in constructing a small boma, in the center of which a thatched hut already had been erected.

They worked almost in silence with only an occasional word of direction or interrogation between them.

Except for a loin cloth, the man was naked, his smooth skin tanned to a deep brown by the action of sun and wind. He moved with the graceful ease of a jungle cat and when he lifted heavy weights, the action seemed as effortless as the raising of empty hands.

When he was not looking at her, and it was seldom that he did, the girl found her eyes wandering toward him, and at such times there was always a puzzled expression upon her face as though she found in him an enigma which she could not solve. As a matter of fact, her feelings toward him were not untinged with awe, since in the brief period of their association she had discovered in this handsome, godlike giant the attributes of the superman and the savage beast closely intermingled. At first she had felt only that unreasoning feminine terror which her unhappy position naturally induced.

To be alone in the heart of an unexplored wilderness of Central Africa with a savage wild man was in itself sufficiently appalling, but to feel also that this man was a blood enemy, that he hated her and her kind and that in addition thereto he owed her a personal grudge for an attack she had made upon him in the past, left no loophole for any hope that he might accord her even the minutest measure of consideration.

She had seen him first months since when he had entered the headquarters of the German high command in East Africa and carried off the luckless Major Schneider, of whose fate no hint had ever reached the German officers; and she had seen him again upon that occasion when he had rescued her from the clutches of the lion and, after explaining to her that he had recognized her in the British camp, had made her prisoner. It was then that she had struck him down with the butt of her pistol and escaped. That he might seek no personal revenge for her act had been evidenced in Wilhelmstal the night that he had killed Hauptmann Fritz Schneider and left without molesting her.

No, she could not fathom him. He hated her and at the same time he had protected her as had been evidenced again

when he had kept the great apes from tearing her to pieces
after she had escaped from the Wamabo village to which
Usanga, the black sergeant, had brought her a captive; but
why was he saving her? For what sinister purpose could this
savage enemy be protecting her from the other denizens of his
cruel jungle? She tried to put from her mind the probable
fate which awaited her, yet it persisted in obtruding itself
upon her thoughts, though always she was forced to admit
that there was nothing in the demeanor of the man to indicate
that her fears were well grounded. She judged him perhaps
by the standards other men had taught her and because she
looked upon him as a savage creature, she felt that she could
not expect more of chivalry from him than was to be found in
the breasts of the civilized men of her acquaintance.

Fräulein Bertha Kircher was by nature a companionable
and cheerful character. She was not given to morbid forebodings, and above all things she craved the society of her
kind and that interchange of thought which is one of the
marked distinctions between man and the lower animals.
Tarzan, on the other hand, was sufficient unto himself. Long
years of semi-solitude among creatures whose powers of oral
expression are extremely limited had thrown him almost entirely upon his own resources for entertainment.

His active mind was never idle, but because his jungle
mates could neither follow nor grasp the vivid train of imaginings that his man-mind wrought, he had long since learned
to keep them to himself; and so now he found no need for
confiding them in others. This fact, linked with that of his
dislike for the girl, was sufficient to seal his lips for other than
necessary conversation, and so they worked on together in
comparative silence. Bertha Kircher, however, was nothing if
not feminine and she soon found that having someone to talk
to who would not talk was extremely irksome. Her fear of
the man was gradually departing, and she was full of a thousand unsatisfied curiosities as to his plans for the future in so
far as they related to her, as well as more personal questions
regarding himself, since she could not but wonder as to his
antecedents and his strange and solitary life in the jungle, as
well as his friendly intercourse with the savage apes among
which she had found him.

With the waning of her fears she became sufficiently emboldened to question him, and so she asked him what he intended doing after the hut and boma were completed.

"I am going to the west coast where I was born," replied
Tarzan. "I do not know when. I have all my life before me
and in the jungle there is no reason for haste. We are not
forever running as fast as we can from one place to another

as are you of the outer world. When I have been here long
enough I will go on toward the west, but first I must see that
you have a safe place in which to sleep, and that you have
learned how to provide yourself with necessaries. That will
take time."

"You are going to leave me here alone?" cried the girl; her
tones marked the fear which the prospect induced. "You are
going to leave me here alone in this terrible jungle, a prey
to wild beasts and savage men, hundreds of miles from a
white settlement and in a country which gives every evidence
of never having been touched by the foot of civilized men?"

"Why not?" asked Tarzan. "I did not bring you here. Would
one of your men accord any better treatment to an enemy
woman?"

"Yes," she exclaimed. "They certainly would. No man of my
race would leave a defenseless white woman alone in this horrible place."

Tarzan shrugged his broad shoulders. The conversation
seemed profitless and it was further distasteful to him for the
reason that it was carried on in German, a tongue which he
detested as much as he did the people who spoke it. He wished
that the girl spoke English and then it occurred to him that as
he had seen her in disguise in the British camp carrying on her
nefarious work as a German spy, she probably did speak English and so he asked her.

"Of course I speak English," she exclaimed, "but I did not
know that you did."

Tarzan looked his wonderment but made no comment. He
only wondered why the girl should have any doubts as to the
ability of an Englishman to speak English, and then suddenly
it occurred to him that she probably looked upon him merely
as a beast of the jungle who by accident had learned to speak
German through frequenting the district which Germany had
colonized. It was there only that she had seen him and so
she might not know that he was an Englishman by birth,
and that he had had a home in British East Africa. It was as
well, he thought, that she knew little of him, as the less she
knew the more he might learn from her as to her activities
in behalf of the Germans and of the German spy system of
which she was a representative; and so it occurred to him to
let her continue to think that he was only what he appeared
to be—a savage denizen of his savage jungle, a man of no
race and no country, hating all white men impartially; and
this in truth, was what she did think of him. It explained perfectly his attacks upon Major Schneider and the Major's
brother, Hauptmann Fritz.

Again they worked on in silence upon the boma which was

now nearly completed, the girl helping the man to the best of her small ability. Tarzan could not but note with grudging approval the spirit of helpfulness she manifested in the ofttimes painful labor of gathering and arranging the thorn bushes which constituted the temporary protection against roaming carnivores. Her hands and arms gave bloody token of the sharpness of the numerous points that had lacerated her soft flesh, and even though she were an enemy Tarzan could not but feel compunction that he had permitted her to do this work, and at last he bade her stop.

"Why?" she asked. "It is no more painful to me than it must be to you, and, as it is solely for my protection that you are building this boma, there is no reason why I should not do my share."

"You are a woman," replied Tarzan. "This is not a woman's work. If you wish to do something, take those gourds I brought this morning and fill them with water at the river. You may need it while I am away."

"While you are away—" she said. "You are going away?"

"When the boma is built I am going out after meat," he replied. "Tomorrow I will go again and take you and show you how you may make your own kills after I am gone."

Without a word she took the gourds and walked toward the river. As she filled them, her mind was occupied with painful forebodings of the future. She knew that Tarzan had passed a death sentence upon her, and that the moment that he left her, her doom was sealed, for it could be but a question of time—a very short time—before the grim jungle would claim her, for how could a lone woman hope successfully to combat the savage forces of destruction which constituted so large a part of existence in the jungle?

So occupied was she with the gloomy prophecies that she had neither ears nor eyes for what went on about her. Mechanically she filled the gourds and, taking them up, turned slowly to retrace her steps to the boma only to voice immediately a half-stifled scream and shrank back from the menacing figure looming before her and blocking her way to the hut.

Go-lat, the king ape, hunting a little apart from his tribe, had seen the woman go to the river for water, and it was he who confronted her when she turned back with her filled gourds. Go-lat was not a pretty creature when judged by standards of civilized humanity, though the shes of his tribe and even Go-lat himself, considered his glossy black coat shot with silver, his huge arms dangling to his knees, his bullet head sunk between his mighty shoulders, marks of great personal beauty. His wicked, bloodshot eyes and broad nose, his ample mouth and great fighting fangs only enhanced the claim of this Adonis of the forest upon the affections of his shes.

Doubtless in the little, savage brain there was a well-formed conviction that this strange she belonging to the Tarmangani must look with admiration upon so handsome a creature as Go-lat, for there could be no doubt in the mind of any that his beauty entirely eclipsed such as the hairless white ape might lay claim to.

But Bertha Kircher saw only a hideous beast, a fierce and terrible caricature of man. Could Go-lat have known what passed through her mind, he must have been terribly chagrined, though the chances are that he would have attributed it to a lack of discernment on her part. Tarzan heard the girl's cry and looking up saw at a glance the cause of her terror. Leaping lightly over the boma, he ran swiftly toward her as Go-lat lumbered closer to the girl the while he voiced his emotions in low gutturals which, while in reality the most amicable of advances, sounded to the girl like the growling of an enraged beast. As Tarzan drew nearer he called aloud to the ape and the girl heard from the human lips the same sounds that had fallen from those of the anthropoid.

"I will not harm your she," Go-lat called to Tarzan.

"I know it," replied the ape-man, "but she does not. She is like Numa and Sheeta, who do not understand our talk. She thinks you come to harm her."

By this time Tarzan was beside the girl. "He will not harm you," he said to her. "You need not be afraid. This ape has learned his lesson. He has learned that Tarzan is lord of the jungle. He will not harm that which is Tarzan's."

The girl cast a quick glance at the man's face. It was evident to her that the words he had spoken meant nothing to him and that the assumed proprietorship over her was, like the boma, only another means for her protection.

"But I am afraid of him," she said.

"You must not show your fear. You will be often surrounded by these apes. At such times you will be safest. Before I leave you I will give you the means of protecting yourself against them should one of them chance to turn upon you. If I were you I would seek their society. Few are the animals of the jungle that dare attack the great apes when there are several of them together. If you let them know that you are afraid of them, they will take advantage of it and your life will be constantly menaced. The shes especially would attack you. I will let them know that you have the means of protecting yourself and of killing them. If necessary, I will show you how and then they will respect and fear you."

"I will try," said the girl, "but I am afraid that it will be difficult. He is the most frightful creature I ever have seen."

Tarzan smiled. "Doubtless he thinks the same of you," he said.

By this time other apes had entered the clearing and they were now the center of a considerable group, among which were several bulls, some young shes, and some older ones with their little balus clinging to their backs or frolicking around at their feet. Though they had seen the girl the night of the Dum-Dum when Sheeta had forced her to leap from her concealment into the arena where the apes were dancing, they still evinced a great curiosity regarding her. Some of the shes came very close and plucked at her garments, commenting upon them to one another in their strange tongue. The girl, by the exercise of all the will power she could command, succeeded in passing through the ordeal without evincing any of the terror and revulsion that she felt. Tarzan watched her closely, a half-smile upon his face. He was not so far removed from recent contact with civilized people that he could not realize the torture that she was undergoing, but he felt no pity for this woman of a cruel enemy who doubtless deserved the worst suffering that could be meted to her. Yet, notwithstanding his sentiments toward her, he was forced to admire her fine display of courage. Suddenly he turned to the apes.

"Tarzan goes to hunt for himself and his she," he said. "The she will remain there," and he pointed toward the hut. "See that no member of the tribe harms her. Do you understand?"

The apes nodded. "We will not harm her," said Go-lat.

"No," said Tarzan. "You will not. For if you do, Tarzan will kill you," and then turning to the girl, "Come," he said, "I am going to hunt now. You had better remain at the hut. The apes have promised not to harm you. I will leave my spear with you. It will be the best weapon you could have in case you should need to protect yourself, but I doubt if you will be in any danger for the short time that I am away."

He walked with her as far as the boma and when she had entered he closed the gap with thorn bushes and turned away toward the forest. She watched him moving across the clearing, noting the easy, catlike tread and the grace of every movement that harmonized so well with the symmetry and perfection of his figure. At the forest's edge she saw him swing lightly into a tree and disappear from view, and then, being a woman, she entered the hut and, throwing herself upon the ground, burst into tears.

10

In the Hands of Savages

TARZAN sought Bara, the deer, or Horta, the boar, for of all
the jungle animals he doubted if any would prove more
palatable to the white woman, but though his keen nostrils were ever on the alert, he traveled far without being rewarded with even the faintest scent spoor of the game he
sought. Keeping close to the river where he hoped to find
Bara or Horta approaching or leaving a drinking place he came
at last upon the strong odor of the Wamabo village and being
ever ready to pay his hereditary enemies, the Gomangani, an
undesired visit, he swung into a detour and came up in the
rear of the village. From a tree which overhung the palisade
he looked down into the street where he saw the preparations
going on which his experience told him indicated the approach
of one of those frightful feasts the *pièce de résistance* of which
is human flesh.

One of Tarzan's chief divertisements was the baiting of the
blacks. He realized more keen enjoyment through annoying
and terrifying them than from any other source of amusement
the grim jungle offered. To rob them of their feast in some
way that would strike terror to their hearts would give him
the keenest of pleasure, and so he searched the village with his
eyes for some indication of the whereabouts of the prisoner.
His view was circumscribed by the dense foliage of the tree
in which he sat, and, so that he might obtain a better view, he
climbed further aloft and moved cautiously out upon a slender
branch.

Tarzan of the Apes possessed a woodcraft scarcely short of
the marvelous but even Tarzan's wondrous senses were not
infallible. The branch upon which he made his way outward
from the bole was no smaller than many that had borne his
weight upon countless other occasions. Outwardly it appeared
strong and healthy and was in full foliage, nor could Tarzan
know that close to the stem a burrowing insect had eaten away
half the heart of the solid wood beneath the bark.

And so when he reached a point far out upon the limb, it snapped close to the bole of the tree without warning. Below him were no larger branches that he might clutch and as he lunged downward his foot caught in a looped creeper so that he turned completely over and alighted on the flat of his back in the center of the village street.

At the sound of the breaking limb and the crashing body falling through the branches the startled blacks scurried to their huts for weapons, and when the braver of them emerged, they saw the still form of an almost naked white man lying where he had fallen. Emboldened by the fact that he did not move they approached more closely, and when their eyes discovered no signs of others of his kind in the tree, they rushed forward until a dozen warriors stood about him with ready spears. At first they thought that the falling had killed him, but upon closer examination they discovered that the man was only stunned. One of the warriors was for thrusting a spear through his heart, but Numabo, the chief, would not permit it.

"Bind him," he said. "We will feed well tonight."

And so they bound his hands and feet with thongs of gut and carried him into the hut where Lieutenant Harold Percy Smith-Oldwick awaited his fate. The Englishman had also been bound hand and foot by this time for fear that at the last moment he might escape and rob them of their feast. A great crowd of natives were gathered about the hut attempting to get a glimpse of the new prisoner, but Numabo doubled the guard before the entrance for fear that some of his people, in the exuberance of their savage joy, might rob the others of the pleasures of the death dance which would precede the killing of the victims.

The young Englishman had heard the sound of Tarzan's body crashing through the tree to the ground and the commotion in the village which immediately followed, and now, as he stood with his back against the wall of the hut, he looked upon the fellow-prisoner that the blacks carried in and laid upon the floor with mixed feelings of surprise and compassion. He realized that he never had seen a more perfect specimen of manhood than that of the unconscious figure before him, and he wondered to what sad circumstances the man owed his capture. It was evident that the new prisoner was himself as much a savage as his captors if apparel and weapons were any criterion by which to judge; yet it was also equally evident that he was a white man and from his well-shaped head and clean-cut features that he was not one of those unhappy half-wits who so often revert to savagery even in the heart of civilized communities.

As he watched the man, he presently noticed that his eyelids were moving. Slowly they opened and a pair of gray eyes looked blankly about. With returning consciousness the eyes assumed their natural expression of keen intelligence, and a moment later, with an effort, the prisoner rolled over upon his side and drew himself to a sitting position. He was facing the Englishman, and as his eyes took in the bound ankles and the arms drawn tightly behind the other's back, a slow smile lighted his features.

"They will fill their bellies tonight," he said.

The Englishman grinned. "From the fuss they made," he said, "the beggars must be awfully hungry. They like to have eaten me alive when they brought me in. How did they get you?"

Tarzan shrugged his head ruefully. "It was my own fault," he replied. "I deserve to be eaten. I crawled out upon a branch that would not bear my weight and when it broke, instead of alighting on my feet, I caught my foot in a trailer and came down on my head. Otherwise they would not have taken me—alive."

"Is there no escape?" asked the Englishman.

"I have escaped them before," replied Tarzan, "and I have seen others escape them. I have seen a man taken away from the stake after a dozen spear thrusts had pierced his body and the fire had been lighted about his feet."

Lieutenant Smith-Oldwick shuddered. "God!" he exclaimed, "I hope I don't have to face that. I believe I could stand anything but the thought of the fire. I should hate like the devil to go into a funk before the devils at the last moment."

"Don't worry," asid Tarzan. "It doesn't last long and you won't funk. It is really not half as bad as it sounds. There is only a brief period of pain before you lose consciousness. I have seen it many times before. It is as good a way to go as another. We must die sometime. What difference whether it be tonight, tomorrow night, or a year hence, just so that we have lived—and I have lived!"

"Your philosophy may be all right, old top," said the young lieutenant, "but I can't say that it is exactly satisfying."

Tarzan laughed. "Roll over here," he said, "where I can get at your bonds with my teeth." The Englishman did as he was bid and presently Tarzan was working at the thongs with his strong white teeth. He felt them giving slowly beneath his efforts. In another moment they would part, and then it would be a comparatively simple thing for the Englishman to remove the remaining bonds from Tarzan and himself.

It was then that one of the guards entered the hut. In an instant he saw what the new prisoner was doing and raising his spear, struck the ape-man a vicious blow across the head with its shaft. Then he called in the other guards and together they fell upon the luckless men, kicking and beating them unmercifully, after which they bound the Englishman more securely than before and tied both men fast on opposite sides of the hut. When they had gone Tarzan looked across at his companion in misery.

"While there is life," he said, "there is hope," but he grinned as he voiced the ancient truism.

Lieutenant Harold Percy Smith-Oldwick returned the other's smile. "I fancy," he said, "that we are getting short on both. It must be close to supper time now."

Zu-tag hunted alone far from the balance of the tribe of Go-lat, the great ape. Zu-tag (Big-neck) was a young bull but recently arrived at maturity. He was large, powerful, and ferocious and at the same time far above the average of his kind in intelligence as was denoted by a fuller and less receding forehead. Already Go-lat saw in this young ape a possible contender for the laurels of his kingship and consequently the old bull looked upon Zu-tag with jealousy and disfavor. It was for this reason, possibly, as much as another that Zu-tag hunted so often alone; but it was his utter fearlessness that permitted him to wander far afield away from the protection which numbers gave the great apes. One of the results of this habit was a greatly increased resourcefulness which found him constantly growing in intelligence and powers of observation.

Today he had been hunting toward the south and was returning along the river upon a path he often followed because it led by the village of the Gomangani whose strange and almost apelike actions and peculiar manners of living had aroused his interest and curiosity. As he had done upon other occasions he took up his position in a tree from which he could overlook the interior of the village and watch the blacks at their vocations in the street below.

Zu-tag had scarcely more than established himself in his tree when, with the blacks, he was startled by the crashing of Tarzan's body from the branches of another jungle giant to the ground within the palisade. He saw the Negroes gather about the prostrate form and later carry it into the hut; and once he rose to his full height upon the limb where he had been squatting and raised his face to the heavens to scream out a savage protest and a challenge, for he had recognized in the brown-skinned Tarmangani the strange white ape who had come among them a night or two before in the midst of their Dum-Dum, and who by so easily mastering the greatest among them, had won the savage respect and admiration of this fierce young bull.

But Zu-tag's ferocity was tempered by a certain native cunning and caution. Before he had voiced his protest there formed in his mind the thought that he would like to save this wonderful white ape from the common enemy, the Gomangani, and so he screamed forth no challenge, wisely determined that more could be accomplished by secrecy and stealth than by force of muscle and fang.

At first he thought to enter the village alone and carry off the Tarmangani; but when he saw how numerous were the warriors and that several sat directly before the entrance to the lair into which the prisoner had been carried, it occurred to him that this was work for many rather than one, and so, as silently as he had come, he slipped away though the foliage toward the north.

The tribe was still loitering about the clearing where stood the hut that Tarzan and Bertha Kircher had built. Some were idly searching for food just within the forest's edge, while others squatted beneath the shade of trees within the clearing.

The girl had emerged from the hut, her tears dried and was gazing anxiously toward the south into the jungle where Tarzan had disappeared. Occasionally she cast suspicious glances in the direction of the huge shaggy anthropoids about her. How easy it would be for one of those great beasts to enter the boma and slay her. How helpless she was, even with the spear that the white man had left her, she realized as she noted for the thousandth time the massive shoulders, the bull necks, and the great muscles gliding so easily beneath the glossy coats. Never, she thought, had she seen such personifications of brute power as were represented by these mighty bulls. Those huge hands would snap her futile spear as she might snap a match in two, while their lightest blow could crush her into insensibility and death.

It was while she was occupied with these depressing thoughts that there dropped suddenly into the clearing from the trees upon the south the figure of a mighty young bull. At that time all of the apes looked much alike to Bertha Kircher, nor was it until some time later that she realized that each differed from the others in individual characteristics of face and figure as do individuals of the human races. Yet even then she could not help but note the wondrous strength and agility of this great beast, and as he approached she even found herself admiring the sheen of his heavy, black, silvershot coat.

It was evident that the newcomer was filled with suppressed excitement. His demeanor and bearing proclaimed this even from afar, nor was the girl the only one to note it. For as they saw him coming many of the apes arose and advanced to meet him, bristling and growling as is their way. Go-lat was among these latter, and he advanced stiffly with the hairs upon his neck and down his spine erect, uttering low growls and baring his fighting fangs, for who might say whether Zu-tag came in peace or otherwise? The old king had seen other young apes come thus in his day filled with a sudden resolution to wrest the kingship from their chief. He had seen bulls about to run amuck burst thus suddenly from the jungle upon the members of the tribe, and so Go-lat took no chances.

Had Zu-tag come indolently, feeding as he came, he might have entered the tribe without arousing notice or suspicion, but when one comes thus precipitately, evidently bursting with some emotion out of the ordinary, let all apes beware. There was a certain amount of preliminary circling, growling, and sniffing, stiff-legged and stiff-haired, before each side discovered that the other had no intention of initiating an attack and then Zu-tag told Go-lat what he had seen among the lairs of the Gomangani.

Go-lat grunted in disgust and turned away. "Let the white ape take care of himself," he said.

"He is a great ape," said Zu-tag. "He came to live in peace with the tribe of Go-lat. Let us save him from the Gomangani."

Go-lat grunted again and continued to move away.

"Zu-tag will go alone and get him," cried the young ape, "if Go-lat is afraid of the Gomangani."

The king ape wheeled in anger, growling loudly and beating upon his breast. "Go-lat is not afraid," he screamed, "but he will not go, for the white ape is not of his tribe. Go yourself and take the Tarmangani's she with you if you wish so much to save the white ape."

"Zu-tag will go," replied the younger bull, "and he will take the Tarmangani's she and all the bulls of Go-lat who are not cowards," and so saying he cast his eyes inquiringly about at the other apes. "Who will go with Zu-tag to fight the Gomangani and bring away our brother," he demanded.

Eight young bulls in the full prime of their vigor pressed forward to Zu-tag's side, but the old bulls with the conservatism and caution of many years upon their gray shoulders, shook their heads and waddled away after Go-lat.

"Good," cried Zu-tag. "We want no old shes to go with us to fight the Gomangani for that is work for the fighters of the tribe."

The old bulls paid no attention to his boastful words, but the eight who had volunteered to accompany him were filled with self-pride so that they stood around vaingloriously beating upon their breasts, baring their fangs and screaming their hideous challenge until the jungle reverberated to the horrid sound.

All this time Bertha Kircher was a wide-eyed and terrified spectator to what, as she thought, could end only in a terrific battle between these frightful beasts, and when Zu-tag and his followers began screaming forth their fearsome challenge, the girl found herself trembling in terror, for of all the sounds of the jungle there is none more awe inspiring than that of the great bull ape when he issues his challenge or shrieks forth his victory cry.

If she had been terrified before she was almost paralyzed with fear now as she saw Zu-tag and his apes turn toward the boma and approach her. With the agility of a cat Zu-tag leaped completely over the protecting wall and stood before her. Valiantly she held her spear before her, pointing it at his breast. He commenced to jabber and gesticulate, and even with her scant acquaintance with the ways of the anthropoids, she realized that he was not menacing her, for there was little or no baring of fighting fangs and his whole expression and attitude was of one attempting to explain a knotty problem or plead a worthy cause. At last he became evidently impatient, for with a sweep of one great paw he struck the spear from her hand and coming close, seized her by the arm, but not roughly. She shrank away in terror and yet some sense within her seemed to be trying to assure her that she was in no danger from this great beast. Zu-tag jabbered loudly, ever and again pointing into the jungle toward the south and moving toward the boma, pulling the girl with him. He seemed almost frantic in his efforts to explain something to her. He pointed toward the boma, herself, and then to the forest, and then, at last, as though by a sudden inspiration, he reached down and, seizing the spear, repeatedly touched it with his forefinger and again pointed toward the south. Suddenly it dawned upon the girl that what the ape was trying to explain to her was related in some way to the white man whose property they thought she was. Possibly her grim protector was in trouble and with this thought firmly established, she no longer held back, but started forward as though to accompany the young bull. At the point in the boma where Tarzan had blocked the entrance, she started to pull away the thorn bushes, and, when Zu-tag saw what she was doing, he fell to and assisted her so that presently they had an opening through the boma through which she passed with the great ape.

Immediately Zu-tag and his eight apes started off rapidly toward the jungle, so rapidly that Bertha Kircher would have had to run at top speed to keep up with them. This she realized she could not do, and so she was forced to lag behind, much to the chagrin of Zu-tag, who constantly kept running back and urging her to greater speed. Once he took her by the arm and tried to draw her along. Her protests were of no avail since the beast could not know that they were protests, nor did he desist until she caught her foot in some tangled grass and fell to the ground. Then indeed was Zu-tag furious and growled hideously. His apes were waiting at the edge of the forest for him to lead them. He suddenly realized that this poor weak she could not keep up with them and that if they traveled at her slow rate they might be too late to render assistance to the Tarmangani, and so without more ado, the giant anthropoid picked Bertha Kircher bodily from the ground and swung her to his back. Her arms were about his neck and in this position he seized her wrists in one great paw so that she could not fall off and started at a rapid rate to join his companions.

Dressed as she was in riding breeches with no entangling skirts to hinder or catch upon passing shrubbery, she soon found that she could cling tightly to the back of the mighty bull and when a moment later he took to the lower branches of the trees, she closed her eyes and clung to him in terror lest she be precipitated to the ground below.

That journey through the primeval forest with the nine great apes will live in the memory of Bertha Kircher for the balance of her life, as clearly delineated as at the moment of its enactment.

The first overwhelming wave of fear having passed, she was at last able to open her eyes and view her surroundings with increased interest and presently the sensation of terror slowly left her to be replaced by one of comparative security when she saw the ease and surety with which these great beasts traveled through the trees; and later her admiration for the young bull increased as it became evident that even burdened with her additional weight, he moved more rapidly and with no greater signs of fatigue than his unburdened fellows.

Not once did Zu-tag pause until he came to a stop among the branches of a tree no great distance from the native village. They could hear the noises of the life within the palisade, the laughing and shouting of the Negroes, and the barking of dogs, and through the foliage the girl caught glimpses of the village from which she had so recently escaped. She shuddered to think of the possibility of having to return to it and of possible recapture, and she wondered why Zu-tag had brought her here.

Now the apes advanced slowly once more and with great caution, moving as noiselessly through the trees as the squirrels themselves until they had reached a point where they could easily overlook the palisade and the village street below.

Zu-tag squatted upon a great branch close to the bole of the tree and by loosening the girl's arms from about his neck, indicated that she was to find a footing for herself and when she had done so, he turned toward her and pointed repeatedly at the open doorway of a hut upon the opposite side of the street below them. By various gestures he seemed to be trying to explain something to her and at last she caught at the germ of his idea—that her white man was a prisoner there.

Beneath them was the roof of a hut onto which she saw that she could easily drop, but what she could do after she had entered the village was beyond her.

Darkness was already falling and the fires beneath the cooking pots had been lighted. The girl saw the stake in the village street and the piles of fagots about it and in terror she suddenly realized the portent of these grisly preparations. Oh, if she but only had some sort of a weapon that might give her even a faint hope, some slight advantage against the blacks. Then she would not hesitate to venture into the village in an attempt to save the man who had upon three different occasions saved her. She knew that he hated her and yet strong within her breast burned the sense of her obligation to him. She could not fathom him. Never in her life had she seen a man at once so paradoxical and dependable. In many of his ways he was more savage than the beasts with which he associated and yet, on the other hand, he was as chivalrous as a knight of old. For several days she had been lost with him in the jungle absolutely at his mercy, yet she had come to trust so implicitly in his honor that any fear she had had of him was rapidly disappearing.

On the other hand, that he might be hideously cruel was evidenced to her by the fact that he was planning to leave her alone in the midst of the frightful dangers which menaced her by night and by day.

Zu-tag was evidently waiting for darkness to fall before carrying out whatever plans had matured in his savage little brain, for he and his fellows sat quietly in the tree about her, watching the preparations of the blacks. Presently it became apparent that some altercation had arisen among the Negroes, for a score or more of them were gathered around one who appeared to be their chief, and all were talking and gesticulating heatedly. The argument lasted for some five or ten minutes when suddenly the little knot broke and two warriors ran to the opposite side of the village from whence they presently returned with a large stake which they soon set up beside the one already in place. The girl wondered what the purpose of the second stake might be, nor did she have long to wait for an explanation.

It was quite dark by this time, the village being lighted by the fitful glare of many fires, and now she saw a number of warriors approach and enter the hut Zu-tag had been watching. A moment later they reappeared, dragging between them two captives, one of whom the girl immediately recognized as her protector and the other as an Englishman in the uniform of an aviator. This, then, was the reason for the two stakes.

Arising quickly she placed a hand upon Zu-tag's shoulder and pointed down into the village. "Come," she said, as if she had been talking to one of her own kind, and with the word she swung lightly to the roof of the hut below. From there to the ground was but a short drop and a moment later she was circling the hut upon the side farthest from the fires, keeping in the dense shadows where there was little likelihood of being discovered. She turned once to see that Zu-tag was directly behind her and could see his huge bulk looming up in the dark, while beyond was another one of his eight. Doubtless they had all followed her and this fact gave her a greater sense of security and hope than she had before experienced.

Pausing beside the hut next to the street, she peered cautiously about the corner. A few inches from her was the open doorway of the structure, and beyond, farther down the village street, the blacks were congregating about the prisoners, who were already being bound to the stakes. All eyes were centered upon the victims, and there was only the remotest chance that she and her companions would be discovered until they were close upon the blacks. She wished, however, that she might have some sort of a weapon with which to lead the attack, for she could not know, of course, for a certainty whether the great apes would follow her or not. Hoping that she might find something within the hut, she slipped quickly around the corner and into the doorway and after her, one by one, came the nine bulls. Searching quickly about the interior, she presently discovered a spear, and, armed with this, she again approached the entrance.

Tarzan of the Apes and Lieutenant Harold Percy Smith-Oldwick were bound securely to their respective stakes. Neither had spoken for some time. The Englishman turned his head so that he could see his companion in misery. Tarzan stood straight against his stake. His face was entirely expressionless in so far as either fear or anger were concerned. His countenance portrayed bored indifference though both men knew that they were about to be tortured.

"Good-bye, old top," whispered the young lieutenant. Tarzan turned his eyes in the direction of the other and smiled. "Good-bye," he said. "If you want to get it over in a hurry, inhale the smoke and flames as rapidly as you can."

"Thanks," replied the aviator and though he made a wry face, he drew himself up very straight and squared his shoulders.

The women and children had seated themselves in a wide circle about the victims while the warriors, hideously painted, were forming slowly to commence the dance of death. Again Tarzan turned to his companion. "If you'd like to spoil their fun," he said, "don't make any fuss no matter how much you suffer. If you can carry on to the end without changing the expression upon your face or uttering a single word, you will deprive them of all the pleasures of this part of the entertainment. Good-bye again and good luck."

The young Englishman made no reply but it was evident from the set of his jaws that the Negroes would get little enjoyment out of him.

The warriors were circling now. Presently Numabo would draw first blood with his sharp spear which would be the signal for the beginning of the torture after a little of which the fagots would be lighted around the feet of the victims.

Closer and closer danced the hideous chief, his yellow, sharp-filed teeth showing in the firelight between his thick, red lips. Now bending double, now stamping furiously upon the ground, now leaping into the air, he danced step by step in the narrowing circle that would presently bring him within spear reach of the intended feast.

At last the spear reached out and touched the ape-man on the breast and when it came away, a little trickle of blood ran down the smooth, brown hide and almost simultaneously there broke from the outer periphery of the expectant audience a woman's shriek which seemed a signal for a series of hideous screamings, growlings, and barkings, and a great commotion upon that side of the circle. The victims could not see the cause of the disturbance, but Tarzan did not have to see, for he knew by the voices of the apes the identity of the disturbers. He only wondered what had brought them and what the purpose of the attack, for he could not believe that they had come to rescue him.

Numabo and his warriors broke quickly from the circle of their dance to see pushing toward them through the ranks of their screaming and terrified people the very white girl who had escaped them a few nights before, and at her back what appeared to their surprised eyes a veritable horde of the huge and hairy forest men upon whom they looked with considerable fear and awe.

Striking to right and left with his heavy fists, tearing with his great fangs, came Zu-tag, the young bull, while at his heels, emulating his example, surged his hideous apes. Quickly they came through the old men and the women and children, for straight toward Numabo and his warriors the girl led them. It was then that they came within range of Tarzan's vision and he saw with unmixed surprise who it was that led the apes to his rescue.

To Zu-tag he shouted: "Go for the big bulls while the she unbinds me," and to Bertha Kircher: "Quick! Cut these bonds. The apes will take care of the blacks."

Turning from her advance the girl ran to his side. She had no knife and the bonds were tied tightly but she worked quickly and coolly and as Zu-tag and his apes closed with the warriors, she succeeded in loosening Tarzan's bonds sufficiently to permit him to extricate his own hands so that in another minute he had freed himself.

"Now unbind the Englishman," he cried, and, leaping forward, ran to join Zu-tag and his fellows in their battle against the blacks. Numabo and his warriors, realizing now the relatively small numbers of the apes against them, had made a determined stand and with spears and other weapons were endeavoring to overcome the invaders. Three of the apes were already down, killed or mortally wounded, when Tarzan, realizing that the battle must eventually go against the apes unless some means could be found to break the morale of the Negroes, cast about him for some means of bringing about the desired end. And suddenly his eye lighted upon a number of weapons which he knew would accomplish the result. A grim smile touched his lips as he snatched a vessel of boiling water from one of the fires and hurled it full in the faces of the warriors. Screaming with terror and pain they fell back though Numabo urged them to rush forward.

Scarcely had the first cauldron of boiling water spilled its contents upon them ere Tarzan deluged them with a second, nor was there any third needed to send them shrieking in every direction to the security of their huts.

By the time Tarzan had recovered his own weapons the girl had released the young Englishman, and, with the six remaining apes, the three Europeans moved slowly toward the village gate, the aviator arming himself with a spear discarded by one of the scalded warriors, as they eagerly advanced toward the outer darkness.

Numabo was unable to rally the now thoroughly terrified and painfully burned warriors so that rescued and rescuers passed out of the village into the blackness of the jungle without further interference.

Tarzan strode through the jungle in silence. Beside him

walked Zu-tag, the great ape, and behind them strung the surviving anthropoids followed by Fräulein Bertha Kircher and Lieutenant Harold Percy Smith-Oldwick, the latter a thoroughly astonished and mystified Englishman.

In all his life Tarzan of the Apes had been obliged to acknowledge but few obligations. He won his way through his savage world by the might of his own muscle, the superior keenness of his five senses and his God-given power to reason. Tonight the greatest of all obligations had been placed upon him—his life had been saved by another and Tarzan shook his head and growled, for it had been saved by one whom he hated above all others.

11

Finding the Airplane

TARZAN of the Apes, returning from a successful hunt, with the body of Bara, the deer, across one sleek, brown shoulder, paused in the branches of a great tree at the edge of a clearing and gazed ruefully at two figures walking from the river to the boma-encircled hut a short distance away.

The ape-man shook his tousled head and sighed. His eyes wandered toward the west and his thoughts to the far-away cabin by the land-locked harbor of the great water that washed the beach of his boyhood home—to the cabin of his long-dead father to which the memories and treasures of a happy childhood lured him. Since the loss of his mate, a great longing had possessed him to return to the haunts of his youth—to the untracked jungle wilderness where he had lived the life he loved best long before man had invaded the precincts of his wild stamping grounds. There he hoped in a renewal of the old life under the old conditions to win surcease from sorrow and perhaps some measure of forgetfulness.

But the little cabin and the land-locked harbor were many long, weary marches away, and he was handicapped by the duty which he felt he owed to the two figures walking in the clearing before him. One was a young man in a worn and ragged uniform of the British Royal Air Forces, the other, a young woman in the even more disreputable remnants of what once had been trim riding togs.

A freak of fate had thrown these three radically different types together. One was a savage, almost naked beast-man, one an English army officer, and the woman, she whom the ape-man knew and hated as a German spy.

How he was to get rid of them Tarzan could not imagine unless he accompanied them upon the weary march back to the east coast, a march that would necessitate his once more retracing the long, weary way he already had covered towards his goal, yet what else could be done? These two had neither the strength, endurance, nor jungle-craft to accompany him

121

through the unknown country to the west, nor did he wish them with him. The man he might have tolerated, but he could not even consider the presence of the girl in the far-off cabin, which had in a way become sacred to him through its memories, without a growl or anger rising to his lips. There remained, then, but the one way, since he could not desert them. He must move by slow and irksome marches back to the east coast, or at least to the first white settlement in that direction.

He had, it is true, contemplated leaving the girl to her fate but that was before she had been instrumental in saving him from torture and death at the hands of the black Wamabos. He chafed under the obligation she had put upon him, but no less did he acknowledge it and as he watched the two, the rueful expression upon his face was lightened by a smile as he thought of the helplessness of them. What a puny thing, indeed, was man! How ill equipped to combat the savage forces of nature and of nature's jungle. Why, even the tiny balu of the tribe of Go-lat, the great ape, was better fitted to survive than these, for a balu could at least escape the numerous creatures that menaced its existence, while with the possible exception of Kota, the tortoise, none moved so slowly as did helpless and feeble man.

Without him these two doubtless would starve in the midst of plenty, should they by some miracle escape the other forces of destruction which constantly threatened them. That morning Tarzan had brought them fruit, nuts, and plantain, and now he was bringing them the flesh of his kill, while the best that they might do was to fetch water from the river. Even now, as they walked across the clearing toward the boma, they were in utter ignorance of the presence of Tarzan near them. They did not know that his sharp eyes were watching them, nor that other eyes less friendly were glaring at them from a clump of bushes close beside the boma entrance. They did not know these things, but Tarzan did. No more than they could he see the creature crouching in the concealment of the foliage, yet he knew that it was there and what it was and what its intentions, precisely as well as though it had been lying in the open.

A slight movement of the leaves at the top of a single stem had apprised him of the presence of a creature there, for the movement was not that imparted by the wind. It came from pressure at the bottom of the stem which communicates a different movement to the leaves than does the wind passing among them, as anyone who has lived his lifetime in the jungle well knows, and the same wind that passed through the foliage of the bush brought to the ape-man's sensitive nostrils indisputable evidence of the fact that Sheeta, the panther, waited there for the two returning from the river.

They had covered half the distance to the boma entrance when Tarzan called to them to stop. They looked in surprise in the direction from which his voice had come to see him drop lightly to the ground and advance toward them.

"Come slowly toward me," he called to them. "Do not run for if you run Sheeta will charge."

They did as he bid, their faces filled with questioning wonderment.

"What do you mean?" asked the young Englishman. "Who is Sheeta?" but for answer the ape-man suddenly hurled the carcass of Bara, the deer, to the ground and leaped quickly toward them, his eyes upon something in their rear; and then it was that the two turned and learned the identity of Sheeta, for behind them was a devil-faced cat charging rapidly toward them.

Sheeta with rising anger and suspicion had seen the ape-man leap from the tree and approach the quarry. His life's experiences backed by instinct told him that the Tarmangani was about to rob him of his prey and as Sheeta was hungry, he had no intention of being thus easily deprived of the flesh he already considered his own.

The girl stifled an involuntary scream as she saw the proximity of the fanged fury bearing down upon them. She shrank close to the man and clung to him and all unarmed and defenseless as he was, the Englishman pushed her behind him and shielding her with his body, stood squarely in the face of the panther's charge. Tarzan noted the act, and though accustomed as he was to acts of courage, he experienced a thrill from the hopeless and futile bravery of the man.

The charging panther moved rapidly, and the distance which separated the bush in which he had concealed himself from the objects of his desire was not great. In the time that one might understandingly read a dozen words the strong-limbed cat could have covered the entire distance and made his kill, yet if Sheeta was quick, quick too was Tarzan. The English lieutenant saw the ape-man flash by him like the wind. He saw the great cat veer in his charge as though to elude the naked savage rushing to meet him, as it was evidently Sheeta's intention to make good his kill before attempting to protect it from Tarzan.

Lieutenant Smith-Oldwick saw these things and then with increasing wonder he saw the ape-man swerve, too, and leap for the spotted cat as a football player leaps for a runner. He saw the strong, brown arms encircling the body of the carnivore, the left arm in front of the beast's left shoulder and the right arm behind his right foreleg, and with the impact the two together rolling over and over upon the turf. He heard the snarls and growls of bestial combat, and it was with a feeling of no little horror that he realized that the sounds coming from the human throat of the battling man could scarce be distinguished from those of the panther.

The first momentary shock of terror over, the girl released her grasp upon the Englishman's arm. "Cannot we do something?" she asked. "Cannot we help him before the beast kills him?"

The Englishman looked upon the ground for some missile with which to attack the panther and then the girl uttered an exclamation and started at a run toward the hut. "Wait there," she called over her shoulder. "I will fetch the spear that he left me."

Smith-Oldwick saw the raking talons of the panther searching for the flesh of the man and the man on his part straining every muscle and using every artifice to keep his body out of range of them. The muscles of his arms knotted under the brown hide. The veins stood out upon his neck and forehead as with ever-increasing power he strove to crush the life from the great cat. The ape-man's teeth were fastened in the back of Sheeta's neck and now he succeeded in encircling the beast's torso with his legs which he crossed and locked beneath the cat's belly. Leaping and snarling, Sheeta sought to dislodge the ape-man's hold upon him. He hurled himself upon the ground and rolled over and over. He reared upon his hind legs and threw himself backwards but always the savage creature upon his back clung tenaciously to him, and always the mighty brown arms crushed tighter and tighter about his chest.

And then the girl, panting from her quick run, returned with the short spear Tarzan had left her as her sole weapon of protection. She did not wait to hand it to the Englishman who ran forward to receive it, but brushed past him and leaped into close quarters beside the growling, tumbling mass of yellow fur and smooth brown hide. Several times she attempted to press the point home into the cat's body, but on both occasions the fear of endangering the ape-man caused her to desist, but at last the two lay motionless for a moment as the carnivore sought a moment's rest from the strenuous exertions of battle, and then it was that Bertha Kircher pressed the point of the spear to the tawny side and drove it deep into the savage heart.

Tarzan rose from the dead body of Sheeta and shook himself after the manner of beasts that are entirely clothed with hair. Like many other of his traits and mannerisms this was the result of environment rather than heredity or reversion, and even though he was outwardly a man, the Englishman and the girl were both impressed with the naturalness of the act. It was as though Numa, emerging from a fight, had shaken himself to straighten his rumpled mane and coat, and yet, too, there was something uncanny about it as there had been when the savage growls and hideous snarls issued from those clean-cut lips.

Tarzan looked at the girl, a quizzical expression upon his face. Again had she placed him under obligations to her, and Tarzan of the Apes did not wish to be obligated to a German spy; yet in his honest heart he could not but admit a certain admiration for her courage, a trait which always greatly impressed the ape-man, he himself the personification of courage.

"Here is the kill," he said, picking the carcass of Bara from the ground. "You will want to cook your portion, I presume, but Tarzan does not spoil his meat with fire."

They followed him to the boma where he cut several pieces of meat from the carcass for them, retaining a joint for himself. The young lieutenant prepared a fire, and the girl presided over the primitive culinary rights of their simple meal. As she worked some little way apart from them, the lieutenant and the ape-man watched her.

"She is wonderful. Is she not?" murmured Smith-Oldwick.

"She is a German and a spy," replied Tarzan.

The Englishman turned quickly upon him. "What do you mean?" he cried.

"I mean what I say," replied the ape-man. "She is a German and a spy."

"I do not believe it!" exclaimed the aviator.

"You do not have to," Tarzan assured him. "It is nothing to me what you believe. I saw her in conference with the Boche general and his staff at the camp near Taveta. They all knew her and called her by name and she handed him a paper. The next time I saw her she was inside the British lines in disguise, and again I saw her bearing word to a German officer at Wilhelmstal. She is a German and a spy, but she is a woman and therefore I cannot destroy her."

"You really believe that what you say is true?" asked the young lieutenant. "My God! I cannot believe it. She is so sweet and brave and good."

The ape-man shrugged his shoulders. "She is brave," he said, "but even Pamba, the rat, must have some good quality, but she is what I have told you and therefore I hate her and you should hate her."

Lieutenant Harold Percy Smith-Oldwick buried his face in his hands. "God forgive me," he said at last. "I cannot hate her."

The ape-man cast a contemptuous look at his companion and arose. "Tarzan goes again to hunt," he said. "You have enough food for two days. By that time he will return."

The two watched him until he had disappeared in the foliage of the trees at the further side of the clearing.

When he had gone the girl felt a vague sense of apprehension that she never experienced when Tarzan was present. The invisible menaces lurking in the grim jungle seemed more real and much more imminent now that the ape-man was no longer near. While he had been there talking with them, the little thatched hut and its surrounding thorn boma had seemed as safe a place as the world might afford. She wished that he had remained—two days seemed an eternity in contemplation— two days of constant fear, two days, every moment of which would be fraught with danger. She turned toward her companion.

"I wish that he had remained," she said. "I always feel so much safer when he is near. He is very grim and very terrible, and yet I feel safer with him than with any man I ever have known. He seems to dislike me and yet I know that he would let no harm befall me. I cannot understand him."

"Neither do I understand him," replied the Englishman; "but I know this much—our presence here is interfering with his plans. He would like to be rid of us, and I half imagine that he rather hopes to find when he returns that we have succumbed to one of the dangers which must always confront us in this savage land.

"I think that we should try to return to the white settlements. This man does not want us here, nor is it reasonable to assume that we could long survive in such a savage wilderness. I have traveled and hunted in several parts of Africa, but never have I seen or heard of any single locality so over-run with savage beasts and dangerous natives. If we set out for the east coast at once we would be in but little more danger than we are here, and if we could survive a day's march, I believe that we will find the means of reaching the coast in a few hours, for my plane must still be in the same place that I landed just before the blacks captured me. Of course there is no one here who could operate it nor is there any reason why they should have destroyed it. As a matter of fact, the natives would be so fearful and suspicious of so strange and incomprehensible a thing that the chances are they would not dare approach it. Yes, it must be where I left it and all ready to carry us safely to the settlements."

"But we cannot leave," said the girl, "until he returns. We could not go away like that without thanking him or bidding him farewell. We are under too great obligations to him."

The man looked at her in silence for a moment. He wondered if she knew how Tarzan felt toward her and then he himself began to speculate upon the truth of the ape-man's charges. The longer he looked at the girl, the less easy was it to entertain the thought that she was an enemy spy. He was upon the point of asking her point-blank but he could not bring himself to do so, finally determining to wait until time and longer acquaintance should reveal the truth or falsity of the accusation.

"I believe," he said as though there had been no pause in their conversation, "that the man would be more than glad to find us gone when he returns. It is not necessary to jeopardize our lives for two more days in order that we may thank him, however much we may apppreciate his services to us. You have more than balanced your obligations to him and from what he told me I feel that you especially should not remain here longer."

The girl looked up at him in astonishment. "What do you mean?" she asked.

"I do not like to tell," said the Englishman, digging nervously at the turf with the point of a stick, "but you have my word that he would rather you were not here."

"Tell me what he said," she insisted, "I have a right to know."

Lieutenant Smith-Oldwick squared his shoulders and raised his eyes to those of the girl. "He said that he hated you," he blurted. "He has only aided you at all from a sense of duty because you are a woman."

The girl paled and then flushed. "I will be ready to go," she said, "in just a moment. We had better take some of this meat with us. There is no telling when we will be able to get more."

And so the two set out down the river toward the south. The man carried the short spear that Tarzan had left with the girl, while she was entirely unarmed except for a stick she had picked up from among those left after the building of the hut. Before departing she had insisted that the man leave a note for Tarzan thanking him for his care of them and bidding him goodbye. This they left pinned to the inside wall of the hut with a little sliver of wood.

It was necessary that they be constantly on the alert since they never knew what might confront them at the next turn of the winding jungle trail or what might lie concealed in the tangled bushes at either side. There was also the ever-present danger of meeting some of Numabo's black warriors and as the village lay directly in their line of march, there was the necessity for making a wide detour before they reached it in order to pass around it without being discovered.

"I am not so much afraid of the native blacks," said the girl, "as I am of Usanga and his people. He and his men were all attached to a German native regiment. They brought me along with them when they deserted, either with the intention of holding me ransom or selling me into the harem of one of the black sultans of the north. Usanga is much more to be feared than Numabo for he has had the advantage of European military training and is armed with more or less modern weapons and ammunition."

"It is lucky for me," remarked the Englishman, "that it was the ignorant Numabo who discovered and captured me rather than the worldly wise Usanga. He would have felt less fear of the giant flying machine and would have known only too well how to wreck it."

"Let us pray that the black sergeant has not discovered it," said the girl.

They made their way to a point which they guessed was about a mile above the village, then they turned into the trackless tangle of undergrowth to the east. So dense was the verdure at many points that it was with the utmost difficulty they wormed their way through, sometimes on hands and knees and again by clambering over numerous fallen tree trunks. Interwoven with dead limbs and living branches were the tough and ropelike creepers which formed a tangled network across their path.

South of them in an open meadowland a number of black warriors were gathered about an object which elicited much wondering comment. The blacks were clothed in fragments of what had once been uniforms of a native German command. They were a most unlovely band and chief among them in authority and repulsiveness was the black sergeant Usanga. The object of their interest was a British aeroplane.

Immediately after the Englishman had been brought to Numabo's village Usanga had gone out in search of the plane, prompted partially by curiosity and partially by an intention to destroy it, but when he had found it, some new thought had deterred him from carrying out his design. The thing represented considerable value as he well knew and it had occurred to him that in some way he might turn his prize to profit. Every day he had returned to it, and while at first it had filled him with considerable awe, he eventually came to look upon it with the accustomed eye of a proprietor, so that he now clambered into the fuseluge and even advanced so far as to wish that he might learn to operate it.

What a feat it would be indeed to fly like a bird far above the highest tree top! How it would fill his less favored companions with awe and admiration! If Usanga could but fly, so great would be the respect of all the tribesmen throughout the scattered villages of the great interior, they would look upon him as little less than a god.

Usanga rubbed his palms together and smacked his thick lips. Then indeed, would he be very rich, for all the villages would pay tribute to him and he could even have as many as a dozen wives. With that thought, however, came a mental picture of Naratu, the black termagant, who ruled him with an iron hand. Usanga made a wry face and tried to forget the extra dozen wives, but the lure of the idea remained and appealed so strongly to him that he presently found himself reasoning most logically that a god would not be much of a god with less than twenty-four wives.

He fingered the instruments and the control, half hoping and half fearing that he would alight upon the combination that would put the machine in flight. Often had he watched the British air-men soaring above the German lines and it looked so simple he was quite sure that he could do it himself if there was somebody who could but once show him how. There was, of course, always the hope that the white man who came in the machine and who had escaped from Numabo's village might fall into Usanga's hands and then indeed would he be able to learn how to fly. It was in this hope that Usanga spent so much time in the vicinity of the plane, reasoning as he did that eventually the white man would return in search of it.

And at last he was rewarded, for upon this very day after he had quit the machine and entered the jungle with his warriors, he heard voices to the north and when he and his men had hidden in the dense foliage upon either side of the trail, Usanga was presently filled with elation by the appearance of the British officer and the white girl whom the black sergeant had coveted and who had escaped him.

The Negro could scarce restrain a shout of elation, for he had not hoped that fate would be so kind as to throw these two whom he most desired into his power at the same time.

As the two came down the trail all unconscious of impending danger, the man was explaining that they must be very close to the point at which the plane had landed. Their entire attention was centered on the trail directly ahead of them, as they momentarily expected it to break into the meadowland where they were sure they would see the plane that would spell life and liberty for them.

The trail was broad, and they were walking side by side so that at a sharp turn the parklike clearing was revealed to them simultaneously with the outlines of the machine they sought.

Exclamations of relief and delight broke from their lips, and at the same instant Usanga and his black warriors rose from the bushes all about them.

12

The Black Flier

THE girl was almost crushed by terror and disappointment. To have been thus close to safety and then to have all hope snatched away by a cruel stroke of fate seemed unendurable. The man was disappointed, too, but more was he angry. He noted the remnants of the uniforms upon the blacks and immediately he demanded to know where were their officers.

"They cannot understand you," said the girl and so in the bastard tongue that is the medium of communication between the Germans and the blacks of their colony, she repeated the white man's question.

Usanga grinned. "You know where they are, white woman," he replied. "They are dead, and if this white man does not do as I tell him, he, too, will be dead."

"What do you want of him?" asked the girl.

"I want him to teach me how to fly like a bird," replied Usanga.

Bertha Kircher looked her astonishment, but repeated the demand to the lieutenant.

The Englishman meditated for a moment. "He wants to learn to fly, does he?" he repeated. "Ask him if he will give us our freedom if I teach him to fly."

The girl put the question to Usanga, who, degraded, cunning, and entirely unprincipled, was always perfectly willing to promise anything whether he had any intentions of fulfilling his promises or not, and so immediately assented to the proposition.

"Let the white man teach me to fly," he said, "and I will take you back close to the settlements of your people, but in return for this I shall keep the great bird," and he waved a black hand in the direction of the aeroplane.

When Bertha Kircher had repeated Usanga's proposition to the aviator, the latter shrugged his shoulders and with a wry face finally agreed. "I fancy there is no other way out of

it," he said. "In any event the plane is lost to the British
government. If I refuse the black scoundrel's request, there is
no doubt but what he will make short work of me with the
result that the machine will lie here until it rots. If I accept
his offer it will at least be the means of assuring your safe
return to civilization and that" he added, "is worth more to
me than all the planes in the British Air Service."

The girl cast a quick glance at him. These were the first
words he had addressed to her that might indicate that his
sentiments toward her were more than those of a companion
in distress. She regretted that he had spoken as he had and
he, too, regretted it almost instantly as he saw the shadow
cross her face and realized that he had unwittingly added to
the difficulties of her already almost unbearable situation.

"Forgive me," he said quickly. "Please forget what that
remark implied. I promise you that I will not offend again,
if it does offend you, until after we are both safely out of this
mess."

She smiled and thanked him, but the thing had been said
and could never be unsaid, and Bertha Kircher knew even
more surely than as though he had fallen upon his knees and
protested undying devotion that the young English officer
loved her.

Usanga was for taking his first lesson in aviation immediately. The Englishman attempted to dissuade him, but immediately the black became threatening and abusive, since,
like all those who are ignorant, he was suspicious that the
intentions of others were always ulterior unless they perfectly
coincided with his wishes.

"All right, old top," muttered the Englishman, "I will give
you the lesson of your life," and then turning to the girl:
"Persuade him to let you accompany us. I shall be afraid to
leave you here with these devilish scoundrels." But when she
put the suggestion to Usanga the black immediately suspected
some plan to thwart him—possibly to carry him against his
will back to the German masters he had traitorously deserted,
and glowering at her savagely, he obstinately refused to entertain the suggestion.

"The white woman will remain here with my people," he
said. "They will not harm her unless you fail to bring me
back safely."

"Tell him," said the Englishman, "that if you are not standing in plain sight in this meadow when I return, I will not
land, but will carry Usanga back to the British camp and
have him hanged."

Usanga promised that the girl would be in evidence upon
their return, and took immediate steps to impress upon his

warriors that under penalty of death they must not harm her. Then, followed by the other members of his party, he crossed the clearing toward the plane with the Englishman. Once seated within what he already considered his new possession, the black's courage began to wane and when the motor was started and the great propeller commenced to whir, he screamed to the Englishman to stop the thing and permit him to alight, but the aviator could neither hear nor understand the black above the noise of the propeller and exhaust. By this time the plane was moving along the ground and even then Usanga was upon the verge of leaping out, and would have done so had he been able to unfasten the strap from about his waist. Then the plane rose from the ground and in a moment soared gracefully in a wide circle until it topped the trees. The black sergeant was in a veritable collapse of terror. He saw the earth dropping rapidly from beneath him. He saw the trees and river and at a distance the little clearing with the thatched huts of Numabo's village. He tried hard not to think of the results of a sudden fall to the rapidly receding ground below. He attempted to concentrate his mind upon the twenty-four wives which this great bird most assuredly would permit him to command. Higher and higher rose the plane, swinging in a wide circle above the forest, river, and meadowland and presently, much to his surprise, Usanga discovered that his terror was rapidly waning, so that it was not long before there was forced upon him a consciousness of utter security, and then it was that he began to take notice of the manner in which the white man guided and manipulated the plane.

After half an hour of skillful maneuvering, the Englishman rose rapidly to a considerable altitude, and then, suddenly, without warning, he looped and flew with the plane inverted for a few seconds.

"I said I'd give this beggar the lesson of his life," he murmured as he heard, even above the whir of the propeller, the shriek of the terrified Negro. A moment later Smith-Oldwick had righted the machine and was dropping rapidly toward the earth. He circled slowly a few times above the meadow until he had assured himself that Bertha Kircher was there and apparently unharmed, then he dropped gently to the ground so that the machine came to a stop a short distance from where the girl and the warriors awaited them.

It was a trembling and ashen-hued Usanga who tumbled out of the fuselage, for his nerves were still on edge as a result of the harrowing experience of the loop, yet with terra firma once more under foot, he quickly regained his composure. Strutting about with great show and braggadocio, he strove

to impress his followers with the mere nothingness of so trivial
a feat as flying birdlike thousands of yards above the jungle,
though it was long until he had thoroughly convinced himself
by the force of autosuggestion that he had enjoyed every
instant of the flight and was already far advanced in the art of
aviation.

So jealous was the black of his new-found toy that he would
not return to the village of Numabo, but insisted on making
camp close beside the plane, lest in some inconceivable fashion
it should be stolen from him. For two days they camped
there, and constantly during daylight hours Usanga compelled
the Englishman to instruct him in the art of flying.

Smith-Oldwick, in recalling the long months of arduous
training he had undergone himself before he had been considered sufficiently adept to be considered a finished flier,
smiled at the conceit of the ignorant African who was already
demanding that he be permitted to make a flight alone.

"If it was not for losing the machine," the Englishman explained to the girl, "I'd let the bounder take it up and break
his fool neck as he would do inside of two minutes."

However, he finally persuaded Usanga to bide his time for
a few more days of instruction, but in the suspicious mind of
the Negro there was a growing conviction that the white man's
advice was prompted by some ulterior motive; that it was in
the hope of escaping with the machine himself by night that
he refused to admit that Usanga was entirely capable of
handling it alone and therefore in no further need of help or
instruction, and so in the mind of the black there formed a
determination to outwit the white man. The lure of the twenty-
four seductive wives proved in itself a sufficient incentive and
there, too, was added his desire for the white girl whom he
had long since determined to possess.

It was with these thoughts in mind that Usanga lay down
to sleep in the evening of the second day. Constantly, however,
the thought of Naratu and her temper arose to take the keen
edge from his pleasant imaginings. If he could but rid himself
of her! The thought having taken form persisted, but always
it was more than outweighed by the fact that the black sergeant
was actually afraid of his woman, so much afraid of her in
fact that he would not have dared to attempt to put her out of
the way unless he could do so secretly while she slept. However, as one plan after another was conjured by the strength of
his desires, he at last hit upon one which came to him almost
with the force of a blow and brought him sitting upright among
his sleeping companions.

When morning dawned Usanga could scarce wait for an
opportunity to put his scheme into execution, and the moment

that he had eaten, he called several of his warriors aside and talked with them for some moments.

The Englishman, who usually kept an eye upon his black captor, saw now that the latter was explaining something in detail to his warriors, and from his gestures and his manner it was apparent that he was persuading them to some new plan as well as giving them instructions as to what they were to do. Several times, too, he saw the eyes of the Negroes turned upon him and once they flashed simultaneously toward the white girl.

Everything about the occurrence, which in itself seemed trivial enough, aroused in the mind of the Englishman a well-defined apprehension that something was afoot that boded ill for him and for the girl. He could not free himself of the idea and so he kept a still closer watch over the black although, as he was forced to admit to himself, he was quite powerless to avert any fate that lay in store for them. Even the spear that he had had when captured had been taken away from him, so that now he was unarmed and absolutely at the mercy of the black sergeant and his followers.

Lieutenant Harold Percy Smith-Oldwick did not have long to wait before discovering something of Usanga's plan, for almost immediately after the sergeant finished giving his instructions, a number of warriors approached the Englishman, while three went directly to the girl.

Without a word of explanation the warriors seized the young officer and threw him to the ground upon his face. For a moment he struggled to free himself and succeeded in landing a few heavy blows among his assailants, but he was too greatly outnumbered to hope to more than delay them in the accomplishment of their object which he soon discovered was to bind him securely hand and foot. When they had finally secured him to their satisfaction, they rolled him over on his side and then it was he saw Bertha Kircher had been similarly trussed.

Smith-Oldwick lay in such a position that he could see nearly the entire expanse of meadow and the aeroplane a short distance away. Usanga was talking to the girl who was shaking her head in vehement negatives.

"What is he saying?" called the Englishman.

"He is going to take me away in the plane," the girl called back. "He is going to take me farther inland to another country where he says that he will be king and I am to be one of his wives," and then to the Englishman's surprise she turned a smiling face toward him, "but there is no danger," she continued, "for we shall both be dead within a few minutes—just give him time enough to get the machine under way, and if he can rise a hundred feet from the ground I shall never need fear him more."

"God!" cried the man. "Is there no way that you can dissuade him? Promise him anything. Anything that you want. I have money, more money than that poor fool could imagine there was in the whole world. With it he can buy anything that money will purchase, fine clothes and food and women, all the women he wants. Tell him this and tell him that if he will spare you I give him my word that I will fetch it all to him."

The girl shook her head. "It is useless," she said. "He would not understand and if he did understand, he would not trust you. The blacks are so unprincipled themselves that they can imagine no such thing as principle or honor in others, and especially do these blacks distrust an Englishman whom the Germans have taught them to believe are the most treacherous and degraded of people. No, it is better thus. I am sorry that you cannot go with us, for if he goes high enough my death will be much easier than that which probably awaits you."

Usanga had been continually interrupting their brief conversation in an attempt to compel the girl to translate it to him, for he feared that they were concocting some plan to thwart him, and to quiet and appease him, she told him that the Englishman was merely bidding her farewell and wishing her good luck. Suddenly she turned to the black. "Will you do something for me?" she asked. "If I go willingly with you?"

"What is it you want?" he inquired.

"Tell your men to free the white man after we are gone. He can never catch us. That is all I ask of you. If you will grant him his freedom and his life, I will go willingly with you."

"You will go with me anyway," growled Usanga. "It is nothing to me whether you go willingly or not. I am going to be a great king and you will do whatever I tell you to do."

He had in mind that he would start properly with this woman. There should be no repetition of his harrowing experience with Naratu. This wife and the twenty-four others should be carefully selected and well trained. Hereafter Usanga would be master in his own house.

Bertha Kircher saw that it was useless to appeal to the brute and so she held her peace though she was filled with sorrow in contemplating the fate that awaited the young officer, scarce more than a boy, who had impulsively revealed his love for her.

At Usanga's order one of the blacks lifted her from the ground and carried her to the machine, and after Usanga had clambered aboard, they lifted her up and he reached down and drew her into the fuselage where he removed the thongs from her wrists and strapped her into her seat and then took his own directly ahead of her.

The girl turned her eyes toward the Englishman. She was very pale but her lips smiled bravely.

"Good-bye!" she cried.

"Good-bye, and God bless you!" he called back—his voice the least bit husky—and then: "The thing I wanted to say—may I say it now, we are so very near the end?"

Her lips moved but whether they voiced consent or refusal he did not know, for the words were drowned in the whir of the propeller.

The black had learned his lesson sufficiently well so that the motor was started without bungling and the machine was soon under way across the meadowland. A groan escaped the lips of the distracted Englishman as he watched the woman he loved being carried to almost certain death. He saw the plane tilt and the machine rise from the ground. It was a good take-off —as good as Lieutenant Harold Percy Smith-Oldwick could make himself but he realized that it was only so by chance. At any instant the machine might plunge to earth and even if, by some miracle of chance, the black could succeed in rising above the tree tops and make a successful flight, there was not one chance in one hundred thousand that he could ever land again without killing his fair captive and himself.

But what was that? His heart stood still.

13

Usanga's Reward

FOR two days Tarzan of the Apes had been hunting leisurely to the north, and swinging in a wide circle, he had returned to within a short distance of the clearing where he had left Bertha Kircher and the young lieutenant. He had spent the night in a large tree that overhung the river only a short distance from the clearing, and now in the early morning hours he was crouching at the water's edge waiting for an opportunity to capture Pisah, the fish, thinking that he would take it back with him to the hut where the girl could cook it for herself and her companion.

Motionless as a bronze statue was the wily ape-man, for well he knew how wary is Pisah, the fish. The slightest movement would frighten him away and only by infinite patience might he be captured at all. Tarzan depended upon his own quickness and the suddenness of his attack, for he had no bait or hook. His knowledge of the ways of the denizens of the water told him where to wait for Pisah. It might be a minute or it might be an hour before the fish would swim into the little pool above which he crouched, but sooner or later one would come. That the ape-man knew, so with the patience of the beast of prey he waited for his quarry.

At last there was a glint of shiny scales. Pisah was coming. In a moment he would be within reach and then with the swiftness of light two strong, brown hands would plunge into the pool and seize him, but, just as the moment that the fish was about to come within reach, there was a great crashing in the underbrush behind the ape-man. Instantly Pisah was gone and Tarzan, growling, had wheeled about to face whatever creature might be menacing him. The moment that he turned he saw that the author of the disturbance was Zu-tag.

"What does Zu-tag want?" asked the ape-man.

"Zu-tag comes to the water to drink," replied the ape.

"Where is the tribe?" asked Tarzan.

"They are hunting for pisangs and scimatines farther back in the forest," replied Zu-tag.

"And the Tarmangani she and bull—" asked Tarzan, "are they safe?"

"They have gone away," replied Zu-tag. "Kudu has come out of his lair twice since they left."

"Did the tribe chase them away?" asked Tarzan.

"No," replied the ape. "We did not see them go. We do not know why they left."

Tarzan swung quickly through the trees toward the clearing. The hut and boma were as he had left them, but there was no sign of either the man or the woman. Crossing the clearing, he entered the boma and then the hut. Both were empty, and his trained nostrils told him that they had been gone for at least two days. As he was about to leave the hut he saw a paper pinned upon the wall with a sliver of wood and taking it down, he read:

After what you told me about Miss Kircher, and knowing that you dislike her, I feel that it is not fair to her and to you that we should impose longer upon you. I know that our presence is keeping you from continuing your journey to the west coast, and so I have decided that it is better for us to try and reach the white settlements immediately without imposing further upon you. We both thank you for your kindness and protection. If there was any way that I might repay the obligation I feel, I should be only too glad to do so.

It was signed by Lieutenant Harold Percy Smith-Oldwick.

Tarzan shrugged his shoulders, crumpled the note in his hand and tossed it aside. He felt a certain sense of relief from responsibility and was glad that they had taken the matter out of his hands. They were gone and would forget, but somehow he could not forget. He walked out across the boma and into the clearing. He felt uneasy and restless. Once he started toward the north in response to a sudden determination to continue his way to the west coast. He would follow the winding river toward the north a few miles where its course turned to the west and then on toward its source across a wooded plateau and up into the foothills and the mountains. Upon the other side of the range he would search for a stream running downward toward the west coast, and thus following the rivers he would be sure of game and water in plenty.

But he did not go far. A dozen steps, perhaps, and he came to a sudden stop. "He is an Englishman," he muttered, "and the other is a woman. They can never reach the settlements without my help. I could not kill her with my own hands when I tried, and if I let them go on alone, I will have killed her just as surely as though I had run my knife into her heart. No," and again he shook his head. "Tarzan of the Apes is a fool and a weak, old woman," and he turned back toward the south.

Manu, the monkey, had seen the two Tarmangani pass two days before. Chattering and scolding, he told Tarzan all about it. They had gone in the direction of the village of the Gomangani, that much had Manu seen with his own eyes, so the ape-man swung on through the jungle in a southerly direction and though with no concentrated effort to follow the spoor of those he trailed, he passed numerous evidences that they had gone this way—faint suggestions of their scent spoor clung lightly to leaf or branch or bole that one or the other had touched, or in the earth of the trail their feet had trod, and where the way wound through the gloomy depth of dank forest, the impress of their shoes still showed occasionally in the damp mass of decaying vegetation that floored the way.

An inexplicable urge spurred Tarzan to increasing speed. The same still, small voice that chided him for having neglected them seemed constantly whispering that they were in dire need of him now. Tarzan's conscience was troubling him, which accounted for the fact that he compared himself to a weak, old woman, for the ape-man, reared in savagery and inured to hardships and cruelty, disliked to admit any of the gentler traits that in reality were his birthright.

The trail made a detour to the east of the village of the Wamabos, and then returned to the wide elephant path nearer to the river, where it continued in a southerly direction for several miles. At last there came to the ears of the ape-man a peculiar whirring, throbbing sound. For an instant he paused, listening intently, "An aeroplane!" he muttered, and hastened forward at greatly increased speed.

When Tarzan of the Apes finally reached the edge of the meadowland where Smith-Oldwick's plane had landed, he took in the entire scene in one quick glance and grasped the situation, although he could scarce give credence to the things he saw. Bound and helpless, the English officer lay upon the ground at one side of the meadow, while around him stood a number of the black deserters from the German command. Tarzan had seen these men before and knew who they were. Coming toward him down the meadow was an aeroplane piloted by the black Usanga and in the seat behind the pilot was the white girl, Bertha Kircher. How it befell that the ignorant savage could operate the plane, Tarzan could not guess nor had he time in which to speculate upon the subject.

His knowledge of Usanga, together with the position of the white man, told him that the black sergeant was attempting to carry off the white girl. Why he should be doing this when he had her in his power and had also captured and secured the only creature in the jungle who might wish to defend her in so far as the black could know, Tarzan could not guess, for he knew nothing of Usanga's twenty-four dream wives nor of the black's fear of the horrid temper of Naratu, his present mate. He did not know, then, that Usanga had determined to fly away with the white girl never to return, and to put so great a distance between himself and Naratu that the latter never could find him again; but it was this very thing that was in the black's mind although not even his own warriors guessed it. He had told them that he would take the captive to a sultan of the north and there obtain a great price for her and that when he returned they should have some of the spoils.

These things Tarzan did not know. All he knew was what he saw—a Negro attempting to fly away with a white girl. Already the machine was slowly leaving the ground. In a moment more it would rise swiftly out of reach. At first Tarzan thought of fitting an arrow to his bow and slaying Usanga, but as quickly he abandoned the idea because he knew that the moment the pilot was slain the machine, running wild, would dash the girl to death among the trees.

There was but one way in which he might hope to succor her—a way which if it failed must send him to instant death and yet he did not hesitate in an attempt to put it into execution.

Usanga did not see him, being too intent upon the unaccustomed duties of a pilot, but the blacks across the meadow saw him and they ran forward with loud and savage cries and menacing rifles to intercept him. They saw a giant white man leap from the branches of a tree to the turf and race rapidly toward the plane. They saw him take a long grass rope from about his shoulders as he ran. They saw the noose swinging in an undulating circle above his head. They saw the white girl in the machine glance down and discover him.

Twenty feet above the running ape-man soared the huge plane. The open noose shot up to meet it, and the girl, half guessing the ape-man's intentions, reached out and caught the noose and, bracing herself, clung tightly to it with both hands. Simultaneously Tarzan was dragged from his feet and the plane lurched sideways in response to the new strain. Usanga clutched wildly at the control and the machine shot upward at a steep angle. Dangling at the end of the rope the ape-man swung pendulum-like in space. The Englishman, lying bound upon the ground, had been a witness of all these happenings. His heart stood still as he saw Tarzan's body hurtling through the air toward the tree tops among which it seemed he must inevitably crash; but the plane was rising rapidly, so that the beast-man cleared the top-most branches. Then slowly, hand over hand, he climbed toward the fuselage. The girl, clinging desperately to the noose, strained every muscle to hold the great weight dangling at the lower end of the rope.

Usanga, all unconscious of what was going on behind him, drove the plane higher and higher into the air.

Tarzan glanced downward. Below him the tree tops and the river passed rapidly to the rear and only a slender grass rope and the muscles of a frail girl stood between him and the death yawning there thousands of feet below.

It seemed to Bertha Kircher that the fingers of her hands were dead. The numbness was running up her arms to her elbows. How much longer she could cling to the straining strands she could not guess. It seemed to her that those lifeless fingers must relax at any instant and then, when she had about given up hope, she saw a strong brown hand reach up and grasp the side of the fuselage. Instantly the weight upon the rope was removed and a moment later Tarzan of the Apes raised his body above the side and threw a leg over the edge. He glanced forward at Usanga and then, placing his mouth close to the girl's ear he cried: "Have you ever piloted a plane?" The girl nodded a quick affirmative.

"Have you the courage to climb up there beside the black and seize the control while I take care of him?"

The girl looked toward Usanga and shuddered. "Yes," she replied, "but my feet are bound."

Tarzan drew his hunting knife from its sheath and reaching down, severed the thongs that bound her ankles. Then the girl unsnapped the strap that held her to her seat. With one hand Tarzan grasped the girls' arm and steadied her as the two crawled slowly across the few feet which intervened between the two seats. A single slight tip of the plane would have cast them both into eternity. Tarzan realized that only through a miracle of chance could they reach Usanga and effect the change in pilots and yet he knew that that chance must be taken, for in the brief moments since he had first seen the plane, he had realized that the black was almost without experience as a pilot and that death surely awaited them in any event should the black sergeant remain at the control.

The first intimation Usanga had that all was not well with him was when the girl slipped suddenly to his side and grasped the control and at the same instant steel-like fingers seized his throat. A brown hand shot down with a keen blade and severed the strap about his waist and giant muscles lifted him bodily from his seat. Usanga clawed the air and shrieked but he was helpless as a babe. Far below the watchers in the meadow could see the aeroplane careening in the sky, for with the change of control it had taken a sudden dive. They saw it right itself and, turning in a short circle, return in their direction, but it was so far above them and the light of the sun so strong that they could see nothing of what was going on within the fuselage; but presently Lieutenant Smith-Oldwick gave a gasp of dismay as he saw a human body plunge downward from the plane. Turning and twisting in mid-air it fell with ever-increasing velocity and the Englishman held his breath as the thing hurtled toward them.

With a muffled thud it flattened upon the turf near the center of the meadow, and when at last the Englishman could gain the courage to again turn his eyes upon it, he breathed a fervent prayer of thanks, for the shapeless mass that lay upon the blood-stained turf was covered with an ebon hide. Usanga had reaped his reward.

Again and again the plane circled above the meadow. The blacks, at first dismayed at the death of their leader, were now worked to a frenzy of rage and a determination to be avenged. The girl and the ape-man saw them gather in a knot about the body of their fallen chief. They saw as they circled above the meadow the black fists shaken at them, and the rifles brandishing a menace toward them. Tarzan still clung to the fuselage directly behind the pilot's seat. His face was close beside Bertha Kircher's, and at the top of his voice, above the noise of propeller, engine and exhaust, he screamed a few words of instruction into her ear.

As the girl grasped the significance of his words she paled, but her lips set in a hard line and her eyes shone with a sudden fire of determination as she dropped the plane to within a few feet of the ground and at the opposite end of the meadow from the blacks and then at full speed bore down upon the savages. So quickly the plane came that Usanga's men had no time to escape it after they realized its menace. It touched the ground just as it struck among them and mowed through them, a veritable juggernaut of destruction. When it came to rest at the edge of the forest the ape-man leaped quickly to the ground and ran toward the young lieutenant, and as he went he glanced at the spot where the warriors had stood, ready to defend himself if necessary, but there was none there to oppose him. Dead and dying they lay strewn for fifty feet along the turf.

By the time Tarzan had freed the Englishman the girl

joined them. She tried to voice her thanks to the ape-man but he silenced her with a gesture.

"You saved yourself," he insisted, "for had you been unable to pilot the plane, I could not have helped you, and now," he said, "you two have the means of returning to the settlements. The day is still young. You can easily cover the distance in a few hours if you have sufficient petrol." He looked inquiringly toward the aviator.

Smith-Oldwick nodded his head affirmatively. "I have plenty," he replied.

"Then go at once," said the ape-man. "Neither of you belong in the jungle." A slight smile touched his lips as he spoke.

The girl and the Englishman smiled too. "This jungle is no place for us at least," said Smith-Oldwick, "and it is no place for any other white man. Why don't you come back to civilization with us?"

Tarzan shook his head. "I prefer the jungle," he said.

The aviator dug his toe into the ground and still looking down, blurted something which he evidently hated to say. "If it is a matter of living, old top," he said, "er—money, er— you know——"

Tarzan laughed. "No" he said. "I know what you are trying to say. It is not that. I was born in the jungle. I have lived all my life in the jungle, and I shall die in the jungle. I do not wish to live or die elsewhere."

The others shook their heads. They could not understand him.

"Go," said the ape-man. "The quicker you go, the quicker you will reach safety."

They walked to the plane together. Smith-Oldwick pressed the ape-man's hand and clambered into the pilot's seat. "Good-bye," said the girl as she extended her hand to Tarzan. "Before I go won't you tell me you don't hate me any more?" Tarzan's face clouded. Without a word he picked her up and lifted her to her place behind the Englishman. An expression of pain crossed Bertha Kircher's face. The motor started and a moment later the two were being borne rapidly toward the east.

In the center of the meadow stood the ape-man watching them. "It is too bad that she is a German and a spy," he said, "for she is very hard to hate."

14

The Black Lion

N UMA, the lion, was hungry. He had come out of the desert country to the east into a land of plenty but though he was young and strong, the wary grass-eaters had managed to elude his mighty talons each time he had thought to make a kill.

Numa, the lion, was hungry and very savage. For two days he had not eaten and now he hunted in the ugliest of humors. No more did Numa roar forth a rumbling challenge to the world but rather he moved silent and grim, stepping softly that no cracking twig might betray his presence to the keen-eared quarry he sought.

Fresh was the spoor of Bara, the deer, that Numa picked up in the well-beaten game trail he was following. No hour had passed since Bara had come this way; the time could be measured in minutes and so the great lion redoubled the cautiousness of his advance as he crept stealthily in pursuit of his quarry.

A light wind was moving through the jungle aisles, and it wafted down now to the nostrils of the eager carnivore the strong scent spoor of the deer, exciting his already avid appetite to a point where it became a gnawing pain. Yet Numa did not permit himself to be carried away by his desires into any premature charge such as had recently lost him the juicy meat of Pacco, the zebra. Increasing his gait but slightly he followed the tortuous windings of the trail until suddenly just before him, where the trail wound about the bole of a huge tree, he saw a young buck moving slowly ahead of him.

Numa judged the distance with his keen eyes, glowing now like two terrible spots of yellow fire in his wrinkled, snarling face. He could do it—this time he was sure. One terrific roar that would paralyze the poor creature ahead of him into momentary inaction, and a simultaneous charge of lightning-like rapidity and Numa, the lion, would feed. The sinuous tail, undulating slowly at its tufted extremity, whipped suddenly erect. It was the signal for the charge and the vocal

organs were shaped for the thunderous roar when, as lightning out of a clear sky, Sheeta, the panther, leaped suddenly
into the trail between Numa and the deer.

A blundering charge made Sheeta, for with the first crash of
his spotted body through the foliage verging the trail, Bara
gave a single startled backward glance and was gone.

The roar that was intended to paralyze the deer broke
horribly from the deep throat of the great cat—an angry roar
of rage against the meddling Sheeta who had robbed him of
his kill, and the charge that was intended for Bara was
launched against the panther; but here too Numa was doomed
to disappointment, for with the first notes of his fearsome
roar Sheeta, considering well the better part of valor, leaped
into a near-by tree.

A half-hour later it was a thoroughly furious Numa who
came unexpectedly upon the scent of man. Heretofore the
lord of the jungle had disdained the unpalatable flesh of the
despised man-thing. Such meat was only for the old, the
toothless, and the decrepit who no longer could make their
kills among the fleet-footed grass-eaters. Bara, the deer, Horta,
the boar, and, best and wariest, Pacco, the zebra, were for the
young, the strong, and the agile, but Numa was hungry—
hungrier than he ever had been in the five short years of
his life.

What if he was a young, powerful, cunning, and ferocious
beast? In the face of hunger, the great leveler, he was as the
old, the toothless, and the decrepit. His belly cried aloud in
anguish and his jowls slavered for flesh. Zebra or deer or
man, what mattered it so that it was warm flesh, red with the
hot juices of life? Even Dango, the hyena, eater of offal,
would, at the moment, have seemed a tidbit to Numa.

The great lion knew the habits and frailties of man, though
he never before had hunted man for food. He knew the
despised Gomangani as the slowest, the most stupid, and the
most defenseless of creatures. No woodcraft, no cunning, no
stealth was necessary in the hunting of man, nor had Numa
any stomach for either delay or silence.

His rage had become an almost equally consuming passion
with his hunger, so that now, as his delicate nostrils apprised
him of the recent passage of man, he lowered his head and
rumbled forth a thunderous roar, and at a swift walk, careless
of the noise he made, set forth upon the trail of his intended
quarry.

Majestic and terrible, regally careless of his sourroundings,
the king of beasts strode down the beaten trail. The natural
caution that is inherent to all creatures of the wild had deserted him. What had he, lord of the jungle, to fear and, with

only man to hunt, what need of caution? And so he did not see or scent what a more wary Numa might readily have discovered until, with the cracking of twigs and a tumbling of earth, he was precipitated into a cunningly devised pit that the wily Wamabos had excavated for just this purpose in the center of the game trail.

Tarzan of the Apes stood in the center of the clearing watching the plane shrinking to diminutive toylike proportions in the eastern sky. He had breathed a sigh of relief as he saw it rise safely with the British flier and Fräulein Bertha Kircher. For weeks he had felt the hampering responsibility of their welfare in this savage wilderness where their utter helplessness would have rendered them easy prey for the savage carnivores or the cruel Wamabos. Tarzan of the Apes loved unfettered freedom, and now that these two were safely off his hands, he felt that he could continue upon his journey toward the west coast and the long-untenanted cabin of his dead father.

And yet, as he stood there watching the tiny speck in the east, another sigh heaved his broad chest, nor was it a sigh of relief, but rather a sensation which Tarzan had never expected to feel again and which he now disliked to admit even to himself. It could not be possible that he, the jungle bred, who had renounced forever the society of man to return to his beloved beasts of the wilds, could be feeling anything akin to regret at the departure of these two, or any slightest loneliness now that they were gone. Lieutenant Harold Percy Smith-Oldwick Tarzan had liked, but the woman whom he had known as a German spy he had hated, though he never had found it in his heart to slay her as he had sworn to slay all Huns. He had attributed this weakness to the fact that she was a woman, although he had been rather troubled by the apparent inconsistency of his hatred for her and his repeated protection of her when danger threatened.

With an irritable toss of his head he wheeled suddenly toward the west as though by turning his back upon the fast disappearing plane he might expunge thoughts of its passengers from his memory. At the edge of the clearing he paused; a giant tree loomed directly ahead of him and, as though actuated by sudden and irresistible impulse, he leaped into the branches and swung himself with apelike agility to the topmost limbs that would sustain his weight. There, balancing lightly upon a swaying bough, he sought in the direction of the eastern horizon for the tiny speck that would be the British plane bearing away from him the last of his own race and kind that he expected ever again to see.

At last his keen eyes picked up the ship flying at a considerable altitude far in the east. For a few seconds he watched it speeding evenly eastward, when, to his horror, he saw the speck dive suddenly downward. The fall seemed interminable to the watcher and he realized how great must have been the altitude of the plane before the drop commenced. Just before it disappeared from sight its downward momentum appeared to abate suddenly, but it was still moving rapidly at a steep angle when it finally disappeared from view behind the far hills.

For half a minute the ape-man stood noting distant landmarks that he judged might be in the vicinity of the fallen plane, for no sooner had he realized that these people were again in trouble than his inherent sense of duty to his own kind impelled him once more to forego his plans and seek to aid them.

The ape-man feared from what he judged of the location of the machine that it had fallen among the almost impassable gorges of the arid country just beyond the fertile basin that was bounded by the hills to the east of him. He had crossed that parched and desolate country of the dead himself and he knew from his own experience and the narrow escape he had had from succumbing to its relentless cruelty no lesser man could hope to win his way to safety from any considerable distance within its borders. Vividly he recalled the bleached bones of the long-dead warrior in the bottom of the precipitous gorge that had all but proved a trap for him as well. He saw the helmet of hammered brass and the corroded breastplate of steel and the long straight sword in its scabbard and the ancient harquebus—mute testimonials to the mighty physique and the warlike spirit on him who had somehow won, thus illy caparisoned and pitifully armed, to the center of savage, ancient Africa; and he saw the slender English youth and the slight figure of the girl cast into the same fateful trap from which this giant of old had been unable to escape —cast there wounded and broken perhaps, if not killed.

His judgment told him that the latter possibility was probably the fact, and yet there was a chance that they might have landed without fatal injuries, and so upon this slim chance he started out upon what he knew would be an arduous journey, fraught with many hardships and unspeakable peril, that he might attempt to save them if they still lived.

He had covered a mile perhaps when his quick ears caught the sound of rapid movement along the game trail ahead of him. The sound, increasing in volume, proclaimed the fact that whatever caused it was moving in his direction and moving rapidly. Nor was it long before his trained senses convinced him that the footfalls were those of Bara, the deer, in rapid flight. Inextricably confused in Tarzan's character were the attributes of man and of beasts. Long experience had taught him that he fights best or travels fastest who is best nourished, and so, with few exceptions, Tarzan could delay his most urgent business to take advantage of an opportunity to kill and feed. This perhaps was the predominant beast trait in him. The transformation from an English gentleman, impelled by the most humanitarian motives, to that of a wild beast crouching in the concealment of a dense bush ready to spring upon its approaching prey, was instantaneous.

And so, when Bara came, escaping the clutches of Numa and Sheeta, his terror and his haste precluded the possibility of his sensing that other equally formidable foe lying in ambush for him. Abreast of the ape-man came the deer; a light-brown body shot from the concealing verdure of the bush, strong arms encircled the sleek neck of the young buck and powerful teeth fastened themselves in the soft flesh. Together the two rolled over in the trail and a moment later the ape-man rose, and, with one foot upon the carcass of his kill, raised his voice in the victory cry of the bull ape.

Like an answering challenge came suddenly to the ears of the ape-man the thunderous roar of a lion, a hideous angry roar in which Tarzan thought that he discerned a note of surprise and terror. In the breast of the wild things of the jungle, as in the breasts of their more enlightened brothers and sisters of the human race, the characteristic of curiosity is well developed. Nor was Tarzan far from innocent of it. The peculiar note in the roar of his hereditary enemy aroused a desire to investigate, and so, throwing the carcass of Bara, the deer, across his shoulder, the ape-man took to the lower terraces of the forest and moved quickly in the direction from which the sound had come, which was in line with the trail he had set out upon

As the distance lessened, the sounds increased in volume, which indicated that he was approaching a very angry lion and presently, where a jungle giant overspread the broad game trail that countless thousands of hoofed and padded feet had worn and trampled into a deep furrow during perhaps countless ages, he saw beneath him the lion pit of the Wamabos and in it, leaping futilely for freedom such a lion as even Tarzan of the Apes never before had beheld. A mighty beast it was that glared up at the ape-man—large, powerful and young, with a huge black mane and a coat so much darker than any Tarzan ever had seen that in the depths of the pit it looked almost black—a black lion!

Tarzan who had been upon the point of taunting and reviling his captive foe was suddenly turned to open admira-

tion for the beauty of the splendid beast. What a creature!
How by comparison the ordinary forest lion was dwarfed into
insignificance! Here indeed was one worthy to be called king
of beasts. With his first sight of the great cat the ape-man
knew that he had heard no note of terror in that initial roar;
surprise doubtless, but the vocal chords of that mighty throat
never had reacted to fear.

With growing admiration came a feeling of quick pity for the
hapless situation of the great brute rendered futile and helpless by the wiles of the Gomangani. Enemy though the beast
was, he was less an enemy to the ape-man than those blacks
who had trapped him, for though Tarzan of the Apes claimed
many fast and loyal friends among certain tribes of African
natives, there were others of degraded character and bestial
habits that he looked upon with utter loathing, and of such
were the human flesh-eaters of Numabo the chief. For a moment Numa, the lion, glared ferociously at the naked man-
thing upon the tree limb above him. Steadily those yellow-
green eyes bored into the clear eyes of the ape-man, and then
the sensitive nostrils caught the scent of the fresh blood of
Bara and the eyes moved to the carcass lying across the brown
shoulder, and there came from the cavernous depths of the
savage throat a low whine.

Tarzan of the Apes smiled. As unmistakably as though a
human voice had spoken, the lion had said to him "I am hungry, even more than hungry. I am starving," and the ape-
man looked down upon the lion beneath him and smiled, a
slow quizzical smile, and then he shifted the carcass from his
shoulder to the branch before him and, drawing the long
blade that had been his father's, deftly cut off a hind quarter
and, wiping the bloody blade upon Bara's smooth coat, he
returned it to its scabbard. Numa, with watering jaws, looked
up at the tempting meat and whined again and the ape-man
smiled down upon him his slow smile and, raising the hind
quarter in his strong brown hands buried his teeth in the tender, juicy flesh.

For the third time Numa, the lion, uttered that low pleading
whine and then, with a rueful and disgusted shake of his
head, Tarzan of the Apes raised the balance of the carcass of
Bara, the deer, and hurled it to the famished beast below.

"Old woman," muttered the ape-man. "Tarzan has become
a weak old woman. Presently he would shed tears because he
has killed Bara, the deer. He cannot see Numa, his enemy,
go hungry, because Tarzan's heart is turning to water by contact with the soft, weak creatures of civilization." But yet he
smiled; nor was he sorry that he had given way to the dic-
tates of a kindly impulse.

As Tarzan tore the flesh from that portion of the kill he had retained for himself his eyes were taking in each detail of the scene below. He saw the avidity with which Numa devoured the carcass; he noted with growing admiration the finer points of the beast, and also the cunning construction of the trap. The ordinary lion pit with which Tarzan was familiar had stakes imbedded in the bottom, upon whose sharpened points the hapless lion would be impaled, but this pit was not so made. Here the short stakes were set at intervals of about a foot around the walls near the top, their sharpened points inclining downward so that the lion had fallen unhurt into the trap but could not leap out because each time he essayed it his head came in contact with the sharp end of a stake above him.

Evidently, then, the purpose of the Wamabos was to capture a lion alive. As this tribe had no contact whatsoever with white men in so far as Tarzan knew, their motive was doubtless due to a desire to torture the beast to death that they might enjoy to the utmost his dying agonies.

Having fed the lion, it presently occurred to Tarzan that his act would be futile were he to leave the beast to the mercies of the blacks, and then too it occurred to him that he could derive more pleasure through causing the blacks discomfiture than by leaving Numa to his fate. But how was he to release him? By removing two stakes there would be left plenty of room for the lion to leap from the pit, which was not of any great depth. However, what assurance had Tarzan that Numa would not leap out instantly the way to freedom was open, and before the ape-man could gain the safety of the trees? Regardless of the fact that Tarzan felt no such fear of the lion as you and I might experience under like circumstances, he yet was imbued with the sense of caution that is necessary to all creatures of the wild if they are to survive. Should necessity require, Tarzan could face Numa in battle, although he was not so egotistical as to think that he could best a full-grown lion in mortal combat other than through accident or the utilization of the cunning of his superior man-mind. To lay himself liable to death futilely, he would have considered as reprehensible as to have shunned danger in time of necessity; but when Tarzan elected to do a thing he usually found the means to accomplish it.

He had now fully determined to liberate Numa, and having so determined, he would accomplish it even though it entailed considerable personal risk. He knew that the lion would be occupied with his feeding for some time, but he also knew that while feeding he would be doubly resentful of any fancied interference. Therefore Tarzan must work with caution.

Coming to the ground at the side of the pit, he examined the stakes and as he did so was rather surprised to note that Numa gave no evidence of anger at his approach. Once he turned a searching gaze upon the ape-man for a moment and then returned to the flesh of Bara. Tarzan felt of the stakes and tested them with his weight. He pulled upon them with the muscles of his strong arms, presently discovering that by working them back and forth he could loosen them: and then a new plan was suggested to him so that he fell to work excavating with his knife at a point above where one of the stakes was imbedded. The loam was soft and easily removed, and it was not long until Tarzan had exposed that part of one of the stakes which was imbedded in the wall of the pit to almost its entire length, leaving only enough imbedded to prevent the stake from falling into the excavation. Then he turned his attention to an adjoining stake and soon had it similarly exposed, after which he threw the noose of his grass rope over the two and swung quickly to the branch of the tree above. Here he gathered in the slack of the rope and, bracing himself against the bole of the tree, pulled steadily upward. Slowly the stakes rose from the trench in which they were imbedded and with them rose Numa's suspicion and growling.

Was this some new encroachment upon his rights and his liberties? He was puzzled and, like all lions, being short of temper, he was irritated. He had not minded it when the Tarmangani squatted upon the verge of the pit and looked down upon him, for had not this Tarmangani fed him? But now something else was afoot and the suspicion of the wild beast was aroused. As he watched, however, Numa saw the stakes rise slowly to an erect position, tumble against each other and then fall backwards out of his sight upon the surface of the ground above. Instantly the lion grasped the possibilities of the situation, and, too, perhaps he sensed the fact that the man-thing had deliberately opened a way for his escape. Seizing the remains of Bara in his great jaws, Numa, the lion, leaped agilely from the pit of the Wamabos and Tarzan of the Apes melted into the jungles to the east.

On the surface of the ground or through the swaying branches of the trees the spoor of man or beast was an open book to the ape-man, but even his acute senses were baffled by the spoorless trail of the airship. Of what good were eyes, or ears, or the sense of smell in following a thing whose path had lain through the shifting air thousands of feet above the tree tops? Only upon his sense of direction could Tarzan depend in his search for the fallen plane. He could not even judge accurately as to the distance it might lie from him, and he knew that from the moment that it disappeared beyond the hills it might have traveled a considerable distance at right angles to its original course before it crashed to earth. If its occupants were killed or badly injured the ape-man might search futilely in their immediately vicinity for some time before finding them.

There was but one thing to do and that was to travel to a point as close as possible to where he judged the plane had landed, and then to follow in ever-widening circles until he picked up their scent spoor. And this he did.

Before he left the valley of plenty he made several kills and carried the choicest cuts of meat with him, leaving all the dead weight of bones behind. The dense vegetation of the jungle terminated at the foot of the western slope, growing less and less abundant as he neared the summit beyond which was a sparse growth of sickly scrub and sunburned grasses, with here and there a gnarled and hardy tree that had withstood the vicissitudes of an almost waterless existence.

From the summit of the hills Tarzan's keen eyes searched the arid landscape before him. In the distance he discerned the ragged tortuous lines that marked the winding course of the hideous gorges which scored the broad plain at intervals—the terrible gorges that had so nearly claimed his life in punishment for his temerity in attempting to invade the sanctity of their ancient solitude.

For two days Tarzan sought futilely for some clew to the whereabouts of the machine or its occupants. He cached portions of his kills at different points, building cairns of rock to mark their locations. He crossed the first deep gorge and circled far beyond it. Occasionally he stopped and called aloud, listening for some response but only silence rewarded him—a sinister silence that his cries only accentuated.

Late in the evening of the second day he came to the well-remembered gorge in which lay the clean-picked bones of the ancient adventurer, and here, for the first time, Ska, the vulture, picked up his trail. "Not this time, Ska," cried the ape-man in a taunting voice, "for now indeed is Tarzan Tarzan. Before, you stalked the grim skeleton of a Tarmangani and even then you lost. Waste not your time upon Tarzan of the Apes in the full of his strength. But still Ska, the vulture, circled and soared above him, and the ape-man, notwithstanding his boasts, felt a shudder of apprehension. Through his brain ran a persistent and doleful chant to which he involuntarily set two words, repeated over and over again in horrible monotony: "Ska knows! Ska knows!" until, shaking himself in anger, he picked up a rock and hurled it at the grim scavenger.

Lowering himself over the precipitous side of the gorge Tarzan half clambered and half slid to the sandy floor beneath.

He had come upon the rift at almost the exact spot at which he had clambered from it weeks before, and there he saw, just as he had left it, just, doubtless, as it had lain for centuries, the mighty skeleton and its mighty armor.

As he stood looking down upon this grim reminder that another man of might had succumbed to the cruel powers of the desert, he was brought to startled attention by the report of a firearm, the sound of which came from the depths of the gorge to the south of him, and reverberated along the steep walls of the narrow rift.

15

Mysterious Footprints

A s THE British plane piloted by Lieutenant Harold Percy
Smith-Oldwick rose above the jungle wilderness where
Bertha Kircher's life had so often been upon the point
of extinction, and sped toward the east, the girl felt a sudden
contraction of the muscles of her throat. She tried very hard
to swallow something that was not there. It seemed strange to
her that she should feel regret in leaving behind her such
hideous perils, and yet it was plain to her that such was the
fact, for she was also leaving behind something beside the
dangers that had menaced her—a unique figure that had entered her life, and for which she felt an unaccountable at-
traction.

Before her in the pilot's seat sat an English officer and gentleman whom, she knew, loved her, and yet she dared to feel
regret in his company at leaving the stamping ground of a
wild beast!

Lieutenant Smith-Oldwick, on his part, was in the seventh
heaven of elation. He was in possession again of his beloved
ship, he was flying swiftly in the direction of his comrades and
his duty, and with him was the woman he loved. The fly in
the ointment, however, was the accusation Tarzan had made
against this woman. He had said that she was a German, and
a spy, and from the heights of bliss the English officer was
occasionally plunged to the depths of despair in contemplation of the inevitable, were the ape-man's charges to prove
true. He found himself torn between sentiments of love and
honor. On the one hand he could not surrender the woman he
loved to the certain fate that must be meted out to her if she
were in truth an enemy spy, while on the other it would be
equally impossible for him as an Englishman and an officer
to give her aid or protection.

The young man contented himself therefore with repeated
mental denials of her guilt. He tried to convince himself that
Tarzan was mistaken, and when he conjured upon the screen

of recollection the face of the girl behind him, he was doubly reassured that those lines of sweet femininity and character, those clear and honest eyes, could not belong to one of the hated alien race.

And so they sped toward the east, each wrapped in his own thoughts. Below them they saw the dense vegetation of the jungle give place to the scantier growth upon the hillside, and then before them there spread the wide expanse of arid waste-lands marked by the deep scarring of the narrow gorges that long-gone rivers had cut there in some forgotten age.

Shortly after they passed the summit of the ridge which formed the boundary between the desert and the fertile coun-try, Ska, the vulture, winging his way at a high altitude toward his aerie, caught sight of a strange new bird of gigantic pro-portions encroaching upon the preserves of his aerial domain. Whether with intent to give battle to the interloper or merely impelled by curiosity, Ska rose suddenly upward to meet the plane. Doubtless he misjudged the speed of the newcomer, but be that as it may, the tip of the propeller blade touched him and simultaneously many things happened. The lifeless body of Ska, torn and bleeding, dropped plummet-like toward the ground; a bit of splintered spruce drove backward to strike the pilot on the forehead; the plane shuddered and trembled and as Lieutenant Harold Percy Smith-Oldwick sank forward in momentary unconsciousness the ship dived headlong toward the earth.

Only for an instant was the pilot unconscious, but that in-stant almost proved their undoing. When he awoke to a reali-zation of their peril it was also to discover that his motor had stalled. The plane had attained frightful momentum, and the ground seemed too close for him to hope to flatten out in time to make a safe landing. Directly beneath him was a deep rift in the plateau, a narrow gorge, the bottom of which appeared comparatively level and sand covered.

In the brief instant in which he must reach a decision, the safest plan seemed to attempt a landing in the gorge, and this he did, but not without considerable damage to the plane and a severe shaking-up for himself and his passenger.

Fortunately neither of them was injured but their condition seemed indeed a hopeless one. It was a grave question as to whether the man could repair his plane and continue the jour-ney, and it seemed equally questionable as to their ability either to proceed on foot to the coast or retrace their way to the country they had just left. The man was confident that they could not hope to cross the desert country to the east in the face of thirst and hunger, while behind them in the valley of plenty lay almost equal danger in the form of carnivores and the warlike natives.

After the plane came to its sudden and disastrous stop, Smith-Oldwick turned quickly to see what the effect of the accident had been on the girl. He found her pale but smiling, and for several seconds the two sat looking at each other in silence.

"This is the end?" the girl asked.

The Englishman shook his head. "It is the end of the first leg, anyway," he replied.

"But you can't hope to make repairs here," she said dubiously.

"No," he said, "not if they amount to anything, but I may be able to patch it up. I will have to look her over a bit first. Let us hope there is nothing serious. It's a long, long way to the Tanga railway."

"We would not get far," said the girl, a slight note of hopelessness in her tone. "Entirely unarmed as we are, it would be little less than a miracle if we covered even a small fraction of the distance."

"But we are not unarmed," replied the man. "I have an extra pistol here, that the beggars didn't discover," and, removing the cover of a compartment, he drew forth an automatic.

Bertha Kircher leaned back in her seat and laughed aloud, a mirthless, half-hysterical laugh. "That popgun!" she exclaimed. "What earthly good would it do other than to infuriate any beast of prey you might happen to hit with it?"

Smith-Oldwick looked rather crestfallen. "But it is a weapon," he said. "You will have to admit that, and certainly I could kill a man with it."

"You could if you happened to hit him," said the girl, "or the thing didn't jam. Really, I haven't much faith in an automatic. I have used them myself."

"Oh, of course," he said ironically, "an express rifle would be better, for who knows but we might meet an elephant here in the desert."

The girl saw that he was hurt, and she was sorry, for she realized that there was nothing he would not do in her service or protection, and that it was through no fault of his that he was so illy armed. Doubtless, too, he realized as well as she the futility of his weapon, and that he had only called attention to it in the hope of reassuring her and lessening her anxiety.

"Forgive me," she said. "I did not mean to be nasty, but this accident is the proverbial last straw. It seems to me that I have borne all that I can. Though I was willing to give my life in the service of my country, I did not imagine that my

death agonies would be so long drawn out, for I realize now
that I have been dying for many weeks."

"What do you mean!" he exclaimed; "what do you mean by
that! You are not dying. There is nothing the matter with you."

"Oh, not that," she said, "I did not mean that. What I mean
is that at the moment the black sergeant, Usanga, and his renegade German native troops captured me and brought me inland, my death warrant was signed. Sometimes I have imagined
that a reprieve has been granted. Sometimes I have hoped
that I might be upon the verge of winning a full pardon, but
really in the depths of my heart I have known that I should
never live to regain civilization. I have done my bit for my
country, and though it was not much I can at least go with the
realization that it was the best I was able to offer. All that I
can hope for now, all that I ask for, is a speedy fulfillment of
the death sentence. I do not wish to linger any more to face
constant terror and apprehension. Even physical torture would
be preferable to what I have passed through. I have no doubt
that you consider me a brave woman, but really my terror has
been boundless. The cries of the carnivores at night fill me
with a dread so tangible that I am in actual pain. I feel the
rending talons in my flesh and the cruel fangs munching upon
my bones—it is as real to me as though I were actually
enduring the horrors of such a death. I doubt if you can understand it—men are so different."

"Yes," he said, "I think I can understand it, and because I
understand I can appreciate more than you imagine the hero-
ism you have shown in your endurance of all that you have
passed through. There can be no bravery where there is no
fear. A child might walk into a lion's den, but it would take
a very brave man to go to its rescue."

"Thank you," she said, "but I am not brave at all, and now
I am very much ashamed of my thoughtlessness for your own
feelings. I will try and take a new grip upon myself and we
will both hope for the best. I will help you all I can if you
will tell me what I may do."

"The first thing," he replied, "is to find out just how serious
our damage is, and then to see what we can do in the way of
repairs."

For two days Smith-Oldwick worked upon the damaged
plane—worked in the face of the fact that from the first he
realized the case was hopeless. And at last he told her.

"I knew it," she said, "but I believe that I felt much as you
must have; that however futile our efforts here might be, it
would be infinitely as fatal to attempt to retrace our way to
the jungle we just left or to go on toward the coast. You know
and I know that we could not reach the Tanga railway on foot.

We should die of thirst and starvation before we had covered half the distance, and if we return to the jungle, even were we able to reach it, it would be but to court an equally certain, though different, fate."

"So we might as well sit here and wait for death as to uselessly waste our energies in what we know would be a futile attempt at escape?" he asked.

"No," she replied, "I shall never give up like that. What I meant was that it was useless to attempt to reach either of the places where we know that there is food and water in abundance, so we must strike out in a new direction. Somewhere there may be water in this wilderness and if there is, the best chance of our finding it would be to follow this gorge downward. We have enough food and water left, if we are careful of it, for a couple of days and in that time we might stumble upon a spring or possibly even reach the fertile country which I know lies to the south. When Usanga brought me to the Wamabo country from the coast he took a southerly route along which there was usually water and game in plenty. It was not until we neared our destination that the country became overrun with carnivores. So there is hope if we can reach the fertile country south of us that we can manage to pull through to the coast."

The man shook his head dubiously. "We can try it," he said. "Personally, I do not fancy sitting here waiting for death."

Smith-Oldwick was leaning against the ship, his dejected gaze directed upon the ground at his feet. The girl was looking south down the gorge in the direction of their one slender chance of life. Suddenly she touched him on the arm.

"Look," she whispered.

The man raised his eyes quickly in the direction of her gaze to see the massive head of a great lion who was regarding them from beyond a rocky projection at the first turning of the gorge.

"Phew!" he exclaimed, "the beggars are everywhere."

"They do not go far from water do they," asked the girl hopefully.

"I should imagine not," he replied; "a lion is not particularly strong on endurance."

"Then he is a harbinger of hope," she exclaimed.

The man laughed. "Cute little harbinger of hope!" he said. "Reminds me of Cock Robin heralding spring."

"The girl cast a quick glance at him. "Don't be silly, and I don't care if you do laugh. He fills me with hope."

"It is probably mutual," replied Smith-Oldwick, "as we doubtless fill him with hope."

The lion evidently having satisfied himself as to the nature of the creatures before him advanced slowly now in their direction.

"Come," said the man, "let's climb aboard," and he helped the girl over the side of the ship.

"Can't he get in here?" she asked.

"I think he can," said the man.

"You are reassuring," she returned.

"I don't feel so." He drew his pistol.

"For heaven's sake," she cried, "don't shoot at him with that thing. You might hit him."

"I don't intend to shoot at him but I might succeed in frightening him away if he attempts to reach us here. Haven't you ever seen a trainer work with lions? He carries a silly little pop-gun loaded with blank cartridges. With that and a kitchen chair he subdues the most ferocious of beasts."

"But you haven't a kitchen chair," she reminded him.

"No," he said, "Government is always muddling things. I have always maintained that airplanes should be equipped with kitchen chairs."

Bertha Kircher laughed as evenly and with as little hysteria as though she were moved by the small talk of an afternoon tea.

Numa, the lion, came steadily toward them; his attitude seemed more that of curiosity than of belligerency. Close to the side of the ship he stopped and stood gazing up at them.

"Magnificent, isn't he?" exclaimed the man.

"I never saw a more beautiful creature," she replied, "nor one with such a dark coat. Why, he is almost black."

The sound of their voices seemed not to please the lord of the jungle, for he suddenly wrinkled his great face into deep furrows as he bared his fangs beneath snarling lips and gave vent to an angry growl. Almost simultaneously he crouched for a spring and immediately Smith-Oldwick discharged his pistol into the ground in front of the lion. The effect of the noise upon Numa seemed but to enrage him further, and with a horrid roar he sprang for the author of the new and disquieting sound that had outraged his ears.

Simultaneously Lieutenant Harold Percy Smith-Oldwick vaulted nimbly out of the cockpit on the opposite side of his plane, calling to the girl to follow his example. The girl, realizing the futility of leaping to the ground, chose the remaining alternative and clambered to the top of the upper plane.

Numa, unaccustomed to the idiosyncrasies of construction of an airship and having gained the forward cockpit, watched the girl clamber out of his reach without at first endeavoring to prevent her. Having taken possession of the plane his anger seemed suddenly to leave him and he made no immediate move toward following Smith-Oldwick. The girl, realizing the comparative safety of her position, had crawled to the outer edge of the wing and was calling to the man to try and reach the opposite end of the upper plane.

It was this scene upon which Tarzan of the Apes looked as he rounded the bend of the gorge above the plane after the pistol shot had attracted his attention. The girl was so intent upon watching the efforts of the Englishman to reach a place of safety, and the latter was so busily occupied in attempting to do so that neither at once noticed the silent approach of the ape-man.

It was Numa who first noticed the intruder. The lion immediately evinced his displeasure by directing toward him a snarling countenance and a series of warning growls. His action called the attention of the two upon the upper plane to the newcomer, eliciting a stifled "Thank God!" from the girl, even though she could scarce credit the evidence of her own eyes that it was indeed the savage man, whose presence always assured her safety, who had come so providentially in the nick of time.

Almost immediately both were horrified to see Numa leap from the cockpit and advance upon Tarzan. The ape-man, carrying his stout spear in readiness, moved deliberately onward to meet the carnivore, which he had recognized as the lion of the Wamabos' pit. He knew from the manner of Numa's approach what neither Bertha Kircher nor Smith-Oldwick knew—that there was more of curiosity than belligerency in it, and he wondered if in that great head there might not be a semblance of gratitude for the kindness that Tarzan had done him.

There was no question in Tarzan's mind but that Numa recognized him, for he knew his fellows of the jungle well enough to know that while they ofttimes forgot certain sensations more quickly than man there are others which remain in their memories for years. A well-defined scent spoor might never be forgotten by a beast if it had first been sensed under unusual circumstances, and so Tarzan was confident that Numa's nose had already reminded him of all the circumstances of their brief connection.

Love of the sporting chance is inherent in the Anglo-Saxon race and it was not now Tarzan of the Apes but rather John Clayton, Lord Greystoke, who smilingly welcomed the sporting chance which he must take to discover how far-reaching was Numa's gratitude.

Smith-Oldwick and the girl saw the two nearing each other. The former swore softly beneath his breath while he nervously fingered the pitiful weapon at his hip. The girl pressed her open palms to her cheeks as she leaned forward in stony-eyed, horror-stricken silence. While she had every confidence in the prowess of the godlike creature who thus dared brazenly to face the king of beasts, she had no false conception of what must certainly happen when they met. She had seen Tarzan battle with Sheeta, the panther, and she had realized then that powerful as the man was, it was only agility, cunning, and chance that placed him upon anywhere near an equal footing with his savage adversary, and that of the three factors upon his side chance was the greatest.

She saw the man and the lion stop simultaneously, not more than a yard apart. She saw the beast's tail whipping from side to side and she could hear his deep-throated growls rumbling from his cavernous breast, but she could read correctly neither the movement of the lashing tail nor the notes of the growl.

To her they seemed to indicate nothing but bestial rage while to Tarzan of the Apes they were conciliatory and reassuring in the extreme. And then she saw Numa move forward again until his nose touched the man's naked leg and she closed her eyes and covered them with her palms. For what seemed an eternity she waited for the horrid sound of the conflict which she knew must come, but all she heard was an explosive sigh of relief from Smith-Oldwick and a half-hysterical "By Jove! Just fancy it!"

She looked up to see the great lion rubbing his shaggy head against the man's hip, and Tarzan's free hand entangled in the black mane as he scratched Numa, the lion, behind a backlaid ear.

Strange friendships are often formed between the lower animals of different species, but less often between man and the savage felidae, because of the former's inherent fear of the great cats. And so after all, therefore, the friendship so suddenly developed between the savage lion and the savage man was not inexplicable.

As Tarzan approached the plane Numa walked at his side, and when Tarzan stopped and looked up at the girl and the man Numa stopped also.

"I had about given up hope of finding you," said the apeman, "and it is evident that I found you just in time."

"But how did you know we were in trouble?" asked the English officer.

"I saw your plane fall," replied Tarzan. "I was watching you from a tree beside the clearing where you took off. I didn't have much to locate you by other than the general direction, but it seems that you volplaned a considerable distance toward the south after you disappeared from my view behind the hills. I have been looking for you further toward the north. I was just about to turn back when I heard your pistol shot. Is your ship beyond repair?"

"Yes," replied Smith-Oldwick, "it is hopeless."

"What are your plans, then? What do you wish to do?" Tarzan directed his question to the girl.

"We want to reach the coast," she said, "but it seems impossible now."

"I should have thought so a little while ago," replied the ape-man, "but if Numa is here there must be water within a reasonable distance. I ran across this lion two days ago in the Wamabo country. I liberated him from one of their pits. To have reached this spot he must have come by some trail unknown to me—at least I crossed no game trail and no spoor of any animal after I came over the hills out of the fertile country. From which direction did he come upon you?"

"It was from the south," replied the girl. "We thought, too, that there must be water in that direction."

"Let's find out then," said Tarzan.

"But how about the lion?" asked Smith-Oldwick.

"That we will have to discover," replied the ape-man, "and we can only do so if you will come down from your perch."

The officer shrugged his shoulders. The girl turned her gaze upon him to note the effect of Tarzan's proposal. The Englishman grew suddenly very white, but there was a smile upon his lips as without a word he slipped over the edge of the plane and clambered to the ground behind Tarzan.

Bertha Kircher realized that the man was afraid nor did she blame him, and she also realized the remarkable courage that he had shown in thus facing a danger that was very real to him.

Numa standing close to Tarzan's side raised his head and glared at the young Englishman, growled once, and looked up at the ape-man. Tarzan retained a hold upon the beast's mane and spoke to him in the language of the great apes. To the girl and Smith-Oldwick the growling gutturals falling from human lips sounded uncanny in the extreme, but whether Numa understood them or not they appeared to have the desired effect upon him, as he ceased growling, and as Tarzan walked to Smith-Oldwick's side Numa accompanied him, nor did he offer to molest the officer.

"What did you say to him?" asked the girl.

Tarzan smiled. "I told him," he replied, "that I am Tarzan of the Apes, mighty hunter, killer of beasts, lord of the jungle, and that you are my friends. I have never been sure that all of the other beasts understand the language of the Mangani. I known that Manu, the monkey, speaks nearly the same tongue and I am sure that Tantor, the elephant, understands all that I say to him. We of the jungle are great boasters. In our speech, in our carriage, in every detail of our demeanor we must impress others with our physical power and our ferocity. That is why we growl at our enemies. We are telling them to beware or we shall fall upon them and tear them to pieces. Perhaps Numa does not understand the words that I use but I believe that my tones and my manner carry the impression that I wish them to convey. Now you may come down and be introduced."

It required all the courage that Bertha Kircher possessed to lower herself to the ground within reach of the talons and fangs of this untamed forest beast, but she did it. Nor did Numa do more than bare his teeth and growl a little as she came close to the ape-man.

"I think you are safe from him as long as I am present," said the ape-man. "The best thing to do is simply to ignore him. Make no advances, but be sure to give no indication of fear and, if possible always keep me between you and him. He will go away presently I am sure and the chances are that we shall not see him again."

At Tarzan's suggestion Smith-Oldwick removed the remaining water and provisions from the plane and, distributing the burden among them, they set off toward the south. Numa did not follow them, but stood by the plane watching until they finally disappeared from view around a bend in the gorge.

Tarzan had picked up Numa's trail with the intention of following it southward in the belief that it would lead to water. In the sand that floored the bottom of the gorge tracks were plain and easily followed. At first only the fresh tracks of Numa were visible, but later in the day the ape-man discovered the older tracks of other lions and just before dark he stopped suddenly in evident surprise. His two companions looked at him questioningly, and in answer to their implied interrogations he pointed at the ground directly in front of him.

"Look at those," he exclaimed.

At first neither Smith-Oldwick nor the girl saw anything but a confusion of intermingled prints of padded feet in the sand, but presently the girl discovered what Tarzan had seen, and an exclamation of surprise broke from her lips.

"The imprint of human feet!" she cried.

Tarzan nodded.

"But there are no toes," the girl pointed out.

"The feet were shod with a soft sandal," explained Tarzan.

"Then there must be a native village somewhere in the vicinity," said Smith-Oldwick.

"Yes," replied the ape-man, "but not the sort of natives which we would expect to find here in this part of Africa where others all go unshod with the exception of a few of

Usanga's renegade German native troops who wear German army shoes. I don't know that you can notice it, but it is evident to me that the foot inside the sandal that made these imprints were not the foot of a Negro. If you will examine them carefully you will notice that the impression of the heel and ball of the foot are well marked even through the sole of the sandal. The weight comes more nearly in the center of a Negro's footprint.

"Then you think these were made by a white person?"

"It looks that way," replied Tarzan, and suddenly, to the surprise of both the girl and Smith-Oldwick, he dropped to his hands and knees and sniffed at the tracks—again a beast utilizing the senses and woodcraft of a beast. Over an area of several square yards his keen nostrils sought the identity of the makers of the tracks. At length he rose to his feet.

"It is not the spoor of the Gomangani," he said, "nor is it exactly like that of white men. There were three who came this way. They were men, but of what race I do not know."

There was no apparent change in the nature of the gorge except that it had steadily grown deeper as they followed it downward until now the rocky and precipitous sides rose far above them. At different points natural caves, which appeared to have been eroded by the action of water in some forgotten age, pitted the side walls at various heights. Near them was such a cavity at the ground's level—an arched cavern floored with white sand. Tarzan indicated it with a gesture of his hand.

"We will lair here tonight," he said, and then with one of his rare, slow smiles. "We will *camp* here tonight."

Having eaten their meager supper Tarzan bade the girl enter the cavern.

"You will sleep inside," he said. "The lieutenant and I will lie outside at the entrance."

16

The Night Attack

A s the girl turned to bid them good night, she thought that she saw a shadowy form moving in the darkness beyond them, and almost simultaneously she was sure that she heard the sounds of stealthy movement in the same direction.

"What is that?" she whispered. "There is something out there in the darkness."

"Yes," replied Tarzan, "it is a lion. It has been there for some time. Hadn't you noticed it before?"

"Oh!" cried the girl, breathing a sigh of relief, "is it our lion?"

"No," said Tarzan, "it is not our lion; it is another lion and he is hunting."

"He is stalking us?" asked the girl.

"He is," replied the ape-man. Smith-Oldwick fingered the grip of his pistol.

Tarzan saw the involuntary movement and shook his head.

"Leave that thing where it is, Lieutenant," he said.

The officer laughed nervously. "I couldn't help it, you know, old man," he said; "instinct of self-preservation and all that."

"It would prove an instinct of self-destruction," said Tarzan. "There are at least three hunting lions out there watching us. If we had a fire or the moon were up you would see their eyes plainly. Presently they may come after us but the chances are that they will not. If you are very anxious that they should, fire your pistol and hit one of them."

"What if they do charge?" asked the girl; "there is no means of escape."

"Why, we should have to fight them," replied Tarzan.

"What chance would we three have against them?" asked the girl.

The ape-man shrugged his shoulders. "One must die sometime," he said. "To you doubtless it may seem terrible—such a death; but Tarzan of the Apes has always expected to go out in some such way. Few of us die of old age in the jungle, nor

166

should I care to die thus. Some day Numa will get me, or Sheeta, or a black warrior. These or some of the others. What difference does it make which it is, or whether it comes tonight or next year or in ten years? After it is over it will be all the same."

The girl shuddered. "Yes," she said in a dull, hopeless voice, "after it is over it will be all the same."

Then she went into the cavern and lay down upon the sand. Smith-Oldwick sat in the entrance and leaned against the cliff. Tarzan squatted on the opposite side.

"May I smoke?" questioned the officer of Tarzan. "I have been hoarding a few cigarettes and if it won't attract those bounders out there I would like to have one last smoke before I cash in. Will you join me?" and he proffered the ape-man a cigarette.

"No, thanks," said Tarzan, "but it will be all right if you smoke. No wild animal is particularly fond of the fumes of tobacco so it certainly won't entice them any closer."

Smith-Oldwick lighted his cigarette and sat puffing slowly upon it. He had proffered one to the girl but she had refused, and thus they sat in silence for some time, the silence of the night ruffled occasionally by the faint crunching of padded feet upon the soft sands of the gorge's floor.

It was Smith-Oldwick who broke the silence. "Aren't they unusually quiet for lions?" he asked.

"No," replied the ape-man; "the lion that goes roaring around the jungle does not do it to attract prey. They are very quiet when they are stalking their quarry."

"I wish they would roar," said the officer. "I wish they would do anything, even charge. Just knowing that they are there and occasionally seeing something like a shadow in the darkness and the faint sounds that come to us from them are getting on my nerves. But I hope," he said, "that all three don't charge at once."

"Three?" said Tarzan. "There are seven of them out there now."

"Good Lord!" exclaimed Smith-Oldwick.

"Couldn't we build a fire," asked the girl, "and frighten them away?"

"I don't know that it would do any good," said Tarzan, "as I have an idea that these lions are a little different from any that we are familiar with and possibly for the same reason which at first puzzled me a little—I refer to the apparent docility in the presence of a man of the lion who was with us today. A man is out there now with those lions."

"It is impossible!" exclaimed Smith-Oldwick. "They would tear him to pieces."

"What makes you think there is a man there?" asked the girl.

Tarzan smiled and shook his head. "I am afraid you would not understand," he replied. "It is difficult for us to understand anything that is beyond our own powers."

"What do you mean by that?" asked the officer.

"Well," said Tarzan, "if you had been born without eyes you could not understand sense impressions that the eyes of others transmit to their brains, and as you have both been born without any sense of smell I am afraid you cannot understand how I can know that there is a man there."

"You mean that you scent a man?" asked the girl.

Tarzan nodded affirmatively.

"And in the same way you know the number of lions?" asked the man.

"Yes," said Tarzan. "No two lions look alike, no two have the same scent."

The young Englishman shook his head. "No," he said, "I cannot understand."

"I doubt if the lions or the man are here necessarily for the purpose of harming us," said Tarzan, "because there has been nothing to prevent their doing so long before had they wished to. I have a theory, but it is utterly preposterous."

"What is it?" asked the girl.

"I think they are here," replied Tarzan, "to prevent us from going some place that they do not wish us to go; in other words we are under surveillance, and possibly as long as we don't go where we are not wanted we shall not be bothered."

"But how are we to know where they don't want us to go?" asked Smith-Oldwick.

"We can't know," replied Tarzan, "and the chances are that the very place we are seeking is the place they don't wish us to trespass on."

"You mean the water?" asked the girl.

"Yes," replied Tarzan.

For some time they sat in silence which was broken only by an occasional sound of movement from the outer darkness. It must have been an hour later that the ape-man rose quietly and drew his long blade from its sheath. Smith-Oldwick was dozing against the rocky wall of the cavern entrance, while the girl, exhausted by the excitement and fatigue of the day, had fallen into deep slumber. An instant after Tarzan arose, Smith-Oldwick and the girl were aroused by a volley of thunderous roars and the noise of many padded feet rushing toward them.

Tarzan of the Apes stood directly before the entrance to the cavern, his knife in his hand, awaiting the charge. The ape-man had not expected any such concerted action as he now realized had been taken by those watching them. He had known for some time that other men had joined those who were with the lions earlier in the evening, and when he arose to his feet it was because he knew that the lions and the men were moving cautiously closer to him and his party. He might easily have eluded them, for he had seen that the face of the cliff rising above the mouth of the cavern might be scaled by as good a climber as himself. It might have been wiser had he tried to escape, for he knew that in the face of such odds even he was helpless, but he stood his ground though I doubt if he could have told why.

He owed nothing either of duty or friendship to the girl sleeping in the cavern, nor could he longer be of any protection to her or her companion. Yet something held him there in futile self-sacrifice.

The great Tarmangani had not even the satisfaction of striking a blow in self-defense. A veritable avalanche of savage beasts rolled over him and threw him heavily to the ground. In falling his head struck the rocky surface of the cliff, stunning him.

It was daylight when he regained consciousness. The first dim impression borne to his awakening mind was a confusion of savage sounds which gradually resolved themselves into the growling of lions, and then, little by little, there came back to him the recollections of what had preceded the blow that had felled him.

Strong in his nostrils was the scent of Numa, the lion, and against one naked leg he could feel the coat of some animal. Slowly Tarzan opened his eyes. He was lying on his side and as he looked down his body, he saw that a great lion stood straddling him—a great lion who growled hideously at something which Tarzan could not see.

With the full return of his senses Tarzan's nose told him that the beast above him was Numa of the Wamabo pit.

Thus reassured, the ape-man spoke to the lion and at the same time made a motion as though he would arise. Immediately Numa stepped from above him. As Tarzan raised his head, he saw that he still lay where he had fallen before the opening of the cliff where the girl had been sleeping and that Numa, backed against the cliffside, was apparently defending him from two other lions who paced to and fro a short distance from their intended victim.

And then Tarzan turned his eyes into the cave and saw that the girl and Smith-Oldwick were gone.

His efforts had been for naught. With an angry toss of his head, the ape-man turned upon the two lions who had continued to pace back and forth a few yards from him. Numa of the lion pit turned a friendly glance in Tarzan's direction, rubbed his head against the ape-man's side, and then directed his snarling countenance toward the two hunters.

"I think," said Tarzan to Numa, "that you and I together can make these beasts very unhappy." He spoke in English, which, of course, Numa did not understand at all, but there must have been something reassuring in the tone, for Numa whined pleadingly and moved impatiently to and fro parallel with their antagonists.

"Come," said Tarzan suddenly and grasping the lion's mane with his left hand he moved toward the other lions, his companion pacing at his side. As the two advanced the others drew slowly back and, finally separating, moved off to either side. Tarzan and Numa passed between them but neither the great black-maned lion nor the man failed to keep an eye upon the beast nearer him so that they were not caught unawares when, as though at some preconcerted signal, the two cats charged simultaneously from opposite directions.

The ape-man met the charge of his antagonist after the same fashion of fighting that he had been accustomed to employing in previous encounters with Numa and Sheeta. To have attempted to meet the full shock of a lion's charge would have been suicidal even for the giant Tarmangani. Instead he resorted to methods of agility and cunning, for quick as are the great cats, even quicker is Tarzan of the Apes.

With outspread, raking talons and bared fangs Numa sprang for the naked chest of the ape-man. Throwing up his left arm as a boxer might ward off a blow, Tarzan struck upward beneath the left forearm of the lion, at the same time rushing in with his shoulder beneath the animal's body and simultaneously drove his blade into the tawny hide behind the shoulder. With a roar of pain Numa wheeled again, the personification of bestial rage. Now indeed would he exterminate this presumptuous man-thing who dared even to think that he could thwart the king of beasts in his desires. But as he wheeled, his intended quarry wheeled with him, brown fingers locked in the heavy mane on the powerful neck and again the blade struck deep into the lion's side.

Then it was that Numa went mad with hate and pain and at the same instant the ape-man leaped full upon his back. Easily before had Tarzan locked his legs beneath the belly of a lion while he clung to its long mane and stabbed it until his point reached its heart. So easy it had seemed before that he experienced a sharp feeling of resentment that he was unable to do so now, for the quick movements of the lion prevented him, and presently, to his dismay, as the lion leaped and threw him about, the ape-man realized that he was swinging inevitably beneath those frightful talons.

With a final effort he threw himself from Numa's back and sought, by his quickness, to elude the frenzied beast for the fraction of an instant that would permit him to regain his feet and meet the animal again upon a more even footing. But this time Numa was too quick for him and he was but partially up when a great paw struck him one the side of the head and bowled him over.

As he fell he saw a black streak shoot above him and another lion close upon his antagonist. Rolling from beneath the two battling lions Tarzan regained his feet, though he was half dazed and staggering from the impact of the terrible blow he had received. Behind him he saw a lifeless lion lying torn and bleeding upon the sand, and before him Numa of the pit was savagely mauling the second lion.

He of the black coat tremendously outclassed his adversary in point of size and strength as well as in ferocity. The battling beasts made a few feints and passes at each other before the larger succeeded in fastening his fangs in the other's throat, and then, as a cat shakes a mouse, the larger lion shook the lesser, and when his dying foe sought to roll beneath and rake his conqueror with his hind claws, the other met him halfway at his own game, and as the great talons buried themselves in the lower part of the other's chest and then were raked downward with all the terrific strength of the mighty hind legs, the battle was ended.

As Numa rose from his second victim and shook himself, Tarzan could not but again note the wondrous proportions and symmetry of the beast. The lions they had bested were splendid specimens themselves and in their coats Tarzan noted a suggestion of the black which was such a strongly marked characteristic of Numa of the pit. Their manes were just a trifle darker than an ordinary black-maned lion but the tawny shade on the balance of their coats predominated. However, the ape-man realized that they were a distinct species from any he had seen as though they had sprung originally from a cross between the forest lion of his acquaintance and a breed of which Numa of the pit might be typical.

The immediate obstruction in his way having been removed, Tarzan was for setting out in search of the spoor of the girl and Smith-Oldwick, that he might discover their fate. He suddenly found himself tremendously hungry and as he circled about over the sandy bottom searching among the tangled network of innumerable tracks for those of his *protégés*, there broke from his lips involuntarily the whine of a hungry beast. Immediately Numa of the pit pricked up his ears and, regard-

ing the ape-man steadily for a moment, he answered the call
of hunger and started briskly off toward the south, stopping
occasionally to see if Tarzan was following.

The ape-man realized that the beast was leading him to
food, and so he followed and as he followed his keen eyes and
sensitive nostrils sought for some indication of the direction
taken by the man and the girl. Presently out of the mass of
lion tracks, Tarzan picked up those of many sandled feet and
the scent spoor of the members of the strange race such as
had been with the lions the night before, and then faintly he
caught the scent spoor of the girl and a little later that of
Smith-Oldwick. Presently the tracks thinned and here those of
the girl and the Englishman became well marked.

They had been walking side by side and there had been
men and lions to the right and left of them, and men and lions
in front and behind. The ape-man was puzzled by the possibilities suggested by the tracks, but in the light of any previous
experience he could not explain satisfactorily to himself what
his perceptions indicated.

There was little change in the formation of the gorge; it still
wound its erratic course between precipitous cliffs. In places
it widened out and again it became very narrow and always
deeper the further south they traveled. Presently the bottom
of the gorge began to slope more rapidly. Here and there were
indications of ancient rapids and waterfalls. The trail became
more difficult but was well marked and showed indications of
great antiquity, and, in places, the handiwork of man. They
had proceeded for a half or three-quarters of a mile when, at
a turning of the gorge, Tarzan saw before him a narrow valley
cut deep into the living rock of the earth's crust, with lofty
mountain ranges bounding it upon the south. How far it extended east and west he could not see, but apparently it was
no more than three or four miles across from north to south.

That it was a well-watered valley was indicated by the
wealth of vegetation that carpeted its floor from the rocky
cliffs upon the north to the mountains on the south.

Over the edge of the cliffs from which the ape-man viewed
the valley a trail had been hewn that led downward to the
base. Preceded by the lion Tarzan descended into the valley,
which, at this point, was forested with large trees. Before him
the trail wound onward toward the center of the valley.
Raucous-voiced birds of brilliant plumage screamed among
the branches while innumerable monkeys chattered and
scolded above him.

The forest teemed with life, and yet there was borne in upon
the ape-man a sense of unutterable loneliness, a sensation that
he never before had felt in his beloved jungles. There was

unreality in everything about him—in the valley itself, lying hidden and forgotten in what was supposed to be an arid waste. The birds and the monkeys, while similar in type to many with which he was familiar, were identical with none, nor was the vegetation without its idiosyncrasies. It was as though he had been suddenly transported to another world and he felt a strange restlessness that might easily have been a premonition of danger.

Fruits were growing among the trees and some of these he saw that Manu, the monkey, ate. Being hungry he swung to the lower branches and, amidst a great chattering of the monkeys, proceeded to eat such of the fruit as he saw the monkeys ate in safety. When he had partially satisfied his hunger, for meat alone could fully do so, he looked about him for Numa of the pit to discover that the lion had gone.

17

The Walled City

DROPPING to the ground once more he picked up the trail of the girl and her captors, which he followed easily along what appeared to be a well-beaten trail. It was not long before he came to a small stream, where he quenched his thirst, and thereafter he saw that the trail followed in the general direction of the stream, which ran southwesterly. Here and there were cross trails and others which joined the main avenue, and always upon each of them were the tracks and scent of the great cats, of Numa, the lion, and Sheeta, the panther.

With the exception of a few small rodents there appeared to be no other wild life on the surface of the valley. There was no indication of Bara, the deer, or Horta, the boar, or of Gorgo, the buffalo, Buto, Tantor, or Duro. Histah, the snake, was there. He saw him in the trees in greater numbers than he ever had seen Histah before; and once beside a reedy pool he caught a scent that could have belonged to none other than Gimla the crocodile, but upon none of these did the Tarmangani care to feed.

And so, as he craved meat, he turned his attention to the birds above him. His assailants of the night before had not disarmed him. Either in the darkness and the rush of the charging lions the human foe had overlooked him or else they had considered him dead; but whatever the reason he still retained his weapons—his spear and his long knife, his bow and arrows, and his grass rope.

Fitting a shaft to his bow Tarzan awaited an opportunity to bring down one of the larger birds, and when the opportunity finally presented itself he drove the arrow straight to its mark. As the gaily plumaged creature fluttered to earth its companions and the little monkeys set up a most terrific chorus of wails and screaming protests. The whole forest became suddenly a babel of hoarse screams and shrill shrieks.

Tarzan would not have been surprised had one or two birds

in the immediate vicinity given voice to terror as they fled, but
that the whole life of the junlgle should set up so weird a protest filled him with disgust. It was an angry face that he turned
up toward the monkeys and the birds as there suddenly stirred
within him a savage inclination to voice his displeasure and
his answer to what he considered their challenge. And so it
was that there broke upon this jungle for the first time Tarzan's
hideous scream of victory and challenge.

The effect upon the creatures above him was instantaneous.
Where before the air had trembled to the din of their voices,
now utter silence reigned and a moment later the ape-man was
alone with his puny kill.

The silence following so closely the previous tumult carried
a sinister impression to the ape-man, which still further
aroused his anger. Picking the bird from where it had fallen
he withdrew his arrow from the body and returned it to his
quiver. Then with his knife he quickly and deftly removed the
skin and feathers together. He ate angrily, growling as though
actually menaced by a near-by foe, and perhaps, too, his
growls were partially induced by the fact that he did not care
for the flesh of birds. Better this, however, than nothing and
from what his senses had told him there was no flesh in the
vicinity such as he was accustomed to and cared most for.
How he would have enjoyed a juicy haunch from Pacco, the
zebra, or a steak from the loin of Gorgo, the buffalo! The very
thought made his mouth water and increased his resentment
against this unnatural forest that harbored no such delicious
quarry.

He had but partially consumed his kill when he suddenly
became aware of a movement in the brush at no great distance
from him and downwind, and a moment later his nostrils
picked up the scent of Numa from the opposite direction, and
then upon either side he caught the fall of padded feet and the
brushing of bodies against leafy branches. The ape-man
smiled. What stupid creature did they think him, to be surprised by such clumsy stalkers? Gradually the sounds and
scents indicated that lions were moving upon him from all
directions, that he was in the center of a steadily converging
circle of beasts. Evidently they were so sure of their prey that
they were making no effort toward stealth, for he heard twigs
crack beneath their feet, and the brushing of their bodies
against the vegetation through which they forced their way.

He wondered what could have brought them. It seemed
unreasonable to believe that the cries of the birds and the
monkeys should have summoned them, and yet, if not, it was
indeed a remarkable coincidence. His judgment told him that
the death of a single bird in this forest which teemed with

birds could scarce be of sufficient moment to warrant that which followed. Yet even in the face of reason and past experience he found that the whole affair perplexed him.

He stood in the center of the trail awaiting the coming of the lions and wondering what would be the method of their attack or if they would indeed attack. Presently a maned lion came into view along the trail below him. At sight of him the lion halted. The beast was similar to those that had attacked him earlier in the day, a trifle larger and a trifle darker than the lions of his native jungles, but neither so large nor so black as Numa of the pit.

Presently he distinguished the outlines of other lions in the surrounding brush and among the trees. Each of them halted as it came within sight of the ape-man and there they stood regarding him in silence. Tarzan wondered how long it would be before they charged and while he waited he resumed his feeding, though with every sense constantly alert.

One by one the lions lay down, but always their faces were toward him and their eyes upon him. There had been no growling and no roaring—just the quiet drawing of the silent circle about him. It was all so entirely foreign to anything that Tarzan ever before had seen lions do that it irritated him so that presently, having finished his repast, he fell to making insulting remarks to first one and then another of the lions, after the habit he had learned from the apes of his childhood.

"Dango, eater of carrion," he called them, and he compared them most unfavorably with Histah, the snake, the most loathed and repulsive creature of the jungle. Finally he threw handfuls of earth at them and bits of broken twigs, and then the lions growled and bared their fangs, but none of them advanced.

"Cowards," Tarzan taunted them. "Numa with a heart of Bara, the deer." He told them who he was, and after the manner of the jungle folk he boasted as to the horrible things he would do to them, but the lions only lay and watched him.

It must have been a half hour after their coming that Tarzan caught in the distance along the trail the sound of footsteps approaching. They were the footsteps of a creature who walked upon two legs, and though Tarzan could catch no scent spoor from that direction he knew that a man was approaching. Nor had he long to wait before his judgment was confirmed by the appearance of a man who halted in the trail directly behind the first lion that Tarzan had seen.

At sight of the newcomer the ape-man realized that here was one similar to those who had given off the unfamiliar scent spoor that he had detected the previous night, and he saw that not only in the matter of scent did the man differ from other human beings with whom Tarzan was familiar.

The fellow was strongly built with skin of a leathery appearance, like parchment yellowed with age. His hair, which was coal black and three or four inches in length, grew out stiffly at right angles to his scalp. His eyes were close set and the irises densely black and very small, so that the white of the eyeball showed around them. The man's face was smooth except for a few straggly hairs on his chin and upper lip. The nose was aquiline and fine, but the hair grew so far down on the forehead as to suggest a very low and brutal type. The upper lip was short and fine while the lower lip was rather heavy and inclined to be pendulous, the chin being equally weak. Altogether the face carried the suggestion of a once strong and handsome countenance entirely altered by physical violence or by degraded habits and thoughts. The man's arms were long, though not abnormally so, while his legs were short, though straight.

He was clothed in tight-fitting nether garments and a loose, sleeveless tunic that fell just below his hips, while his feet were shod in soft-soled sandals, the wrappings of which extended halfway to his knees, closely resembling a modern spiral military legging. He carried a short, heavy spear, and at his side swung a weapon that at first so astonished the ape-man that he could scarcely believe the evidence of his senses —a heavy saber in a leather-covered scabbard. The man's tunic appeared to have been fabricated upon a loom—it was certainly not made of skins, while the garments that covered his legs were quite as evidently made from the hides of rodents.

Tarzan noted the utter unconcern with which the man approached the lions, and the equal indifference of Numa to him. The fellow paused for a moment as though appraising the ape-man and then pushed on past the lions, brushing against the tawny hide as he passed him in the trail.

About twenty feet from Tarzan the man stopped, addressing the former in a strange jargon, no syllable of which was intelligible to the Tarmangani. His gestures indicated numerous references to the lions surrounding them, and once he touched his spear with the forefinger of his left hand and twice he struck the saber at his hip.

While he spoke Tarzan studied the fellow closely, with the result that there fastened itself upon his mind a strange conviction—that the man who addressed him was what might only be described as a rational maniac. As the thought came to the ape-man he could not but smile, so paradoxical the description seemed. Yet a closer study of the man's features, carriage, and the contour of his head carried almost incontrovertibly the assurance that he was insane, while the tones of his voice and his gestures resembled those of a sane and intelligent mortal.

Presently the man had concluded his speech and appeared to be waiting questioningly Tarzan's reply. The ape-man spoke to the other first in the language of the great apes, but he soon saw that the words carried no conviction to his listener. Then with equal futility he tried several native dialects but to none of these did the man respond.

By this time Tarzan began to lose patience. He had wasted sufficient time by the road, and as he had never depended much upon speech in the accomplishment of his ends, he now raised his spear and advanced toward the other. This, evidently, was a language common to both, for instantly the fellow raised his own weapon and at the same time a low call broke from his lips, a call which instantly brought to action every lion in the hitherto silent circle. A volley of roars shattered the silence of the forest and simultaneously lions sprang into view upon all sides as they closed in rapidly upon their quarry. The man who had called them stepped back, his teeth bared in a mirthless grin.

It was then that Tarzan first noticed that the fellow's upper canines were unusually long and exceedingly sharp. It was just a flashing glimpse he got of them as he leaped agilely from the ground and, to the consternation of both the lions and their master, disappeared in the foliage of the lower terrace, flinging back over his shoulder as he swung rapidly away: "I am Tarzan of the Apes; mighty hunter; mighty fighter! None in the jungle more powerful, none more cunning than Tarzan!"

A short distance beyond the point at which they had surrounded him, Tarzan came to the trail again and sought for the spoor of Bertha Kircher and Lieutenant Smith-Oldwick. He found them quickly and continued upon his search for the two. The spoor lay directly along the trail for another half-mile when the way suddenly debouched from the forest into open land and there broke upon the astonished view of the ape-man the domes and minarets of a walled city.

Directly before him in the wall nearest him Tarzan saw a low-arched gateway to which a well-beaten trail led from that which he had been following. In the open space between the forest and the city walls, quantities of garden stuff was growing, while before him at his feet, in an open man-made ditch, ran a stream of water! The plants in the garden were laid out in well-spaced, symmetrical rows and appeared to have been given excellent attention and cultivation. Tiny streams were trickling between the rows from the main ditch before him and at some distance to his right he could see people at work among the plants.

The city wall appeared to be about thirty feet in height, its plastered expanse unbroken except by occasional embrasures. Beyond the wall rose the domes of several structures and numerous minarets dotted the sky line of the city. The largest and central dome appeared to be gilded, while others were red, or blue, or yellow. The architecture of the wall itself was of uncompromising simplicity. It was of a cream shade and appeared to be plastered and painted. At its base was a line of well-tended shrubs and at some distance towards its eastern extremity it was vine covered to the top.

As he stood in the shadow of the trail, his keen eyes taking in every detail of the picture before him, he became aware of the approach of a party in his rear and there was borne to him the scent of the man and the lions whom he had so readily escaped. Taking to the trees Tarzan moved a short distance to the west and, finding a comfortable crotch at the edge of the forest where he could watch the trail leading through the gardens to the city gate, he awaited the return of his would-be captors. And soon they came—the strange man followed by the pack of great lions. Like dogs they moved along behind him down the trail among the gardens to the gate.

Here the man struck upon the panels of the door with the butt of his spear, and when it opened in response to his signal he passed in with his lions. Beyond the open door Tarzan, from his distant perch, caught but a fleeting glimpse of life within the city, just enough to indicate that there were other human creatures who abode there, and then the door closed.

Through that door he knew that the girl and the man whom he sought to succor had been taken into the city. What fate lay in store for them or whether already it had been meted out to them he could not even guess, nor where, within that forbidding wall, they were incarcerated he could not know. But of one thing he was assured: that if he were to aid them he could not do it from outside the wall. He must gain entrance to the city first, nor did he doubt, that once within, his keen senses would eventually reveal the whereabouts of those whom he sought.

The low sun was casting long shadows across the gardens when Tarzan saw the workers returning from the eastern field. A man came first, and as he came he lowered little gates along the large ditch of running water, shutting off the streams that had run between the rows of growing plants; and behind him came other men carrying burdens of fresh vegetables in great

woven baskets upon their shoulders. Tarzan had not realized
that there had been so many men working in the field, but
now as he sat there at the close of the day he saw a procession
filing in from the east, bearing the tools and the produce back
into the city.

And then, to gain a better view, the ape-man ascended to
the topmost branches of a tall tree where he overlooked the
nearer wall. From this point of vantage he saw that the city
was long and narrow, and that while the outer walls formed
a perfect rectangle, the streets within were winding. Toward
the center of the city there appeared to be a low, white
building around which the larger edifices of the city had been
built, and here, in the fast-waning light, Tarzan thought that
between two buildings he caught the glint of water, but of
that he was not sure. His experience of the centers of civilization naturally inclined him to believe that this central area
was a plaza about which the larger buildings were grouped
and that there would be the most logical place to search first
for Bertha Kircher and her companion.

And then the sun went down and darkness quickly en-
veloped the city—a darkness that was accentuated for the
ape-man rather than relieved by the artificial lights which
immediately appeared in many of the windows visible to him.

Tarzan had noticed that the roofs of most of the buildings
were flat, the few exceptions being those of what he imagined
to be the more pretentious public structures. How this city
had come to exist in this forgotten part of unexplored Africa
the ape-man could not conceive. Better than another, he
realized something of the unsolved secrets of the Great Dark
Continent, enormous areas of which have as yet been untouched by the foot of civilized man. Yet he could scarce
believe that a city of this size and apparently thus well con-
structed could have existed for the generations that it must
have been there, without intercourse with the outer world.
Even though it was surrounded by a trackless desert waste, as
he knew it to be, he could not conceive that generation after
generation of men could be born and die there without attempting to solve the mysteries of the world beyond the
confines of their little valley.

And yet, here was the city surrounded by tilled land and
filled with people!

With the coming of night there arose throughout the jungle
the cries of the great cats, the voice of Numa blended with
that of Sheeta, and the thunderous roars of the great males
reverberated through the forest until the earth trembled, and
from within the city came the answering roars of other lions.

A simple plan for gaining entrance to the city had occurred

to Tarzan, and now that darkness had fallen he set about to put it into effect. Its success hinged entirely upon the strength of the vines he had seen surmounting the wall toward the east. In this direction he made his way, while from out of the forest about him the cries of the flesh-eaters increased in volume and ferocity. A quarter of a mile intervened between the forest and the city wall—a quarter of a mile of cultivated land unrelieved by a single tree. Tarzan of the Apes realized his limitations and so he knew that it would undoubtedly spell death for him to be caught in the open space by one of the great black lions of the forest if, as he had already surmised, Numa of the pit was a specimen of the forest lion of the valley.

He must, therefore, depend entirely upon his cunning and his speed, and upon the chance that the vine would sustain his weight.

He moved through the middle terrace, where the way is always easiest, until he reached a point opposite the vine-clad portion of the wall, and there he waited, listening and scenting, until he might assure himself that there was no Numa within his immediate vicinity, or, at least, none that sought him. And when he was quite sure that there was no lion close by in the forest, and none in the clearing between himself and the wall, he dropped lightly to the ground and moved stealthily out into the open.

The rising moon, just topping the eastern cliffs, cast its bright rays upon the long stretch of open garden beneath the wall. And, too, it picked out in clear relief for any curious eyes that chanced to be cast in that direction, the figure of the giant ape-man moving across the clearing. It was only chance, of course, that a great lion hunting at the edge of the forest saw the figure of the man halfway between the forest and the wall. Suddenly there broke upon Tarzan's ears a menacing sound. It was not the roar of a hungry lion, but the roar of a lion in rage, and, as he glanced back in the direction from which the sound came, he saw a huge beast moving out from the shadow of the forest toward him.

Even in the moonlight and at a distance Tarzan saw that the lion was huge; that it was indeed another of the black-maned monsters similar to Numa of the pit. For an instant he was impelled to turn and fight, but at the same time the thought of the helpless girl imprisoned in the city flashed through his brain and, without an instant's hesitation, Tarzan of the Apes wheeled and ran for the wall. Then it was that Numa charged.

Numa, the lion, can run swifty for a short distance, but he lacks endurance. For the period of an ordinary charge he

can cover the ground with greater rapidity possibly than any
other creature in the world. Tarzan, on the other hand, could
run at great speed for long distances, though never as rapidly
as Numa when the latter charged.

The question of his fate, then, rested upon whether, with
his start, he could elude Numa for a few seconds; and, if so,
if the lion would then have sufficient stamina remaining to
pursue him at a reduced gait for the balance of the distance
to the wall.

Never before, perhaps, was staged a more thrilling race,
and yet it was run with only the moon and stars to see. Alone
and in silence the two beasts sped across the moonlit clearing.
Numa gained with appalling rapidity upon the fleeing man,
yet at every bound Tarzan was nearer to the vine-clad wall.
Once the ape-man glanced back. Numa was so close upon
him that it seemed inevitable that at the next bound he should
drag him down; so close was he that the ape-man drew his
knife as he ran, that he might at least give a good account of
himself in the last moments of his life.

But Numa had reached the limit of his speed and endurance.
Gradually he dropped behind but he did not give up the
pursuit, and now Tarzan realized how much hinged upon the
strength of the untested vines.

If, at the inception of the race, only Goro and the stars had
looked down upon the contestants, such was not the case at
its finish, since from an embrasure near the summit of the
wall two close-set black eyes peered down upon the two.
Tarzan was a dozen yards ahead of Numa when he reached
the wall. There was no time to stop and institute a search
for sturdy stems and safe handholds. His fate was in the
hands of chance and with the realization he gave a final spurt
and running catlike up the side of the wall among the vines,
sought with his hands for something that would sustain his
weight. Below him Numa leaped also.

18

Among the Maniacs

A s the lions swarmed over her protectors, Bertha Kircher shrank back in the cave in a momentary paralysis of fright superinduced, perhaps, by the long days of terrific nerve strain which she had undergone.

Mingled with the roars of the lions had been the voices of men, and presently out of the confusion and turmoil she felt the near presence of a human being, and then hands reached forth and seized her. It was dark and she could see but little, nor any sign of the English officer or the ape-man. The man who seized her kept the lions from her with what appeared to be a stout spear, the haft of which he used to beat off the beasts. The fellow dragged her from the cavern the while he shouted what appeared to be commands and warnings to the lions.

Once out upon the light sands of the bottom of the gorge objects became more distinguishable, and then she saw that there were other men in the party and that two half led and half carried the stumbling figure of a third, whom she guessed must be Smith-Oldwick.

For a time the lions made frenzied efforts to reach the two captives but always the men with them succeeded in beating them off. The fellows seemed utterly unafraid of the great beasts leaping and snarling about them, handling them much the same as one might handle a pack of obstreperous dogs. Along the bed of the old watercourse that once ran through the gorge they made their way, and as the first faint lightening of the eastern horizon presaged the coming dawn, they paused for a moment upon the edge of a declivity, which appeared to the girl in the strange light of the waning night as a vast, bottomless pit; but, as their captors resumed their way and the light of the new day became stronger, she saw that they were moving downward toward a dense forest.

Once beneath the over-arching trees all was again Cimmerian darkness, nor was the gloom relieved until the sun finally arose beyond the eastern cliffs, when she saw that they were following what appeared to be a broad and well-beaten game trail through a forest of great trees. The ground was unusually dry for an African forest and the underbrush, while heavily foliaged, was not nearly so rank and impenetrable as that which she had been accustomed to find in similar woods. It was as though the trees and the bushes grew in a waterless country, nor was there the musty odor of decaying vegetation or the myriads of tiny insects such as are bred in damp places.

As they proceeded and the sun rose higher, the voices of the arboreal jungle life rose in discordant notes and loud chattering about them. Innumerable monkeys scolded and screamed in the branches overhead, while harsh-voiced birds of brilliant plumage darted hither and thither. She noticed presently that their captors often cast apprehensive glances in the direction of the birds and on numerous occasions seemed to be addressing the winged denizens of the forest.

One incident made a marked impression on her. The man who immediately preceded her was a fellow of powerful build, yet, when a brilliantly colored parrot swooped downward toward him, he dropped upon his knees and covering his face with his arms bent forward until his head touched the ground. Some of the others looked at him and laughed nervously. Presently the man glanced upward and seeing that the bird had gone, rose to his feet and continued along the trail.

It was at this brief halt that Smith-Oldwick was brought to her side by the men who had been supporting him. He had been rather badly mauled by one of the lions; but was now able to walk alone, though he was extremely weak from shock and loss of blood.

"Pretty mess, what?" he remarked with a wry smile, indicating his bloody and disheveled state.

"It is terrible," said the girl. "I hope you are not suffering."

"Not as much as I should have expected," he replied, "but I feel as weak as a fool. What sort of creatures are these beggars, anyway?"

"I don't know," she replied, "there is something terribly uncanny about their appearance."

The man regarded one of their captors closely for a moment and then, turning to the girl asked, "Did you ever visit a madhouse?"

She looked up at him in quick understanding and with a horrified expression in her eyes. "That's it!" she cried.

"They have all the earmarks," he said. "Whites of the eyes showing all around the irises, hair growing stiffly erect from the scalp and low down upon the forehead—even their mannerisms and their carriage are those of maniacs."

The girl shuddered.

"Another thing about them," continued the Englishman, "that doesn't appear normal is that they are afraid of parrots and utterly fearless of lions."

"Yes," said the girl; "and did you notice that the birds seem utterly fearless of them—really seem to hold them in contempt? Have you any idea what language they speak?"

"No," said the man, "I have been trying to figure that out. It's not like any of the few native dialects of which I have any knowledge."

"It doesn't sound at all like the native language," said the girl, "but there is something familiar about it. You know, every now and then I feel that I am just on the verge of understanding what they are saying, or at least that somewhere I have heard their tongue before, but final recognition always eludes me."

"I doubt if you ever heard their language spoken," said the man. "These people must have lived in this out-of-the-way valley for ages and even if they had retained the original language of their ancestors without change, which is doubtful, it must be some tongue that is no longer spoken in the outer world."

At one point where a stream of water crossed the trail the party halted while the lions and the men drank. They motioned to their captors to drink too, and as Bertha Kircher and Smith-Oldwick, lying prone upon the ground drank from the clear, cool water of the rivulet, they were suddenly startled by the thunderous roar of a lion a short distance ahead of them. Instantly the lions with them set up a hideous response, moving restlessly to and fro with their eyes always either turned in the direction from which the roar had come or toward their masters, against whom the tawny beasts slunk. The men loosened the sabers in their scabbards, the weapons that had aroused Smith-Oldwick's curiosity as they had Tarzan's, and grasped their spears more firmly.

Evidently there were lions and lions, and while they evinced no fear of the beasts which accompanied them, it was quite evident that the voice of the newcomer had an entirely different effect upon them, although the men seemed less terrified than the lions. Neither, however, showed any indication of an inclination to flee; on the contrary the entire party advanced along the trail in the direction of the menacing roars, and presently there appeared in the center of the path a black lion of gigantic proportions. To Smith-Oldwick and the girl he appeared to be the same lion that they had encountered at the plane and from which Tarzan had rescued them. But it was not Numa of the pit, although he resembled him closely.

The black beast stood directly in the center of the trail lashing his tail and growling menacingly at the advancing party. The men urged on their own beasts, who growled and whined but hesitated to charge. Evidently becoming impatient, and in full consciousness of his might the intruder raised his tail stiffly erect and shot forward. Several of the defending lions made a half-hearted attempt to obstruct his passage, but they might as well have placed themselves in the path of an express train, as hurling them aside the great beast leaped straight for one of the men. A dozen spears were launched at him and a dozen sabers leaped from their scabbards; gleaming, razor-edged weapons they were, but for the instant rendered futile by the terrific speed of the charging beast.

Two of the spears entering his body but served to further enrage him as, with demoniacal roars, he sprang upon the hapless man he had singled out for his prey. Scarcely pausing in his charge he seized the fellow by the shoulder and, turning quickly at right angles, leaped into the concealing foliage that flanked the trail, and was gone, bearing his victim with him.

So quickly had the whole occurrence transpired that the formation of the little party was scarcely altered. There had been no opportunity for flight, even if it had been contemplated; and now that the lion was gone with his prey the men made no move to pursue him. They paused only long enough to recall the two or three of their lions that had scattered and then resumed the march along the trail.

"Might be an everyday occurrence from all the effect it has on them," remarked Smith-Oldwick to the girl.

"Yes," she said. "They seem to be neither surprised nor disconcerted, and evidently they are quite sure that the lion, having got what he came for, will not molest them further."

"I had thought," said the Englishman, "that the lions of the Wamabo country were about the most ferocious in existence, but they are regular tabby cats by comparison with these big black fellows. Did you ever see anything more utterly fearless or more terribly irresistible than that charge?"

For a while, as they walked side by side, their thoughts and conversation centered upon this latest experience, until the trail emerging from the forest opened to their view a walled city and an area of cultivated land. Neither could suppress an exclamation of surprise.

"Why, that wall is a regular engineering job," exclaimed Smith-Oldwick.

"And look at the domes and minarets of the city beyond," cried the girl. "There must be a civilized people beyond that wall. Possibly we are fortunate to have fallen into their hands."

Smith-Oldwick shrugged his shoulders. "I hope so," he said, "though I am not at all sure about people who travel about with lions and are afraid of parrots. There must be something wrong with them."

The party followed the trail across the field to an arched gateway which opened at the summons of one of their captors, who beat upon the heavy wooden panels with his spear. Beyond, the gate opened into a narrow street which seemed but a continuation of the jungle trail leading from the forest. Buildings on either hand adjoined the wall and fronted the narrow, winding street, which was only visible for a short distance ahead. The houses were practically all two-storied structures, the upper stories flush with the street while the walls of the first story were set back some ten feet, a series of simple columns and arches supporting the front of the second story and forming an arcade on either side of the narrow thoroughfare.

The pathway in the center of the street was unpaved, but the floors of the arcades were cut stone of various shapes and sizes but all carefully fitted and laid without mortar. These floors gave evidence of great antiquity, there being a distinct depression down the center as though the stone had been worn away by the passage of countless sandaled feet during the ages that it had lain there.

There were few people astir at this early hour, and these were of the same type as their captors. At first those whom they saw were only men, but as they went deeper into the city they came upon a few naked children playing in the soft dust of the roadway. Many they passed showed the greatest surprise and curiosity in the prisoners, and often made inquiries of the guards, which the two assumed must have been in relation to themselves, while others appeared not to notice them at all.

"I wish we could understand their bally language," exclaimed Smith-Oldwick.

"Yes," said the girl, "I would like to ask them what they are going to do with us."

"That would be interesting," said the man. "I have been doing considerable wondering along that line myself."

"I don't like the way their canine teeth are filed," said the girl. "It's too suggestive of some of the cannibals I have seen."

"You don't really believe they are cannibals, do you?" asked the man. "You don't think white people are ever cannibals, do you?"

"Are these people white?" asked the girl.

"They're not Negroes, that's certain," rejoined the man. "Their skin is yellow, but yet it doesn't resemble the Chinese exactly, nor are any of their features Chinese."

It was at this juncture that they caught their first glimpse of a native woman. She was similar in most respects to the men though her stature was smaller and her figure more symmetrical. Her face was more repulsive than that of the men, possibly because of the fact that she was a woman, which rather accentuated the idiosyncrasies of eyes, pendulous lip, pointed tusks and stiff, low-growing hair. The latter was longer than that of the men and much heavier. It hung about her shoulders and was confined by a colored bit of some lacy fabric. Her single garment appeared to be nothing more than a filmy scarf which was wound tightly around her body from below her naked breasts, being caught up some way at the bottom near her ankles. Bits of shiny metal resembling gold, ornamented both the headdress and the skirt. Otherwise the woman was entirely without jewelry. Her bare arms were slender and shapely and her hands and feet well proportioned and symmetrical.

She came close to the party as they passed her, jabbering to the guards who paid no attention to her. The prisoners had an opportunity to observe her closely as she followed at their side for a short distance.

"The figure of a houri," remarked Smith-Oldwick, "with the face of an imbecile."

The street they followed was intersected at irregular intervals by crossroads which, as they glanced down them, proved to be equally as tortuous as that through which they were being conducted. The houses varied but little in design. Occasionally there were bits of color, or some attempt at other architectural ornamentation. Through open windows and doors they could see that the walls of the houses were very thick and that all apertures were quite small, as though the people had built against extreme heat, which they realized must have been necessary in this valley buried deep in an African desert.

Ahead they occasionally caught glimpses of larger structures, and as they approached them, came upon what was evidently a part of the business section of the city. There were numerous small shops and bazaars interspersed among the residences, and over the doors of these were signs painted in characters strongly suggesting Greek origin and yet it was not Greek as both the Englishman and the girl knew.

Smith-Oldwick was by this time beginning to feel more acutely the pain of his wounds and the consequent weakness that was greatly aggravated by loss of blood. He staggered now occasionally and the girl, seeing his plight, offered him her arm.

"No," he expostulated, "you have passed through too much yourself to have any extra burden imposed upon you." But though he made a valiant effort to keep up with their captors he occasionally lagged, and upon one such occasion the guards for the first time showed any disposition toward brutality.

It was a big fellow who walked at Smith-Oldwick's left. Several times he took hold of the Englishman's arm and pushed him forward not ungently, but when the captive lagged again and again the fellow suddenly, and certainly with no just provocation, flew into a perfect frenzy of rage. He leaped upon the wounded man, striking him viciously with his fists and, bearing him to the ground, grasped his throat in his left hand while with his right he drew his long sharp saber. Screaming terribly he waved the blade above his head.

The others stopped and turned to look upon the encounter with no particular show of interest. It was as though one of the party had paused to readjust a sandal and the others merely waited until he was ready to march on again.

But if their captors were indifferent, Bertha Kircher was not. The close-set blazing eyes, the snarling fanged face, and the frightful screams filled her with horror, while the brutal and wanton attack upon the wounded man aroused within her the spirit of protection for the weak that is inherent in all women. Forgetful of everything other than that a weak and defenseless man was being brutally murdered before her eyes, the girl cast aside discretion and, rushing to Smith-Oldwick's assistance, seized the uplifted sword arm of the shrieking creature upon the prostrate Englishman.

Clinging desperately to the fellow she surged backward with all her weight and strength with the result that she overbalanced him and sent him sprawling to the pavement upon his back. In his efforts to save himself he relaxed his grasp upon the grip of his saber which had no sooner fallen to the ground than it was seized upon by the girl. Standing erect beside the prostrate form of the English officer Bertha Kircher, the razor-edged weapon grasped firmly in her hand, faced their captors.

She was a brave figure; even her soiled and torn riding togs and disheveled hair detracted nothing from her appearance. The creature she had felled scrambled quickly to his feet and in the instant his whole demeanor changed. From demoniacal rage he became suddenly convulsed with hysterical laughter although it was a question in the girl's mind as to which was the more terrifying. His companions stood looking on with vacuous grins upon their countenances, while he from whom the girl had wrested the weapon leaped up and down shrieking with laughter. If Bertha Kircher had needed further evidence to assure her that they were in the hands of a mentally deranged people the man's present actions would have been sufficient to convince her. The sudden uncontrolled rage and now the equally uncontrolled and mirthless laughter but emphasized the facial attributes of idiocy.

Suddenly realizing how helpless she was in the event any one of the men should seek to overpower her, and moved by a sudden revulsion of feeling that brought on almost a nausea of disgust, the girl hurled the weapon upon the ground at the feet of the laughing maniac and, turning, kneeled beside the Englishman.

"It was wonderful of you," he said, "but you shouldn't have done it. Don't antagonize them: I believe that they are all mad and you know they say that one should always humor a madman."

She shook her head. "I couldn't see him kill you," she said.

A sudden light sprang to the man's eyes as he reached out a hand and grasped the girl's fingers. "Do you care a little now?" he asked. "Can't you tell me that you do—just a bit?"

She did not withdraw her hand from his but she shook her head sadly. "Please don't," she said. "I am sorry that I can only like you very much."

The light died from his eyes and his fingers relaxed their grasp on hers. "Please forgive me," he murmured. "I intended waiting until we got out of this mess and you were safe among your own people. It must have been the shock or something like that, and seeing you defending me as you did. Anyway, I couldn't help it and really it doesn't make much difference what I say now, does it?"

"What do you mean?" she asked quickly.

He shrugged and smiled ruefully. "I will never leave this city alive," he said. "I wouldn't mention it except that I realize that you must know it as well as I. I was pretty badly torn up by the lion and this fellow here has about finished me. There might be some hope if we were among civilized people, but here with these frightful creatures what care could we get even if they were friendly?"

Bertha Kircher knew that he spoke the truth, and yet she could not bring herself to an admission that Smith-Oldwick would die. She was very fond of him, in fact her great regret was that she did not love him, but she knew that she did not.

It seemed to her that it could be such an easy thing for any girl to love Lieutenant Harold Percy Smith-Oldwick—an English officer and a gentleman, the scion of an old family and himself a man of ample means, young, good-looking and affable. What more could a girl ask for than to have such a man love her and that she possessed Smith-Oldwick's love there was no doubt in Bertha Kircher's mind.

She sighed, and then, laying her hand impulsively on his forehead, she whispered, "Do not give up hope, though. Try to live for my sake and for your sake I will try to love you."

It was as though new life had suddenly been injected into the man's veins. His face lightened instantly and with strength that he himself did not know he possessed he rose slowly to his feet, albeit somewhat unsteadily. The girl helped him and supported him after he had arisen.

For the moment they had been entirely unconscious of their surroundings and now as she looked at their captors she saw that they had fallen again into their almost habitual manner of stolid indifference, and at a gesture from one of them the march was resumed as though no untoward incident had occurred.

Bertha Kircher experienced a sudden reaction from the momentary exaltation of her recent promise to the Englishman. She knew that she had spoken more for him than for herself but now that it was over she realized, as she had realized the moment before she had spoken, that it was unlikely she would ever care for him the way he wished. But what had she promised? Only that she would try to love him. "And now?" she asked herself.

She realized that there might be little hope of their ever returning to civilization. Even if these people should prove friendly and willing to let them depart in peace, how were they to find their way back to the coast? With Tarzan dead, as she fully believed him after having seen his body lying lifeless at the mouth of the cave when she had been dragged forth by her captor, there seemed no power at their command which could guide them safely.

The two had scarcely mentioned the ape-man since their capture, for each realized fully what his loss meant to them. They had compared notes relative to those few exciting moments of the final attack and capture and had found that they agreed perfectly upon all that had occurred. Smith-Oldwick had even seen the lion leap upon Tarzan at the instant that the former was awakened by the roars of the charging beasts, and though the night had been dark, he had been able to see that the body of the savage ape-man had never moved from the instant that it had come down beneath the beast.

And so, if at other times within the past few weeks Bertha Kircher had felt that her situation was particularly hopeless, she was now ready to admit that hope was absolutely extinct.

The streets were beginning to fill with the strange men and women of this strange city. Sometimes individuals would notice them and seem to take a great interest in them, and again others would pass with vacant stares, seemingly unconscious of their immediate surroundings and paying no attention whatsoever to the prisoners. Once they heard hideous screams up a side street, and looking they saw a man in the throes of a demoniacal outburst of rage, similar to that which they had witnessed in the recent attack upon Smith-Oldwick. This creature was venting his insane rage upon a child which he repeatedly struck and bit, pausing only long enough to shriek at frequent intervals. Finally, just before they passed out of sight the creature raised the limp body of the child high above his head and cast it down with all his strength upon the pavement, and then, wheeling and screaming madly at the top of his lungs, he dashed headlong up the winding street.

Two women and several men had stood looking on at the cruel attack. They were at too great a distance for the Europeans to know whether their facial expressions portrayed pity or rage, but be that as it may, none offered to interfere.

A few yards farther on a hideous hag leaned from a second story window where she laughed and jibbered and made horrid grimaces at all who passed her. Others went their ways apparently attending to whatever duties called them, as soberly as the inhabitants of any civilized community.

"God," muttered Smith-Oldwick, "what an awful place!"

The girl turned suddenly toward him. "You still have your pistol?" she asked him.

"Yes," he replied. "I tucked it inside my shirt. They did not search me and it was too dark for them to see whether I carried any weapons or not. So I hid it in the hope that I might get through with it."

She moved closer to him and took hold of his hand. "Save one cartridge for me, please?" she begged.

Smith-Oldwick looked down at her and blinked his eyes very rapidly. An unfamiliar and disconcerting moisture had come into them. He had realized, of course, how bad a plight was theirs but somehow it had seemed to affect him only: it did not seem possible that anyone could harm this sweet and beautiful girl.

And that she should have to be destroyed—destroyed by him! It was too hideous: it was unbelievable, unthinkable! If he had been filled with apprehension before, he was doubly perturbed now.

"I don't believe I could do it, Bertha," he said.

"Not even to save me from something worse?" she asked.

He shook his head dismally. "I could never do it," he replied.

The street that they were following suddenly opened upon a wide avenue, and before them spread a broad and beautiful lagoon, the quiet surface of which mirrored the clear cerulean of the sky. Here the aspect of all their surroundings changed. The buildings were higher and much more pretentious in design and ornamentation. The street itself was paved in mosaics of barbaric but stunningly beautiful design. In the ornamentation of the buildings there was considerable color and a great deal of what appeared to be gold leaf. In all the decorations there was utilized in various ways the conventional figure of the parrot, and, to a lesser extent, that of the lion and the monkey.

Their captors led them along the pavement beside the lagoon for a short distance and then through an arched doorway into one of the buildings facing the avenue. Here, directly within the entrance was a large room furnished with massive benches and tables, many of which were elaborately hand carved with the figures of the inevitable parrot, the lion, or the monkey, the parrot always predominating.

Behind one of the tables sat a man who differed in no way that the captives could discover from those who accompanied them. Before this person the party halted, and one of the men who had brought them made what seemed to be an oral report. Whether they were before a judge, a military officer, or a civil dignitary they could not know, but evidently he was a man of authority, for, after listening to whatever recital was being made to him the while he closely scrutinized the two captives, he made a single futile attempt to converse with them and then issued some curt orders to him who had made the report.

Almost immediately two of the men approached Bertha Kircher and signaled her to accompany them. Smith-Oldwick started to follow her but was intercepted by one of their guards. The girl stopped then and turned back, at the same time looking at the man at the table and making signs with her hands, indicating, as best she could, that she wished Smith-Oldwick to remain with her, but the fellow only shook his head negatively and motioned to the guards to remove her. The Englishman again attempted to follow but was restrained. He was too weak and helpless even to make an attempt to enforce his wishes. He thought of the pistol inside his shirt and then of the futility of attempting to overcome an entire city with the few rounds of ammunition left to him.

So far, with the single exception of the attack made upon him, they had no reason to believe that they might not receive fair treatment from their captors, and so he reasoned that it might be wiser to avoid antagonizing them until such a time as he became thoroughly convinced that their intentions were entirely hostile. He saw the girl led from the building and just before she disappeared from his view she turned and waved her hand to him:

"Good luck!" she cried, and was gone.

The lions that had entered the building with the party had, during their examination by the man at the table, been driven from the apartment through a doorway behind him. Toward this same doorway two of the men now led Smith-Oldwick. He found himself in a long corridor from the sides of which other doorways opened, presumably into other apartments of the building. At the far end of the corridor he saw a heavy grating beyond which appeared an open courtyard. Into this courtyard the prisoner was conducted, and as he entered it with the two guards he found himself in an opening which was bounded by the inner walls of the building. It was in the nature of a garden in which a number of trees and flowering shrubs grew. Beneath several of the trees were benches and there was a bench along the south wall, but what aroused his most immediate attention was the fact that the lions who had assisted in their capture and who had accompanied them upon the return to the city, lay sprawled about upon the ground or wandered restlessly to and fro.

Just inside the gate his guard halted. The two men exchanged a few words and then turned and reentered the corridor. The Englishman was horror-stricken as the full realization of his terrible plight forced itself upon his tired brain. He turned and seized the grating in an attempt to open it and gain the safety of the corridor, but he found it securely locked against his every effort, and then he called aloud to the retreating figure of the men within. The only reply he received was a high-pitched, mirthless laugh, and then the two passed through the doorway at the far end of the corridor and he was alone with the lions.

19

The Queen's Story

IN THE meantime Bertha Kircher was conducted the length of the plaza toward the largest and most pretentious of the buildings surrounding it. This edifice covered the entire width of one end of the plaza. It was several stories in height, the main entrance being approached by a wide flight of stone steps, the bottom of which was guarded by enormous stone lions, while at the top there were two pedestals flanking the entrance and of the same height, upon each of which was the stone image of a large parrot. As the girl neared these latter images she saw that the capital of each column was hewn into the semblance of a human skull upon which the parrots perched. Above the arched doorway and upon the walls of the building were the figures of other parrots, of lions, and of monkeys. Some of these were carved in bas-relief; others were delineated in mosaics, while still others appeared to have been painted upon the surface of the wall.

The colorings of the last were apparently much subdued by age with the result that the general effect was soft and beautiful. The sculpturing and mosaic work were both finely executed, giving evidence of a high degree of artistic skill. Unlike the first building into which she had been conducted, the entrance to which had been doorless, massive doors closed the entrance which she now approached. In the niches formed by the columns which supported the door's arch, and about the base of the pedestals of the stone parrots, as well as in various other places on the broad stairway, lolled some score of armed men. The tunics of these were all of a vivid yellow and upon the breast and back of each was embroidered the figure of a parrot.

As she was conducted up the stairway one of these yellow-coated warriors approached and halted her guides at the top of the steps. Here they exchanged a few words and while they were talking the girl noticed that he who had halted them, as well as those whom she could see of his companions, appeared to be, if possible, of a lower mentality than her original captors.

Their coarse, bristling hair grew so low upon their foreheads as, in some instances, to almost join their eyebrows, while the irises were smaller, exposing more of the white of the eyeball.

After a short parley the man in charge of the doorway, for such he seemed to be, turned and struck upon one of the panels with the butt of his spear, at the same time calling to several of his companions, who rose and came forward at his command. Soon the great doors commenced slowly to swing creakingly open, and presently, as they separated, the girl saw behind them the motive force which operated the massive doors—to each door a half-dozen naked Negroes.

At the doorway her two guards were turned back and their places taken by a half-dozen of the yellow-coated soldiery. These conducted her through the doorway which the blacks, pulling upon heavy chains, closed behind them. And as the girl watched them she noted with horror that the poor creatures were chained by the neck to the doors.

Before her led a broad hallway in the center of which was a little pool of clear water. Here again in floor and walls was repeated in new and ever-changing combinations and designs, the parrots, the monkeys, and the lions, but now many of the figures were of what the girl was convinced must be gold. The walls of the corridor consisted of a series of open archways through which, upon either side, other spacious apartments were visible. The hallway was entirely unfurnished, but the rooms on either side contained benches and tables. Glimpses of some of the walls revealed the fact that they were covered with hangings of some colored fabric, while upon the floors were thick rugs of barbaric design and the skins of black lions and beautifully marked leopards.

The room directly to the right of the entrance was filled with men wearing the yellow tunics of her new guard while the walls were hung with numerous spears and sabers. At the far end of the corridor a low flight of steps led to another closed doorway. Here the guard was again halted. One of the guards at this doorway, after receiving the report of one of those who accompanied her, passed through the door, leaving them standing outside. It was fully fifteen minutes before he returned, when the guard was again changed and the girl conducted into the chamber beyond.

Through three other chambers and past three more massive doors, at each of which her guard was changed, the girl was conducted before she was ushered into a comparatively small room, back and forth across the floor of which paced a man in a scarlet tunic, upon the front and back of which was embroidered an enormous parrot and upon whose head was a barbaric headdress surmounted by a stuffed parrot.

The walls of this room were entirely hidden by hangings upon which hundreds, even thousands, of parrots were embroidered. Inlaid in the floor were golden parrots, while, as thickly as they could be painted, upon the ceiling were brilliant-hued parrots with wings outspread as though in the act of flying.

The man himself was larger of stature than any she had yet seen within the city. His parchment-like skin was wrinkled with age and he was much fatter than any other of his kind that she had seen. His bared arms, however, gave evidence of great strength and his gait was not that of an old man. His facial expression denoted almost utter imbecility and he was quite the most repulsive creature that ever Bertha Kircher had looked upon.

For several minutes after she was conducted into his presence he appeared not to be aware that she was there but continued his restless pacing to and fro. Suddenly, without the slightest warning, and while he was at the far end of the room from her with his back toward her, he wheeled and rushed madly at her. Involuntarily the girl shrank back, extending her open palms toward the frightful creature as though to hold him aloof but a man upon either side of her, the two who had conducted her into the apartment, seized and held her.

Although he rushed violently toward her the man stopped without touching her. For a moment his horrid white-rimmed eyes glared searchingly into her face, immediately following which he burst into maniacal laughter. For two or three minutes the creature gave himself over to merriment and then, stopping as suddenly as he had commenced to laugh, he fell to examining the prisoner. He felt of her hair, her skin, the texture of the garment she wore and by means of signs made her understand she was to open her mouth. In the latter he seemed much interested, calling the attention of one of the guards to her canine teeth and then baring his own sharp fangs for the prisoner to see.

Presently he resumed pacing to and fro across the floor, and it was fully fifteen minutes before he again noticed the prisoner, and then it was to issue a curt order to her guards, who immediately conducted her from the apartment.

The guards now led the girl through a series of corridors and apartments to a narrow stone stairway which led to the floor above, finally stopping before a small door where stood a naked Negro armed with a spear. At a word from one of her guards the Negro opened the door and the party passed into a low-ceiled apartment, the windows of which immediately caught the girl's attention through the fact that they were heavily barred. The room was furnished similarly to those that she had seen in other parts of the building; the same carved tables and benches, the rugs upon the floor, the decorations upon the walls, although in every respect it was simpler than anything she had seen on the floor below. In one corner was a low couch covered with a rug similar to those on the floor except that it was of a lighter texture, and upon this sat a woman.

As Bertha Kircher's eyes alighted upon the occupant of the room the girl gave a little gasp of astonishment, for she recognized immediately that here was a creature more nearly of her own kind than any she had seen within the city's walls. An old woman it was who looked at her through faded blue eyes, sunken deep in a wrinkled and toothless face. But the eyes were those of a sane and intelligent creature, and the wrinkled face was the face of a white woman.

At sight of the girl the woman rose and came forward, her gait so feeble and unsteady that she was forced to support herself with a long staff which she grasped in both her hands. One of the guards spoke a few words to her and then the men turned and left the apartment. The girl stood just within the door waiting in silence for what might next befall her.

The old woman crossed the room and stopped before her, raising her weak and watery eyes to the fresh young face of the newcomer. Then she scanned her from head to foot and once again the old eyes returned to the girl's face. Bertha Kircher on her part was not less frank in her survey of the little old woman. It was the latter who spoke first. In a thin, cracked voice she spoke, hesitatingly, falteringly, as though she were using unfamiliar words and speaking a strange tongue.

"You are from the outer world?" she asked in English. "God grant that you may speak and understand this tongue."

"English?" the girl exclaimed, "Yes, of course, I speak English."

"Thank God!" cried the little old woman. "I did not know whether I myself might speak it so that another could understand. For sixty years I have spoken only their accursed gibberish. For sixty years I have not heard a word in my native language. Poor creature! Poor creature!" she mumbled. "What accursed misfortune threw you into their hands?"

"You are an English woman?" asked Bertha Kircher. "Did I understand you aright that you are an English woman and have been here for sixty years?"

The old woman nodded her head affirmatively. "For sixty years I have never been outside of this palace. "Come," she said, stretching forth a bony hand. "I am very old and cannot stand long. Come and sit with me on my couch."

The girl took the proffered hand and assisted the old lady back to the opposite side of the room and when she was seated the girl sat down beside her.

"Poor child! Poor child!" moaned the old woman. "Far better to have died than to have let them bring you here. At first I might have destroyed myself but there was always the hope that someone would come who would take me away, but none ever comes. Tell me how they got you."

Very briefly the girl narrated the principal incidents which led up to her capture by some of the creatures of the city.

"Then there is a man with you in the city?" asked the old woman.

"Yes," said the girl, "but I do not know where he is nor what are their intentions in regard to him. In fact, I do not know what their intentions toward me are."

"No one might even guess," said the old woman. "They do not know themselves from one minute to the next what their intentions are, but I think you can rest assured, my poor child, that you will never see your friend again."

"But they haven't slain you," the girl reminded her, "and you have been their prisoner, you say, for sixty years."

"No," replied her companion, "they have not killed me, nor will they kill you, though God knows before you have lived long in this horrible place you will beg them to kill you."

"Who are they—" asked Bertha Kircher, "what kind of people? They differ from any that I ever have seen. And tell me, too, how you came here."

"It was long ago," said the old woman, rocking back and forth on the couch. "It was long ago. Oh, how long it was! I was only twenty then. Think of it, child! Look at me. I have no mirror other than my bath, I cannot see what I look like for my eyes are old, but with my fingers I can feel my old and wrinkled face, my sunken eyes, and these flabby lips drawn in over toothless gums. I am old and bent and hideous, but then I was young and they said that I was beautiful. No, I will not be a hypocrite; I was beautiful. My glass told me that.

"My father was a missionary in the interior and one day there came a band of Arabian slave raiders. They took the men and women of the little native village where my father labored, and they took me, too. They did not know much about our part of the country so they were compelled to rely upon the men of our village whom they had captured to guide them. They told me that they never before had been so far south and that they had heard there was a country rich in ivory and slaves west of us. They wanted to go there and from there they would take us north, where I was to be sold into the harem of some black sultan.

"They often discussed the price I would bring, and that that price might not lessen, they guarded me jealously from one another so the journeys were made as little fatiguing for me as possible. I was given the best food at their command and I was not harmed.

"But after a short time, when we had reached the confines of the country with which the men of our village were familiar and had entered upon a desolate and arid desert waste, the Arabs realized at last that we were lost. But they still kept on, ever toward the west, crossing hideous gorges and marching across the face of a burning land beneath the pitiless sun. The poor slaves they had captured were, of course, compelled to carry all the camp equipage and loot and thus heavily burdened, half starved and without water, they soon commenced to die like flies.

"We had not been in the desert land long before the Arabs were forced to kill their horses for food, and when we reached the first gorge, across which it would have been impossible to transport the animals, the balance of them were slaughtered and the meat loaded upon the poor staggering blacks who still survived.

"Thus we continued for two more days and now all but a handful of blacks were dead, and the Arabs themselves had commenced to succumb to hunger and thirst and the intense heat of the desert. As far as the eye could reach back toward the land of plenty from whence we had come, our route was marked by circling vultures in the sky and by the bodies of the dead who lay down in the trackless waste for the last time. The ivory had been abandoned tusk by tusk as the blacks gave out, and along the trail of death was strewn the camp equipage and the horse trappings of a hundred men.

"For some reason the Arab chief favored me to the last, possibly with the idea that of all his other treasures I could be most easily transported, for I was young and strong and after the horses were killed I had walked and kept up with the best of the men. We English, you know, are great walkers, while these Arabians had never walked since they were old enough to ride a horse.

"I cannot tell you how much longer we kept on but at last, with our strength almost gone, a handful of us reached the bottom of a deep gorge. To scale the opposite side was out of the question and so we kept on down along the sands of what must have been the bed of an ancient river, until finally we came to a point where we looked out upon what appeared to be a beautiful valley in which we felt assured that we would find game in plenty.

"By then there were only two of us left—the chief and myself. I do not need to tell you what the valley was, for you found it in much the same way as I did. So quickly were we captured that it seemed they must have been waiting for us, and I learned later that such was the case, just as they were waiting for you.

"As you came through the forest you must have seen the monkeys and parrots and since you have entered the palace, how constantly these animals, and the lions, are used in the decorations. At home we were all familiar with talking parrots who repeated the things that they were taught to say, but these parrots are different in that they all talk in the same language that the people of the city use, and they say that the monkeys talk to the parrots and the parrots fly to the city and tell the people what the monkeys say. And, although it is hard to believe, I have learned that this is so, for I have lived here among them for sixty years in the palace of their king.

"They brought me, as they brought you, directly to the palace. The Arabian chief was taken elsewhere. I never knew what became of him. Ago XXV was king then. I have seen many kings since that day. He was a terrible man; but then, they are all terrible."

"What is the matter with them?" asked the girl.

"They are a race of maniacs," replied the old woman. "Had you not guessed it? Among them are excellent craftsmen and good farmers and a certain amount of law and order, such as it is.

"They reverence all birds, but the parrot is their chief deity. There is one who is held here in the palace in a very beautiful apartment. He is their god of gods. He is a very old bird. If what Ago told me when I came is true, he must be nearly three hundred years old by now. Their religious rites are revolting in the extreme, and I believe that it may be the practice of these rites through ages that has brought the race to its present condition of imbecility.

"And yet, as I said, they are not without some redeeming qualities. If legend may be credited, their forebears—a little handful of men and women who came from somewhere out of the north and became lost in the wilderness of central Africa—found here only a barren desert valley. To my own knowledge rain seldom, if ever, falls here, and yet you have seen a great forest and luxuriant vegetation outside of the city as well as within. This miracle is accomplished by the utilization of natural springs which their ancestors developed, and upon which they have improved to such an extent that the entire valley receives an adequate amount of moisture at all times.

"Ago told me that many generations before his time the

forest was irrigated by changing the course of the streams which carried the spring water to the city but that when the trees had sent their roots down to the natural moisture of the soil and required no further irrigation, the course of the stream was changed and other trees were planted. And so the forest grew until today it covers almost the entire floor of the valley except for the open space where the city stands. I do not know that this is true. It may be that the forest has always been here, but it is one of their legends and it is borne out by the fact that there is not sufficient rainfall here to support vegetation.

"They are peculiar people in many respects, not only in their form of worship and religious rites but also in that they breed lions as other people breed cattle. You have seen how they use some of these lions but the majority of them they fatten and eat. At first, I imagine, they ate lion meat as a part of their religious ceremony but after many generations they came to crave it so that now it is practically the only flesh they eat. They would, of course, rather die than eat the flesh of a bird, nor will they eat monkey's meat, while the herbivorous animals they raise only for milk, hides, and flesh for the lions. Upon the south side of the city are the corrals and pastures where the herbivorous animals are raised. Boar, deer, and antelope are used principally for the lions, while goats are kept for milk for the human inhabitants of the city."

"And you have lived here all these years," exclaimed the girl, "without ever seeing one of your own kind?"

The old woman nodded affirmatively.

"For sixty years you have lived here," continued Bertha Kircher, "and they have not harmed you!"

"I did not say they had not harmed me," said the old woman, "they did not kill me, that is all."

"What"—the girl hesitated—"what," she continued at last, "was your position among them? Pardon me," she added quickly, "I think I know but I should like to hear from your own lips, for whatever your position was, mine will doubtless be the same."

The old woman nodded. "Yes," she said, "doubtless; if they can keep you away from the women."

"What do you mean?" asked the girl.

"For sixty years I have never been allowed near a woman. They would kill me, even now, if they could reach me. The men are frightful, God knows they are frightful! But heaven keep you from the women!"

"You mean," asked the girl, "that the men will not harm me?"

"Ago XXV made me his queen," said the old woman. "But

he had many other queens, nor were they all human. He was not murdered for ten years after I came here. Then the next king took me, and so it has been always. I am the oldest queen now. Very few of their women live to a great age. Not only are they constantly liable to assassination but, owing to their subnormal mentalities, they are subject to periods of depression during which they are very likely to destroy themselves."

She turned suddenly and pointed to the barred windows. "You see this room," she said, "with the black eunuch outside? Wherever you see these you will know that there are women, for with very few exceptions they are never allowed out of captivity. They are considered and really are more violent than the men."

For several minutes the two sat in silence, and then the younger woman turned to the older.

"Is there no way to escape?" she asked.

The old woman pointed again to the barred windows and then to the door, saying: "And there is the armed eunuch. And if you should pass him, how could you reach the street? And if you reached the street, how could you pass through the city to the outer wall? And even if, by some miracle, you should gain the outer wall, and, by another miracle, you should be permitted to pass through the gate, could you ever hope to traverse the forest where the great black lions roam and feed upon men? No!" she exclaimed, answering her own question, "there is no escape, for after one had escaped from the palace and the city and the forest it would be but to invite death in the frightful desert land beyond.

"In sixty years you are the first to find this buried city. In a thousand no denizen of this valley has ever left it, and within the memory of man, or even in their legends, none had found them prior to my coming other than a single warlike giant, the story of whom has been handed down from father to son.

"I think from the description that he must have been a Spaniard, a giant of a man in buckler and helmet, who fought his way through the terrible forest to the city gate, who fell upon those who were sent out to capture him and slew them with his mighty sword. And when he had eaten of the vegetables from the gardens, and the fruit from the trees and drank of the water from the stream, he turned about and fought his way back through the forest to the mouth of the gorge. But though he escaped the city and the forest he did not escape the desert. For a legend runs that the king, fearful that he would bring others to attack them, sent a party after him to slay him.

"For three weeks they did not find him, for they went in the wrong direction, but at last they came upon his bones picked clean by the vultures, lying a day's march up the same gorge through which you and I entered the valley. I do not know," continued the old woman, "that this is true. It is just one of their many legends."

"Yes," said the girl, "it is true. I am sure it is true, for I have seen the skeleton and the corroded armor of this great giant."

At this juncture the door was thrown open without ceremony and a Negro entered bearing two flat vessels in which were several smaller ones. These he set down on one of the tables near the women, and, without a word, turned and left. With the entrance of the man with the vessels, a delightful odor of cooked food had aroused the realization in the girl's mind that she was very hungry, and at a word from the old woman she walked to the table to examine the viands. The larger vessels which contained the smaller ones were of pottery while those within them were quite evidently of hammered gold. To her intense surprise she found lying between the smaller vessels a spoon and a fork, which, while of quaint design, were quite as serviceable as any she had seen in more civilized communities. The tines of the fork were quite evidently of iron or steel, the girl did not know which, while the handle and the spoon were of the same material as the smaller vessels.

There was a highly seasoned stew with meat and vegetables, a dish of fresh fruit, and a bowl of milk beside which was a little jug containing something which resembled marmalade. So ravenous was she that she did not even wait for her companion to reach the table, and as she ate she could have sworn that never before had she tasted more palatable food. The old woman came slowly and sat down on one of the benches opposite her.

As she removed the smaller vessels from the larger and arranged them before her on the table a crooked smile twisted her lips as she watched the younger woman eat.

"Hunger is a great leveler," she said with a laugh.

"What do you mean?" asked the girl.

"I venture to say that a few weeks ago you would have been nauseated at the idea of eating cat."

"Cat?" exclaimed the girl.

"Yes," said the old woman. "What is the difference—a lion is a cat."

"You mean I am eating lion now?"

"Yes," said the old woman, "and as they prepare it, it is very palatable. You will grow very fond of it."

Bertha Kircher smiled a trifle dubiously. "I could not tell it," she said, "from lamb or veal."

"No," said the woman, "it tastes as good to me. But these lions are very carefully kept and very carefully fed and their flesh is so seasoned and prepared that it might be anything so far as taste is concerned."

And so Bertha Kircher broke her long fast upon strange fruits, lion meat, and goat's milk.

Scarcely had she finished when again the door opened and there entered a yellow-coated soldier. He spoke to the old woman.

"The king," she said, "has commanded that you be prepared and brought to him. You are to share these apartments with me. The king knows that I am not like his other women. He never would have dared to put you with them. Herog XVI has occasional lucid intervals. You must have been brought to him during one of these. Like the rest of them he thinks that he alone of all the community is sane, but more than once I have thought that the various men with whom I have come in contact here, including the kings themselves, looked upon me as, at least, less mad than the others. Yet how I have retained my senses all these years is beyond me."

"What do you mean by prepare?" asked Bertha Kircher. "You said that the king had commanded I be prepared and brought to him."

"You will be bathed and furnished with a robe similar to that which I wear."

"Is there no escape?" asked the girl. "Is there no way even in which I can kill myself?"

The woman handed her the fork. "This is the only way," she said, "and you will notice that the tines are very short and blunt."

The girl shuddered and the old woman laid a hand gently upon her shoulder. "He may only look at you and send you away," she said. "Ago XXV sent for me once, tried to talk with me, discovered that I could not understand him and that he could not understand me, ordered that I be taught the language of his people, and then apparently forgot me for a year. Sometimes I do not see the king for a long period. There was one king who ruled for five years whom I never saw. There is always hope; even I whose very memory has doubtless been forgotten beyond these palace walls still hope, though none knows better how futilely."

The old woman led Bertha Kircher to an adjoining apartment in the floor of which was a pool of water. Here the girl bathed and afterward her companion brought her one of the clinging garments of the native women and adjusted it about her figure. The material of the robe was of a gauzy fabric which accentuated the rounded beauty of the girlish form.

"There," said the old woman, as she gave a final pat to one of the folds of the garment, "you are a queen indeed!"

The girl looked down at her naked breasts and but half-concealed limbs in horror. "They are going to lead me into the presence of men in this half-nude condition!" she exclaimed.

The old woman smiled her crooked smile. "It is nothing," she said. "You will become accustomed to it as did I who was brought up in the home of a minister of the gospel, where it was considered little short of a crime for a woman to expose her stockinged ankle. By comparison with what you will doubtless see and the things that you may be called upon to undergo, this is but a trifle."

For what seemed hours to the distraught girl she paced the floor of her apartment, awaiting the final summons to the presence of the mad king. Darkness had fallen and the oil flares within the palace had been lighted long before two messengers appeared with instructions that Herog demanded her immediate presence and that the old woman, whom they called Xanila, was to accompany her. The girl felt some slight relief when she discovered that she was to have at least one friend with her, however powerless to assist her the old woman might be.

The messengers conducted the two to a small apartment on the floor below. Xanila explained that this was one of the anterooms off the main throneroom in which the king was accustomed to hold court with his entire retinue. A number of yellow-tunicked warriors sat about upon the benches within the room. For the most part their eyes were bent upon the floor and their attitudes that of moody dejection. As the two women entered several glanced indifferently at them, but for the most part no attention was paid to them.

While they were waiting in the anteroom there entered from another apartment a young man uniformed similarly to the others with the exception that upon his head was a fillet of gold, in the front of which a single parrot feather rose erectly above his forehead. As he entered, the other soldiers in the room rose to their feet.

"That is Metak, one of the king's sons," Xanila whispered to the girl.

The prince was crossing the room toward the audience chamber when his glance happened to fall upon Bertha Kircher. He halted in his tracks and stood looking at her for a full minute without speaking. The girl, embarrassed by his bold stare and her scant attire, flushed and, dropping her gaze to the floor, turned away. Metak suddenly commenced to tremble from head to foot and then, without warning, other than a loud, hoarse scream he sprang forward and seized the girl in his arms.

Instantly pandemonium ensued. The two messengers who had been charged with the duty of conducting the girl to the king's presence danced, shrieking, about the prince, waving their arms and gesticulating wildly as though they would force him to relinquish her, the while they dared not lay hands upon royalty. The other guardsmen, as though suffering in sympathy the madness of their prince, ran forward screaming and brandishing their sabers.

The girl fought to release herself from the horrid embrace of the maniac, but with his left arm about her he held her as easily as though she had been but a babe, while with his free hand he drew his saber and struck viciously at those nearest him.

One of the messengers was the first to feel the keen edge of Metak's blade. With a single fierce cut the prince drove through the fellow's collar bone and downward to the center of his chest. With a shrill shriek that rose above the screaming of the other guardsmen the man dropped to the floor, and as the blood gushed from the frightful wound he struggled to rise once more to his feet and then sank back again and died in a great pool of his own blood.

In the meantime Metak, still clinging desperately to the girl, had backed toward the opposite door. At the sight of the blood two of the guardsmen, as though suddenly aroused to maniacal frenzy, dropped their sabers to the floor and fell upon each other with nails and teeth, while some sought to reach the prince and some to defend him. In a corner of the room sat one of the guardsmen laughing uproariously and just as Metak succeeded in reaching the door and taking the girl through, she thought that she saw another of the men spring upon the corpse of the dead messenger and bury his teeth in its flesh.

During the orgy of madness Xanila had kept closely at the girl's side but at the door of the room Metak had seen her and, wheeling suddenly, cut viciously at her. Fortunately for Xanila she was halfway through the door at the time, so that Metak's blade but dented itself upon the stone arch of the portal, and then Xanila, guided doubtless by the wisdom of sixty years of similar experiences, fled down the corridor as fast as her old and tottering legs would carry her.

Metak, once outside the door, returned his saber to its scabbard and lifting the girl bodily from the ground carried her off in the opposite direction from that taken by Xanila.

20

Came Tarzan

JUST before dark that evening, an almost exhausted flier entered the headquarters of Colonel Capell of the Second Rhodesians and saluted.

"Well, Thompson," asked the superior, "what luck? The others have all returned. Never saw a thing of Oldwick or his plane. I guess we shall have to give it up unless you were more successful."

"I was," replied the young officer. "I found the plane."

"No!" ejaculated Colonel Capell. "Where was it? Any sign of Oldwick?"

"It is in the rottenest hole in the ground you ever saw, quite a bit inland. Narrow gorge. Saw the plane all right but can't reach it. There was a regular devil of a lion wandering around it. I landed near the edge of the cliff and was going to climb down and take a look at the plane. But this fellow hung around for an hour or more and I finally had to give it up."

"Do you think the lions got Oldwick?" asked the colonel.

"I doubt it," replied Lieutenant Thompson, "from the fact that there was no indication that the lion had fed anywhere about the plane. I arose after I found it was impossible to get down around the plane and reconnoitered up and down the gorge. Several miles to the south I found a small, wooded valley in the center of which—please don't think me crazy, sir —is a regular city—streets, buildings, a central plaza with a lagoon, good-sized buildings with domes and minarets and all that sort of stuff."

The elder officer looked at the younger compassionately. "You're all wrought up, Thompson," he said. "Go and take a good sleep. You have been on this job now for a long while and it must have gotten on your nerves."

The young man shook his head a bit irritably. "Pardon me, sir," he said, "but I am telling you the truth. I am not mistaken. I circled over the place several times. It may be that

208

Oldwick has found his way there—or has been captured by these people."

"Were there people in the city?" asked the colonel.

"Yes, I saw them in the streets."

"Do you think cavalry could reach the valley?" asked the colonel.

"No," replied Thompson, "the country is all cut up with these deep gorges. Even infantry would have a devil of a time of it, and there is absolutely no water that I could discover for at least a two days' march."

It was at this juncture that a big Vauxhall drew up in front of the headquarters of the Second Rhodesians and a moment later General Smuts alighted and entered. Colonel Capell arose from his chair and saluted his superior, and the young lieutenant saluted and stood at attention.

"I was passing," said the general, "and I thought I would stop for a chat. By the way, how is the search for Lieutenant Smith-Oldwick progressing? I see Thompson here and I believe he was one of those detailed to the search."

"Yes," said Capell, "he was. He is the last to come in. He found the lieutenant's ship," and then he repeated what Lieutenant Thompson had reported to him. The general sat down at the table with Colonel Capell, and together the two officers, with the assistance of the flier, marked the approximate location of the city which Thompson had reported he'd discovered.

"It's a mighty rough country," remarked Smuts, "but we can't leave a stone unturned until we have exhausted every resource to find that boy. We will send out a small force; a small one will be more likely to succeed than a large one. About one company, Colonel, or say two, with sufficient motor lorries for transport of rations and water. Put a good man in command and let him establish a base as far to the west as the motors can travel. You can leave one company there and send the other forward. I am inclined to believe you can establish your base within a day's march of the city and if such is the case the force you send ahead should have no trouble on the score of lack of water as there certainly must be water in the valley where the city lies. Detail a couple of planes for reconnaissance and messenger service so that the base can keep in touch at all times with the advance party. When can your force move out?"

"We can load the lorries tonight," replied Capell, "and march about one o'clock tomorrow morning."

"Good," said the general, "keep me advised," and returning the others' salutes he departed.

As Tarzan leaped for the vines he realized that the lion was close upon him and that his life depended upon the strength of the creepers clinging to the city walls; but to his intense relief he found the stems as large around as a man's arm, and the tendrils which had fastened themselves to the wall so firmly fixed, that his weight upon the stem appeared to have no appreciable effect upon them.

He heard Numa's baffled roar as the lion slipped downward clawing futilely at the leafy creepers, and then with the agility of the apes who had reared him, Tarzan bounded nimbly aloft to the summit of the wall.

A few feet below him was the flat roof of the adjoining building and as he dropped to it his back was toward the niche from which an embrasure looked out upon the gardens and the forest beyond, so that he did not see the figure crouching there in the dark shadow. But if he did not see he was not long in ignorance of the fact that he was not alone, for scarcely had his feet touched the roof when a heavy body leaped upon him from behind and brawny arms encircled him about the waist.

Taken at a disadvantage and lifted from his feet, the ape-man was, for the time being, helpless. Whatever the creature was that had seized him, it apparently had a well-defined purpose in mind, for it walked directly toward the edge of the roof so that it was soon apparent to Tarzan that he was to be hurled to the pavement below—a most efficacious manner of disposing of an intruder. That he would be either maimed or killed the ape-man was confident; but he had no intention of permitting his assailant to carry out the plan.

Tarzan's arms and legs were free but he was in such a disadvantageous position that he could not use them to any good effect. His only hope lay in throwing the creature off its balance, and to this end Tarzan straightened his body and leaned as far back against his captor as he could, and then suddenly lunged forward. The result was as satisfactory as he could possibly have hoped. The great weight of the ape-man thrown suddenly out from an erect position caused the other also to lunge violently forward with the result that to save himself he involuntarily released his grasp. Catlike in his movements, the ape-man had no sooner touched the roof than he was upon his feet again, facing his adversary, a man almost as large as himself and armed with a saber which he now whipped from its scabbard. Tarzan, however, had no mind to allow the use of this formidable weapon and so he dove for the other's legs beneath the vicious cut that was directed at him from the side, and as a football player tackles an opposing runner, Tarzan tackled his antagonist, carrying him backward several yards and throwing him heavily to the roof upon his back.

No sooner had the man touched the roof than the ape-man was upon his chest, one brawny hand sought and found the sword wrist and the other the throat of the yellow-tunicked guardsman. Until then the fellow had fought in silence but just as Tarzan's fingers touched his throat he emitted a single piercing shriek that the brown fingers cut off almost instantly. The fellow struggled to escape the clutch of the naked creature upon his breast but equally as well might he have fought to escape the talons of Numa, the lion.

Gradually his struggles lessened, his pin-point eyes popped from their sockets, rolling horribly upward, while from his foam-flecked lips his swollen tongue protruded. As his struggles ceased Tarzan arose, and placing a foot upon the carcass of his kill, was upon the point of screaming forth his victory cry when the thought that the work before him required the utmost caution sealed his lips.

Walking to the edge of the roof he looked down into the narrow, winding street below. At intervals, apparently at each street intersection, an oil flare sputtered dimly from brackets set in the walls a trifle higher than a man's head. For the most part the winding alleys were in dense shadow and even in the immediate vicinity of the flares the illumination was far from brilliant. In the restricted area of his vision he could see that there were still a few of the strange inhabitants moving about the narrow thoroughfares.

To prosecute his search for the young officer and the girl he must be able to move about the city as freely as possible, but to pass beneath one of the corner flares, naked as he was except for a loin cloth, and in every other respect markedly different from the inhabitants of the city, would be but to court almost immediate discovery. As these thoughts flashed through his mind and he cast about for some feasible plan of action, his eyes fell upon the corpse upon the roof near him, and immediately there occurred to him the possibility of disguising himself in the raiment of his conquered adversary.

It required but a few moments for the ape-man to clothe himself in the tights, sandals, and parrot emblazoned yellow tunic of the dead soldier. Around his waist he buckled the saber belt but beneath the tunic he retained the hunting knife of his dead father. His other weapons he could not lightly discard, and so, in the hope that he might eventually recover them, he carried them to the edge of the wall and dropped them among the foliage at its base. At the last moment he found it difficult to part with his rope, which, with his knife, was his most accustomed weapon, and one which he had used for the greatest length of time. He found that by removing the saber belt he could wind the rope about his waist beneath his tunic, and then replacing the belt still retain it entirely concealed from chance observation.

At last, satisfactorily disguised, and with even his shock of black hair adding to the verisimilitude of his likeness to the natives of the city, he sought for some means of reaching the street below. While he might have risked a drop from the eaves of the roof he feared to do so lest he attract the attention of passers-by, and probable discovery. The roofs of the buildings varied in height but as the ceilings were all low he found that he could easily travel along the roof tops and this he did for some little distance, until he suddenly discovered just ahead of him several figures reclining upon the roof of a near-by building.

He had noticed openings in each roof, evidently giving ingress to the apartments below, and now, his advance cut off by those ahead of him, he decided to risk the chance of reaching the street through the interior of one of the buildings. Approaching one of the openings he leaned over the black hole and, listened for sounds of life in the apartment below. Neither his ears nor his nose registered evidence of the presence of any living creature in the immediate vicinity, and so without further hesitation the ape-man lowered his body through the aperture and was about to drop when his foot came in contact with the rung of a ladder, which he immediately took advantage of to descend to the floor of the room below.

Here, all was almost total darkness until his eyes became accustomed to the interior, the darkness of which was slightly alleviated by the reflected light from a distant street flare which shone intermittently through the narrow windows fronting the thoroughfare. Finally, assured that the apartment was unoccupied, Tarzan sought for a stairway to the ground floor. This he found in a dark hallway upon which the room opened —a flight of narrow stone steps leading downward toward the street. Chance favored him so that he reached the shadows of the arcade without encountering any of the inmates of the house.

Once on the street he was not at a loss as to the direction in which he wished to go, for he had tracked the two Europeans practically to the gate, which he felt assured must have given them entry to the city. His keen sense of direction and location made it possible for him to judge with considerable accuracy the point within the city where he might hope to pick up the spoor of those whom he sought.

The first need, however, was to discover a street paralleling the northern wall along which he could make his way in the direction of the gate he had seen from the forest. Realizing that his greatest hope of success lay in the boldness of his operations he moved off in the direction of the nearest street flare without making any other attempt at concealment than keeping in the shadows of the arcade, which he judged would draw no particular attention to him in that he saw other pedestrians doing likewise. The few he passed gave him no heed, and he had almost reached the nearest intersection when he saw several men wearing yellow tunics identical to that which he had taken from his prisoner.

They were coming directly toward him and the ape-man saw that should he continue on he would meet them directly at the intersection of the two streets in the full light of the flare. His first inclination was to go steadily on, for personally he had no objection to chancing a scrimmage with them; but a sudden recollection of the girl, possibly a helpless prisoner in the hands of these people, caused him to seek some other and less hazardous plan of action.

He had almost emerged from the shadow of the arcade into the full light of the flare and the approaching men were but a few yards from him, when he suddenly kneeled and pretended to adjust the wrappings of his sandals—wrappings, which, by the way, he was not at all sure that he had adjusted as their makers had intended them to be adjusted. He was still kneeling when the soldiers came abreast of him. Like the others he had passed they paid no attention to him and the moment they were behind him he continued upon his way, turning to the right at the intersection of the two streets.

The street he now took was, at this point, so extremely winding that, for the most part, it received no benefit from the flares at either corner, so that he was forced practically to grope his way in the dense shadows of the arcade. The street became a little straighter just before he reached the next flare, and as he came within sight of it he saw silhouetted against a patch of light the figure of a lion. The beast was coming slowly down the street in Tarzan's direction.

A woman crossed the way directly in front of it and the lion paid no attention to her, nor she to the lion. An instant later a little child ran after the woman and so close did he run before the lion that the beast was forced to turn out of its way a step to avoid colliding with the little one. The ape-man grinned and crossed quickly to the opposite side of the street, for his delicate senses indicated that at this point the breeze stirring through the city streets and deflected by the opposite wall would now blow from the lion toward him as the beast passed, whereas if he remained upon the side of the street upon which he had been walking when he discovered the carnivore, his scent would have been borne to the nostrils of the animal, and Tarzan was sufficiently jungle-wise to realize that while he might deceive the eyes of man and beast he could not so easily disguise from the nostrils of one of the great cats that he was a creature of a different species from the inhabitants of the city, the only human beings, possibly, that Numa was familiar with. In him the cat would recognize a stranger, and, therefore, an enemy, and Tarzan had no desire to be delayed by an encounter with a savage lion. His ruse worked successfully, the lion passing him with not more than a side glance in his direction.

He had proceeded for some little distance and had about reached a point where he judged he would find the street which led up from the city gate when, at an intersection of two streets, his nostrils caught the scent spoor of the girl. Out of a maze of other scent spoors the ape-man picked the familiar odor of the girl and, a second later, that of Smith-Oldwick. He had been forced to accomplish it, however, by bending very low at each street intersection in repeated attention to his sandal wrappings, bringing his nostrils as close to the pavement as possible.

As he advanced along the street through which the two had been conducted earlier in the day he noted, as had they, the change in the type of buildings as he passed from a residence district into that portion occupied by shops and bazaars. Here the number of flares was increased so that they appeared not only at street intersections but midway between as well, and there were many more people abroad. The shops were open and lighted, for with the setting of the sun the intense heat of the day had given place to a pleasant coolness. Here also the number of lions, roaming loose through the thoroughfares, increased, and also for the first time Tarzan noted the idiosyncrasies of the people.

Once he was nearly upset by a naked man running rapidly through the street screaming at the top of his voice. And again he nearly stumbled over a woman who was making her way in the shadows of one of the arcades upon all fours. At first the ape-man thought she was hunting for something she had dropped, but as he drew to one side to watch her, he saw that she was doing nothing of the kind—that she had merely elected to walk upon her hands and knees rather than erect upon her feet. In another block he saw two creatures struggling upon the roof of an adjacent building until finally one of them, wrenching himself free from the grasp of the other, gave his adversary a mighty push which hurled him to the pavement below, where he lay motionless upon the dusty road. For an instant a wild shriek re-echoed through the city from the lungs of the victor and then, without an instant's hesitation, the fellow leaped headfirst to the street beside the body of his victim. A lion moved out from the dense shadows of a doorway and approached the two bloody and lifeless things before him. Tarzan wondered what effect the odor of blood would have upon the beast and was surprised to see that the animal only sniffed at the corpses and the hot red blood and then lay down beside the two dead men.

He had passed the lion but a short distance when his attention was called to the figure of a man lowering himself laboriously from the roof of a building upon the east side of the thoroughfare. Tarzan's curiosity was aroused.

21

In the Alcove

As SMITH-OLDWICK realized that he was alone and practically defenseless in an enclosure filled with great lions he was, in his weakened condition, almost in a state verging upon hysterical terror. Clinging to the grating for support he dared not turn his head in the direction of the beasts behind him. He felt his knees giving weakly beneath him. Something within his head spun rapidly around. He became very dizzy and nauseated and then suddenly all went black before his eyes as his limp body collapsed at the foot of the grating.

How long he lay there unconscious he never knew; but as reason slowly reasserted itself in his semi-conscious state he was aware that he lay in a cool bed upon the whitest of linen in a bright and cheery room, and that upon one side close to him was an open window, the delicate hangings of which were fluttering in a soft summer breeze which blew in from a sun-kissed orchard of ripening fruit which he could see without—an old orchard in which soft, green grass grew between the laden trees, and where the sun filtered through the foliage; and upon the dappled greensward a little child was playing with a frolicsome puppy.

"God," thought the man, "what a horrible nightmare I have passed through!" and then he felt a hand stroking his brow and cheek—a cool and gentle hand that smoothed away his troubled recollections. For a long minute Smith-Oldwick lay in utter peace and content until gradually there was forced upon his sensibilities the fact that the hand had become rough, and that it was no longer cool but hot and moist; and suddenly he opened his eyes and looked up into the face of a huge lion.

Lieutenant Harold Percy Smith-Oldwick was not only an English gentleman and an officer in name, he was also what these implied—a brave man; but when he realized that the sweet picture he had looked upon was but the figment of a dream, and that in reality he still lay where he had fallen at the foot of the grating with a lion standing over him licking his face, the tears sprang to his eyes and ran down his cheeks. Never, he thought, had an unkind fate played so cruel a joke upon a human being.

For some time he lay feigning death while the lion, having ceased to lick him, sniffed about his body. There are some things than which death is to be preferred; and there came at last to the Englishman the realization that it would be better to die swiftly than to lie in this horrible predicament until his mind broke beneath the strain and he went mad.

And so, deliberately and without haste, he rose, clinging to the grating for support. At his first move the lion growled, but after that he paid no further attention to the man, and when at last Smith-Oldwick had regained his feet the lion moved indifferently away. Then it was that the man turned and looked about the enclosure.

Sprawled beneath the shade of the trees and lying upon the long bench beside the south wall the great beasts rested, with the exception of two or three who moved restlessly about. It was these that the man feared and yet when two more of them had passed him by he began to feel reassured, recalling the fact that they were accustomed to the presence of man.

And yet he dared not move from the grating. As the man examined his surroundings he noted that the branches of one of the trees near the further wall spread close beneath an open window. If he could reach that tree and had strength to do so, he could easily climb out upon the branch and escape, at least, from the enclosure of the lions. But in order to reach the tree he must pass the full length of the enclosure, and at the very bole of the tree itself two lions lay sprawled out in slumber.

For half an hour the man stood gazing longingly at this seeming avenue of escape, and at last, with a muttered oath, he straightened up and throwing back his shoulders in a gesture of defiance, he walked slowly and deliberately down the center of the courtyard. One of the prowling lions turned from the side wall and moved toward the center directly in the man's path, but Smith-Oldwick was committed to what he considered his one chance, for even temporary safety, and so he kept on, ignoring the presence of the beast. The lion slouched to his side and sniffed him and then, growling, he bared his teeth.

Smith-Oldwick drew the pistol from his shirt. "If he has made up his mind to kill me," he thought. "I can't see that it will make any difference in the long run whether I infuriate him or not. The beggar can't kill me any deader in one mood than another."

But with the man's movement in withdrawing the weapon from his shirt the lion's attitude suddenly altered and though he still growled he turned and sprang away, and then at last the Englishman stood almost at the foot of the tree that was his goal, and between him and safety sprawled a sleeping lion.

Above him was a limb that ordinarily he could have leaped for and reached with ease; but weak from his wounds and loss of blood he doubted his ability to do so now. There was even a question as to whether he would be able to ascend the tree at all. There was just one chance: the lowest branch left the bole within easy reach of a man standing on the ground close to the tree's stem, but to reach a position where the branch would be accessible he must step over the body of a lion. Taking a deep breath he placed one foot between the sprawled legs of the beast and gingerly raised the other to plant it upon the opposite side of the tawny body. "What," he thought, "if the beggar should happen to wake now?" The suggestion sent a shudder through his frame but he did not hesitate or withdraw his foot. Gingerly he planted it beyond the lion, threw his weight forward upon it and cautiously brought his other foot to the side of the first. He had passed and the lion had not awakened.

Smith-Oldwick was weak from loss of blood and the hardships he had undergone, but the realization of his situation impelled him to a show of agility and energy which he probably could scarcely have equaled when in possession of his normal strength. With his life depending upon the success of his efforts, he swung himself quickly to the lower branches of the tree and scrambled upward out of reach of possible harm from the lions below—though the sudden movement in the branches above them awakened both the sleeping beasts. The animals raised their heads and looked questioningly up for a moment and then lay back again to resume their broken slumber.

So easily had the Englishman succeeded thus far that he suddenly began to question as to whether he had at any time been in real danger. The lions, as he knew, were accustomed to the presence of men; but yet they were still lions and he was free to admit that he breathed more easily now that he was safe above their clutches.

Before him lay the open window he had seen from the ground. He was now on a level with it and could see an apparently unoccupied chamber beyond, and toward this he made his way along a stout branch that swung beneath the opening. It was not a difficult feat to reach the window, and a moment later he drew himself over the still and dropped into the room.

He found himself in a rather spacious apartment, the floor of which was covered with rugs of barbaric design, while the few pieces of furniture were of a similar type to that which he had seen in the room on the first floor into which he and Bertha Kircher had been ushered at the conclusion of their journey. At one end of the room was what appeared to be a curtained alcove, the heavy hangings of which completely hid the interior. In the wall opposite the window and near the alcove was a closed door, apparently the only exit from the room.

He could see, in the waning light without, that the close of the day was fast approaching, and he hesitated while he deliberated the advisability of waiting until darkness had fallen, or of immediately searching for some means of escape from the building and the city. He at last decided that it would do no harm to investigate beyond the room, that he might have some idea as how best to plan his escape after dark. To this end he crossed the room toward the door but he had taken only a few steps when the hangings before the alcove separated and the figure of a woman appeared in the opening.

She was young and beautifully formed; the single drapery wound around her body from below her breasts left no detail of her symmetrical proportions unrevealed, but her face was the face of an imbecile. At sight of her Smith-Oldwick halted, momentarily expecting that his presence would elicit screams for help from her. On the contrary she came toward him smiling, and when she was close her slender, shapely fingers touched the sleeve of his torn blouse as a curious child might handle a new toy, and still with the same smile she examined him from head to foot, taking in, in childish wonderment, every detail of his apparel.

Presently she spoke to him in a soft, well-modulated voice which contrasted sharply with her facial appearance. The voice and the girlish figure harmonized perfectly and seemed to belong to each other, while the head and face were those of another creature. Smith-Oldwick could understand no word of what she said, but nevertheless he spoke to her in his own cultured tone, the effect of which upon her was evidently most gratifying, for before he realized her intentions or could prevent her she had thrown both arms about his neck and was kissing him with the utmost abandon.

The man tried to free himself from her rather surprising attentions, but she only clung more tightly to him, and suddenly, as he recalled that he had always heard that one must humor the mentally deficient, and at the same time seeing in

her a possible agency of escape, he closed his eyes and returned her embraces.

It was at this juncture that the door opened and a man
entered. With the sound from the first movement of the latch,
Smith-Oldwick opened his eyes, but though he endeavored to
disengage himself from the girl he realized that the newcomer
had seen their rather compromising position. The girl, whose
back was toward the door, seemed at first not to realize that
someone had entered, but when she did she turned quickly
and as her eyes fell upon the man whose terrible face was now
distorted with an expression of hideous rage she turned,
screaming, and fled toward the alcove. The Englishman,
flushed and embarrassed, stood where she had left him. With
the sudden realization of the futility of attempting an explanation, came that of the menacing appearance of the man, whom
he now recognized as the official who had received them in the
room below. The fellow's face, livid with insane rage and,
possibly, jealousy, was twitching violently, accentuating the
maniacal expression that it habitually wore.

For a moment he seemed paralyzed by anger, and then with
a loud shriek that rose into an uncanny wail, he drew his
curved saber and sprang toward the Englishman. To Smith-
Oldwick there seemed no possible hope of escaping the keen-
edged weapon in the hands of the infuriated man, and though
he felt assured that it would draw down upon him an equally
sudden and possibly more terrible death, he did the only thing
that remained for him to do—drew his pistol and fired straight
for the heart of the oncoming man. Without even so much as
a groan the fellow lunged forward upon the floor at Smith-
Oldwick's feet—killed instantly with a bullet through the
heart. For several seconds the silence of the tomb reigned in
the apartment.

The Englishman, standing over the prostrate figure of the
dead man, watched the door with drawn weapon, expecting
momentarily to hear the rush of feet of those whom he was
sure would immediately investigate the report of the pistol.
But no sounds came from below to indicate that anyone there
had heard the explosion, and presently the man's attention
was distracted from the door to the alcove, between the hangings of which the face of the girl appeared. The eyes were
widely dilated and the lower jaw dropped in an expression of
surprise and awe.

The girl's gaze was riveted upon the figure upon the floor,
and presently she crept stealthily into the room and tiptoed
toward the corpse. She appeared as though constantly poised
for flight, and when she had come to within two or three feet
of the body she stopped and, looking up at Smith-Oldwick,

voiced some interrogation which he could not, of course, understand. Then she came close to the side of the dead man and kneeling upon the floor felt gingerly of the body.

Presently she shook the corpse by the shoulder, and then with a show of strength which her tenderly girlish form belied, she turned the body over on its back. If she had been in doubt before, one glance at the hideous features set in death must have convinced her that life was extinct, and with the realization there broke from her lips peal after peal of mad, maniacal laughter as with her little hands she beat upon the upturned face and breast of the dead man. It was a gruesome sight from which the Englishman involuntarily drew back— a gruesome, disgusting sight such as, he realized, might never be witnessed outside a madhouse or this frightful city.

In the midst of her frenzied rejoicing at the death of the man, and Smith-Oldwick could attribute her actions to no other cause, she suddenly desisted from her futile attacks upon the insensate flesh and, leaping to her feet, ran quickly to the door, where she shot a wooden bolt into its socket, thus securing them from interference from without. Then she returned to the center of the room and spoke rapidly to the Englishman, gesturing occasionally toward the body of the slain man. When he could not understand, she presently became provoked and in a sudden hysteria of madness she rushed forward as though to strike the Englishman. Smith-Oldwick dropped back a few steps and leveled his pistol upon her. Mad though she must have been, she evidently was not so mad but what she had connected the loud report, the diminutive weapon, and the sudden death of the man in whose house she dwelt, for she instantly desisted and quite as suddenly as it had come upon her, her homicidal mood departed.

Again the vacuous, imbecile smile took possession of her features, and her voice, dropping its harshness, resumed the soft, well-modulated tones with which she had first addressed him. Now she attempted by signs to indicate her wishes, and motioning Smith-Oldwick to follow her she went to the hangings and opening them disclosed the alcove. It was rather more than an alcove, being a fair-sized room heavy with rugs and hangings and soft, pillowed couches. Turning at the entrance she pointed to the corpse upon the floor of the outer room, and then crossing the alcove she raised some draperies which covered a couch and fell to the floor upon all sides, disclosing an opening beneath the furniture.

To this opening she pointed and then again to the corpse, indicating plainly to the Englishman that it was her desire that the body be hidden here. But if he had been in doubt, she essayed to dispel it by grasping his sleeve and urging him

in the direction of the body which the two of them then lifted
and half carried and half dragged into the alcove. At first
they encountered some difficulty when they endeavored to
force the body of the man into the small space she had selected
for it, but eventually they succeeded in doing so. Smith-Oldwick was again impressed by the fiendish brutality of the girl.
In the center of the room lay a blood-stained rug which the
girl quickly gathered up and draped over a piece of furniture
in such a way that the stain was hidden. By rearranging the
other rugs and by bringing one from the alcove she restored
the room to order so no outward indication of the tragedy so
recently enacted there was apparent.

These things attended to, and the hangings draped once
more about the couch that they might hide the gruesome thing
beneath, the girl once more threw her arms about the Englishman's neck and dragged him toward the soft and luxurious
pillows above the dead man. Acutely conscious of the horror
of his position, filled with loathing, disgust, and an outraged
sense of decency, Smith-Oldwick was also acutely alive to the
demands of self-preservation. He felt that he was warranted
in buying his life at almost any price; but there was a point at
which his finer nature rebelled.

It was at this juncture that a loud knock sounded upon the
door of the outer room. Springing from the couch, the girl
seized the man by the arm and dragged him after her to the
wall close by the head of the couch. Here she drew back one
of the hangings, revealing a little niche behind, into which she
shoved the Englishman and dropped the hangings before him,
effectually hiding him from observation from the rooms beyond.

He heard her cross the alcove to the door of the outer room,
and heard the bolt withdrawn followed by the voice of a man
mingled with that of the girl. The tones of both seemed
rational so that he might have been listening to an ordinary
conversation in some foreign tongue. Yet with the gruesome
experiences of the day behind him, he could not but momentarily expect some insane outbreak from beyond the hangings.

He was aware from the sounds that the two had entered
the alcove, and, prompted by a desire to know what manner
of man he might next have to contend with, he slightly parted
the heavy folds that hid the two from his view and looking out
saw them sitting on the couch with their arms about each
other, the girl with the same expressionless smile upon her
face that she had vouchsafed him. He found he could so
arrange the hangings that a very narrow slit between two of
them permitted him to watch the actions of those in the alcove

without revealing himself or increasing his liability of detection.

He saw the girl lavishing her kisses upon the newcomer, a much younger man than he whom Smith-Oldwick had dispatched. Presently the girl disengaged herself from the embrace of her lover as though struck by a sudden memory. Her brows puckered as in labored thought and then with a startled expression, she threw a glance backward toward the hidden niche where the Englishman stood, after which she whispered rapidly to her companion, occasionally jerking her head in the direction of the niche and on several occasions making a move with one hand and forefinger, which Smith-Oldwick could not mistake as other than an attempt to describe his pistol and its use.

It was evident then to him that she was betraying him, and without further loss of time he turned his back toward the hangings and commenced a rapid examination of his hiding place. In the alcove the man and the girl whispered, and then cautiously and with great stealth, the man rose and drew his curved saber. On tiptoe he approached the hangings, the girl creeping at his side. Neither spoke now, nor was there any sound in the room as the girl sprang forward and with outstretched arm and pointing finger indicated a point upon the curtain at the height of a man's breast. Then she stepped to one side, and her companion, raising his blade to a horizontal position, lunged suddenly forward and with the full weight of his body and his right arm, drove the sharp point through the hangings and into the niche behind for its full length.

Bertha Kircher, finding her struggles futile and realizing that she must conserve her strength for some chance opportunity of escape, desisted from her efforts to break from the grasp of Prince Metak as the fellow fled with her through the dimly lighted corridors of the palace. Through many chambers the prince fled, bearing his prize. It was evident to the girl that, though her captor was the king's son, he was not above capture and punishment for his deeds, as otherwise he would not have shown such evident anxiety to escape with her, as well as from the results of his act.

From the fact that he was constantly turning affrighted eyes behind them, and glancing suspiciously into every nook and corner that they passed, she guessed that the prince's punishment might be both speedy and terrible were he caught.

She knew from their route that they must have doubled back several times although she had quite lost all sense of direction; but she did not know that the prince was as equally confused as she, and that really he was running in an aimless, erratic manner, hoping that he might stumble eventually upon a place of refuge.

Nor is it to be wondered at that this offspring of maniacs should have difficulty in orienting himself in the winding mazes of a palace designed by maniacs for a maniac king. Now a corridor turned gradually and almost imperceptibly in a new direction, again one doubled back upon and crossed itself; here the floor rose gradually to the level of another story, or again there might be a spiral stairway down which the mad prince rushed dizzily with his burden. Upon what floor they were or in what part of the palace even Metak had no idea until, halting abruptly at a closed door, he pushed it open to step into a brilliantly lighted chamber filled with warriors, at one end of which sat the king upon a great throne; beside this, to the girl's surprise, she saw another throne where was seated a huge lioness, recalling to her the words of Xanila which, at the time, had made no impression on her: "But he had many other queens, nor were they all human."

At sight of Metak and the girl, the king rose from his throne and started across the chamber, all semblance of royalty vanishing in the maniac's uncontrollable passion. And as he came he shrieked orders and commands at the top of his voice. No sooner had Metak so unwarily opened the door to this hornets' nest than he immediately withdrew and, turning, fled again in a new direction. But now a hundred men were close upon his heels, laughing, shrieking, and possibly cursing. He dodged hither and thither, distancing them for several minutes until, at the bottom of a long runway that inclined steeply downward from a higher level, he burst into a subterranean apartment lighted by many flares.

In the center of the room was a pool of considerable size, the level of the water being but a few inches below the floor. Those behind the fleeing prince and his captive entered the chamber in time to see Metak leap into the water with the girl and disappear beneath the surface taking his captive with him, nor, though they waited excitedly around the rim of the pool, did either of the two again emerge.

When Smith-Oldwick turned to investigate his hiding place, his hands, groping upon the rear wall, immediately came in contact with the wooden panels of a door and a bolt such as that which secured the door of the outer room. Cautiously and silently drawing the wooden bar he pushed gently against the panel to find that the door swung easily and noiselessly outward into utter darkness. Moving carefully and feeling forward for each step he passed out of the niche, closing the door behind him.

Feeling about, he discovered that he was in a narrow corridor which he followed cautiously for a few yards to be brought up suddenly by what appeared to be a ladder across the passageway. He felt of the obstruction carefully with his hands until he was assured that it was indeed a ladder and that a solid wall was just beyond it, ending the corridor. Therefore, as he could not go forward and as the ladder ended at the floor upon which he stood, and as he did not care to retrace his steps, there was no alternative but to climb upward, and this he did, his pistol ready in a side pocket of his blouse.

He had ascended but two or three rungs when his head came suddenly and painfully in contact with a hard surface above him. Groping about with one hand over his head he discovered that the obstacle seemed to be the covering to a trap door in the ceiling which, with a little effort, he succeeded in raising a couple of inches, revealing through the cracks the stars of a clear African night.

With a sigh or relief, but with unabated caution, he gently slid the trapdoor to one side far enough to permit him to raise his eyes above the level of the roof. A quick glance assured him that there was none near enough to observe his movements, nor, in fact, as far as he could see, was anyone in sight.

Drawing himself quickly through the aperture he replaced the cover and endeavored to regain his bearings. Directly to the south of him the low roof he stood upon adjoined a much loftier portion of the building, which rose several stories above his head. A few yards to the west he could see the flickering light of the flares of a winding street, and toward this he made his way.

From the edge of the roof he looked down upon the night life of the mad city. He saw men and women and children and lions, and of all that he saw it was quite evident to him that only the lions were sane. With the aid of the stars he easily picked out the points of the compass, and following carefully in his memory the steps that had led him into the city and to the roof upon which he now stood, he knew that the thoroughfare upon which he looked was the same along which he and Bertha Kircher had been led as prisoners earlier in the day.

If he could reach this he might be able to pass undetected in the shadows of the arcade to the city gate. He had already given up as futile the thought of seeking out the girl and attempting to succor her, for he knew that alone and with the few remaining rounds of ammunition he possessed, he could do nothing against this city-full of armed men. That he could live to cross the lion-infested forest beyond the city was doubtful, and having, by some miracle, won to the desert beyond, his fate would be certainly sealed; but yet he was consumed with but one desire—to leave behind him as far as possible this horrid city of maniacs.

He saw that the roofs rose to the same level as that upon which he stood unbroken to the north to the next street intersection. Directly below him was a flare. To reach the pavement in safety it was necessary that he find as dark a portion of the avenue as possible. And so he sought along the edge of the roofs for a place where he might descend in comparative concealment.

He had proceeded some little way beyond a point where the street curved abruptly to the east before he discovered a location sufficiently to his liking. But even here he was compelled to wait a considerable time for a satisfactory moment for his descent, which he had decided to make down one of the pillars of the arcade. Each time he prepared to lower himself over the edge of the roofs, footsteps approaching in one direction or another deterred him until at last he had almost come to the conclusion that he would have to wait for the entire city to sleep before continuing his flight.

But finally came a moment which he felt propitious and though with inward qualms, it was with outward calm that he commenced the descent to the street below.

When at last he stood beneath the arcade he was congratulating himself upon the success that had attended his efforts up to this point when, at a slight sound behind him, he turned to see a tall figure in the yellow tunic of a warrior confronting him.

22

Out of the Niche

NUMA, the lion, growled futilely in baffled rage as he slipped back to the ground at the foot of the wall after his unsuccessful attempt to drag down the fleeing ape-man. He poised to make a second effort to follow his escaping quarry when his nose picked up a hitherto unnoticed quality in the scent spoor of his intended prey. Sniffing at the ground that Tarzan's feet had barely touched, Numa's growl changed to a low whine, for he had recognized the scent spoor of the man-thing that had rescued him from the pit of the Wamabos.

What thoughts passed through that massive head? Who may say? But now there was no indication of baffled rage as the great lion turned and moved majestically eastward along the wall. At the eastern end of the city he turned toward the south, continuing his way to the south side of the wall along which were the pens and corrals where the herbivorous flocks were fattened for the herds of domesticated lions within the city. The great black lions of the forest fed with almost equal impartiality upon the flesh of the grass-eaters and man. Like Numa of the pit they occasionaly made excursions across the desert to the fertile valley of the Wamabos, but principally they took their toll of meat from the herds of the walled city of Herog, the mad king, or seized upon some of his luckless subjects.

Numa of the pit was in some respect an exception to the rule which guided his fellows of the forest in that as a cub he had been trapped and carried into the city, where he was kept for breeding purposes, only to escape in his second year. They had tried to teach him in the city of maniacs that he must not eat the flesh of man, and the result of their schooling was that only when aroused to anger or upon that one occasion that he had been impelled by the pangs of hunger, did he ever attack man.

The animal corrals of the maniacs are protected by an outer

227

wall or palisade of upright logs, the lower ends of which are imbedded in the ground, the logs themselves being placed as close together as possible and further reinforced and bound together by withes. At intervals there are gates through which the flocks are turned on to the gazing land south of the city during the daytime. It is at such times that the black lions of the forest take their greatest toll from the herds, and it is infrequent that a lion attempts to enter the corrals at night. But Numa of the pit, having scented the spoor of his benefactor, was minded again to pass into the walled city, and with that idea in his cunning brain he crept stealthily along the outer side of the palisade, testing each gateway with a padded foot until at last he discovered one which seemed insecurely fastened. Lowering his great head he pressed against the gate, surging forward with all the weight of his huge body and the strength of his giant sinews—one mighty effort and Numa was within the corral.

The enclosure contained a herd of goats which immediately upon the advent of the carnivore started a mad stampede to the opposite end of the corral which was bounded by the south wall of the city. Numa had been within such a corral as this before, so that he knew that somewhere in the wall was a small door through which the goatherd might pass from the city to his flock; toward this door he made his way, whether by plan or accident it is difficult to say, though in the light of ensuing events it seems possible that the former was the case.

To reach the gate he must pass directly through the herd which had huddled affrightedly close to the opening so that once again there was a furious rush of hoofs as Numa strode quickly to the side of the portal. If Numa had planned, he had planned well, for scarcely had he reached his position when the door opened and a herder's head was projected into the enclosure, the fellow evidently seeking an explanation of the disturbance among his flock. Possibly he discovered the cause of the commotion, but it is doubtful, for it was dark and the great, taloned paw that reached up and struck downward a mighty blow that almost severed his head from his body, moved so quickly and silently that the man was dead within a fraction of a second from the moment that he opened the door, and then Numa, knowing now his way, passed through the wall into the dimly lighted streets of the city beyond.

Smith-Oldwick's first thought when he was accosted by the figure in the yellow tunic of a soldier was to shoot the man dead and trust to his legs and the dimly lighted, winding streets to permit his escape, for he knew that to be accosted was equivalent to recapture since no inhabitant of this weird city but would recognize him as an alien. It would be a simple thing to shoot the man from the pocket where the pistol lay without drawing the weapon, and with this purpose in mind the Englishman slipped his hands into the side pocket of his blouse, but simultaneously with this action his wrist was seized in a powerful grasp and a low voice whispered in English: "Lieutenant, it is I, Tarzan of the Apes."

The relief from the nervous strain under which he had been laboring for so long, left Smith-Oldwick suddenly as weak as a babe, so that he was forced to grasp the ape-man's arm for support—and when he found his voice all he could do was to repeat: "You? You? I thought you were dead!"

"No, not dead," replied Tarzan, "and I see that you are not either. But how about the girl?"

"I haven't seen her," replied the Englishman, "since we were brought here. We were taken into a building on the plaza close by and there we were separated. She was led away by guards and I was put into a den of lions. I haven't seen her since."

"How did you escape?" asked the ape-man.

"The lions didn't seem to pay much attention to me and I climbed out of the place by way of a tree and through a window into a room on the second floor. Had a little scrimmage there with a fellow and was hidden by one of their women in a hole in the wall. The loony thing then betrayed me to another bounder who happened in, but I found a way out and up onto the roof where I have been for quite some time now waiting for a chance to get down into the street without being seen. That's all I know, but I haven't the slightest idea in the world where to look for Miss Kircher."

"Where were you going now?" asked Tarzan.

Smith-Oldwick hesitated. "I—well, I couldn't do anything here alone and I was going to try to get out of the city and in some way reach the British forces east and bring help."

"You couldn't do it," said Tarzan. "Even if you got through the forest alive you could never cross the desert country without food or water."

"What shall we do, then?" asked the Englishman.

"We will see if we can find the girl," replied the ape-man, and then, as though he had forgotten the presence of the Englishman and was arguing to convince himself, "She may be a German and a spy, but she is a woman—a white woman—I can't leave her here."

"But how are we going to find her?" asked the Englishman.

"I have followed her this far," replied Tarzan, "and unless I am greatly mistaken I can follow her still farther."

"But I cannot accompany you in these clothes without exposing us both to detection and arrest," argued Smith-Oldwick.

"We will get you other clothes, then," said Tarzan.

"How?" asked the Englishman.

"Go back to the roof beside the city wall where I entered," replied the ape-man with a grim smile, "and ask the naked dead man there how I got my disguise."

Smith-Oldwick looked quickly up at his companion. "I have it," he exclaimed. "I know where there is a fellow who doesn't need his clothes anymore, and if we can get back on this roof I think we can find him and get his apparel without much resistance. Only a girl and a young fellow whom we could easily surprise and overcome."

"What do you mean?" asked Tarzan. "How do you know that the man doesn't need his clothes any more."

"I know he doesn't need them," replied the Englishman, "because I killed him."

"Oh!" exclaimed the ape-man, "I see. I guess it might be easier that way than to tackle one of these fellows in the street where there is more chance of our being interrupted."

"But how are we going to reach the roof again, after all?" queried Smith-Oldwick.

"The same way you came down," replied Tarzan. "This roof is low and there is a little ledge formed by the capital of each column; I noticed that when you descended. Some of the buildings wouldn't have been so easy to negotiate."

Smith-Oldwick looked up toward the eaves of the low roof. "It's not very high," he said, "but I am afraid I can't make it. I'll try—I've been pretty weak since a lion mauled me and the guards beat me up, and too, I haven't eaten since yesterday."

Tarzan thought a moment. "You've got to go with me," he said at last. "I can't leave you here. The only chance you have of escape is through me and I can't go with you now until we have found the girl."

"I want to go with you," replied Smith-Oldwick. "I'm not much good now but at that two of us may be better than one."

"All right," said Tarzan, "come on," and before the Englishman realized what the other contemplated Tarzan had picked him up and thrown him across his shoulder. "Now, hang on," whispered the ape-man, and with a short run he clambered apelike up the front of the low arcade. So quickly and easily was it done that the Englishman scarcely had time to realize what was happening before he was deposited safely upon the roof.

"There," remarked Tarzan. "Now, lead me to the place you speak of."

Smith-Oldwick had no difficulty in locating the trap in the roof through which he had escaped. Removing the cover the ape-man bent low, listening and sniffing. "Come," he said after a moment's investigation and lowered himself to the floor beneath. Smith-Oldwick followed him, and together the two crept through the darkness toward the door in the back wall of the niche in which the Englishman had been hidden by the girl. They found the door ajar and opening it Tarzan saw a streak of light showing through the hangings that separated it from the alcove.

Placing his eye close to the aperture he saw the girl and the young man of which the Englishman had spoken seated on opposite sides of a low table upon which food was spread. Serving them was a giant Negro and it was he whom the ape-man watched most closely. Familiar with the tribal idiosyncrasies of a great number of African tribes over a considerable proportion of the Dark Continent, the Tarmangani at last felt reasonably assured that he knew from what part of Africa this slave had come, and the dialect of his people. There was, however, the chance that the fellow had been captured in childhood and that through long years of non-use his native language had become lost to him, but then there always had been an element of chance connected with nearly every event of Tarzan's life, so he waited patiently until in the performance of his duties the black man approached a little table which stood near the niche in which Tarzan and the Englishman hid.

As the slave bent over some dish which stood upon the table his ear was not far from the aperture through which Tarzan looked. Apparently from a solid wall, for the Negro had no knowledge of the existence of the niche, came to him in the tongue of his own people, the whispered words: "If you would return to the land of the Wamabo say nothing, but do as I bid you."

The black rolled terrified eyes toward the hangings at his side. The ape-man could see him tremble and for a moment was fearful that in his terror he would betray them. "Fear not," he whispered, "we are your friends."

At last the Negro spoke in a low whisper, scarcely audible even to the keen ears of the ape-man. "What," he asked, "can poor Otobu do for the god who speaks to him out of the solid wall?"

"This," replied Tarzan. "Two of us are coming into this room. Help us prevent this man and woman from escaping or raising an outcry that will bring others to their aid."

"I will help you," replied the Negro, "to keep them within

this room, but do not fear that their outcries will bring others. These walls are built so that no sound may pass through, and even if it did what difference would it make in this village which is constantly filled with the screams of its mad people. Do not fear their cries. No one will notice them. I go to do your bidding."

Tarzan saw the black cross the room to the table upon which he placed another dish of food before the feasters. Then he stepped to a place behind the man and as he did so raised his eyes to the point in the wall from which the ape-man's voice had come to him, as much as to say, "Master, I am ready."

Without more delay Tarzan threw aside the hangings and stepped into the room. As he did so the young man rose from the table to be instantly seized from behind by the black slave. The girl, whose back was toward the ape-man and his companion, was not at first aware of their presence but saw only the attack of the slave upon her lover, and with a loud scream she leaped forward to assist the latter. Tarzan sprang to her side and laid a heavy hand upon her arm before she could interfere with Otobu's attentions to the young man. At first, as she turned toward the ape-man, her face reflected only mad rage, but almost instantly this changed into the vapid smile with which Smith-Oldwick was already familiar and her slim fingers commenced their soft appraisement of the newcomer.

Almost immediately she discovered Smith-Oldwick but there was neither surprise nor anger upon her countenance. Evidently the poor mad creature knew but two principal moods, from one to the other of which she changed with lightning-like rapidity.

"Watch her a moment," said Tarzan to the Englishman, "while I disarm that fellow," and stepping to the side of the young man whom Otobu was having difficulty in subduing Tarzan relieved him of his saber. "Tell them," he said to the Negro, "if you speak their language, that we will not harm them if they leave us alone and let us depart in peace."

The black had been looking at Tarzan with wide eyes, evidently not comprehending how this god could appear in so material a form, and with the voice of a white bwana and the uniform of a warrior of this city to which he quite evidently did not belong. But nevertheless his first confidence in the voice that offered him freedom was not lessened and he did as Tarzan bid him.

"They want to know what you want," said Otobu, after he had spoken to the man and the girl.

"Tell them that we want food for one thing," said Tarzan, "and something else that we know where to find in this room. Take the man's spear, Otobu; I see it leaning against the wall in the corner of the room. And you, Lieutenant, take his saber," and then again to Otobu, "I will watch the man while you go and bring forth that which is beneath the couch over against this wall," and Tarzan indicated the location of the piece of furniture.

Otobu, trained to obey, did as he was bid. The eyes of the man and the girl followed him, and as he drew back the hangings and dragged forth the corpse of the man Smith-Oldwick had slain, the girl's lover voiced a loud scream and attempted to leap forward to the side of the corpse. Tarzan, however, seized him and then the fellow turned upon him with teeth and nails. It was with no little difficulty that Tarzan finally subdued the man, and while Otobu was removing the outer clothing from the corpse, Tarzan asked the black to question the young man as to his evident excitement at the sight of the body.

"I can tell you Bwana," replied Otobu. "This man was his father."

"What is he saying to the girl?" asked Tarzan.

"He is asking her if she knew that the body of his father was under the couch. And she is saying that she did not know it."

Tarzan repeated the conversation to Smith-Oldwick, who smiled. "If the chap could have seen her removing all evidence of the crime and arranging the hangings of the couch so that the body was concealed after she had helped me drag it across the room, he wouldn't have very much doubt as to her knowledge of the affair. The rug you see draped over the bench in the corner was arranged to hide the blood stain—in some ways they are not so loony after all."

The black man had now removed the outer garments from the dead man, and Smith-Oldwick was hastily drawing them on over his own clothing. "And now," said Tarzan, "we will sit down and eat. One accomplishes little on an empty stomach." As they ate the ape-man attempted to carry on a conversation with the two natives through Otobu. He learned that they were in the palace which had belonged to the dead man lying upon the floor beside them. He had held an official position of some nature, and he and his family were of the ruling class but were not members of the court.

When Tarzan questioned them about Bertha Kircher, the young man said that she had been taken to the king's palace; and when asked why replied: "For the king, of course."

During the conversation both the man and the girl appeared quite rational, even asking some questions as to the country from which their uninvited guests had come, and evidencing much surprise when informed that there was anything but waterless wastes beyond their own valley.

When Otobu asked the man, at Tarzan's suggestion, if he

was familiar with the interior of the king's palace, he replied
that he was; that he was a friend of Prince Metak, one of the
king's sons, and that he often visited the palace and that Metak
also came here to his father's palace frequently. As Tarzan
ate he racked his brain for some plan whereby he might utilize
the knowledge of the young man to gain entrance to the
palace, but he had arrived at nothing which he considered
feasible when there came a loud knocking upon the door of
the outer room.

For a moment no one spoke and then the young man raised
his voice and cried aloud to those without. Immediately
Otobu sprang for the fellow and attempted to smother his
words by clapping a palm over his mouth.

"What is he saying?" asked Tarzan.

"He is telling them to break down the door and rescue him
and the girl from two strangers who entered and made them
prisoners. If they enter they will kill us all."

"Tell him," said Tarzan, "to hold his peace or I will slay
him."

Otobu did as he was instructed and the young maniac lapsed
into scowling silence. Tarzan crossed the alcove and entered
the outer room to note the effect of the assaults upon the door.
Smith-Oldwick followed him a few steps, leaving Otobu to
guard the two prisoners. The ape-man saw that the door could
not long withstand the heavy blows being dealt the panels
from without. "I wanted to use that fellow in the other room,"
he said to Smith-Oldwick, "but I am afraid we will have to get
out of here the way we came. We can't accomplish anything
by waiting here and meeting these fellows. From the noise out
there there must be a dozen of them. Come," he said, "you go
first and I will follow."

As the two turned back from the alcove they witnessed an
entirely different scene from that upon which they had turned
their backs but a moment or two before. Stretched on the
floor and apparently lifeless lay the body of the black slave,
while the two prisoners had vanished completely.

23

The Flight from Xuja

A s METAK bore Bertha Kircher toward the edge of the
pool, the girl at first had no conception of the deed he
contemplated but when, as they approached the edge,
he did not lessen his speed she guessed the frightful truth. As
he leaped head foremost with her into the water, she closed
her eyes and breathed a silent prayer, for she was confident
that the maniac had no other purpose than to drown himself
and her. And yet, so potent is the first law of nature that even
in the face of certain death, as she surely believed herself, she
clung tenaciously to life, and while she struggled to free herself from the powerful clutches of the madman, she held her
breath against the final moment when the asphyxiating waters
must inevitably flood her lungs.

Through the frightful ordeal she maintained absolute control of her senses so that, after the first plunge, she was aware
that the man was swimming with her beneath the surface. He
took perhaps not more than a dozen strokes directly toward
the end wall of the pool and then he arose; and once again she
knew that her head was above the surface. She opened her
eyes to see that they were in a corridor dimly lighted by grat-
ings set in its roof—a winding corridor, water filled from wall
to wall.

Along this the man was swimming with easy powerful
strokes, at the same time holding her chin above the water.
For ten minutes he swam thus without stopping and the girl
heard him speak to her, though she could not understand what
he said, as he evidently immediately realized, for, half floating,
he shifted his hold upon her so that he could touch her nose
and mouth with the fingers of one hand. She grasped what he
meant and immediately took a deep breath, whereat he dove
quickly beneath the surface pulling her down with him and
again for a dozen strokes or more he swam thus wholly
submerged.

When they again came to the surface, Bertha Kircher saw that they were in a large lagoon and that the bright stars were shining high above them, while on either hand domed and minareted buildings were silhouetted sharply against the star-lit sky. Metak swam swiftly to the north side of the lagoon where, by means of a ladder, the two climbed out upon the embankment. There were others in the plaza but they paid but little if any attention to the two bedraggled figures. As Metak walked quickly across the pavement with the girl at his side, Bertha Kircher could only guess at the man's intentions. She could see no way in which to escape and so she went docilely with him, hoping against hope that some fortuitous circumstance might eventually arise that would give her the coveted chance for freedom and life.

Metak led her toward a building which, as she entered, she recognized as the same to which she and Lieutenant Smith-Oldwick had been led when they were brought into the city. There was no man sitting behind the carved desk now, but about the room were a dozen or more warriors in the tunics of the house to which they were attached, in this case white with a small lion in the form of a crest or badge upon the breast and back of each.

As Metak entered and the men recognized him they arose, and in answer to a query he put, they pointed to an arched doorway at the rear of the room. Toward this Metak led the girl, and then, as though filled with a sudden suspicion, his eyes narrowed cunningly and turning toward the soldiery he issued an order which resulted in their all preceding him through the small doorway and up a flight of stairs a short distance beyond.

The stairway and the corridor above were lighted by small flares which revealed several doors in the walls of the upper passageway. To one of these the men led the prince. Bertha Kircher saw them knock upon the door and heard a voice reply faintly through the thick door to the summons. The effect upon those about her was electrical. Instantly excitement reigned, and in response to orders from the king's son the soldiers commenced to beat heavily upon the door, to throw their bodies against it and to attempt to hew away the panels with their sabers. The girl wondered at the cause of the evident excitement of her captors.

She saw the door giving to each renewed assault, but what she did not see just before it crashed inward was the figures of the two men who alone, in all the world, might have saved her, pass between the heavy hangings in an adjoining alcove and disappear into a dark corridor.

As the door gave and the warriors rushed into the apartment followed by the prince, the latter became immediately filled with baffled rage, for the rooms were deserted except for the dead body of the owner of the palace, and the still form of the black slave, Otobu, where they lay stretched upon the floor of the alcove.

The prince rushed to the windows and looked out, but as the suite overlooked the barred den of lions from which, the prince thought, there could be no escape, his puzzlement was only increased. Though he searched about the room for some clue to the whereabouts of its former occupants he did not discover the niche behind the hangings. With the fickleness of insanity he qiuckly tired of the search, and, turning to the soldiers who had accompanied him from the floor below, dismissed them.

After setting up the broken door as best they could, the men left the apartment and when they were again alone Metak turned toward the girl. As he opproached her, his face distorted by a hideous leer, his features worked rapidly in spasmodic twitches. The girl, who was standing at the entrance of the alcove, shrank back, her horror reflected in her face. Step by step she backed across the room, while the crouching maniac crept stealthily after her with clawlike fingers poised in anticipation of the moment they should leap forth and seize her.

As she passed the body of the Negro, her foot touched some obstacle at her side, and glancing down she saw the spear with which Otobu had been supposed to hold the prisoners. Instantly she leaned forward and snatched it from the floor with its sharp point directed at the body of the madman. The effect upon Metak was electrical. From stealthy silence he broke into harsh peals of laughter, and drawing his saber danced to and fro before the girl, but whichever way he went the point of the spear still threatened him.

Gradually the girl noticed a change in the tone of the creature's screams that was also reflected in the changing expression upon his hideous countenance. His hysterical laughter was slowly changing into cries of rage while the silly leer upon his face was supplanted by a ferocious scowl and upcurled lips, which revealed the sharpened fangs beneath.

He now ran rapidly in almost to the spear's point, only to jump away, run a few steps to one side and again attempt to make an entrance, the while he slashed and hewed at the spear with such violence that it was with difficulty the girl maintained her guard, and all the time was forced to give ground step by step. She had reached the point where she was standing squarely against the couch at the side of the room when, with an incredibly swift movement, Metak stooped and grasping a low stool hurled it directly at her head.

She raised the spear to fend off the heavy missile, but she was not entirely successful, and the impact of the blow carried her backward upon the couch, and instantly Metak was upon her.

Tarzan and Smith-Oldwick gave little thought as to what had become of the other two occupants of the room. They were gone, and so far as these two were concerned they might never return. Tarzan's one desire was to reach the street again, where, now that both of them were in some sort of disguise, they should be able to proceed with comparative safety to the palace and continue their search for the girl.

Smith-Oldwick preceded Tarzan along the corridor and as they reached the ladder he climbed aloft to remove the trap. He worked for a moment and then, turning, addressed Tarzan. "Did we replace the cover on this trap when we came down? I don't recall that we did."

"No," said Tarzan, "it was left open."

"So I thought," said Smith-Oldwick, "but it's closed now and locked. I cannot move it. Possibly you can," and he descended the ladder.

Even Tarzan's immense strength, however, had no effect other than to break one of the rungs of the ladder against which he was pushing, nearly precipitating him to the floor below. After the rung broke he rested for a moment before renewing his efforts, and as he stood with his head near the cover of the trap, he distinctly heard voices on the roof above him.

Dropping down to Oldwick's side he told him what he had heard. "We had better find some other way out," he said, and the two started to retrace their steps toward the alcove. Tarzan was again in the lead, and as he opened the door in the back of the niche, he was suddenly startled to hear, in tones of terror and in a woman's voice, the words: "O God, be merciful" from just beyond the hangings.

Here was no time for cautious investigation and, not even waiting to find the aperture and part the hangings, but with one sweep of a brawny hand dragging them from their support, the ape-man leaped from the niche into the alcove.

At the sound of his entry the maniac looked up, and as he saw at first only a man in the uniform of his father's soldiers, he shrieked forth an angry order, but at the second glance, which revealed the face of the newcomer, the madman leaped from the prostrate form of his victim and, apparently forgetful of the saber which he had dropped upon the floor beside the couch as he leaped to grapple with the girl, closed with bare hands upon his antagonist, his sharp-filed teeth searching for the other's throat.

Metak, the son of Herog, was no weakling. Powerful by nature and rendered still more so in the throes of one of his maniacal fits of fury he was no mean antagonist, even for the mighty ape-man, and to this a distinct advantage for him was added by the fact that almost at the outset of their battle Tarzan, in stepping backward, struck his heel against the corpse of the man whom Smith-Oldwick had killed, and fell heavily backward to the floor with Metak upon his breast.

With the quickness of a cat the maniac made an attempt to fasten his teeth in Tarzan's jugular, but a quick movement of the latter resulted in his finding a hold only upon the Tarmangani's shoulder. Here he clung while his fingers sought Tarzan's throat, and it was then that the ape-man, realizing the possibility of defeat, called to Smith-Oldwick to take the girl and seek to escape.

The Englishman looked questioningly at Bertha Kircher, who had now risen from the couch, shaking and trembling. She saw the question in his eyes and with an effort she drew herself to her full height. "No," she cried, "if he dies here I shall die with him. Go if you wish to. You can do nothing here, but I—I cannot go."

Tarzan had now regained his feet, but the maniac still clung to him tenaciously. The girl turned suddenly to Smith-Oldwick. "Your pistol!" she cried. "Why don't you shoot him?"

The man drew the weapon from his pocket and approached the two antagonists, but by this time they were moving so rapidly that there was no opportunity for shooting one without the danger of hitting the other. At the same time Bertha Kircher circled about them with the prince's saber, but neither could she find an opening. Again and again the two men fell to the floor, until presently Tarzan found a hold upon the other's throat, against which contingency Metak had been constantly battling, and slowly, as the giant fingers closed, the other's mad eyes protruded from his livid face, his jaws gaped and released their hold upon Tarzan's shoulder, and then in a sudden excess of disgust and rage the ape-man lifted the body of the prince high above his head and with all the strength of his great arms hurled it across the room and through the window where it fell with a sickening thud into the pit of lions beneath.

As Tarzan turned again toward his companions, the girl was standing with the saber still in her hand and an expression upon her face that he never had seen there before. Her eyes were wide and misty with unshed tears, while her sensitive lips trembled as though she were upon the point of giving way to some pent emotion which her rapidly rising and falling bosom plainly indicated she was fighting to control.

"If we are going to get out of here," said the ape-man, "we can't lose any time. We are together at last and nothing can be gained by delay. The question now is the safest way. The couple who escaped us evidently departed through the passageway to the roof and secured the trap against us so that we are cut off in that direction. What chance have we below? You came that way," and he turned toward the girl.

"At the foot of the stairs," she said, "is a room full of armed men. I doubt if we could pass that way."

It was then that Otobu raised himself to a sitting posture. "So you are not dead after all," exclaimed the ape-man. "Come, how badly are you hurt?"

The Negro rose gingerly to his feet, moved his arms and legs and felt of his head.

"Otobu does not seem to be hurt at all, Bwana," he replied, "only for a great ache in his head."

"Good," said the ape-man. "You want to return to the Wamabo country?"

"Yes, Bwana."

"Then lead us from the city by the safest way."

"There is no safe way," replied the black, "and even if we reach the gates we shall have to fight. I can lead you from this building to a side street with little danger of meeting anyone on the way. Beyond that we must take our chance of discovery. You are all dressed as are the people of this wicked city so perhaps we may pass unnoticed, but at the gate it will be a different matter, for none is permitted to leave the city at night."

"Very well," replied the ape-man, "let us be on our way."

Otobu led them through the broken door of the outer room, and part way down the corridor he turned into another apartment at the right. This they crossed to a passageway beyond, and, finally, traversing several rooms and corridors, he led them down a flight of steps to a door which opened directly upon a side street in rear of the palace.

Two men, a woman, and a black slave were not so extraordinary a sight upon the streets of the city as to arouse comment. When passing beneath the flares the three Europeans were careful to choose a moment when no chance pedestrian might happen to get a view of their features, but in the shadow of the arcades there seemed little danger of detection. They had covered a good portion of the distance to the gate without mishap when there came to their ears from the central portion of the city sounds of a great commotion.

"What does that mean?" Tarzan asked of Otobu, who was now trembling violently.

"Master," he replied, "they have discovered that which has happened in the palace of Veza, mayor of the city. His son and the girl escaped and summoned soldiers who have now doubtless discovered the body of Veza."

"I wonder," said Tarzan, "if they have discovered the party I threw through the window."

Bertha Kircher, who understood enough of the dialect to follow their conversation, asked Tarzan if he knew that the man he had thrown from the window was the king's son. The ape-man laughed. "No," he said, "I did not. That rather complicates matters—at least if they have found him."

Suddenly there broke above the turmoil behind them the clear strains of a bugle. Otobu increased his pace. "Hurry, Master," he cried, "it is worse than I had thought."

"What do you mean?" asked Tarzan.

"For some reason the king's guard and the king's lions are being called out. I fear, O Bwana, that we cannot escape them. But why they should be called out for us I do not know."

But if Otobu did not know, Tarzan at least guessed that they had found the body of the king's son. Once again the notes of the bugle rose high and clear upon the night air. "Calling more lions?" asked Tarzan.

"No, Master," replied Otobu. "It is the parrots they are calling."

They moved on rapidly in silence for a few minutes when their attention was attracted by the flapping of the wings of a bird above them. They looked up to discover a parrot circling about over their heads.

"Here are the parrots, Otobu," said Tarzan with a grin. "Do they expect to kill us with parrots?"

The Negro moaned as the bird darted suddenly ahead of them toward the city wall. "Now indeed are we lost, Master," cried the black. "The bird that found us has flown to the gate to warn the guard."

"Come, Otobu, what are you talking about?" exclaimed Tarzan irritably. "Have you lived among these lunatics so long that you are yourself mad?"

"No, Master," replied Otobu. "I am not mad. You do not know them. These terrible birds are like human beings without hearts or souls. They speak the language of the people of this city of Xuja. They are demons, Master, and when in sufficient numbers they might even attack and kill us."

"How far are we from the gate?" asked Tarzan.

"We are not very far," replied the Negro. "Beyond this next turn we will see it a few paces ahead of us. But the bird has reached it before us and by now they are summoning the guard," the truth of which statement was almost immediately indicated by sounds of many voices raised evidently in commands just ahead of them, while from behind came increased evidence of approaching pursuit—loud screams and the roars of lions.

A few steps ahead a narrow alley opened from the east into the thoroughfare they were following and as they approached it there emerged from its dark shadows the figure of a mighty lion. Otobu halted in his tracks and shrank back against Tarzan. "Look, Master," he whimpered, "a great black lion of the forest!"

Tarzan drew the saber which still hung at his side. "We cannot go back," he said. "Lions, parrots, or men, it must be all the same," and he moved steadily forward in the direction of the gate. What wind was stirring in the city street moved from Tarzan toward the lion and when the ape-man had approached to within a few yards of the beast, who had stood silently eyeing them up to this time, instead of the expected roar, a whine broke from the beast's throat. The ape-man was conscious of a very decided feeling of relief. "It's Numa of the pit," he called back to his companions, and to Otobu, "Do not fear, this lion will not harm us."

Numa moved forward to the ape-man's side and then turning, paced beside him along the narrow street. At the next turn they came in sight of the gate, where, beneath several flares, they saw a group of at least twenty warriors prepared to seize them, while from the opposite direction the roars of the pursuing lions sounded close upon them, mingling with the screams of numerous parrots which now circled about their heads. Tarzan halted and turned to the young aviator. "How many rounds of ammunition have you left?" he asked.

"I have seven in the pistol," replied Smith-Oldwick, "and perhaps a dozen more cartridges in my blouse pocket."

"I'm going to rush them," said Tarzan. "Otobu, you stay at the side of the woman. Oldwick, you and I will go ahead, you upon my left. I think we need not try to tell Numa what to do," for even then the great lion was baring his fangs and growling ferociously at the guardsmen, who appeared uneasy in the face of this creature which, above all others, they feared.

"As we advance, Oldwick," said the ape-man, "fire one shot. It may frighten them; and after that fire only when necessary. All ready? Let's go!" and he moved forward toward the gate. At the same time, Smith-Oldwick discharged his weapon and a yellow-coated warrior screamed and crumpled forward upon his face. For a minute the others showed symptoms of panic but one, who seemed to be an officer, rallied them. "Now," said Tarzan, "all together!" and he started at a run for the gate. Simultaneously the lion, evidently scenting the purpose of the Tarmangani, broke into a full charge toward the guard.

Shaken by the report of the unfamiliar weapon, the ranks of the guardsmen broke before the furious assault of the great beast. The officer screamed forth a volley of commands in a mad fury of uncontrolled rage but the guardsmen, obeying the first law of nature as well as actuated by their inherent fear of the black denizen of the forest, scattered to right and left to elude the monster. With ferocious growls Numa wheeled to the right, and with raking talons struck right and left among a little handful of terrified guardsmen who were endeavoring to elude him, and then Tarzan and Smith-Oldwick closed with the others.

For a moment their most formidable antagonist was the officer in command. He wielded his curved saber as only an adept might as he faced Tarzan, to whom the similar weapon is his own hand was most unfamiliar. Smith-Oldwick could not fire for fear of hitting the ape-man when suddenly to his dismay he saw Tarzan's weapon fly from his grasp as the Xujan warrior neatly disarmed his opponent. With a scream the fellow raised his saber for the final cut that would terminate the earthly career of Tarzan of the Apes when, to the astonishment of both the ape-man and Smith-Oldwick, the fellow stiffened rigidly, his weapon dropped from the nerveless fingers of his upraised hand, his mad eyes rolled upward and foam flecked his bared lip. Gasping as though in the throes of strangulation the fellow pitched forward at Tarzan's feet.

Tarzan stooped and picked up the dead man's weapon, a smile upon his face as he turned and glanced toward the young Englishman.

"The fellow is an epileptic," said Smith-Oldwick. "I suppose many of them are. Their nervous condition is not without its good points—a normal man would have gotten you."

The other guardsmen seemed utterly demoralized at the loss of their leader. They were huddled upon the opposite side of the street at the left of the gate, screaming at the tops of their voices and looking in the direction from which sounds of reinforcements were coming, as though urging on the men and lions that were already too close for the comfort of the fugitives. Six guardsmen still stood with their backs against the gate, their weapons flashing in the light of the flares and their parchment-like faces distorted in horrid grimaces of rage and terror.

Numa had pursued two fleeing warriors down the street which paralleled the wall for a short distance at this point. The ape-man turned to Smith-Oldwick. "You will have to use your pistol now," he said, "and we must get by these fellows at once;" and as the young Englishman fired, Tarzan rushed in to close quarters as though he had not already discovered that with the saber he was no match for these trained swordsmen. Two men fell to Smith-Oldwick's first two shots and then he missed, while the four remaining divided, two leaping for the aviator and two for Tarzan.

The ape-man rushed in in an effort to close with one of his antagonists where the other's saber would be comparatively useless. Smith-Oldwick dropped one of his assailants with a bullet through the chest and pulled his trigger on the second, only to have the hammer fall futilely upon an empty chamber. The cartridges in his weapon were exhausted and the warrior with his razor-edged, gleaming saber was upon him.

Tarzan raised his own weapon but once and that to divert a vicious cut for his head. Then he was upon one of his assailants and before the fellow could regain his equilibrium and leap back after delivering his cut, the ape-man had seized him by the neck and crotch. Tarzan's other antagonist was edging around to one side where he might use his weapon, and as he raised the blade to strike at the back of the Tarmangani's neck, the latter swung the body of his comrade upward so that it received the full force of the blow. The blade sank deep into the body of the warrior, eliciting a single frightful scream, and then Tarzan hurled the dying man in the face of his final adversary.

Smith-Oldwick, hard pressed and now utterly defenseless, had given up all hope in the instant that he realized his weapon was empty, when, from his left, a living bolt of black-maned ferocity shot past him to the breast of his opponent. Down went the Xujan, his face bitten away by one snap of the powerful jaws of Numa of the pit.

In the few second that had been required for the consummation of these rapidly ensuing events, Otobu had dragged Bertha Kircher to the gate which he had unbarred and thrown open, and with the vanishing of the last of the active guardsmen, the party passed out of the maniac city of Xuja into the outer darkness beyond. At the same moment a half dozen lions rounded the last turn in the road leading back toward the plaza, and at sight of them Numa of the pit wheeled and charged. For a moment the lions of the city stood their ground, but only for a moment, and then before the black beast was upon them, they turned and fled, while Tarzan and his party moved rapidly toward the blackness of the forest beyond the garden.

"Will they follow us out of the city?" Tarzan asked Otobu.

"Not at night," replied the black. "I have been a slave here for five years but never have I known these people to leave the city by night. If they go beyond the forest in the daytime they usually wait until the dawn of another day before they return, as they fear to pass through the country of the black lions after dark. No, I think, Master, that they will not follow us tonight, but tomorrow they will come, and, O Bwana, then will they surely get us, or those that are left of us, for at least one among us must be the toll of the black lions as we pass through their forest."

As they crossed the garden, Smith-Oldwick refilled the magazine of his pistol and inserted a cartridge in the chamber. The girl moved silently at Tarzan's left, between him and the aviator. Suddenly the ape-man stopped and turned toward the city, his mighty frame, clothed in the yellow tunic of Herog's soldiery, plainly visible to the others beneath the light of the stars. They saw him raise his head and they heard break from his lips the plaintive note of a lion calling to his fellows. Smith-Oldwick felt a distinct shudder pass through his frame, while Otobu, rolling the whites of his eyes in terrified surprise, sank tremblingly to his knees. But the girl thrilled and she felt her heart beat in a strange exultation, and then she drew nearer to the beast-man until her shoulder touched his arm. The act was involuntary and for a moment she scarce realized what she had done, and then she stepped silently back, thankful that the light of the stars was not sufficient to reveal to the eyes of her companions the flush which she felt mantling her cheek. Yet she was not ashamed of the impulse that had prompted her, but rather of the act itself which she knew, had Tarzan noticed it, would have been repulsive to him.

From the open gate of the city of maniacs came the answering cry of a lion. The little group waited where they stood until presently they saw the majestic proportions of the black lion as he approached them along the trail. When he had rejoined them Tarzan fastened the fingers of one hand in the black mane and started on once more toward the forest. Behind them, from the city, rose a bedlam of horrid sounds, the roaring of lions mingling with the raucous voices of the screaming parrots and the mad shrieks of the maniacs. As they entered the Stygian darkness of the forest the girl once again involuntarily shrank closer to the ape-man, and this time Tarzan was aware of the contact.

Himself without fear, he yet instinctively appreciated how terrified the girl must be. Actuated by a sudden kindly impulse he found her hand and took it in his own and thus they continued upon their way, groping through the blackness of the trail. Twice they were approached by forest lions, but upon both occasions the deep growls of Numa of the pit drove off their assailants. Several times they were compelled to rest, for Smith-Oldwick was constantly upon the verge of exhaustion, and toward morning Tarzan was forced to carry him on the steep ascent from the bed of the valley.

24

The Tommies

DAYLIGHT overtook them after they had entered the gorge, but, tired as they all were with the exception of Tarzan, they realized that they must keep on at all costs until they found a spot where they might ascend the precipitous side of the gorge to the floor of the plateau above. Tarzan and Otobu were both equally confident that the Xujans would not follow them beyond the gorge, but though they scanned every inch of the frowning cliffs upon either hand noon came and there was still no indication of any avenue of escape to right or left. There were places where the ape-man alone might have negotiated the ascent but none where the others could hope successfully to reach the plateau, nor where Tarzan, powerful and agile as he was, could have ventured safely to carry them aloft.

For half a day the ape-man had been either carrying or supporting Smith-Oldwick and now, to his chagrin, he saw that the girl was faltering. He had realized well how much she had undergone and how greatly the hardships and dangers and the fatigue of the past weeks must have told upon her vitality. He saw how bravely she attempted to keep up, yet how often she stumbled and staggered as she labored through the sand and gravel of the gorge. Nor could he help but admire her fortitude and the uncomplaining effort she was making to push on.

The Englishman must have noticed her condition too, for some time after noon, he stopped suddenly and sat down in the sand. "It's no use," he said to Tarzan. "I can go no farther. Miss Kircher is rapidly weakening. You will have to go on without me."

"No," said the girl, "we cannot do that. We have all been through so much together and the chances of our escape are still so remote that whatever comes, let us remain together, unless," and she looked up at Tarzan, "you, who have done so much for us to whom you are under no obligations, will go on without us. I for one wish that you would. It must be as evident to you as it is to me that you cannot save us, for though you succeeded in dragging us from the path of our pursuers, even your great strength and endurance could never take one of us across the desert waste which lies between here and the nearest fertile country."

The ape-man returned her serious look with a smile. "You are not dead," he said to her, "nor is the lieutenant, nor Otobu, nor myself. One is either dead or alive, and until we are dead we should plan only upon continuing to live. Because we remain here and rest is no indication that we shall die here. I cannot carry you both to the country of the Wamabos, which is the nearest spot at which we may expect to find game and water, but we shall not give up on that account. So far we have found a way. Let us take things as they come. Let us rest now because you and Lieutenant Smith-Oldwick need the rest, and when you are stronger we will go on again."

"But the Xujans—?" she asked, "may they not follow us here?"

"Yes," he said, "they probably will. But we need not be concerned with them until they come."

"I wish," said the girl, "that I possessed your philosophy but I am afraid it is beyond me."

"You were not born and reared in the jungle by wild beasts and among wild beasts, or you would possess, as I do, the fatalism of the jungle."

And so they moved to the side of the gorge beneath the shade of an overhanging rock and lay down in the hot sand to rest. Numa wandered restlessly to and fro and finally, after sprawling for a moment close beside the ape-man, rose and moved off up the gorge to be lost to view a moment later beyond the nearest turn.

For an hour the little party rested and then Tarzan suddenly rose and, motioning the others to silence, listened. For a minute he stood motionless, his keen ears acutely receptive to sounds so faint and distant that none of the other three could detect the slightest break in the utter and deathlike quiet of the gorge. Finally the ape-man relaxed and turned toward them. "What is it?" asked the girl.

"They are coming," he replied. "They are yet some distance away, though not far, for the sandaled feet of the men and the pads of the lions make little noise upon the soft sands."

"What shall we do—try to go on?" asked Smith-Oldwick. "I believe I could make a go of it now for a short way. I am much rested. How about you Miss Kircher?"

"Oh, yes," she said, "I am much stronger. Yes, surely I can go on."

Tarzan knew that neither of them quite spoke the truth, that people do not recover so quickly from utter exhaustion, but he saw no other way and there was always the hope that just beyond the next turn would be a way out of the gorge.

"You help the lieutenant, Otobu," he said, turning to the black, "and I will carry Miss Kircher," and though the girl objected, saying that he must not waste his strength, he lifted her lightly in his arms and moved off up the canyon, followed by Otobu and the Englishman. They had gone no great distance when the others of the party became aware of the sounds of pursuit, for now the lions were whining as though the fresh scent spoor of their quarry had reached their nostrils.

"I wish that your Numa would return," said the girl.

"Yes," said Tarzan, "but we shall have to do the best we can without him. I should like to find some place where we can barricade ourselves against attack from all sides. Possibly then we might hold them off. Smith-Oldwick is a good shot and if there are not too many men he might be able to dispose of them provided they can only come at him one at a time. The lions don't bother me so much. Sometimes they are stupid animals, and I am sure that these that pursue us, and who are so dependent upon the masters that have raised and trained them, will be easily handled after the warriors are disposed of."

"You think there is some hope, then?" she asked.

"We are still alive," was his only answer.

"There," he said presently, "I thought I recalled this very spot." He pointed toward a fragment that had evidently fallen from the summit of the cliff and which now lay imbedded in the sand a few feet from the base. It was a jagged fragment of rock which rose some ten feet above the surface of the sand, leaving a narrow aperture between it and the cliff behind. Toward this they directed their steps and when finally they reached their goal they found a space about two feet wide and ten feet long between the rock and the cliff. To be sure it was open at both ends but at least they could not be attacked upon all sides at once.

They had scarcely concealed themselves before Tarzan's quick ears caught a sound upon the face of the cliff above them, and looking up he saw a diminutive monkey perched upon a slight projection—an ugly-faced little monkey who looked down upon them for a moment and then scampered away toward the south in the direction from which their pursuers were coming. Otobu had seen the monkey too. "He will tell the parrots," said the black, "and the parrots will tell the madmen."

"It is all the same," replied Tarzan; "the lions would have found us here. We could not hope to hide from them."

He placed Smith-Oldwick, with his pistol, at the north open-ing of their haven and told Otobu to stand with his spear at the Englishman's shoulder, while he himself prepared to guard the southern approach. Between them he had the girl lie down in the sand. "You will be safe there in the event that they use their spears," he said.

The minutes that dragged by seemed veritable eternities to Bertha Kircher and then at last, and almost with relief, she knew that the pursuers were upon them. She heard the angry roaring of the lions and the cries of the madmen. For several minutes the men seemed to be investigating the stronghold which their quarry had discovered. She could hear them both to the north and south and then from where she lay she saw a lion charging for the ape-man before her. She saw the giant arm swing back with the curved saber and she saw it fall with terrific velocity and meet the lion as he rose to grapple with the man, cleaving his skull as cleanly as a butcher opens up a sheep.

Then she heard footsteps running rapidly toward Smith-Oldwick and, as his pistol spoke, there was a scream and the sound of a falling body. Evidently disheartened by the failure of their first attempt the assaulters drew off, but only for a short time. Again they came, this time a man opposing Tar-zan and a lion seeking to overcome Smith-Oldwick. Tarzan had cautioned the young Englishman not to waste his car-tridges upon the lions and it was Otobu with the Xujan spear who met the beast, which was not subdued until both he and Smith-Oldwick had been mauled, and the latter had succeeded in running the point of the saber the girl had carried, into the beast's heart. The man who opposed Tarzan inadvertently came too close in an attempt to cut at the ape-man's head, with the result that an instant later his corpse lay with the neck broken upon the body of the lion.

Once again the enemy withdrew, but again only for a short time, and now they came in full force, the lions and the men, possibly a half dozen of each, the men casting their spears and the lions waiting just behind, evidently for the signal to charge.

"Is this the end?" asked the girl.

"No," cried the ape-man, "for we still live!"

The words had scarcely passed his lips when the remaining warriors, rushing in, cast their spears simultaneously from both sides. In attempting to shield the girl, Tarzan received one of the shafts in the shoulder, and so heavily had the weapon been hurled that it bore him backward to the ground. Smith-Oldwick fired his pistol twice when he too was struck down, the weapon entering his right leg midway between hip and knee. Only Otobu remained to face the enemy, for the Englishman, already weak from his wounds and from the latest mauling he had received at the claws of the lion, had lost consciousness as he sank to the ground with this new hurt.

As he fell his pistol dropped from his fingers, and the girl, seeing, snatched it up. As Tarzan struggled to rise, one of the warriors leaped full upon his breast and bore him back as, with fiendish shrieks, he raised the point of his saber above the other's heart. Before he could drive it home the girl leveled Smith-Oldwick's pistol and fired point-blank at the fiend's face.

Simultaneously there broke upon the astonished ears of both attackers and attacked a volley of shots from the gorge. With the sweetness of the voice of an angel from heaven the Europeans heard the sharp-barked commands of an English noncom. Even above the roars of the lions and the screams of the maniacs, those beloved tones reached the ears of Tarzan and the girl at the very moment that even the ape-man had given up the last vestige of hope.

Rolling the body of the warrior to one side Tarzan struggled to his feet, the spear still protruding from his shoulder. The girl rose too, and as Tarzan wrenched the weapon from his flesh and stepped out from behind the concealment of their refuge, she followed at his side. The skirmish that had resulted in their rescue was soon over. Most of the lions escaped but all of the pursuing Xujans had been slain. As Tarzan and the girl came into full view of the group, a British Tommy leveled his rifle at the ape-man. Seeing the fellow's actions and realizing instantly the natural error that Tarzan's yellow tunic had occasioned the girl sprang between him and the soldier. "Don't shoot," she cried to the latter, "we are both friends."

"Hold up your hands, you, then," he commanded Tarzan. "I ain't taking no chances with any duffer with a yellow shirt."

At this juncture the British sergeant who had been in command of the advance guard approached and when Tarzan and the girl spoke to him in English, explaining their disguises, he accepted their word, since they were evidently not of the same race as the creatures which lay dead about them. Ten minutes later the main body of the expedition came into view. Smith-Oldwick's wounds were dressed, as well as were those of the ape-man, and in half an hour they were on their way to the camp of their rescuers.

That night it was arranged that the following day Smith-Oldwick and Bertha Kircher should be transported to British headquarters near the coast by aeroplane, the two planes attached to the expeditionary force being requisitioned for the purpose. Tarzan and Otobu declined the offers of the British captain to accompany his force overland on the return march as Tarzan explained that his country lay to the west, as did Otobu's, and that they would travel together as far as the country of the Wamabos.

"You are not going back with us, then?" asked the girl.

"No," replied the ape-man. "My home is upon the west coast. I will continue my journey in that direction."

She cast appealing eyes toward him. "You will go back into that terrible jungle?" she asked. "We shall never see you again?"

He looked at her a moment in silence. "Never," he said, and without another word turned and walked away.

In the morning Colonel Capell came from the base camp in one of the planes that was to carry Smith-Oldwick and the girl to the east. Tarzan was standing some distance away as the ship landed and the officer descended to the ground. He saw the colonel greet his junior in command of the advance detachment, and then he saw him turn toward Bertha Kircher who was standing a few paces behind the captain. Tarzan wondered how the German spy felt in this situation, especially when she must know that there was one there who knew her real status. He saw Colonel Capell walk toward her with outstretched hands and smiling face and, although he could not hear the words of his greeting, he saw that it was friendly and cordial to a degree.

Tarzan turned away scowling, and if any had been close by they might have heard a low growl rumble from his chest. He knew that his country was at war with Germany and that not only his duty to the land of his fathers, but also his personal grievance against the enemy people and his hatred of them, demanded that he expose the girl's perfidy, and yet he hesitated, and because he hesitated he growled—not at the German spy but at himself for his weakness.

He did not see her again before she entered a plane and was borne away toward the east. He bid farewell to Smith-Oldwick and received again the oft-repeated thanks of the young Englishman. And then he saw him too borne aloft in the high circling plane and watched until the ship became a speck far above the eastern horizon to disappear at last high in air.

The Tommies, their packs and accouterments slung, were waiting the summons to continue their return march. Colonel Capell had, through a desire to personally observe the stretch of country between the camp of the advance detachment and the base, decided to march back his troops. Now that all was in readiness for departure he turned to Tarzan. "I wish you would come back with us, Greystoke," he said, "and if my appeal carries no inducement possibly that of Smith-Oldwick and the young lady who just left us may. They asked me to urge you to return to civilization."

"No," said Tarzan, "I shall go my own way. Miss Kircher and Lieutenant Smith-Oldwick were only prompted by a sense of gratitude in considering my welfare."

"Miss Kircher?" exclaimed Capell and then he laughed. "You know her then as Bertha Kircher, the German spy?"

Tarzan looked at the other a moment in silence. It was beyond him to conceive that a British officer should thus laconically speak of an enemy spy whom he had had within his power and permitted to escape. "Yes," he replied, "I knew that she was Bertha Kircher, the German spy?"

"Is that all you knew?" asked Capell.

"That is all," said the ape-man.

"She is the Honorable Patricia Canby," said Capell; "one of the most valuable members of the British Intelligence Service attached to the East African forces. Her father and I served in India together and I have known her ever since she was born.

"Why, here's a packet of papers she took from a German officer and has been carrying it through all her vicissitudes— single-minded in the performance of her duty. Look! I haven't yet had time to examine them but as you see here is a military sketch map, a bundle of reports, and the diary of one Hauptmann Fritz Schneider."

"The diary of Hauptmann Fritz Schneider!" repeated Tarzan in a constrained voice. "May I see it, Capell? He is the man who murdered Lady Greystoke."

The Englishman handed the little volume over to the other without a word. Tarzan ran through the pages quickly looking for a certain date—the date that the horror had been committed—and when he found it he read rapidly. Suddenly a gasp of incredulity burst from his lips. Capell looked at him questioningly.

"God!" exclaimed the ape-man. "Can this be true? Listen!" and he read an excerpt from the closely written page:

" 'Played a little joke on the English pig. When he comes home he will find the burned body of his wife in her boudoir— but he will only *think* it is his wife. Had von Goss substitute the body of a dead Negress and char it after putting Lady Greystoke's rings on it—Lady G will be of more value to the High Command alive than dead.' "

"She lives!" cried Tarzan.

"Thank God!" exclaimed Capell. "And now?"

"I will return with you, of course. How terribly I have

wronged Miss Canby, but how could I know? I even told
Smith-Oldwick, who loves her, that she was a German spy.

"Not only must I return to find my wife but I must right
this wrong."

"Don't worry about that," said Capell, "she must have convinced him that she is no enemy spy, for just before they left
this morning he told me she had promised to marry him."

About Edgar Rice Burroughs

Edgar Rice Burroughs is one of the world's most popular authors. With no previous experience as an author, he wrote and sold his first novel—*A Princess of Mars*—in 1912. In the ensuing thirty-eight years until his death in 1950, Burroughs wrote 91 books and a host of short stories and articles. Although best known as the creator of the classic *Tarzan of the Apes* and *John Carter of Mars,* his restless imagination knew few bounds. Burroughs' prolific pen ranged from the American West to primitive Africa and on to romantic adventure on the moon, the planets, and even beyond the farthest star.

No one knows how many copies of ERB books have been published throughout the world. It is conservative to say, however, that of the translations into 32 known languages, including Braille, the number must run into the hundreds of millions. When one considers the additional world-wide following of the Tarzan newspaper feature, radio programs, comic magazines, motion pictures and television, Burroughs must have been known and loved by literally a thousand million or more.

IN 1942 THE U.S. RATIONED GASOLINE

The basic ration for passenger cars

A

MILEAGE RATION

"A" DRIVERS
MUST DISPLAY
THIS STICKER

That was wartime and the spirit of sacrifice was in the air. No one liked it, but everyone went along. Today we need a wartime spirit to solve our energy problems. A spirit of thrift in our use of all fuels, especially gasoline. We Americans pump over 200 million gallons of gasoline into our automobiles each day. That is nearly one-third the nation's total daily oil consumption and more than half of the oil we import every day . . . at a cost of some $40 billion a year. So conserving gasoline is more than a way to save money at the pump and help solve the nation's balance of payments; it also can tackle a major portion of the nation's energy problem. And that is something we all have a stake in doing . . . with the wartime spirit, but without the devastation of war or the inconvenience of rationing.

ENERGY CONSERVATION -
IT'S YOUR CHANCE TO SAVE, AMERICA
Department of Energy, Washington, D.C.